ChangelingPress.com

Vendetta/Shade Duet

Hounds Of Hell MC

Jamie Targaet

Vendetta/Shade Duet
Hounds Of Hell MC
Jamie Targaet

All rights reserved.
Copyright ©2026 Jamie Targaet

ISBN: 978-1-60521-970-7

Publisher:
Changeling Press LLC
315 N. Centre St.
Martinsburg, WV 25404
ChangelingPress.com

Printed in the U.S.A.

Editor: Treva Harte
Cover Artist: Bryan Keller

The individual stories in this anthology have been previously released in E-Book format.

No part of this publication may be reproduced or shared by any electronic or mechanical means, including but not limited to reprinting, photocopying, or digital reproduction, without prior written permission from Changeling Press LLC.

This book contains sexually explicit scenes and adult language which some may find offensive and which is not appropriate for a young audience. Changeling Press books are for sale to adults, only, as defined by the laws of the country in which you made your purchase.

Table of Contents

Vendetta (Cottonmouth MC 1)
A Hounds of Hell MC Romance
Jamie Targaet

They betrayed me. They tried to sell my woman. But I'm the man they couldn't kill. Now I'm the darkness coming for them.

Dylan -- I thought I could handle my uncle's world. I thought I could survive with the help of the mysterious man who'd slipped into my bed like a secret I didn't want to question. But one night everything shattered. My uncle Eli handed me off to a trafficker like I was nothing, and the man I trusted turned out to be the ghost Eli thought he'd left hanging in the woods -- the man who would kill to keep me safe.

Vendetta -- I used to be Tank, proud to wear the Cottonmouth patch, until I spoke out against the rot poisoning our MC. Now I'm back to burn the criminal empire infecting Oak Grove, and the Cottonmouths that invited it in, to the ground.

Dylan was never supposed to be part of the plan. Hell, she's the niece of the man who betrayed me. But I'll die before I let him hurt her again. And when Eli and his men try to finish what they started, they'll see I'm not the same man they tried to bury.

Prologue

Oak Grove
A Few Months Ago

Stepping into the compound's meeting room, Tank felt like a soldier entering enemy territory.

Eli Crizer sat at the head of the table, the Oak Grove chapter's president and now the face of everything Tank had just witnessed. Tall and broad-shouldered, Eli was built like a man who spent his entire life fighting to stay on top. Hell, the man had killed his own son a couple of years back. His white hair was cut close, making the dark hazel of his eyes stand out like polished brass, cold and shrewd. A black and gray tattoo snaked up the left side of his neck, disappearing beneath his collar. The man's face was hard, weathered by years of violence and command, with a thin slit of a mouth that never really smiled unless someone else was bleeding. Leaning back in his chair, his face an unreadable mask, Eli draped his arms over the sides like a king holding court.

To Eli's left sat Trucker, Oak Grove's enforcer. The man sat stone-faced with his arms crossed and eyes like flint. On Eli's right was Grudge, who didn't look like much because he was painfully thin and always dirty, with his fingers drumming restlessly on the table. On the right, Creep and Eagle nursed beers, their expressions unreadable. Then finally there was Nate, the youngest patch in their club, who wouldn't even look up from the scarred wood of the table when someone entered the club's space.

They weren't there to engage in a meaningful discussion anyway. It wasn't even really about club business. Tank had been asking too many questions, and they'd given him an opportunity to see for himself what they were all part of. Maybe they wanted to watch him squirm. Or it could be that they thought seeing the truth would shut him up.

No. What he'd seen had lit a fuse they couldn't put out. And fucking cowards that they were, not a single one of them spoke. Tank could have heard a pin drop in the room.

"I'm out," Tank said in a low, firm voice. "I'm done being any fucking part of *this*."

Tank glanced around. Half the men there wouldn't meet his gaze. The others stared at him incredulously, like he'd lost his mind.

"You done?" Eli asked, slowly rising. "Just like that?"

"Just like that," Tank shot back. "When you put out the word that you needed more Cottonmouths for a good opportunity, I thought it was regular club business."

Tank had come over from Abingdon a few weeks ago. When the Oak Grove chapter of Cottonmouth MC put out the call for backup, extra muscle for a new "opportunity," he rode out with a couple of his brothers from the Abingdon chapter, thinking it would be business as usual. Dealing guns, protection details, and maybe a little heat with the local law. But now that Tank found out what was really going on, he knew he'd made a mistake. A fucking big one.

"I didn't know you meant caging up girls barely old enough to drive and selling them to monsters. And the drugs? I've seen firsthand what that shit does to neighborhoods, to *families*. I didn't fight for this country just to come back here to protect traffickers and fucking cowards. This isn't the Cottonmouth MC I pledged my life to. This isn't brotherhood. It's a Goddamn pipeline for filth."

"You think you're better than us?" Eli's voice dropped an octave, laced with threat.

"No. But I'm above doing evil shit like that." Tank stared him down.

He'd walked out of the warehouse that no one was supposed to talk about just before coming here. Inside, girls, barely more than kids, were locked in back rooms like livestock. Some of them were chained to rusty bed frames, others were kept behind reinforced doors with nothing but a dirty old mattress and a bucket. The air there was thick with fear, sweat, and the sickening smell of the horrible things that had happened to them. Vacant eyes, hollowed out by whatever they'd been through, acknowledging his presence without recognition. One young woman being held in the warehouse had tried to speak to him, probably reading the outrage and empathy on his face. But one of the guards barked a warning and she flinched so hard she fell back against the wall.

It was the kind of evil shit you couldn't possibly unsee. Tank felt sick to realize the club was balls deep in it.

Drugs were packaged right beside crates of stolen guns. He saw meth, heroin, fentanyl. Brick after brick of narcotics covered the tables, all organized, shrink-wrapped and tagged as inventory. Some of it was already weighed and bagged, ready for the streets. Some of it was boxed and ready for transport. The guns were military-grade assault rifles and semi-automatics, not the handguns they usually ran. They were still oiled and gleaming, packed carefully in crates using fake serial numbers and counterfeit shipping tags. The entire operation, efficient and organized, felt like hell's supply chain.

Every last bit of it was protected under the

Cottonmouth patch. *His* patch.

A long, tense moment passed. Eli didn't move. No one else in the room said or did anything else either.

Finally, Eli said, "Then go. If you're done, walk. Ain't nobody stopping you."

Nodding, Tank turned to leave. He'd faced some fucked-up shit before, but this took the cake. For a moment, he told himself it was over. Maybe, just *maybe,* Eli would let him walk. He kept his stride even, his back straight, refusing to show an ounce of doubt.

But something gnawed at him. A flash of instinct from his Marine days. Just walking out was too quiet, too easy. Tank elected to ignore it. He chose to believe he'd be leaving with his honor intact.

* * *

Bones, the VP of the Oak Grove chapter, called him later that evening and said they wanted to talk, to part ways like brothers. He gave Tank a time and a meeting place. It was just outside of town, tucked back in the trees off an old service road no one really used anymore. It wasn't the place where you patched things up. It was where you went to end them.

Tank stared at his phone for a while after the call ended. A gut instinct fired a warning shot like it had back in the sandbox right before the convoy got hit. Did they think he was stupid? This wasn't a peace talk. It was a death sentence. No way he was going. He was getting the hell out of Oak Grove. *Tonight.*

He was halfway to the garage when the hairs on the back of his neck stood up. The air had shifted, and it was too quiet. No crickets. No dogs barking. Just that uneasy stillness that meant eyes were on him.

Tank froze in the shadow of the side door, one hand on his keys, the other hovering near the grip of the Glock tucked into the waist of his jeans. His mind raced through every step. Bike fueled, gear packed, back route planned.

Someone knew.

That thought dropped hard into his gut as he locked the door behind him and stepped onto the porch, duffel slung over his shoulder. The night was too still, the air too heavy, like the world was holding its breath.

Tank scanned the street. He saw nothing. His bike was parked at the edge of the gravel drive, just beyond the reach of the porch light. He took a step forward.

A crunch of gravel behind him made him spin around, but it was too late.

A blunt object slammed into his ribs from the side, driving the breath out of him. He stumbled off the porch, hit the ground hard, and rolled, just in time to avoid a second strike.

They were waiting. Five of them, moving out of the shadows like wolves. Bandanas up, no colors. No names. But he recognized the size of one. The stance of another.

Cottonmouths.

Tank scrambled to his feet, reached for the Glock, but a boot caught his jaw, sending him reeling back into the side of his truck. They didn't shoot him. That would be too loud, too messy. Eli didn't want a corpse. He wanted silence.

"What's this?" one of them said, yanking the duffel away and tossing it aside. "Planning a little trip?"

Another one spotted his gun and grabbed it as Tank wiped the blood from his mouth, bracing against the wheel well.

"Fuck you," Tank muttered.

The biggest one cracked his knuckles. "Heard you were thinking about running. Can't have that."

A fist drove into his gut, punching the air from his lungs. Tank doubled over as another blow caught him in the jaw, another fist split his lip. The assault was fast and brutal, all boots, fists, and elbows. They didn't speak or shout. They beat him down with cold, mechanical violence like they were taking out the trash. Tank tried to fight back, but he was outnumbered, and their betrayal cut deeper than any blow or knife. Their silence was the worst part. No one called him brother or tried to warn him. It was like he'd never been one of them.

The beating continued mercilessly. Someone ripped his cut right off his back. Spit hit the ground beside his head. "Piece of shit don't deserve to wear it."

His arms were yanked viciously behind him and bound with chain, cold metal biting deep into raw skin. Then gravel, the scuff of boots. A grunt of effort as they dragged him by the arms toward a waiting truck. Creep's truck.

They threw him into the bed like dead weight, the ridged metal slamming against his ribs. One of them hopped up beside him, boot planted on his spine as the engine turned over and they rolled out slowly into the dark.

No words then, only the thrum of the engine and the rhythmic clink of the chain bouncing with every bump in the road. Trees blurred past. He lifted his head once, just enough to see stars above the canopy and a sliver of moonlight. It was the last thing he remembered before the truck stopped and the boots started again.

Eli's voice echoed in the dark. "Brothers don't betray brothers."

Tank was barely able to lift his head, blood dripping from his mouth. "Since when is disagreement a betrayal?" he asked bitterly.

Eli didn't answer. Just stared at him with cold, dead eyes.

"Standing up for what's right makes me a traitor?" Tank choked out.

Silence was the only answer he was getting.

Tank fought them but by then it wasn't much. Every movement sent flashes of pain shooting through his ribs, cracked and grinding with every painful breath. Blood streamed from a gash above his brow, hot and blinding, filling one eye until he could barely see. His jaw throbbed where a boot had caught him, and waves of nausea rolled through his stomach. His body screamed with every jolt, but he wouldn't fucking beg. Tank gritted his teeth through the agony, rage and betrayal burning hotter than the pain ever could.

By the time they dragged him to the trees, the only thing Tank knew for certain was that the brotherhood he'd believed in was dead in Oak Grove.

Someone pulled a splintered crate over and shoved him up onto it. His knees nearly buckled, but they kept him steady just long enough. They looped a noose over a low-hanging branch of a huge, gnarled oak tree. Its limbs twisted upward like crooked fingers, and its bark was scarred and blackened in patches like it had survived both rot and fire. Standing alone at the edge of the clearing, it loomed like a sentinel to every dirty secret or dealing that ever passed through its woods. A crude wooden sign had been nailed to the tree trunk, the words "Price of Betrayal" were painted on it in crooked letters and blood-red paint.

Eli stepped closer.

Outrage surged through Tank's chest, colliding with rage and betrayal until it all became one searing heat. His heart pounded hard against cracked ribs, and it was hard to breathe. Tank glared up at the man he'd once followed, feeling the last of his trust crumble like ash. The noose scratched his skin, but the weight of it was real.

Yet, at that moment, what burned hottest wasn't fear. It was the promise he made at that moment. *You'll regret this.*

"Tank's dead weight. And this club don't need dead weight," Eli told his helpers.

They kicked the crate out from under him.

* * *

Everything went black.

It took Tank a minute to figure out if he was still alive. The world was silent and felt distant, like he was floating just beneath the surface of a dark lake. There was no pain at first. Just a cold, creeping numbness that sank deep into his bones. He couldn't move, couldn't breathe. For a second, he thought maybe he was done. But some deep, primal instinct had him clawing back. Awareness returned to him slowly. He could hear rustling leaves around him, feel the wind. He tasted blood, sharp and metallic on his tongue. The pain eventually drifted back in, dragging his awareness along with it.

He should've died. But somehow, he hadn't.

The crushing weight of silence and the burn of rope biting into his throat, cutting off air, thought, and hope was all he knew outside the pain. It was quiet. No voices. No shuffling boots or revving engines. They left him there. Whether they were too cowardly to watch, or something spooked them, he didn't know. But the stillness wrapped around him like an eerie shroud, and somehow, it made the betrayal so much worse. Tank's world narrowed to pressure and panic, the rope squeezing the life out of him. The noose held firm, digging deeper by the second, and his body convulsed against it, desperate for air. Stars burst behind his eyes. His body became numb, and he felt his mind begin to drift.

Then out of nowhere there was a snap. An unexpected, jarring fall. His body slammed into the cold ground and the gasp ripped from his chest, air burning like fire as it sucked into his starving lungs. Maybe the branch cracked. Maybe someone had a shred of humanity and cut him down after the rest walked away. He'd never know. And he didn't fucking care. All he knew was the taste of blood and dirt in his mouth and the agony of that first breath.

His body was broken and everything hurt. Every breath felt like a razor in his chest. His wrists screamed from where the chains had bitten into them, slick with his blood. He wasn't sure how they'd come loose. Had it happened in the fall? Somehow, they'd given way. The metal still clinked with every move he made, dragging behind him.

But he moved slowly, with intention. Crawling through the cold dirt and winter's dead leaves. Blood dripped from his face and his muscles shook with each inch forward. Dragging his body over the forest floor was pure agony, his fingers bleeding now as he clawed at the ground. Still, he pushed himself on. Instinct urged him to drag himself out of that patch of woods. Rage and the will to survive fueled every single motion.

He didn't know where he was going. He only

knew that if he managed to survive this, he couldn't stay *here*. He wouldn't fucking die like that. Not by their hands. Not discarded in the woods like a piece of garbage they were done with. He would never be just another secret buried in the dirt behind their clubhouse. Every inch he crawled was a solemn vow. *You failed. You should've made sure I was dead.*

Tank *was* dead. He left that name in the dirt beneath the hanging tree, with the blood they'd spilled and the brotherhood they'd shattered. That man had believed in loyalty and brotherhood.

That man was gone. He buried the name.

And from the ashes, Vendetta rose, scarred, silent, and born of vengeance.

Chapter One

Vendetta

The sun was barely visible on the horizon when Vendetta rolled into Oak Grove in his courier van. It was early enough that the roads were still quiet and held little traffic, but late enough that the night's shadows still clung to the edges of buildings and businesses. It was a typical small Southern town, and it honestly hadn't changed much in the months since he was last here.

Oak Grove wore the ghost of its better days like an old, threadbare coat. There were hints that it had once thrived. Maybe a couple of decades back when the factories still ran and every porch on Main Street was filled with families and the elderly in the grace of their retirement. There were no newer buildings that he could see as he drove down its main street. The small collection of buildings that made up the town were weather-beaten and worn, with paint peeling off brick like old skin. Half the storefronts were tagged with graffiti, and the windows that weren't busted out were fogged from the inside with neglect. The people he saw starting their day just looked older and tired. Some walked with hunched shoulders and hollow eyes, some with faces aged beyond their years. It was like everyone in Oak Grove had seen too much. They'd stopped looking for hope long ago.

He didn't have to be here. He could have moved on and tried to put his life back together in another town like Oak Grove, under another name. It would have been easier. Most people, if told what had happened to him here just a few short months ago, wouldn't have blamed him if that had been his choice.

What happened to Tank? The story the Oak

Grove Cottonmouths fed the Abingdon chapter was clean and quiet. They said Tank didn't agree with the club's new direction and hit the road and went nomad. Just like that.

And Abingdon bought it. No questions or pushback. They accepted the lie like it was gospel, like Tank walking away without a word made any damn sense. Maybe they believed it. Maybe they were too afraid to challenge Oak Grove. Either way, no one came looking. No one checked on him.

It was a second betrayal, colder than the first. They buried him without a body, without even realizing it. And that, more than the noose or the chain, was the wound that never stopped bleeding.

The new name fit him like armor. *Vendetta.* He was no longer Tank. No longer the man who believed in doing the right thing and expected others to feel the same way. No longer the man who believed brotherhood still meant something. For now, he kept his scars hidden beneath the ordinary clothes he wore as a delivery driver. The long scar around his neck still ached in the cold, a chilling reminder of how close he'd come to death. He wore hoodies, jackets, and bandanas and left his hair down when he could to hide it.

What gnawed at him in his quiet moments, the ones that hit hardest late at night, was this: no one ever found a body. That made their story believable. Tank had just disappeared, gone nomad. But what if he *hadn't* survived that night? What if his heart had stopped out there under the trees, lungs crushed, neck broken?

Would they have come back for him? Would they have buried him? Or just left him there to rot like nothing? And if they *had* come back for the body and found it missing… That meant he could still be alive.

Did Eli suspect he was alive? Was he haunted by the possibility that his ghost still walked? He hoped so. He liked the idea of that. The fear creeping in, the doubt festering. Let Eli feel hunted for once.

He'd been doing his homework. The criminal organization that had infected the Oak Grove Cottonmouths used the name Sinister Skin Holdings. They'd tried really hard to infiltrate Mercy too, a neighboring county, awhile back. The Hounds kicked them out, protecting the town and its people from the corruption and filth that Eli Crizer and his followers welcomed. For now. It wasn't nearly as easy as it sounded to be rid of the fuckers, so he waited.

When the word went out on certain channels that they were looking for a Hound out of Mercy traveling with a young woman, Vendetta had set out to find them and he did. Knowing what they were up against, and to gather a little intel, he'd helped Outcast and his girl Anya escape the assholes. The fact that the woman had been the captive of Sebastian Six, one of Sinister Skin Holdings' top dogs, made it all the sweeter for him. He helped get them back to Mercy in one piece when the odds were stacked against them. Someone had to.

There was a final showdown, and Vendetta had been there for it, helping the Hounds with their common enemy. Watching Outcast shoot Six in the face had given Vendetta back his fire, his need to make things right. When they parted ways that night, Outcast had looked him in the eye and said, "If you ever need us, you call. We'll come." A nod from their president, Razor, confirmed it.

Vendetta hadn't called in that favor yet. But he would. When the time came, and the reckoning hit Oak Grove like a bullet hitting bone, he'd want the Hounds at his back.

Until then, Vendetta would be just another shadow. He'd scored himself a job working for a delivery service in and around Oak Grove, and that would have its uses. He found himself staying in a rundown motel at the edge of town, cash only, no questions asked. It smelled like bad sex, mildew, and cigarettes, but the lock on the door was solid and the window faced the lot. It was all he needed.

Sinister Skin Holdings had failed to root in Mercy, but they'd found fresh soil here. Eli Crizer had let the fuckers in. The Oak Grove Cottonmouths had sold out for blood money, dirty deals, and human cargo. They'd taken the offer the Hounds solidly rejected.

He promised himself it wouldn't last long. Vendetta would move through Oak Grove like smoke. He would watch everything. After all, he knew how they operated and where they trafficked. Vendetta even knew who they leaned on and all the locations where product was moved and stored. If he could control the fury that clawed inside his chest whenever he thought about it, he could find a way to end them and their entire fucking operation.

That was his mission now.

When Vendetta pulled his van into the cracked lot behind *INeeda Medical Supply* just after seven, the morning fog was still clinging to the pavement. His was a pre-owned cargo van with a few dings in its white paint, but he'd gotten a deal on it at the city auction. Stepping out of the van, he took in the warehouse where he'd be working. The building looked like it had been repurposed. It looked like it could have been a tire shop or auto body place. Someone'd slapped a vinyl sign over the front and started pushing boxes of wound care kits and portable oxygen tanks.

Vendetta met Freddie, the manager, at his one interview for the job. People weren't showing up in droves to work as a delivery driver and he didn't get the impression that he'd been up against anyone else for the job. Freddie met him at the door just as he said he would. He looked like the kind of guy who told the same three jokes at every company get-together. Mid-fifties, thinning hair slicked back, probably the same way he wore it in the '90s. The man's stomach pressed a little too tight against his neatly tucked button-down and he wore khakis like they were tactical gear. He seemed friendly enough, but he had the kind of humor that made people laugh more out of habit than actual amusement. It didn't make him a bad guy. Just the kind of man who thought charm and authority came from a tucked shirt and a clipboard.

The man grinned as he approached the loading dock, clipboard in hand. "You're early, Jason Evans," he said. "Didn't figure a guy with that much beard would be punctual."

The long beard wasn't something he'd worn as Tank. It gave him a different look and that was useful. Vendetta gave a tight smile and said nothing. He wasn't here to make friends. He was here to work, to watch, and when the time came, to strike. He towered over Freddie who had to glance up to hold his gaze. The lack of friendly banter had the man skipping more talk and moving ahead to the work. Vendetta was anxious to get on with that.

Freddie grabbed a folded uniform shirt from the table behind him, squinting at the chest like he was already picturing the embroidery. "We do names here. Customers like it. And it helps the drivers feel like part of the team. You want 'Jason' stitched on yours, or something cooler?" He grinned like he thought that was hilarious.

Vendetta shook his head. "No name. I'm good."

Freddie paused in folding the shirt. "C'mon, man, makes it official."

Vendetta met his gaze. "Still Jason. Just don't stitch it."

Freddie looked like he wanted to push, but something in Vendetta's expression must've told him not to. Shrugging, he laughed and handed him the shirt. "All right. Suit yourself, mystery man."

Vendetta didn't answer, just pulled the shirt on right over the long-sleeved T-shirt he wore to conceal his scars; the one around his neck along with those from service, and any identifying tattoos. He followed Freddie out the warehouse doors. Leading him through the back of the warehouse, his new boss pointed out shelves stacked with everything from wound dressings to portable oxygen tanks.

"The back wall is for scheduled clinic runs. Dialysis stuff, diabetic supplies, the usual," Freddie said. "You'll load up over here. Zone 3. That'll be your area for now. There are a few nursing homes, assisted living places, and a couple clinics."

Vendetta followed him, listening, not talking, taking it all in. To his new boss, this was just inventory. Boxes with barcodes, delivery routes, and time windows. To Vendetta, it was intel. Each stop would be a new opportunity. Each facility was a chance for him to ask the right question or overhear the wrong name. If the criminal network was funneling victims through Oak Grove, someone would have to be patching them up. And he was about to be the guy who delivered straight to their doors.

Freddie pointed to a clipboard with route sheets, still yammering about mileage logs and signoffs. Vendetta wasn't really paying attention. He wasn't here for the paycheck. He was here to look for the cracks. And the second they started turning up? He'd wedge it wide fucking open.

"Oh, I should mention that since you're the new guy, you also get stuck with the restaurant and bar deliveries," Freddie continued, gesturing toward a separate rack of clearly labeled boxes. They were smaller, but still under the *INeeda* logo. "There's not a lot of those, fortunately. It's mostly first aid kits, gloves, and hand sanitizer. A couple places just like to keep up appearances, I guess."

Vendetta's attention snapped to that rack. Bars and restaurants, not medical centers or clinics. Regular public places. Why the hell would some dive bar need hospital-grade medical supplies?

"What kind of places are we talking about?" Vendetta asked, keeping his tone casual.

Freddie shrugged. "Just a handful. That Irish pub off Highway 8, the pizza place in town, and some bar over on Main. Uh, what's it called now… *Ned's Sundown Lounge*? Something like that. Just got bought out recently."

That had Vendetta's full attention. He didn't say anything, just nodded like it was nothing. But his thoughts were coming together.

Bars weren't supposed to be on this route. But if the Cottonmouths were using any of them as a front, keeping injured victims somewhere, laundering money through food service, even staging meetings, it made sense to stock them with basic supplies to avoid raising suspicion. And now he had an excuse to walk through the front door of every one of them.

Perfect.

Vendetta half-listened to the rest of what Freddie had to say. But his mind was already spinning with plans. There were routes and schedules to study. There were building layouts, security habits -- all of it a mental blueprint taking shape while his new boss rambled on about clipboard protocol and break room etiquette. He caught the end of it, just as Freddie clapped a hand on another man's shoulder.

"Jason, meet Alan Perkins. He's one of our best. You'll ride along with him for a couple days."

Alan was mid-forties, wiry, friendly in that small-town way. He had a smoker's voice and a habit of talking too much when the cab went quiet. But he was efficient, knew every stop by heart, and didn't ask too many questions. Vendetta kept his answers short, stuck to the basics, and watched everything closely.

By the time they wrapped up the route and rolled back into the warehouse, he already knew which clinics ran tight on inventory. He knew which ones had loose security, and which doors were always left cracked open in the back.

That night, back in his motel room, Vendetta ate lukewarm takeout straight from the container. The TV played the local news in the background. They reported something about a school board dispute and a car fire near the interstate. But his mind was consumed with everything he'd learned that day. Every face he'd seen, every note Alan made on the log sheet all looped through his head like puzzle pieces waiting for a match.

Oak Grove had no idea he was back. And soon enough, it wouldn't matter.

* * *

Dylan

Ned's Sundown Lounge looked rougher in the light of day than it ever did at night.

Dylan Crizer waited across the street with her keys clenched in her hand, taking it all in. The building looked old, dressed in faded black brick. The same flickering neon sign that barely spelled the word "Open" was still there. She remembered it from passing by that building as a child. The tinted windows smeared with fingerprints and smoke stains were new. While the building wasn't falling apart just yet, it had clearly seen better days. Maybe better decades.

Yeah, it was as bad as her Uncle Eli had said it was. It blew her mind that he was now co-owner of the bar that had been there most of her life. Eli Crizer was a big bad biker, president of the Cottonmouths and all that, but he'd never been well-off before. How did a biker get that kind of money? Did he dip into his retirement account? Did he even have one of those?

Not long after she returned to Oak Grove, she found out her uncle had bought the place with a "business associate." How did he get a business associate? The place had always fascinated her, so when she saw the "help wanted" sign in the window, she marched herself in and applied right away. Not surprisingly, her uncle, who hadn't made time to reach out to her so far, called her the same day about her application.

"It's not the place for you, Dylan," he said right off the bat. When she asked why, he countered with, "It's gonna be full of drunks, ex-cons, and worse."

She thought the fact that she'd been a waitress for years would guarantee her the job. Although she wasn't the best at making drinks consistently good in a rough environment, she had bartender experience, too.

Her uncle didn't agree. "You're a Crizer. You're better than serving drinks to scummy people."

But here she was anyway. Not just because she had something to prove. She now had something to rebuild. Her entire life basically. Maybe she wouldn't be starting a new job today; Eli as a co-owner could cut her off. But she had to try.

Dylan had spent five years with a man who wanted to control her every move. Five years pretending she was happy in a dead-end relationship in Richmond. When she left, she made up her mind that she'd come back to Oak Grove and figure it out from the ground up. She'd start over. Hell, she was only twenty-five. She had time.

She was starting over right here at *Ned's Sundown Lounge.*

Pushing through the front door, Dylan blinked as her eyes adjusted to the low light inside the bar. The entire place smelled of old leather, cheap whiskey, and stale beer. It appeared to be well stocked and mostly clean despite all the scuff marks and the sticky spots along the floor. The tables were roomy and spaced out well around its central dance floor. A narrow hallway led off in the direction of the restrooms and the back offices. *Ned's Sundown Lounge* had its own unique charm. If you squinted.

"Good afternoon," came a voice from behind the bar. A tall, older woman with a sharp jaw and leopard-print eyeglasses worked at polishing glasses, watching Dylan with a smile. "You must be Eli's niece."

"Dylan," she said, stepping up to the bar. "Here for my first day."

At least she hoped she was. If Eli told them she couldn't work there, what would she do? She really needed the job and had already told him that.

"I'm Peggy," the woman said in the way of introduction as she gave her a once-over and nodded like she approved of what she saw. "You got the job. Just stay aware and don't take shit from anyone. Even the regulars. You'll be fine."

Dylan didn't hesitate. "Wasn't planning on it."

"Come on." Peggy put the last glass she polished on the bar and motioned for Dylan to follow her.

Down that narrow hallway and to the left was a line of really old lockers outside the business offices. All of them had huge padlocks, protecting the personal items the employees wanted to tuck away. Just one, at the far end, had a small key stuck in the bottom of its padlock. Peggy pointed to that one.

"There's only one key," Peggy warned. "If you lose it, you're responsible for getting a new lock, okay?"

Dylan nodded, tucking her purse into the locker and securing it with the padlock before sliding its tiny silver key into the front pocket of her jeans.

Peggy jerked a thumb in the opposite direction. "The kitchen is that way. There's not a lot of menu options to memorize. Burgers, fries, nachos. I think they have chili a couple of times a week. None of it is that great."

Good to know. Pulling the hair tie from her wrist, she pulled her hair up into a ponytail as she followed the woman back through the bar, taking in every corner as she went. Dylan was many things but naive wasn't one of them.

Her Uncle Eli had influence here and he led a shady biker club. And now he was a co-owner of this place. People didn't just "run bars" these days. Bars were often covers for other things. More shady shit.

She'd left a couple of bars after learning they were running drugs out of them. The second one had a full police raid one night and it took hours for it to be cleared up so everyone could go home. She never returned because drugs were dangerous and brought dangerous people. No job was worth putting herself in the line of fire.

But until she had proof that something wasn't right here at her uncle's bar, she was going to do the damn job. Unfortunately, she needed the money to get back on her feet.

Smile. Hustle. Listen. It had been her mantra since her first job in a bar.

Peggy looked to be somewhere in her forties. She had a no-nonsense attitude that had to come in handy in a place as rough as this. "House rules. Keep the regulars' drinks full and staff are *not* allowed to talk politics. Or religion. People don't want to think about religion when they're drinking and partying, you know? The jukebox plays when it fucking wants to, so no beating it or kicking it. If Ned's here and he sees you do it, he'll lose his mind."

"Who's Ned?" Dylan asked.

"The other co-owner," Peggy replied. "Try not to piss him off, even if you are Eli's family."

"Understood," Dylan said.

"Now, if a fight breaks out and there's usually one each fucking week," Peggy explained, "don't be a hero. Just try and get clear and wave down one of the bouncers. We usually have at least two of them scheduled each night. It's not a bad idea to check the schedule. It's on the whiteboard with the lockers. See who's on duty each night so you know who you're looking for." She jerked her chin in the direction of the far end of the bar.

Dylan followed her gaze to the two huge guys leaning against the back wall near the hallway, perfectly still and silent. One of them was built like a refrigerator with tattoos creeping up both sides of his neck. The other looked mean even though he wasn't actively trying to at that moment. He was leaner with an angular face and a body you could only get from hours each week in the gym. The gym rats were hit-or-miss as bouncers. Dylan would be willing to bet money that the fridge was the one to flag down in a fight.

"They don't talk much, but they move fast, let me tell you. If some shit goes down, make eye contact, give a nod, and then get out of the way. Got it?"

"Got it," Dylan said, scanning the room as Peggy handed her an apron and a notepad. "Is there a panic button or something? I've worked in other places that had them."

Peggy snorted. "This ain't Applebee's, sweetheart. You see something coming, you move. *Fast*."

It wasn't the serious lack of formal safety protocols that raised Dylan's eyebrows. It was the way Peggy said it, like fights weren't just a possibility, they were expected. Like there was a rhythm to them and they were allowed. She nodded and kept listening, but something about that rubbed her wrong.

"Most of our business is on the weekends, of course, but the VIPs come in all during the week," Peggy went on, already moving back to the bar to stock napkins in old-fashioned metal boxes. "You'll know them when you see them. They don't tip, but don't piss them off. Eli likes to keep them happy."

Dylan paused, notebook in hand. "VIPs?"

"Locals. Out-of-towners. Some are from his MC. Doesn't matter," Peggy said, without looking up. "You serve what they order and stay out of their conversations. That's not me being rude. That's me keeping you employed."

The words hit her like a warning. Something about all of it, the emphasis, the look in Peggy's eyes, the way she didn't offer names made Dylan's stomach tighten as she kept listening, wondering what else she was going to hear. Nodding, she filed it all away and forced a smile.

"Thanks for showing me the ropes," Dylan said. "I appreciate it."

Peggy finally looked at her, a long, assessing stare. Then she shrugged. "You've got the eyes for this place. You watch everything. That's good. Just make sure you don't watch too closely, yeah?"

Dylan didn't answer. But she was definitely paying attention.

"One last thing." Peggy spoke quietly. "You're one of the owner's family members which probably means you'd have to *really* fuck up to get fired. But just keep in mind, you're still expendable."

"I'll do my best to remember that."

The evening crowd was light, just as Peggy explained it would be. It was Thursday night, and *Ned's Sundown Lounge* always did look better at night. The dim lighting and the fact that the sun had already set, covered the bar's many imperfections better than paint ever could. The jukebox was working tonight, playing songs that were moody and lazy, and they filled the space without drawing attention.

The regulars were easy to spot, planted on barstools like fixtures, beers in front of them. Some of them talked to each other in low voices, some were there on their own. Dylan had just finished clearing one of her tables when the cool night air blew a newcomer through the front doors.

Dylan glanced up and paused.

The newest patron was tall and built. She didn't think she'd seen him before. That didn't necessarily mean anything. She was just back in town after having been gone several years.

The man who just walked in didn't look like a local. Six-four, easy, with broad shoulders under a worn jean jacket and a dark hoodie that had definitely seen better days. His long dark hair was pulled back low at the neck, and a beat-up baseball cap shadowed most of his face. Not that it helped much. He was *fine* and pretty hard to miss.

Dark eyes scanned the room once, slow and deliberate. He didn't come across as cocky, just aware. Like he was used to being in places where trouble could find him in a hurry. When his gaze finally landed on her, it lingered for half a second longer than it needed to. Not creepy or flirty. Maybe interested.

Dylan straightened and stepped behind the bar, already reaching for a clean glass. But the new guy didn't sit at the bar like most of them. No, he picked out a booth near the back, one that gave him the best line of sight on both the bar's exits.

Shit, they really must have fights often here.

Dylan clocked that and noticed how relaxed his movements were. Like someone trained not to draw attention but fully capable of handling it if he had to.

She walked over with a notepad in hand, smiling when his gaze met hers. "You look like a bourbon guy," she said by way of greeting.

"It depends on who's pouring," he said, voice deep and gravel smooth.

She raised an eyebrow. "So, you're one of those."

He smirked. "One of what?"

"One of those mysterious types with a tragic backstory and specific taste in whiskey."

That smirk turned into a smile and when he turned it on her, well, it froze her to the spot. "Would I be less exciting if I say beer?"

"Beer's not as exciting," she replied, scribbling his order. "But you seem like anything but a boring guy."

That earned her a look. Something warmer flickered behind those dark eyes before it faded.

"Do you have a beer preference?"

"Whatever you have on draft," he told her.

Nodding, she walked off to grab his drink, curiosity crawling under her skin. There was something about tall, dark, and handsome back there. He just didn't seem like he was local. He was too quiet, observant. He just seemed like the kind of man who had a story written all over him in scars he didn't show. And if she was being honest? Whatever that story was, she wanted to hear it.

When she returned with his beer, she caught him giving her the once-over, the hint of a grin playing about his lips. She had a feeling he just might be her next favorite mistake. Setting down a coaster then the beer mug, she smiled. "Can I get you anything else? Some chips or nachos?"

He tilted his head at that. "You have nachos? I think you're the first waitress that ever offered me that."

"They might suck," she said with a laugh. "It's my first shift here so..."

"Yeah, well let me try 'em," he said, eyes still on her. "I'll give you a review."

"Deal," she said.

As she headed back to give her order to the

kitchen, she saw a group of bikers walking into the bar. They came in loud, laughing too hard, and walking like they owned the place. From a certain point of view, she guessed they did. The snakes on their patches told her they were Cottonmouths, probably from her uncle's club.

Well, this should be interesting.

At the kitchen window, a short, pudgy guy with a great smile introduced himself to her as Bart. He explained that he'd been at the bar for a decade, he was practically a manager there. *Yeah, right.* And if she had any questions to let him know. It was all she could do to get away from him to get back to her table. And the bikers had, of course, found a booth in her section.

And her mystery man? He fucking left. At first, she thought he stiffed her, but she spotted a note on the table laid over cash.

Dylan headed for the bikers. They smelled like road dust, booze, and arrogance. The youngest one was the loud one, probably three drinks deep from wherever they'd been before. Mid-twenties, shaggy dark hair, arms covered in faded ink and cigarette burns. He sprawled in the booth, legs spread wide, arm thrown over the backrest like he was already getting comfortable. Next to him was a beefy biker with gun-metal gray hair and eyes nearly the same color. If he'd been drinking, she couldn't tell. She assumed he was a higher-up in the club based on his demeanor.

The biker across from him was tall and wiry with a crooked nose that looked like it had been broken at least twice and never reset properly. He scanned the bar like he was looking for a fight, twitchy hands tapping a beat against the table. Next to him in the aisle seat was the biggest of the bunch, built like a semi-truck with his leather vest stretched tight across his chest and deep scowl etched into his face. He had nothing to say. He didn't even acknowledge she was there.

But the gray-haired biker did, acknowledging her with a toothy grin that made her feel like she needed a shower.

"Well, hello there," he said, voice oily-smooth. "What's your name, sweet thing?"

Dylan didn't flinch. She set her notepad on the table, pen poised and gave him a flat look. "Eli's niece."

The table erupted at that, with the other three bikers laughing and the one who spoke to her loving the attention. Then he leaned back, raising his hands in mock surrender. "Didn't realize royalty was working tonight."

"You gonna order," she said calmly, "or should I come back?"

That earned a low chuckle from the younger guy. But the way they looked at her changed. Not with less interest but more caution.

"We'll order," the gray-haired biker said. "I'm Trucker. This little shithead next to me is Nate because he's not cool enough for a biker name. Over there is Grudge." He pointed to the thin, dirty one. "And Creep."

Since they were in her uncle's club, it wasn't in her best interest to be rude. Now they knew who she was, they'd leave her alone. "Dylan," she told them.

"Dylan," Trucker snapped. "We need a bottle of Jack and clean glasses."

"You've got it."

She'd met her first VIPs. She walked back to the table tall, dark, and handsome abandoned, wondering what happened there. He'd left her a twenty and a note on the back of a paper receipt from somewhere else.

Sorry, I got called back to work. If this isn't enough, text me.

A phone number was written at the bottom.

Chapter Two

Vendetta

A week was all he needed. Vendetta had the delivery routes down cold, knew which clinics were careless with sign-ins, and which drivers cut corners. He also knew which facilities had back doors that stayed mysteriously propped open during late-night drop-offs. He kept his mouth shut and his head down. He made his deliveries, nodded when he was expected to, and kept his eyes wide open.

But he wasn't just doing the job. He was using it to shadow the Cottonmouths, to hunt down all their dirty little secrets. And once he'd collected enough, he'd create a plan for how he was going to bring the motherfuckers down.

Oak Grove looked the same as it always did on the surface. He didn't know until he came over from Abingdon that this new town pulsed with something putrid, like a wound beneath the surface that never quite healed, just festered. In the six months he'd been there, he'd seen deals made out in the open like nothing mattered. Cash moved in broad daylight, and people looked the other way like they'd been taught not to ask questions. Maybe they were too afraid. The deeper Vendetta dug, the more he came to realize that the town wasn't just turning a blind eye. It was bought and paid for.

There were meetings that didn't show up on the schedule and unmarked vans parked behind *Ned's Sundown Lounge* around the clock. There were young faces that he never saw twice, just a glimpse through tinted windows before they were gone. It made him sick to his stomach and more determined to put an end to the rotten fucking bunch of them.

He'd been tailing a few of the Cottonmouths after hours, always careful to stay at a distance. Trucker and Creep. Eagle and Grudge. He couldn't decide if they were cocky, or they just didn't give a shit. They didn't know they were being watched yet. But they would.

Vendetta hadn't been back to *Ned's Sundown Lounge* since that night when he'd met that gorgeous, curvy little waitress who had told him it was her first night on the job. He thought about her, more than he ever should. He couldn't allow himself to get distracted. But, fuck, he sure wanted that distraction.

She was curvy in a way that made a man want to slow down and take his time. Her honey-blonde hair had been pulled back at work. He couldn't help but imagine what it must look like falling around her shoulders. She had the biggest blue eyes that were too damn honest for a hellhole like *that* bar. She watched the room like she didn't miss a thing, even when she pretended not to notice anything at all. She carried herself with purpose, chin high even when facing down a table full of patch-wearing bastards without blinking.

He hadn't gotten her name. He just knew she didn't belong in a place like that. That made her even harder to forget.

The number he left her? His phone still hadn't rung. He tried to convince himself that was good thing. It was safer that way. But part of him had to wonder if she'd tucked it away. Or if she'd already thrown it out. Maybe it didn't matter.

He had a trap to build. And when that trap snapped shut, every single fucking one of them -- Eli and the whole Goddamn operation -- were going down.

As if his thoughts had conjured it, his phone buzzed just as he reached the motel parking lot. One short vibration and a number he didn't recognize.

Was it her?

Vendetta glanced at the screen, thumb hovering for half a second before he tapped it open.

Hey mystery guy, u coming back to the bar? I'm working tonight. Did i do something wrong or u just not that into beer and awkward charm?

Vendetta stared at the screen, the faintest pull at the corners of his mouth. But he knew exactly who it was. It was *her.* He could just picture that sassy smile on her face when she hit send. He remembered that body he'd love to take a slow tour of.

As he walked to his motel room, he couldn't help grinning. Well, that answered that question. Honestly, he'd assumed he'd never hear from her and that she'd tossed out his number that night. Now that she had reached out to him, instinct told him it was a bad idea. Maybe he needed to take a step back. Getting involved with her could be dangerous for them both.

But ignoring her? That didn't sit right with him either. He read the message again, slower this time. Setting the phone down on the cheap motel table when he walked in, he took a seat, leaning back in the chair. He stared at the screen like it might offer him an easier answer than the one in his gut.

Getting involved with her was risky. But she'd been on his mind all fucking week. *That smile.* Plus, he loved a big-eyed girl.

But getting closer to her might be a way of getting information faster, getting him closer to the truth. *Ned's Sundown Lounge* was a prime Cottonmouth hangout. Guys like Trucker and Creep came and went like it was their clubhouse. If there were side deals happening, drop-offs being arranged, or names being passed around, just maybe it would start there. And the waitress? She worked on the floor. She struck him as observant. She'd hear and see everything while she was there.

Vendetta tried telling himself *that* was the reason he was going to text her back. But as he picked up the phone, reading her message once more, the knot in his chest said otherwise. His thumb hovered over the screen for only a second before he typed out a reply.

didn't do anything wrong. been busy. might stop by tonight.

It was short and to the point. He kept it neutral. Then he hit send before tossing the phone on the bed and rising from the chair, stretching.

Vendetta hadn't planned on going back to the bar yet, much less tonight. But something about her message stuck with him. Was it curiosity tugging at his chest? Or that he couldn't admit to himself what he really wanted wasn't part of his strategy?

Stripping off his work clothes, he took a quick shower and pulled on a clean hoodie with a heavier denim jacket. He slid the knife into his boot more out of habit than worry. By the time he stepped out into the chilly night air, he'd made his decision. Vendetta was going to *Ned's Sundown Lounge*. And he'd be lying to himself if he thought he was just going for information, for his revenge. But he wasn't ready to admit that to himself just yet.

* * *

Ned's was quieter than usual when Vendetta arrived. There were no Cottonmouths now. No loud laughter or obnoxious posturing from the back tables. Just a low hum of conversation, a few locals nursing drinks, and an old country song drifting from the jukebox that sounded like heartbreak wrapped in twang. Maybe it was ordinary for a weeknight.

Out of habit, he scanned the room as he headed for the bar. The waitress he came to see was behind it, wiping down the counter with a rag that had seen better days. Her hair was up again, a few blonde strands falling loose around her face. She only wore a hint of makeup, but she didn't need even that. She was one gorgeous little lady. He just had to make sure she didn't end up being a gorgeous distraction for what he was back in Oak Grove to do.

She'd spotted him when the door opened, and her entire demeanor shifted. The fatigue in her eyes faded. It was just a spark instead of a big leap. But he saw it. And for whatever reason, it hit him harder than he expected.

"There you are," she said, setting the rag aside. "I was starting to think I imagined the whole 'mystery guy with a beer preference' thing."

Vendetta leaned an elbow on the bar. "Didn't want to spoil the mystery too fast."

That earned him a grin, and damned if it didn't stop him cold for just a beat. "Well, I'm glad you're here. It's slower tonight. Less chaos, more time for conversation… Unless that's too forward."

He shook his head. "Conversation sounds good."

She reached for a clean glass. "Beer, right? Same as last time?"

Vendetta nodded, watching her move confidently behind the bar. But now that he was looking closer, he noticed the tension beneath the surface. Like she was carrying a secret weight no one else could see. And didn't he fucking know that feeling?

Setting the glass down gently in front of him, she

smiled. "I was beginning to think you weren't coming back."

"I wasn't," he said, though he wasn't sure that was entirely true. Lifting the drink to his lips, he said, "Then I got a text," before he took a drink.

Her smile was just short of playful. "Sounds like whoever sent it must've been pretty persuasive."

Vendetta didn't smile, but he'd play along. "Yeah, she was."

Leaning her arms on the bar, she watched him. "So, mystery man, what do you do when you're not ghosting small-town dive bars?"

Vendetta tapped a finger on the rim of his glass. "Independent courier," he said after a moment. "Medical supplies."

Her fair brows lifted. "Like hospitals and clinics?"

He nodded, took another sip. "Rehab centers. Some pharmacies. Anything under the *INeeda Medical* umbrella."

Her mouth parted slightly in surprise. "That's the place that used to be a tire shop, right?"

"Yeah."

"We get stuff from them sometimes," she said, polishing glasses while she had the time. "First aid kits, sanitizer, gloves. Boring stuff, I know. But they keep the health inspector from shutting us down."

"Boring's not so bad," he said, his gaze on her hands. For how pretty she was, hair and makeup subtle, but enhancing what she already had. Her hands were an interesting counterpoint. Her fingernails were short and unpainted. It showed she wasn't afraid of hard work.

"Maybe not," she agreed, then tilted her head. "Will you be making any of our deliveries? Usually, not always, they send Alan. Do you know him?"

Vendetta nodded. "Alan trained me. And maybe so."

The waitress leaned in a just a little closer. "If you are, I might have to start using a lot more gloves."

Why the fuck did he have to meet her now? While he was on a quest for revenge? Why couldn't he have met her after *that*?

Vendetta's gaze held hers for a long beat. Oh, he fucking liked her. A *lot*. But this was dangerous. Those big blue eyes would make it way too easy to forget the reason he was really here.

Or was it possibly a good thing? Whatever was going on between them, it was real enough to make him forget the mission for half a second. Since his own MC tried to fucking kill him, he'd been totally absorbed with his need for revenge. The constant drag of it left him feeling broken, like his quest for payback was the only thing holding what was left of him together. It left him drained most days, emotionally and physically.

Once he had his revenge, he was going to guaran-damn-tee every part of Cottonmouths and the motherfucking criminal network who bought them was dismantled, the victims set free.

But right now? The way she smiled at him, the way those big eyes took him in? It was the first time in a while he'd felt anything close to being human again.

Vendetta knew that the last thing he should be doing right now was to involve an innocent woman in the mess that was his life and resurrection. But maybe he could take it really slow, keep her out of everything until it was done.

"What time do you get off?" he asked her.

The smile she rewarded him was beautiful.

"Nine tonight," she said.

It was 8:45.

"We could go back to my place," she said, as she finished with the glasses. "It will take me twenty minutes to help close everything down."

Vendetta nodded. Going to hers was perfect. Pulling another twenty from his pocket, he slid it across the counter, finished off his beer.

She took it, getting in the register and appeared to be making change.

"Keep it," he told her. "I can wait in the parking lot. What do you drive?"

"I walk," she told him. "My place is a couple of blocks over."

"You walk?" Was she serious? "In this town?"

"Yeah, that's what my uncle says." She shook her head.

"I'll drive us," he said in a way that didn't leave room for argument. "Mine's the white Transit in the lot."

"I'll be out there shortly," she told him before getting back to closing the place down.

* * *

Dylan

Tall, dark, and mysterious drove them from the bar to her apartment building. The walk up the stairs to her apartment on the top floor didn't take long, but she felt every step of it.

He didn't say much, and she didn't fill the silence. Not because it was awkward, but because it wasn't. It felt oddly natural, like they were both saying plenty without saying a word.

Dylan's building sat on the east edge of Oak Grove, tucked between a closed-down Laundromat and a vape shop that never seemed to be open. It was three stories tall and built sometime in the eighties. The hallway lights flickered, the carpet was worn and uneven, and the stairwell always smelled vaguely of burnt toast and someone else's regrets.

It was her home now.

Dylan led him up to the third floor, down a narrow hallway that creaked underfoot. Hers was the unit with a weathered brass "3B" on the door. Dylan didn't look at him as she unlocked it, just pushed it open and stepped inside.

Her apartment wasn't much, but it was clean. It had one bedroom with a small bathroom and kitchen and a decent-sized living room. It held a thrifted couch with a throw blanket folded neatly over the arm, a secondhand coffee table she'd repainted herself, and a flat-screen TV. The TV had been one of the few things she'd taken with her from her previous apartment. There was no art on the walls, but there were a few framed photos on a shelf, just nothing recent. There were pictures of her in college, with her mom. A lake trip with friends she hadn't spoken to in far too long. A couple of other photos with family.

The kitchen was tucked into the corner. It was tiny, but she kept it spotless. She kept a candle that she burned low on the windowsill, cinnamon and vanilla softening the lingering scent of takeout.

"I don't have much," she said, locking the door behind him. "But it's mine."

She didn't say it defensively. She didn't want to explain that she was someone who had tied everything up in someone else for too long. She was finally learning how to build something for herself. She had to start somewhere, right?

Tossing her keys into the bowl by the door,

Dylan finally turned to her guest.

"So," she said with a soft smile, "you want a drink or something to eat?"

Tall, dark, and handsome shook his head.

The lighting in her apartment was better than at the bar. Her mystery man really was handsome. She turned toward him and found him standing near the door, just inside her space, still and quiet like he wasn't sure if he belonged there. He looked like trouble dressed in denim. He was built like someone who'd carried weight, literally and emotionally, for a long time. His dark hair brushed his shoulders, slightly damp from the night air, and the long beard only made him look more dangerous, but not in a way that scared her.

He wore his jeans with an old hoodie under a broken-in jean jacket. It was like he'd walked out of a backroad and into her life without warning. The cap shadowed his eyes, but not enough to hide the intensity in them. They were dark and sharp, like he saw everything and forgot nothing.

The man made her feel things she shouldn't be feeling. It was rare that she took someone home on a whim. But when he asked when her shift ended, what was she supposed to do? She'd learned that if you said no to the right thing, you usually didn't get a second chance.

He hadn't told her much. She didn't know his name or where he came from. And she hadn't pushed. But there was something steady about him. Like whatever storms he'd walked through had taught him how to stay calm in the middle of chaos.

The only thing she was sure of? He wasn't like anyone she'd met so far.

"Well, come in," she told him, motioning to her

couch. "You promised me conversation."

That earned her a smile that made her weak in the knees. Pulling off his cap, he hung it on one of the coat pegs next to her front door. Then he shed the denim jacket for good measure. Even with the hoodie he wore, she could tell there was a great body under there. She knew there had to be. His thighs were thick and heavily muscled, straining the jeans he wore. She watched patiently, thinking she'd be fine if he wanted to take more things off.

Walking around, he took a seat next to her on the couch. Right next to her.

Holding out a hand, she grinned at him. "I'm Dylan."

He shook her hand, his gaze on her mouth now. "Jason."

"Now that that's out of the way." She leaned into him, kissing his mouth. Yeah, she knew she could be reading the situation wrong, but she didn't think so.

Jason kissed her back, slowly, not matching her hurried pace. His hands came up to cup her face as he deepened the kiss and she let him, loving the way one hand moved to pull the tie from her hair so it would fall heavily around her shoulders. He wasted no time getting both hands in it, clutching the strands to pull her closer.

And the man sure knew how to kiss. *Damn.*

Dylan was a curvy girl, but Jason let go of her hair, grabbing her hips and pulling her to straddle his lap like she weighed nothing at all. While she was caught off guard, he began peppering kisses over her throat, over her chest. He wasn't playing. When those big hands slid up from her hips to her breasts, she pressed herself into him. The scratch of his beard sent shivers down her spine. The way his hands handled her breasts had her nipples rock hard as she tried to catch her breath.

Wrapping her arms around his neck, she got her hands into the thick locks of his hair. When he grabbed the hem of her peasant top and pulled it up and off her, she helped him, grateful she'd worn a nice bra and panty set. Had she hoped things would go like this? *Yes*. Jason's hands went for the back of her bra, and she took the opportunity to grind down on him, not disappointed in the bulge she encountered. Her panties were a soaked mess under her jeans as he got the bra off, got his hands and mouth on her breasts.

"That feels so fucking good," she said with a gasp. The way his tongue danced over her nipple had her squirming on his lap. Little nips of his teeth pushed her desire through the roof.

Grabbing his hair, she just enjoyed what he was offering, hanging on tight.

Jason took his time with her, not hitting the gas pedal the way she wanted him to. His touch was rough, but he didn't cross the line to pain. He started rolling his hips under her, wanting her to feel what she was doing to him. Yes, she wanted that. Impatient as she was, she couldn't hurry him, but the slow torture was what she needed and hadn't known it until this minute. It had been so long since she'd last had sex, and she couldn't remember anyone working her up the way he was now.

He pressed warm kisses up her chest, over her throat. By the time his lips made it to her ear, Dylan was trembling with need. The brush of his beard over her ear made her shiver.

"Are we covered here?" His breath was hot in her ear. "I didn't exactly plan ahead. Not that I'm disappointed by how this is going."

"IUD," she managed, struggling for air. "I've been tested. I'm clean."

"Me too. Hang on," he said, rising from the couch with her like he didn't have her wrapped around his body. "Where am I going?"

There were only two other rooms, a bathroom and her bedroom which she pointed to. Jason headed for it, again, not in a rush.

It was cooler in her bedroom and dark, with only the light from the streetlamps shining through her one small window. When he lowered her onto her bed it felt heavenly, cool against her skin. She didn't have long to enjoy it because Jason's hands went to the front of her jeans, and he began working them off her lower body, pulling off her panties. When she was completely revealed to him, those dark eyes took her in slowly, like he was committing her to memory. The man hovered above her, taking her all in and it was driving her crazy.

While he was eye-fucking her, she pawed at his hoodie. "Your turn. Take stuff off," she said, flashing him a smile.

Grabbing the hem of that hoodie, he pulled it off like an experienced stripper, smiling the entire time. She'd underestimated what he had under there. *Damn.* Jason was cut with huge biceps and a wide expanse of muscular chest. He had a few tattoos scattered over his torso and arms, but it was too dark to make out any details. And considering the bulge at the front of his jeans right now, she didn't give a damn what tattoos he had.

"Now the rest," she prompted him, running a bare foot along his denim-covered thigh.

"Yes, ma'am," he said, making quick work of his jeans. And he was commando under there, so she got a look at what he was packing earlier than she would have. It was well-proportioned to the rest of him. Damn.

"See something you like?" Jason asked, taking himself in hand and working his cock with leisurely strokes.

Jason rolled to her side, stretching out on his back. He winked at her, still working himself. "Save a bike, ride a biker," he said. "Hop on."

Well, she wasn't turning *that* down. Dylan straddled him, sliding down on him and gasping as her walls spread around him. She took it slowly, enjoying the burn and stretch. His big hands were on her hips, but he wasn't trying to hurry her. The way those deep, dark eyes drank her in, she could tell he was enjoying the show.

When Dylan made it all the way down, she rotated her hips, causing him to rotate up into her. It was a nice start, but she wanted more. Planting her hands on his chest, she switched up her position. He said ride a biker, didn't he? When she found a comfortable place, she started moving up and down on him. Being on top was a huge turn on for her and as a curvier girl, she didn't get the opportunity often.

Jason was the perfect size to hit all the right places, feeling so good as she moved on him. The way his gaze moved over her face and breasts had her libido growing fangs. The way he focused on where their bodies joined as she rode him made her weak in the knees.

Sliding a hand between them, he delicately started working her clit with his thumb. It wasn't the all-out rub fest that most men thought was sexy. No, his touch was delicate with just the right amount of pressure. He kept up with her, making her fuck herself on his cock as she was. It drove her crazy.

"You feel so good squeezing me," he growled, the pleasure making his deep voice gravelly, and the sound sent shivers down her spine.

Dylan was beyond speech at that point. Her nails were scratching over the light sprinkling of hair on his massive chest, her vision fading out as she got closer to the orgasm she was chasing. When it hit her, she closed her eyes and stars exploded behind her eyelids as all that sensation rocked her. Her movements were erratic, slowing.

Beneath her, Jason finally grabbed her hips and started pulling her down on his cock as he thrust up. She tried not to scream because of her neighbors but… fuck her neighbors. His moves drew her release out, taking it from a quiet riot to full-on fireworks exploding in her body. She clawed at his chest, fighting to breathe. She wasn't aware that he'd rolled her under him until she was coming back down.

Having him on top? What more could a girl want? Jason was big and her world darkened as she was lost in his shadow. He was already fucking her, slowly. His cock was harder now.

Leaning down, he chained kisses up her neck, up to her ear. "You got quiet, Dylan," he whispered hotly. "You good?"

Still fighting to catch her breath, she grinned. "I'm fan-fucking-tastic, big guy. What else you got?"

His laugh was a deep rumble that sent a shiver running through her. "I was hoping you'd say that."

His movements within her slowed as he captured each of her hands in his. Lacing his fingers through hers, he pressed them into the bed on either side of her head. His hold was firm, but not too hard and it didn't hurt. Jason came closer, dropping to his elbows so he could kiss her mouth, taste her skin. And he did as his thrusts gained in speed and momentum. Dylan's knees came up to cradle his hips, as he worked himself in her. His thrusts were faster, a little harder. Pinned beneath him, she just enjoyed the ride, wishing she'd turned on the lamp on her bedside table. The view of him was gorgeous with wide shoulders, all that muscle, and his dark hair hanging around his face as he fucked her.

Jason pushed her back up to the edge again, breathing fast, but he didn't appear to be close to coming himself. He dropped kisses over her face, down to her chest. When his lips found her nipple, and he didn't break his stride, she braced for impact. He traced over that tiny peak, and at the same time, his thrusts grew stronger. Her cry was raspy and low as he made her come again on his cock, still pushing into her as her walls fluttered around his driving length.

He was still going, and she felt him smile above her in the dark more than she actually saw it. "You know how beautiful you look when you come?" His voice was rougher. "Want to go for one more?"

Was he kidding? She was about to pass out, cock-drunk and dizzy. She wasn't even moving right now.

Dylan winced as he pulled free of her, shifting on the bed.

"Over," he said, as he easily pushed her over onto her stomach. Despite how sated she was, Dylan was curious to see what he'd do next. She was super grateful she had the day off tomorrow because she couldn't imagine she'd be walking straight for a couple of days.

"Up," Jason said, hauling her hips up with her knees tucked under her.

When she went to push up with her arms, a firm

hand pressed her head back down to the pillow.

"Stay," he said, his fingers running through her hair for just a moment.

She wouldn't have thought she had anything else to give, but she'd never tried the position before, so she wanted to let that play out. He might be scraping her off her own bed later, but it would be worth it.

Jason's hands grabbed her hips, then he speared right into her from behind. For a moment, he barely moved, giving her time to adjust. Her thighs were shaking now, and she just hoped her knees would hold her up for this. Because when he started moving faster, driving into her from behind, pleasure blended with just a shade of pain. It was working her up again.

"I knew you had one more to give me," he said, one hand smoothing over her ass, as if it were apologizing for the growing force of his cock.

Dylan wouldn't have thought she had one more, but she was heading for it anyway. She just hoped she survived it. He'd reached a rhythm that had her squeezing around him, mindlessly chanting "please" over and over as he kept going.

The slap on her ass was a complete surprise, the sharp sting warming up her skin. Jason did it again, making her clench around his cock despite herself.

"That's too good," he drawled, sounding breathless now.

When his hand fisted in her hair, she barely noticed. When he tugged on it sharply, her blissed-out mind somehow figured out what he wanted. Pushing up on her hands, she was into doggy-style. He was holding onto her hair tight enough to sting but not to hurt. Then he took her for a ride. Holding onto her hair with one hand, the other gripping her hips, Jason rocked her world, slamming into her over and over.

She told herself she was just hanging on until he could get off but only a couple of minutes later, he shifted his angle until he hit her in just the right spot.

Dylan's knees and elbows shook, sweat dotted her brow. He was adding spanks here and there, not in any discernible rhythm so she didn't know when the next was coming. Her heart was flying when that wave hit her and she collapsed, screaming into her pillow as he worked himself through it behind her, meeting his own end with her hips in his hands.

Dylan felt him rolling to one side of her, the heavy cadence of his breath matching hers. One of his large hands slid over her ass, content to settle there as she eased down from all that stimulation. Still, he'd exceeded her expectations. Not only was he completely charming, he'd worked her over in a way no man ever had before. She had no doubt she'd be sore tomorrow, but she was smiling because every sore spot or movement would just be a reminder of tonight. And tonight blew her away.

"That smile for me?" Jason asked and she loved his whiskey-deep voice.

Dylan nodded, still smiling. "Are you staying tonight?" she asked, hoping she didn't sound completely needy but knowing she probably did.

"I'd like to." He kept his voice low. "As long as it's not going to create a problem."

She sighed. "Not at all. I had an ex for several months and the only person I know in town is my uncle." His hand was rubbing her lower back now and she hummed, enjoying that touch. "He's never even been to my place. Too busy running his biker gang."

If she'd opened her eyes, she would have seen Jason freeze next to her. But she was too blissed out at that point.

"Oh, yeah?" he asked. "You know which biker gang? There are a few around in these areas."

"The Cottonmouths," she whispered. "My uncle Eli is their president."

Chapter Three

Vendetta

The morning light just started to spill through the blinds when Vendetta pulled his hoodie back over his head, careful not to make a sound. Dylan was still asleep, curled on her side. She had one arm under the pillow, sleeping peacefully with her blonde hair tangled against her cheek. Her full figure was wrapped in sheets like she was posing for a boudoir photo shoot. Dylan was beautiful.

He shouldn't have stayed the night; he knew that, and he sure as hell shouldn't have touched her. But the damage was done now, and all he could do was control what happened next. He moved through the apartment with muscle memory. Grabbing his jacket and boots in hand, he didn't look back until he reached the door.

That's when he saw it. Not that he needed it for verification because he believed her. A photo on the edge of her small shelf. A handful of people. Her, a few years younger, smiling widely in front of a birthday cake with candles in the shape of two and one. The man standing right behind her? None other than Eli Crizer.

The recognition hit like a gut punch. It was *true*. Same cold stare and crooked smile. The same fucking monster behind the charm. Vendetta's stomach flipped as he stared at that photo for one long, stunned second before turning the handle and slipping out the door of her apartment.

Outside, the air was cold and sharp in his lungs. *Crizer's fucking niece*. The woman he was trying hard not to fall for? She shared blood with the man he came back to destroy. And the worst part was that he couldn't wait to see her again.

Last night was one of the best nights he'd had in years. Vendetta knew he should have walked away and never looked back, but he just couldn't shake her. The way she looked at him, like she wasn't afraid, like she saw something in him worth knowing. She didn't see the ghosts or the scars and he had plenty. Just *him.*

Dylan didn't know who he really was or what happened to him. Hell, she didn't even know his real name. But when she smiled at him, when she touched him, he didn't feel like Vendetta the ghost. He felt like the man he used to be. And no one had made him feel like that in a long damn time. Vendetta knew it was dangerous. That getting close to her could cost them both by the end.

After a quick stop at his motel room, Vendetta showered and changed clothes, making it to work right on time. He didn't linger with Alan and Freddie and the other drivers. They stood around for a good half hour each morning as they drank coffee, shared gossip, and pretended to laugh at Freddie's lame-ass jokes. He wouldn't linger. He needed to get to the heart of the Cottonmouth's corrupt partnership with the dark crime syndicate. He wouldn't drag it out a minute longer than he had to.

Vendetta rolled into the alley behind *Ned's Sundown Lounge* around 11:00 that morning, the van tires crunching over gravel and scattered trash in the lot. The back door of the bar was propped open with a cinder block, the same lazy setup as usual. No Cottonmouth bikes out front. And Dylan told him she had the day off.

Good. He wasn't in the mood for pretending. Grabbing the box of medical supplies from the back, he headed for the door. It was basic stuff. Gloves, alcohol wipes, first aid kits. The kind of order that didn't raise red flags unless you knew who was doing the ordering.

Peggy Campbell met him at the door, arms crossed, sunglasses pushed up on her head like she hadn't slept much either.

"Didn't think *you'd* be doing the drop today," she muttered, stepping aside.

"Lucky you," he replied. He was just about to walk in when Peggy spoke again in a low voice, but sharp enough to cut through the air between them.

"I saw you leave with Dylan last night."

Vendetta paused, hand on the doorframe. He turned just enough to see her expression. It wasn't smug or curious. It felt like a warning.

He met her gaze. "You see a lot for someone who keeps their head down most of the time."

Peggy crossed her arms. "I'm not blind. And I've been here long enough to know that getting close to anything with the name Crizer stamped on it usually ends bad."

She had no fucking idea.

"She seems nice," Peggy added, tone edged. "Does a good job. But she's almost too nice for *this* place."

Vendetta didn't fire off a quick answer. He needed to be careful, not just for his sake but Dylan's. He nodded. "She doesn't belong here," he said finally.

Peggy watched him, her expression unreadable. "Most don't. But some figure it out too late."

Vendetta knew that already. It gave him a lot to think about because he didn't want Dylan to be a casualty of this place. She didn't know it, but the fact that she was Eli's niece wouldn't help her. The man killed his own son a couple of years back in some bad blood with the Hounds in Mercy. In the right circumstances, Eli wouldn't hesitate to kill her either. And Vendetta would be damned if he let that happen. When all this went down, he had no intention of leaving her behind.

With that, he walked into the back as he normally did.

"Put it near the back fridge," Peggy called. "Outta the way."

He started toward the hallway, passing the kitchen and bar storage before reaching the cooler room. As instructed, he set the box down and turned to leave. But then he heard a low, male voice coming from the other side of the wall.

"They're moving two more tonight… Eli… van leaves after midnight."

Vendetta froze, eyes narrowing. The voice was muffled so he had no chance of identifying the speaker or making out all the words, but he got the gist of it.

"Girl last week put up a fight… drop point. Tell 'em… dose 'em fucking earlier."

Another voice laughed. "Hell, let 'em fight. Makes the payout better… sickos down the line."

With his pulse pounding in his ears, his hands clenched at his sides. He'd known the bar had a basement, but he didn't realize that they were using it for their trafficking activities. Was this a hub for their activities? Vendetta didn't think for a single minute that it was the *only* hub. Eli was smarter than that.

Moving quietly, he traced the edge of the wall toward a half-open door leading down to a narrow flight of stairs. A customer wouldn't notice it unless they were looking for it. Vendetta couldn't go down, not without revealing himself. But he stayed, watching and listening.

From what he could tell there were two of them. Cottonmouth jackets tossed over chairs and there was a packing case next to those. He also saw a clipboard with neat columns. He was too far to see exactly what was written on the paper it held. But if he had to guess, there were names, drop points, and dollar amounts. He could make out dollar signs. Trafficking manifests?

There was more laughter as the conversation turned into something crude. *Disgusting.*

The sight of the clipboard turned his blood to ice. He'd seen lists like that overseas, different language but with the same intent. Humans mercilessly turned into inventory. Numbers attached to young people's lives. Fury coiled tight in his chest, and he had to control it until he was ready. It was like drinking battery acid and hoping you didn't die.

But at that moment, any lingering doubt he had about what had to be done burned away. This wasn't just revenge anymore. It was justice. And when he was done, there wouldn't be enough left of Eli Crizer's operation to sweep under the rug.

Going back the way he came, he kept his footsteps silent, trying to contain the storm of emotions that just hit him. When he returned to the hallway, Peggy was waiting. She gave him a hard look.

"What took you so long?" she asked, trying to sound like she wasn't interested in the answer. The wariness in the woman's eyes suggested otherwise.

"My boss called." As a lie it worked because if she thought he was on the phone, she would think he didn't hear anything he wasn't supposed to hear.

"Have a good one," she said, tone flat.

"You too," he muttered, walking toward his van.

Yes, he knew what they were doing. But now, he needed to figure out where their other hot spots were and get his hands on solid proof. Once he had it all plotted out, he'd dismantle the whole fucking operation from the inside and then, and only then, he'd let them know who destroyed them. A man they thought long dead, risen from the ashes.

* * *

Dylan

The bar was quiet at her next shift a couple of days later. For now.

Dylan wiped down the counter for the second time, more out of nerves than necessity. Her phone buzzed in her apron pocket. Just a quick check-in from Jason. While it was nothing heavy or flirtatious, it had her heart skipping a beat.

Jason hadn't ghosted her. When she woke up alone in bed the next morning, she assumed he had. There was no note or text. Nothing. It would have ruined her entire day except for the text he sent her around lunchtime while she was in the grocery store.

Hope you slept well, beautiful.

More texts arrived after that. Always short, because Jason wasn't a big talker, and he absolutely didn't do emojis. She'd thought about him too much since that night they spent together. It felt good to breathe next to someone who didn't expect anything from her for once. Someone who looked at her like he actually saw her. He hadn't asked about seeing her again, which gave her a few doubts, but she kept hearing from him so there was hope.

Sometimes Dylan still questioned why she had come back to Oak Grove of all places. She had a small, cramped apartment and a job at her uncle's bar. The only way she was better off than when she lived in Richmond was that she didn't have a loser boyfriend.

Honestly, she shouldn't even be considering another relationship just yet.

Ah, but Jason made her want things. Right now, it would be worth it if he'd walked through that door again.

Instead, the door opened and the temperature in the room shifted. A group of Cottonmouths swaggered in like they owned the place. Coiled snakes on their cuts, the boots, the body language, the presence. And then she saw her uncle, Eli. He caught sight of her instantly and gave a nod. He moved toward the bar, toward her, while the rest of his crew scattered to their usual table like hyenas to a carcass.

"Didn't expect to see you tonight," Eli said, taking a seat at the bar, expression unreadable.

"I'm scheduled," Dylan replied, grabbing a clean glass and setting it in front of him. "Same as last week."

"You know this place gets rough after dark." His voice was calm, but there was an undercurrent. He wasn't just making conversation.

"I can handle rough," she said, meeting his eyes. "You never gave me a chance to tell you about my work experience."

Eli gave a short, dry laugh as she poured him a beer. "You're a Crizer, I'll give you that. Stubborn as fuck."

He watched her a moment longer, then lowered his voice just enough to make her lean in. "You're smart. You've got options. You don't need to be here, Dylan."

"I *want* to be here."

Her uncle's eyes narrowed at her. "Wanting something doesn't mean it's good for you."

Before she could answer, one of the guys at the

table hollered for a round of beers, and Eli pulled back, voice lighter. "Go take care of them."

She nodded, forcing a polite smile as he walked to their table. But her stomach dropped after that very short conversation. She could have assumed that his advice was meant to keep her safe and protect her. But that wasn't what it felt like. It felt like a warning. And the way he said it left a cold weight in her stomach she couldn't shake. Why was he trying to warn her? Was there something going on that she wasn't supposed to know about?

Dylan got a round of beers ready, carrying the tray over with practiced ease, balancing bottles and short glasses like second nature. The laughter at the table swelled as she approached. They were the kind of sounds men made when they were trying to look like they ran the room.

"Careful there, sweetheart," Trucker said as she leaned in to set down the drinks. "Don't spill any on me. This jacket's older than you."

Dylan gave him a tight smile, unfazed. "Then maybe don't lean so close to the edge of the table."

That got a few snickers from the others. Grudge, lounging with his boots up, muttered something to Creep beside him, and they exchanged a glance. "Girl's got teeth," Eagle said, louder this time. "Might want to watch that."

Eli didn't say a word.

What the fuck is that supposed to mean?

Setting down the last glass, Dylan turned to walk away when she caught it, almost a whisper.

Trucker kicked him hard under the table as she started walking.

Creep leaned toward the center of the table, voice pitched just above a whisper. "Midnight drop is behind the lot again. Same place as last week. Crates are marked."

Dylan didn't stop walking, and hoped to God she didn't give any indication she'd heard anything. But the words lodged in her brain like a splinter. What was happening at midnight that the big bad bikers had to whisper about? She didn't know what any of it meant, but the tone used *wasn't* bar business.

Back behind the counter, Dylan took a slow breath and focused on restocking straws just to keep her hands busy. She didn't know why but she just couldn't get the coded comment out of her head.

Uncle Eli hadn't said a word when they talked to her like that. He hadn't even blinked when they tossed around whatever the hell that was. And for the first time since taking this job, Dylan wondered if her uncle had been trying to protect her from whatever shady shit was going on there.

Or trying to keep her from seeing too much.

The crowd came in even though her uncle and his men stayed a long time. It was almost ten before they left. Once the bar began emptying out, she stepped outside for a quick break. The cool night air bit her skin as she leaned against the brick wall out back. The door shut behind her with a thud, cutting off the noise from inside. *Much better.*

Pulling out her phone, Dylan's thumb hovered for a long minute before she typed out a text to Jason.

Dylan: *you ever get the feeling you're not supposed to hear something*?

It didn't take him long to reply.

Jason: *you okay*?

Staring at the screen for a second, she debated how much to say.

Dylan: *yeah. just… weird vibe at work tonight. uncle*

showed up with his crew. it was weird.

There was a pause. Longer this time.

Jason: *you wanna talk about it? i can bring pizza to your place.*

Her lips curved before she realized it, looking down at her phone again.

Dylan: *yeah. that'd be nice. pineapple okay*?

Jason: *real pizzas dont have pineapple*

Dylan laughed. Oh, he was one of *those.*

Dylan: *fine. no sausage*

She laughed, tucking her phone back in her pocket. She wasn't sure what was happening at *Ned's Sundown Lounge*, or what exactly she'd stumbled into. But for now, knowing someone was willing to show up with food and no questions made the world feel a little less twisted.

* * *

Dylan

Ned's Sundown Lounge was still buzzing behind her, but Dylan's shift was over, and that was all she cared about. She pulled her coat tighter around her as she stepped into the cool night and spotted Jason's van idling under the streetlight across the lot.

The headlights were off, but she could see him through the windshield, quietly waiting. Something about that made her heart squeeze in her chest. In a world full of noise, his silence felt like safety. She opened the passenger door when she reached him, and the scent of pizza hit her before she even got in. After the day she had, climbing into the van with him and the smell of warm pizza was literally heaven. Did she smell…

"Pineapple?" she asked, sliding inside and closing the door behind her.

He handed her the warm box without a word, and she smiled. "You're good."

"I try," Jason said, his voice low and even.

She set the box on her lap and buckled up. "You really didn't have to do this."

"I wanted to."

That was all he said, and that was all she needed. The drive to her apartment was quiet, just the hum of the tires. By the time they pulled into her lot, the pizza box had warmed her lap, and her nerves had settled just a little. Upstairs, inside her apartment, she kicked off her boots. Jason set the pizza on the table while she grabbed two plates and a couple of drinks. There was no small talk or pressure. When was the last time she shared comfortable silence with anyone?

She sat next to him on the couch, eyes scanning his face as she chewed on her bottom lip. But he beat her to the punch.

"So…" he said gently. "What happened earlier?"

Dylan leaned back, blowing out a sigh, and finally let it spill. "My uncle came in with his crew. You know, his Cottonmouths. They were rowdy but… not in a drunk way. Like something was going on. I brought them drinks and overheard one of them mention something I really wasn't trying to hear when I walked back to the bar."

Jason wasn't looking at her, just eating a slice of pizza. It made it easier to get it out.

"One of them said something about a midnight drop behind a lot and…" She paused, watching him carefully. "I don't know what that means, but it didn't sound like beer deliveries."

Finishing up his pizza slice, Jason kept listening.

"And the way they acted…" She shook her head. "They were different with me. Like I was a piece of furniture. And my uncle didn't say a damn word to stop it." She looked down, her voice softer now. "Eli doesn't want me working there. Did I tell you that? When he came to the bar tonight, he was *still* trying to get that message across. I guess that's what has me overthinking all this. I mean, I know things go on behind the scenes at sketchy bars. I've quit a couple. But it makes me wonder."

Jason leaned back slightly, his gaze steady on her. "If your uncle doesn't want you working there, maybe you should listen to him," he said quietly.

Dylan looked up at him. "You think he's right?"

"I think," Jason said, carefully, "that places like that don't get better just because good people walk through the door."

The silence that followed said more than any warning could.

Thinking he probably hadn't come there to listen to her talk about her job, she reached for the pizza box and flipped it open again. Like the silence between them didn't feel like a loaded gun resting on the table.

"Ham and pineapple," she said, trying for light. "Don't judge."

Jason's mouth twitched, just slightly. "Wouldn't dream of it."

They ate at a quiet rhythm for a few moments, comfortable, but not quite relaxed. He watched her carefully, like he was trying to understand more than just her taste in pizza. "You mentioned your uncle," he said finally, tone still casual. "You two close?"

Dylan shrugged, swallowing her bite. "As close as you can be when you move back home at twenty-five and ask for a job at the one place he doesn't want you to work."

He nodded slowly, waiting.

Dylan took a sip of her drink. "We were close when I was a kid. My dad was his brother, and *not* a biker. He died in a car accident when I was little. He always kept an eye on me after my mom passed. That was a week before my twenty-first birthday."

Something flashed in Jason's dark eyes, but it was gone so fast she wondered if she'd imagined it.

"He's always been protective, but… this time, I don't know. It felt different. Like he wasn't just worried I'd get hit on or stiffed on tips. Like he knew something I didn't, and he didn't want me to know. I've worked in bars before," she went on, trying to shrug it off. "College town spots. Rough crowds. But nothing like this. This place… I'm not going to lie, it's a little scary."

"And yet you're still there," he pointed out.

"I didn't want to back down just because it made him uncomfortable," she said, lifting her eyes to his. "I wanted to prove I could handle it."

He studied her for a beat longer. "And now?"

She hesitated, brushing her fingers over the edge of the pizza box. "Now I'm not so sure."

Jason grabbed a plate and put his half slice of pizza down. Now his gaze was on her, his voice low but direct. "Is proving your uncle wrong the right reason to stay in a place that feels dangerous?"

The question stretched out between them. It wasn't judgmental, but honest. Thinking about the answer to that only pushed her anxiety higher. She exhaled slowly. "No. It's not."

Jason waited, still listening.

"I guess…" she started, then stopped. Took a breath and tried again. "A few months ago, I walked away from a five-year relationship. We weren't married, but it kind of felt like it sometimes. Lived together, built a life together… or tried to. I don't think he ever really saw me."

"Was he as young as you?" Jason asked.

Dylan shook her head. "Maybe that was the problem. I'm into older men, but he wanted to control my every move, my every thought." Her voice went soft. "When I left, I told myself I was done shrinking to fit inside someone else's expectations. I came back here because I needed space to figure out who I am again. And yeah, part of me wanted to prove I could handle this job. That I didn't need anyone telling me what I could or couldn't do anymore."

She looked up at him, her gaze steadier now. "I didn't come back to be reckless. I came back to be me. I just didn't expect 'me' to feel this damn complicated."

Jason held her eyes for a long moment, something unreadable flickering behind his own. Then he nodded, quiet. "Complicated's okay," he said. "So long as it doesn't get you killed."

"What else am I going to do?" she asked. She'd posed the question to herself dozens of times with no answer coming. "Working at the bar is what I'm used to. I don't really want to work as a checkout girl or in an office. That's just not me."

"There are more options than that, you know." Laying his arm along the back of the couch behind her, his fingers started toying with a lock of her hair idly. "Why not a waitress?"

Dylan had to laugh at that. "Yeah, you think *we* get treated like shit sometimes? Waitresses have it much worse, believe me."

"I don't know," he said, studying her now. "There's a family-owned Greek restaurant near where I'm staying. Nice place. The waitresses there look like they do pretty well."

"Where do you live by the way?" She hoped it wasn't too forward a question. She wasn't trying to scare him away.

"Renting a room by the day," he explained.

Oh. *Wait*. He was just here temporarily?

Now his entire hand was playing with her hair, and he smiled. "I'm here temporarily. For now. If things go the way I want them to, I could make a case for staying here or staying next door in Mercy."

That was better. Still, she hated that he saw her reaction to the news he might *not* stick around. It made her look desperate. *Fuck.*

"Get out of your head, pretty girl," he told her. "Why worry about tomorrow? I try to live in the moment."

Dylan wanted to think that way, but she just couldn't pull it off. Maybe it was because she was in a place of transition with her relationship ending and moving back to Oak Grove.

Jason's hand cupped the back of her head, pulling her in for a kiss. Dylan went along. It wasn't a half-hearted effort to move things along to what he really wanted. He took his time, kissing her softly. She liked the way his hands moved in her hair or over her body. She loved that he kissed like it was the best part of his day and he'd been looking forward to it all day.

Yeah, she *wished*.

But for now, he was hers. And he was gorgeous so why not enjoy it while she could? So far, they'd only had one night together, and the next day she'd barely wanted to get out of bed, she was so sleepy and sated.

He wasn't wearing a cap today and his hair was down, just touching his shoulders in thick locks of rich brown. She got her hands in his hair as he deepened the kiss. His beefy arms wrapped around her, dragging her close to him and she was here for it. He kissed her breathless, until she was running her hands over his body as much as he was hers. When her hand finally settled over the bulge at the front of his jeans, the deep groan that earned her was so satisfying.

Dylan pulled out of his grip to stand, taking his hand and trying to get him to her bedroom. But he didn't look like he had any intention of going anywhere. He shook his head, wrapping his hands behind her knees and pulling her in until she straddled his lap.

He was as breathless as she was as the center of her dropped snugly over him. "You really like cowgirl, huh?" she teased.

"When the view's as beautiful as this one? Yeah," he told her, claiming her mouth for another heated kiss.

"I've got another idea," she told him, grinning.

A flash of disappointment crossed his features as she pulled out of his grasp. It faded as she got on her knees between his spread thighs. He huffed out a laugh as she worked at his belt and finally got his jeans open. He was more than happy to push them all the way down for her, his dark-eyed gaze heated as he watched her.

"I'm still fucking you after this," he said bluntly.

The scent of him rose as he offered his cock to her. Dylan loved that he was just a little longer, just a little wider than she was used to. And she'd been looking forward to this. Working him carefully with her hands, she gripped the base firmly with one hand, stroked the shaft with the other. As if he needed to be worked up. He was so warm and hard in her hands.

When she pressed a kiss to the head of his cock, she felt his gaze on her. She took her time, teasing him.

When her lips spread around the head and she teased him with the tip of her tongue, his head dropped back onto the sofa, his breath rushing out in a hiss.

He liked that, huh? Dylan really got to work then. She broke out her best moves, working him further into her mouth until he hit the back of her throat. Just as he settled into that, she changed it up, tracing his shaft, all his ridges carefully with her tongue. The way he huffed impatiently had her smiling around him. The way his hands sank into her hair as she continued teasing him had her plenty wet, hoping he'd keep the promise he made about later.

Considering how insatiable he'd been on their first night together, she was pretty sure it was a safe bet. By the time she was working him back into her throat again, those big hands took control of her head. He was careful with her but ended up fucking her face just the same. It was worth the tears spilling from her eyes, the fight to suck in air at any opportunity. He was close…

When he literally pulled her off him, she was sure she looked a mess, staring at him with her mouth open. So much heat in his expression as he kissed her like his life depended on it, tasting himself on her tongue. He broke the kiss as he stood, pulling her up with him. He undid her jeans before she could react. He pulled them and her panties off, with the fury of a storm.

Dylan still had her peasant top on, her bright fuzzy socks. He came at her, backing her against the nearest wall with the intent, she hoped, of fucking her senseless.

She braced for him to grab her caveman style and haul her up the wall. Instead, he took a knee and held her hips in his hands, getting his mouth on her. After a minute -- and a lot of obscene noises -- he hauled one of her legs over his shoulder, digging in. All she could do was hold onto his broad shoulders as he tasted her, working her up with his lips and tongue. He didn't stop until she was right there on the edge, arching her back against the wall and literally begging him for it with words she barely had the breath to say.

Jason stopped right before she could come. The whine he pulled from her would have been embarrassing if she hadn't been so desperate to climax. She had to fight to stay upright as need gripped her hard. It was *then* that he grabbed her legs, hauling them up around his waist and pushing her up the wall like she weighed nothing at all. Jason wasted no time sliding inside her in one smooth thrust.

Dylan came on his cock before he made the second thrust, crying out. Jason's hand clamped over her mouth, muting her cries as he began to nail her into the wall. Pinned to the wall, she just hung on for the ride.

Her orgasm bled into another as his thrusts gained in speed and power. He came with her the second time, his face buried in her shoulder. A slice of pain had her jerking in his hold. He'd *bitten* her. Not hard enough to break the skin but enough for her to feel it, for the pinch of pain to blend with the pleasure flooding her entire body.

As they came down, Jason dropped a kiss over the bite mark he left on her shoulder, layered more kisses over her neck. When his lips met hers, they were gentle, unhurried.

"Are you staying the night?" she asked, hoping the answer was yes. "I'm sleepy."

A sharp slap landed on her ass before he eased her to her feet. Jason's grin was downright sinful.

"Sleepy?" He shook his head. "Time for round two."

He threw her over his shoulder and hustled them into her bedroom. Dylan just laughed and held on.

Chapter Four

Vendetta

The morning air was crisp, cold enough to keep his window rolled halfway up, but not cold enough to stop the fog from clinging to the edges of the glass. The van hummed beneath him, its tires eating up the pavement as he made his way through the first leg of his route. A rehab clinic, an assisted living, and a small pharmacy with a back door and no security cameras.

The usual.

Vendetta kept the van steady, one hand on the wheel, the other resting on his thigh. His fingers twitched out of habit more than restlessness.

But his mind wasn't on the road. It was on *her*. The girl with the knockout smile, kind eyes, and a voice that had a way of cutting through his walls without even trying. The girl who'd invited him into her story. She had no idea she was living in the middle of a battlefield. He hadn't planned on seeing her again, not until he accomplished what he'd set out to do. He sure hadn't counted on sitting in her apartment eating pizza and listening to her question her whole damn world. But the more he got to know her, the more he *had* her, the more he craved.

All it took was her mention of her uncle, Eli, and he had his excuse to see her again. His gut warned him not to answer her text. Every instinct honed from years of surviving betrayal, blood, and backroom lies screamed that getting closer to her was a bad idea. That the second he got tangled up with Dylan Crizer, he'd lose the edge he needed to finish what he came back here to do.

But there was no walking away from it now. When the truth in all this came for her -- and it would -

- who would she have left to trust but *him*? It didn't matter how bad an idea it was. She was his responsibility from the moment he'd touched her. She was his to protect, his to watch over. He would be the one to protect her when she inevitably faced her uncle's betrayal.

Eli Crizer was good at doling out betrayal. Vendetta hadn't asked for the betrayal Eli and his sworn brothers had dealt him. But it was his, and he'd burn Oak Grove down before he let them, let *Eli*, touch her.

Vendetta's anger rose at the thought of her uncle not speaking up while his crew disrespected his niece right in front of him. That silence said everything. Either he didn't care, or he couldn't afford to show it. Neither one sat right. And the way Dylan talked about him? Like she was still trying to give him the benefit of the doubt. Dylan hadn't seen who he really was yet. But she would. And when she did, she'd break. Which meant Vendetta had to be ready to make sure she didn't shatter alone. Another reason he needed to stay close to her.

Turning down a narrow access road, *Noesner Medical Clinic* was the kind of place that looked respectable from the front but hadn't seen a paint job in five years. It sat on the edge of the industrial strip, boxed in by chain-link fencing and loading docks that hadn't been used for anything legal in a long time.

His stop here was simple. He was dropping off one box of wound care kits and IV-line replacements. He'd been in and out a half-dozen times already. He'd never seen more than a tired receptionist or a delivery driver from the lab.

Something was different today.

As Vendetta rounded the back lot, he slowed the

van to a crawl. Another vehicle was already there. A dark, unmarked van. No company logos. Just dust, dents, and tinted windows. Outside of it, two men stood, one of them wearing a Cottonmouth cut. He was too young to be a higher up. Young and jumpy, he was one of the hang-arounds Vendetta had noticed lurking near *Ned*'s a few times. The other man was older and in casual clothes, and he looked really pissed off.

Vendetta parked in the lot, his van facing in the opposite direction of the men, but it provided a perfect angle to watch them in his side mirror. He slid the driver's side window down on the off chance he could hear anything. And he could. Their voices carried, sharp and angry.

"You said the shipment was clean!" the older man hissed.

"Yeah, I said it would be clean," the Cottonmouth snapped back. "But it's not. What the fuck do you want me to do about it now?"

Vendetta killed the engine and slid down in his seat just enough to stay out of view.

The older guy shoved a clipboard at the biker. "They flagged it. Said half the barcodes don't match the shipment. You trying to get me fired? Or raided?"

"Keep your fuckin' voice down," the Cottonmouth growled, grabbing the clipboard and glancing around. "We'll fix it. Just move the rest of it to *Ned*'s. Tell them it was rerouted."

The man spat on the ground. "You're lucky I owe Eli."

Vendetta's eyes narrowed. *There it is*. Maybe a lead?

Whatever they were moving, it wasn't medical supplies. And whatever had gone wrong was happening under Eli Crizer's name.

Vendetta waited until the argument died down and the other van pulled away before climbing out of his own. He dropped the box at the back door of *Noesner Medical* like nothing was wrong. He smiled, signed, and drove off.

But his next stop wasn't on the delivery sheet. He was going back to the warehouse. To the logbooks and digital records. Because if what he just heard was the tip of something bigger? He was going to dig until the whole damn thing collapsed.

Rolling the van back into the *INeeda* warehouse lot like it was just another day on the job, he parked where he always did. He gave Freddie the usual nod as he passed the office window. There was no need to draw attention or move too fast. Inside, the air smelled like cardboard and bleach. The fluorescent lights overhead buzzed faintly, and the shelves stood stacked in neat, harmless rows. A dozen employees moved like clockwork, handling boxes, checking orders, and scanning barcodes.

And just like that, he disappeared into the system. Vendetta made his way to the records room under the guise of a restock. No one questioned him. New guy or not, he'd already learned how to stay off the radar. People didn't look twice if you looked like you belonged there.

He stepped into the back office where they kept the printed records. They were filed by date, destination, and client account. It was mostly digitized now, but the paper trail still mattered. He pulled records from the past four weeks for *Noesner Medical*. He sorted through them one by one. At first, he saw exactly what he expected -- bandages, alcohol wipes, cold packs, and gloves.

But the red flags soon began to emerge.

A record from two weeks ago:

* 400-count sterile surgical gloves.

* IV sedation kits, unboxed.

* Sterile wraps ordered under a third-party billing name SS Holdings.

That same name again. *SS. Sinister Skin.*

Flipping back through the records, there was a separate account for *Ned's Sundown Lounge.*

Officially, they'd only ordered standard supplies. But three days ago, an order had been placed under a personal pickup listing. No driver name. Just initials: SH.

And the contents?

Wound sealants

Two field-use medical kits

Naltrexone injectors

What the hell was a bar doing with opioid blockers? Vendetta's mind was racing. This wasn't just shady. This was medical gear ordered in preparation for damage control. The contents were for sedation, patching up trauma, and keeping people alive, just long enough.

Vendetta carefully tucked the copies back exactly as he'd found them, his heart pounding cold and steady in his chest. He tucked the last document back into place, closed the cabinet with the same casual care he'd use if nothing had changed. But everything *had.* They were moving people, and Dylan Crizer was right in the middle of it without even realizing it. He couldn't afford to make a mistake now. Couldn't afford to spook the Cottonmouths too early -- or Dylan.

Still... He knew he needed to try and convince her to get a job somewhere else. Somewhere safer, far from *Ned*'s and the shady dealings happening every night. Vendetta knew it wouldn't work. She was so damn stubborn, the kind of stubborn that grew from being hurt too many times and still choosing to stand up straight. Dylan wouldn't run just because he told her to.

But shouldn't he at least try? Even if she stayed, even if she fought him on it, maybe hearing it from someone else, someone who saw the warning signs would plant a seed. Maybe it would remind her that she wasn't as safe as she wanted to believe.

Meanwhile, first things first. He needed to know her schedule better than she did. If things turned ugly fast, and they would, her safety would depend on him knowing exactly where she was, and when. He rolled the van out of the warehouse with his last set of deliveries like nothing was wrong, every movement calm and practiced. But his mind was already working the angles.

Where did Dylan go when she wasn't at *Ned*'s? When were her shifts? He'd never liked the idea of her walking back and forth to work at the bar… or anywhere for that matter. Who did she trust enough to talk to beside him? He'd been remiss in not paying close enough attention before. But he sure would now.

No more late-night distractions or pretending he could just drift in and out of her life like it didn't matter. It damn well did matter. More than it should. And he'd start tonight.

Vendetta would need to map her routines, watch the corners she didn't know she needed to watch. He'd like to think he was the only one she'd told about her uncle's behavior and what she heard at the Cottonmouths' table. If she'd told someone else, like Peggy who knew something, it could put her in the line of fire. If Eli's operation realized she was asking the wrong questions or just standing in the wrong hallway at the wrong time, she'd become disposable.

Did she know her cousin, who was known as Baby Face to his MC, well at all? Did she know what had really happened to him? Or did she think he was alive somewhere out there?

Vendetta had already buried one life at the hands of traitors. He wasn't about to bury another.

* * *

Dylan

Her night started like any other. Business was slow and steady with locals filtering in for cheap beer and cheaper conversation. Dylan moved from table to table, refilling drinks, clearing away the empty ones, and smiling when she had to. Otherwise, she kept her head down.

She had an hour to go when the front door creaked open and Uncle Eli stepped inside, his broad shoulders filling the frame. Tonight, he walked like the worn leather of his cut was weighing him down. And he wasn't alone. The man with him didn't belong in a bar like *Ned*'s. He looked like he was somewhere in his forties with his hair styled and neat. His coat was tailored, his boots polished. The expensive watch circling his wrist caught the light as they walked to the back with her uncle. They took a booth in the corner.

The man scanned the room just like Eli did every time he walked in, but the *way* this guy did it made her skin crawl. It was almost like he was cataloging everything around him, trying to decide if it was good enough for him.

They were talking, heads close and voices low. It was her section, but some gut instinct told her she didn't want to go back there. But it was her job. Swallowing hard, she grabbed a tray and forced herself to walk to the back toward them. She approached the table with a smile she didn't feel, pad and pen ready. "What can I get you?"

The wealthy-looking man glanced up, and immediately, his attention locked on her. His gaze swept over her slowly, like he was memorizing every curve of her body, the tilt of her smile, and the way her hands fidgeted with the pen.

Now, she really wanted to be anywhere else.

"I'll take a bourbon," he said in a smooth voice. His gaze didn't leave her.

She scribbled it down, avoiding direct eye contact. "And for you?" she asked Eli, her voice tightening.

Eli didn't even look at her. No acknowledgement at all. *What the fuck*?

Just muttered, "Same," without lifting his eyes from the conversation.

Dylan's heart twisted in her chest. *What had she done to deserve this*? She turned and walked away quickly. She could feel the other man's gaze follow her the whole way back to the bar. Something about him unnerved her. She tried to shake it off as she poured their drinks. *You're reading too much into it. It's nothing*. It wasn't the first time a stranger had looked at her a little too long. It wasn't the first time her uncle had acted like she didn't exist while he was doing business in the bar.

But this was different. It *felt* different. There was something wrong under the surface tonight, something she couldn't put her finger on. But she'd felt it the entire shift.

For the first time since she took the job at *Ned*'s, a terrible thought crossed her mind. Maybe Eli hadn't wanted her working here because he knew exactly the kind of men he'd be sitting across from.

Wiping her hands on a towel after she set the glasses onto a tray, she felt her phone buzz in her pocket. It was Jason. She didn't even have to check. Somehow, he always seemed to know when something wasn't right. Deciding she'd read his text as soon as she served the drinks to her uncle and his guest, she put her game face on and headed in that direction. The second she approached, the tension sharpened. The wealthy man's smile widened in a way that gave her the creeps. Eli barely spared her a glance, still focused on whatever low, urgent conversation they were having. She set the bourbon in front of her uncle first, then his guest. He caught her wrist before she could pull away; not tightly, but enough to get her attention.

"You're wasted in a place like this, sweetheart," he said, voice smooth and heavy like syrup.

Every muscle in Dylan's body went rigid. She forced a smile, trying to keep composed until she could get away from the table. "Enjoy your drink," she said in a calm voice, as she carefully tried to pull her wrist free of his grip, but the man didn't let go.

Eli didn't react or say a word, like he didn't notice it was happening. He didn't even lift his head.

The man leaned in closer, dropping his voice low enough that only she could hear it. "Maybe you'd like to work someplace better. It would be safer and a helluva lot cleaner. Bet your uncle here wouldn't mind."

Dylan's stomach turned as the realization hit her. *Uncle.* The man doing this knew exactly who she was. Yanking her wrist free, not hard enough to cause a scene, but enough to make it clear she wasn't interested, she backed away fast with the tray clutched tightly to her chest and her heart pounding in her ears.

She didn't stop until she slipped behind the bar with trembling hands. It was all she could do to pull her phone from her pocket, to see Jason's text waiting.

Jason: *how's it going beautiful?*

Dylan fumbled over the keyboard, her heart racing.

Dylan: *weird night.cant wait tosee you*

She hit send before she could second-guess herself, trying to calm her breathing as she kept one eye on that booth in the back… where her uncle still talked to that man and pretended she didn't exist.

Peggy was off tonight but she asked one of the newer waitresses, Rose, if she'd finish that table for her. Rose, who was going through a divorce and had kids to feed, told her she could take off early if she wanted to. Dylan needed the money too, but just now, she had no problem getting away from *Ned*'s, her uncle, and whoever that man was.

By the time she slipped out the back door of *Ned*'s, Jason's van was already there, idling under the same broken streetlight that barely lit the alley. He unlocked the passenger door as she approached, giving her that smile she had come to love. Like it was just another night and everything was normal.

Only it wasn't normal. She slid into the passenger seat, throwing on the seatbelt and clutching her bag tight against her lap. The second the door shut, the weight of the world outside stayed locked on the other side of the glass.

Jason didn't press her, though she felt his gaze on her. He just pulled out onto the street, the radio low, the heater kicking on with a low hum.

After a minute, he glanced over at her, keeping his voice light. "Busy night?"

Normally, Dylan would've laughed and teased

him. Usually, she had some story to tell, about old bikers getting rowdy over jukebox picks or the regulars ordering one too many cheap whiskeys. But tonight, she was engulfed in a serious sense of dread. Staring out the windshield, she just watched the darkness rush past and swallowed hard before answering.

"Busy's not the word I'd use."

Jason didn't say anything right away. But she noticed his grip tightening on the steering wheel as he drove. His gaze darted to her and back to the road, brief but not sharp. It was like he knew she wasn't telling him everything. And he wasn't asking, but then he never did. Somehow, that made it worse, because part of her wanted to spill everything, right now in the dark cab of the van, in the safety of his presence. She wanted to tell him about the stranger who'd come in with Eli, how he'd grabbed her and how Eli hadn't reacted at all when it happened. She wanted to explain that she felt, deep down, she was noticing strange things at *Ned*'s, and just maybe she'd made a mistake in staying there.

They drove in silence for a few more minutes, and it was the kind of silence that said more than words ever could. When they pulled into her apartment lot, Jason shifted the van into park but didn't kill the engine. He didn't look at her right away, just stared through the windshield like he was working through something.

"I don't have to stay tonight," he said, "if it's a bad night and you need space." His voice was careful, like he didn't want to spook her. But he sounded so sincere. He rubbed a hand along the back of his neck, the movement almost shy. "And I'm not expecting anything. Not ever."

The words hung there, soft and steady, giving

her all the room in the world to say no. But Dylan didn't want him to leave. Not tonight. Not when it felt like there was a weight on her chest and she wouldn't be able to breathe if she sat with it alone. Turning toward him, her hands knotted in her lap.

"I don't need space," she said quietly. She *needed* him. "I just… I don't have anyone else I can really talk to."

Jason's mouth twitched, almost a smile, but not quite. It seemed like he was relieved by her answer, which surprised her. *No sex but please listen to me blather about all my problems.* Where had this guy been all her life?

Reaching over, he gently brushed the backs of his knuckles across hers. "Then talk to me, sweetheart," he said, voice rough. "I'm right here."

"Let's go up," she said.

As he usually did, Jason followed her up to her apartment. Dylan moved automatically, turning on the soft lamp in the corner, kicking off her boots, tossing her keys into the bowl by the door. Jason toed off his own boots near the entryway without a word. He made it clear he was here for however long she needed him.

"Anything you want for dinner?" he asked, pulling his phone out of his pocket.

"Anything but pizza. I think I'm turning into a slice at this point."

He grinned. "Burgers and fries, okay?"

Dylan nodded, her chest easing just a little. "Yeah. Thanks."

While Jason ordered takeout, Dylan sank onto her worn couch, pulling a blanket loosely over her lap even though the apartment wasn't cold. She wasn't shivering from the chilly night.

When he finished ordering, Jason moved into the kitchen, grabbed two sodas from her fridge without asking, and brought one to her. Settling into the chair across from her, the space between them was wide open, but the connection was unmistakable. He just cracked open his drink, waited. And somehow, that patience made it easier.

Wrapping her hands around her soda can, drawing slow circles against the condensation, she took a deep breath and found her voice. "So tonight," she said quietly. "My uncle came in with some guy. I don't know who he was. But he was --" She shook her head. "Rich, obviously. Someone important. Types like him don't come into *Ned's*."

Jason nodded, his gaze locked on her.

The words came easier to her now. "At first, they were just talking, keeping their voices down. I brought them their drinks, and…" She hesitated, taking a breath. "That rich guy grabbed my wrist. Not hard. But he didn't let go right away. He --" Her hands clenched tighter around the can. "He said I didn't belong in a place like that. That my uncle wouldn't mind if I went somewhere else. It was like some kind of inside joke or something."

Jason visibly tensed but kept listening.

"And Eli," she continued, her voice cracking slightly, "he didn't say anything. He didn't stop it. He didn't even look at me."

Her gaze dropped to her lap, her face burning with anger and shame. For a long moment, the only sound was the soft hum of her fridge kicking on.

"You didn't do anything wrong, Dylan," Jason said firmly. "You didn't invite that, and you didn't deserve it."

Tears stung her eyes at his words. She wanted to

believe that.

Leaning forward, Jason rested his forearms on his knees, his voice gentler now. "And I know you don't want to hear this," he added, "but maybe it's time to think about finding another job."

Dylan nodded. "Yeah," she whispered. "Maybe." But deep down, she knew it wouldn't be that easy. Not when the place, and apparently her uncle, were tangled up in things she wasn't supposed to know about. Still, for tonight, she didn't have all the answers. She just needed to breathe and to hear someone say she hadn't read too much into what happened. That she wasn't overreacting.

When their food arrived, Jason rose smoothly, pulling a few crumpled bills from his pocket. Locking the door behind him, he carried the order over to the coffee table, tossing a wrapped burger into Dylan's lap with a wink. He joined her on the couch, and they ate for a couple of minutes.

But it didn't last long. Dylan set her half-eaten burger down and wiped her hands on a napkin. Nerves made it impossible to eat anything else.

"My uncle," she said quietly. "I just…" Dylan stared at her hands for a long moment before finding the words. "I know my uncle's not perfect," she said, voice low. "And he's always had that rough side to him. I never thought he'd act like this. I don't understand what he wants. Or what I did wrong." She blew out a breath, tried to push past the tension. "You know he looked right through me, like I wasn't even worth acknowledging."

Some emotion flashed in Jason's eyes.

"He's the only family I have left." She shook her head, feeling stupid. "I always thought that even if he didn't like my choices, he cared. That somewhere under the biker persona, he still saw me. You know, he was there for me when my mom passed. And now?"

Jason slowly sets his food aside and leaned forward next to her.

"You're not nothing," he said, voice rougher now, like it cost him something to say it. "Not even close."

When her gaze met his, she saw it again. Anger held in check, protectiveness he didn't voice. The tension in her body eased. Even if her uncle had forgotten who she was, Jason hadn't.

"Is it just your uncle?" Jason asked. "Or is there an aunt? Cousins?"

Dylan blew out another breath. "There wasn't an aunt. Just a baby mama, my cousin's mother. Not sure I ever even met her."

"You know your cousin?"

"Jared?" Dylan nodded. "Yeah, I've seen him a few times. He's really intense. He became a biker like his dad, but he ran off somewhere a couple of years ago."

"Did he?" Jason asked.

She shrugged. "I heard something about gambling debts. Probably a good thing he moved on, really. Him and Eli didn't get along."

The silence stretched between them for a long moment. Dylan tucked her legs up under her, pulling the blanket tighter around her shoulders. She studied Jason, really studied him now -- the quiet strength, the patience, the way he never looked away when she needed him most.

It was then that she noticed the scar on his neck. It was long and pale, twisting beneath his jaw. It wasn't really obvious unless you were close to him, in the light. Now that she saw it, looking away was hard.

It didn't look that old, but it had healed. The skin around it looked tight in places, uneven. *What happened to you*? But she wasn't going to ask. Instead, she looked back into his eyes and softened her tone, like maybe if she offered him trust, he'd offer her the truth one day.

"You've seen your share of bad, haven't you?" she asked quietly.

Jason's gaze held hers, a shadow behind his eyes now. And even though he didn't say it out loud, she saw it clear as day. Yes, he'd seen bad. And maybe done worse. It wasn't her right to ask what it was or how close it had come to killing him. She couldn't help but feel that whatever left that scar on his neck didn't just tear skin. It took something else too. Something he hadn't gotten back.

She traced the rim of her soda can with her fingertip, her voice hesitant. "Can I ask you something?"

Jason's mouth twitched at the corner, almost a smile. "You can ask," he said.

"Who are you? Really?"

His gaze didn't waver. But something in his posture stiffened, a barely-there tension she wouldn't have caught from nights spent together. "Someone who knows what it's like to look around and realize the people you trusted the most… aren't who you thought they were."

Her heart skipped a beat. It wasn't the full answer, but it was enough for tonight. "Okay," she whispered.

Jason leaned back against the couch, one arm draped over its back. "You don't have to figure all this out tonight," he said. "I'm not telling you what to do but I'd think really hard before I walked back in that bar."

There was an underlying warning to his words. Instinct told her that maybe he was right.

"But whatever you decide to do, I'll be right here," he said.

Dylan let herself believe it, just for tonight. Let herself believe that not everyone would look away when it counted. Moving closer to him on the couch, she snuggled into his side, and he just held her. When she closed her eyes, the darkness didn't feel so lonely.

Chapter Five

Vendetta

The town of Oak Grove hadn't changed, at least not on the outside. The sidewalks were still cracked, the same boarded-up storefronts were trying to look like they hadn't completely given up. The people still went about their days, heads bowed, eyes cast down. Like maybe if they pretended not to notice the rot crawling beneath the surface, it didn't really exist.

But it did exist, and Vendetta was done watching it spread.

He leaned against the hood of his van behind the *INeeda* warehouse, a cigarette burning low between his fingers. It had been a while since he'd smoked, and today he only did it for the small shot of comfort. He'd already reviewed his manifest copies twice today. The sedatives, syringes, and wound kits were all ordered through shell accounts and rerouted to drop points that didn't exist on public maps. All were ordered under vague supplier aliases, but the trail led back to one name buried in the purchase routing: SS Holdings. He'd seen that name too many times to count now.

The same name was tied to a false construction permit in Mercy. The same name that popped up on *Ned*'s "cleaning supply" invoices, and on more than one rerouted delivery that didn't match what was logged. SS wasn't a company; it was a shield. A front for the real operation that was slowly poisoning Oak Grove every damn day.

The same network had tried to infiltrate Mercy under a different name. The one that used tattoo shops, clinics, and bars; anything that let them move bodies without drawing attention. Yet, unlike the Cottonmouths of Oak Grove, the Hounds of Hell had held the line and forced the fuckers out of Mercy. That charge had been led by their president, Razor, and Outcast, who Vendetta had helped get back to Mercy safe with his girl. If the Hounds could pull that off, surely to God the Cottonmouths could too. At least the decent ones, if there were any left in that chapter. By now, maybe some of them might be willing to turn on Eli and his corrupt inner circle.

When SS had come to Oak Grove, Eli Crizer had handed them the fucking keys.

After all, they weren't just moving products anymore. They were moving *people*. He had the paper trail to prove it, as if he needed much. It wasn't like he was going to the police. He'd seen it with his own eyes when he was still Tank, and he thought he belonged to an MC. He'd seen those young men and women. Hell, he should have done more than try to walk away that day. He'd made it all about getting payback for what was done to him. But how many young lives had been betrayed while he brooded and recovered, while he planned to confront them like their fucking ghost of Christmas past?

And now, Dylan. She hadn't seen the worst of it yet, but she was intuitive, he'd give her that. She knew something was wrong, just like she knew *Ned*'s was no longer just a bar. And Eli's silence spoke volumes.

But she still didn't see Eli for what he really was, had no idea of what her uncle was capable of. Hell, she didn't know that her cousin, the brute everyone knew as Baby Face, was gone. Maybe she didn't know because she'd been living in Richmond at the time that happened? Put into the ground by his father's own hand. And if Eli'd had no issue with taking out his own son for whatever the fuck went down there, he would have no qualms about hurting his niece.

If she kept trusting the man who she'd counted on since her mother's death, she would end up dead like her cousin. Or worse.

What the hell was he going to do to keep her alive? Because whether she knew it or not, she'd become the one thing Vendetta couldn't afford to lose. When he finished what he'd set out to do here in Oak Grove, Dylan was his. She just didn't know it yet. No way was he leaving her behind, not when she occupied as many of his thoughts now as his plans for her uncle.

Vendetta was running out of time. Now Dylan was caught up in this. He kept seeing her face from last night. Her tight smile, trembling hands, and that forced calm in her voice when she told him what happened at *Ned*'s. The way she'd described how that rich bastard had looked at her, grabbed her like she was something to own. Vendetta saw the panic behind her eyes, even after she tried to laugh it off. He knew that look from the trafficked girls he saw in the warehouse that day -- the day Tank died.

Vendetta was done watching and waiting.

Flicking the cigarette away, he straightened up and scanned the lot as he moved to his van's driver's door. He was done gathering intel. It was time to find the fault lines inside the Cottonmouths; namely the ones who didn't like what they were seeing, the ones who had nightmares about what they were doing. Someone would crack. And when they did? He'd blow this whole thing wide fucking open.

Climbing into the van, he started the engine. The low rumble rolled through his chest like a war drum.

Time's up.

* * *

Dylan

She almost didn't come in. She'd spent half the afternoon before her shift staring at the worn heels of her work boots by the door, seriously considering leaving them there forever. Walking away from *Ned*'s, from her uncle, from all of it.

Jason had warned her that maybe it was time to get out. He hadn't said it like a lecture or tried to push her. But the look in his eyes, the weight of his voice when he'd said, *"Places like that don't get better just because good people walk through the door…"* That had stuck with her. She knew he was genuinely worried about her. He'd stayed over that night, but he hadn't asked for anything. She'd needed someone to keep the shadows from creeping in, and he'd done that for her. That mattered a lot more than she'd let herself admit. She'd never known a guy who could just quietly be there for her, even when she knew he was concerned.

Dylan wasn't sure what to call what was happening between them, but it felt real. It was steady and stronger than anything she'd had in a long time.

Which made walking into the bar again tonight feel like a betrayal; not just of herself but of him. But she still did it. Old habits were hard to break, and she wasn't ready to face what it meant if she really walked away. Walking away from Oak Grove wouldn't be as easy this time. She was older now and coming home had come with comfort and happiness she'd never felt in Richmond. Explaining to herself why she still clung to the hope that her uncle wasn't the man people whispered about when his back was turned wasn't easy, either. Now he made her nervous.

But she showed up, just like always. Eli didn't come into *Ned*'s every night. And if he came back in with that gentleman, she'd get someone else to cover her table. If her uncle got mad or even fired her for that, so be it. At least the decision would be out of her hands.

The second she walked through the back door of the bar, something felt different. The lights were dimmer than usual. The regulars weren't as rowdy as they normally were. And the silence that followed her entrance wasn't the good kind.

Peggy was at the bar in her usual spot, wiping down glasses that didn't need wiping. She looked up when Dylan entered, her smile faltering for just a heartbeat before returning, tight and too bright. "You made it in," Peggy said, like that was a surprise.

Dylan forced a smile. "Yeah. Barely." She headed to the back to grab her apron and stash her bag in her locker, but even her footsteps sounded too loud on the warped wood floor. Her gut wasn't settling. The air felt heavy and too still, like a storm was rolling in.

Out of habit, she checked the roster. No big party tonight. No events. So why did it feel like something was coming?

When Dylan stepped back out front, her uncle was there. Eli stood near the end of the bar, talking low to a man she didn't recognize. Another tall guy in a sharp jacket and expensive shoes that definitely didn't belong anywhere near Oak Grove. Just the sight of him had her anxiety escalating. She couldn't hear what they were saying, but she didn't need to. She recognized that posture, the closed-off body language. Eli didn't even acknowledge her walking past.

Again.

The stranger, though? He did look at her. No, he watched her, then he smiled, and it wasn't friendly.

Dylan moved behind the bar, her hands suddenly colder than they normally were.

Peggy leaned in, her voice low. "That guy's not

local. Big money from Nashville maybe? Maybe farther. He came in last week too."

Dylan nodded slowly, not trusting her voice. Eli caught her eye from across the room and motioned her over.

She went but moved slowly. She didn't have a good feeling about the entire situation.

"Dylan, I need you to cover a special shift tonight," he said. "Our client wants a little extra attention. Private setting. High tip potential."

She blinked. A private shift? "I -- I'm not scheduled for that," she said.

Eli shrugged. "You are now."

Her stomach flipped, and she wasn't sure if it was panic or rage. Private shift? Since when? Looking past him, she found the other man watching her like she was already his.

And that's when her instincts started screaming. She agreed, but not with a smile. Not with confidence. She gave a small nod and a tight breath, her agreement more out of obligation than willingness. That last fragile thread of belief still held. The one that said, *he's your uncle; he wouldn't let anything happen to you.*

Even after everything, his silence to the way he looked right through her and let that other man touch her last week, she'd still wanted to believe Eli gave a damn. She should have known better.

Eli handed her a black, zip-up jacket, new, branded with the bar's logo, and a card with an address scrawled across it in bold, sharp handwriting. "Client wants a one-on-one setting. Just drinks, small talk. You're there to make the guy feel welcome. That's it," he said.

His tone was too cool. And he still didn't look her in the eyes.

Dylan frowned, turning the card over in her hand. "Why out there?" she asked quietly.

Eli shrugged like it didn't matter. "Client's request. He wanted privacy."

"I don't have a car," she reminded him, liking the situation less by the second.

"That's been taken care of," he told her.

What was that supposed to mean?

"How long am I supposed to be there?" she asked. "Why just me? You've got a lot of other girls."

That got his attention, but not in the way she wanted it. His expression was hard to read. "Because he asked for you," Eli said flatly. "You can handle yourself, remember? That's what you said."

Her stomach dropped when he threw her own words back at her. The way he dismissed every reasonable concern, like this wasn't a favor. It was already a done deal.

"Is this safe?" Dylan had to ask.

"You think I'd send my niece somewhere dangerous?" he asked with a smirk.

She wanted to believe him. But something in his voice left her feeling cold and uneasy. Dylan slipped the jacket on like it could protect her.

"Just drinks?" she asked under her breath. But deep down, she was already starting to wonder if she'd just made the biggest mistake of her life. Her stomach curled in on itself as she read the address on the card. It wasn't in town or near anything familiar. Just a private road outside Oak Grove.

Peggy watched from behind the bar, but she didn't say a word. Her gaze followed Dylan as she went back to grab her bag. When Dylan came back, strong headlights flared through the side window of the bar. Was the car already there? She saw a black sedan with tinted windows. Everything was happening way too fucking fast.

"Your ride," Eli said, not even glancing up. "Client requested no phones. It's his policy for private sessions. No distractions. No recording."

Dylan blinked. "You want me to go out there without a phone?"

Eli held out his hand. "You'll get it back after. Or I'll bring it to you. You're fine."

She looked down at her phone. Jason's name lit up at the top of the screen. He'd texted earlier asking if she wanted him to pick up Greek food for tonight.

Every part of her screamed not to go.

But Eli's eyes were hard now. His mouth a firm line.

And some piece of her, the part that still didn't want to believe Eli would do anything to harm her, overrode everything else. Taking her phone out of her bag and turning it off, she placed it in Eli's waiting hand.

"Good girl," he muttered.

The words made her skin crawl as she walked out of the bar.

* * *

Vendetta

Vendetta sat in the van, parked in the shadow of a broken streetlight two blocks from *Ned*'s. The engine was off, the lights out. Just him, his notebook, and a clear view of the bar's back lot. He'd been tailing Eli's top guys for days now. Trucker, Nate, Eagle, and Creep first and then others who he was sure were Eli's disciples in the MC. Vendetta watched how they moved, paid attention to who they talked to. He made notes of what they *didn't* say.

Nate always left first, jumpy and fast walking. The kid looked over his shoulder every few minutes, everywhere he went. Creep usually lingered, making late-night runs that didn't match any shift schedule. And Trucker, the one with the tattoo crawling up the back of his neck, argued on his burner phone like someone was squeezing him.

He flipped to the next page and scribbled a few new notes on Eagle. He was a quiet one, observant, and never the first to speak in meetings. But he was always listening carefully. From what Vendetta knew, he was the kind of guy who didn't like getting his hands dirty but knew where every body was buried. His name was underlined twice.

Weak link.

Closing the notebook, Vendetta leaned back in his seat and exhaled through his nose. It was time to make a loop past *Ned*'s. Just in case. He pulled out slowly, headlights off, windows down to catch anything that didn't sound right. As he rolled into the lot behind the bar, he spotted movement by the back door, a flash of a familiar shape. *Peggy*.

The woman was pacing, phone in one hand, her other hand tangled in her apron like she was trying to anchor herself. Then she looked up, spotted his van, and her whole body shifted. She made a beeline for him. Vendetta rolled the window down before she could knock.

He knew. Before she even spoke, he knew. The way she moved, fast and desperate, told him everything.

Dylan was gone. And whatever had happened tonight, he was already too late. The words hit like a punch to the ribs before they were even said.

Peggy gripped the edge of the window, her

knuckles white. "She's gone," she said, her breath hitching. "Dylan. She left in a black car not even twenty minutes ago."

Vendetta's fingers curled tight around the steering wheel. "Where?"

"Some private client thing. Eli said it was just a shift, but off-site. A high roller. He told her no phones, took hers before she could leave."

Vendetta's vision narrowed, everything inside him going cold and quiet. "And she just went?" he asked in a low voice.

"She didn't want to," Peggy whispered. "She looked scared. But she went."

Vendetta's jaw clenched.

Peggy hesitated, then added, "I… I snapped a picture of the car. I got the license plate."

His eyes cut to her sharply.

She held up her phone with shaking hands. "Something about it just felt wrong. I didn't know what else to do."

Vendetta took the phone, glancing at the image she captured. A low-profile black sedan with tinted windows and Virginia plates. Clean but forgettable to anyone but him. He texted the image from her phone to his before handing it back.

"This is good," he said, his voice tight. "This helps."

She nodded, swallowing hard. "You're gonna bring her back, right?"

"Yeah," he said, already shifting into gear. "I am." He didn't say it. The look in Peggy's eyes said she understood.

For half a second, time froze. Then Vendetta dropped the gear into drive, tires spitting gravel as he shot out of the lot and into the night. He didn't know where she was. But he'd find her. Because if they'd laid one hand on her -- Eli, the client, any of them -- he was going to make what they did to him look like a sweet memory.

Vendetta took the first corner fast, his mind racing even faster. *Private event. High roller. No phones. Off-site.* Eli wouldn't have sent her far, not with a client like that. That kind of man wanted control, but he also wanted to stay close to the product. Close to the network. That helped him narrow options around Oak Grove quite a bit. The location could be a nearby luxury rental used for "private parties." It could also be one of the out-of-town properties Eli had access to. Worst case, it could be one of the holding houses tied to the shipments he'd already traced.

He gunned the engine as he pulled up the list of locations in his mind. Three spots rising to the top of his mental list. There was a rural cabin upstate, a warehouse in East Oak Grove, and a lakefront Airbnb that had been getting too much SS traffic for weeks. And he planned to check each and every one of them, even if he had to kick every door in.

But he'd start at the lake. If Dylan was there, he'd bring her out safe. And whoever was inside? Well, they'd never touch another woman again.

* * *

Dylan

The car ride was silent. No music was playing, and the driver didn't say a word. There was just the hum of the engine and the blur of dark trees flashing past the window like shadows.

When the car finally slowed, Dylan leaned forward, squinting through the windshield. They'd pulled up to a house, and it was beautiful. All modern glass and sharp lines, tucked back at the edge of a private lake. She'd gone to school with kids of the people who lived in this area. Needless to say, they hadn't been her friends.

Every light was on around that house like it had been staged for a photo shoot. The apprehension she felt about this situation grew as she took it all in. It was way too nice for a bar gig.

The driver got out and opened her door without a word. Dylan hesitated, her heart already racing in her chest as she wondered just what situation she'd allowed herself to be delivered to. She stepped out. She should've taken the time to get a text off to Jason. She should have listened to him. She shouldn't have walked back through *Ned*'s door.

The wind off the lake felt colder than it should have. When she glanced back at the house, she now saw a man waiting for her on the porch. As she walked in his direction and got closer, she recognized him. It was the man who'd come in that night with Eli. The man was too rich for Oak Grove, with his polished clothes and wolf smile. It was the man who'd grabbed her, scared her.

"Miss Crizer," he said smoothly, like they were already old friends. "Welcome. Come in."

She forced a tight smile and followed him inside, her boots clicking too loudly on the hardwood floors. She didn't see a bar or trays. No setup of any kind. No, there was just low music, moody lighting, and a table with two glasses already poured.

She hesitated. Her heart raced in her chest. Had her uncle set her up?

"I thought I was here to… work," she said slowly.

The man gave her a smile that didn't quite reach

his eyes. "You are," he said, gesturing toward one of the glasses. "But not the kind that needs a uniform."

Her throat went dry.

She didn't sit. "Where's Eli?"

"Busy," he said. "But you're in good hands. Come, sit. Relax. You must be tired."

Dylan didn't move. "I'd like to call him."

"No need," the man said easily. "You're with me now."

With me. The words echoed in her skull like a siren. Her eyes darted to the door she'd just walked through. It was already closed. She crossed to it, trying the handle. It was locked tight.

There had to be other exits if she could find them.

"Why am I here?" she asked, voice tight.

The man's smile widened as he stepped closer. "Because you're exactly what I asked for," he said. "And your uncle is a very generous man."

Panic hit her hard. It was a cold, creeping thing sliding down her spine. She wasn't really here for a job or a shift. This was a handoff, and she was the product.

Dylan took a slow step back from him, keeping the locked door in her peripheral vision. He was still smiling at her like she was some new toy he couldn't wait to unwrap. Forcing herself to breathe evenly, she focused on staying calm.

"I think there's been a mistake," she said, voice steady, but cold. "I'm not here for this."

The man laughed softly, almost admiringly. "That's cute," he said. "But we both know your uncle doesn't make mistakes."

She didn't blink. "Then he's not the man I thought he was."

He took another step forward. "You'll see things

differently after a drink. And maybe a night's rest." The man reached for her arm, his touch light, almost polite even.

Dylan slapped his hand away hard enough that it echoed. "No."

His eyes darkened, the smile slipping just slightly. "I suggest you remember where you are, Dylan."

"I know exactly where I am," she snapped. "In a stranger's house, without a phone, and locked in. And if you think I won't scream loud enough to shatter every window in this place, try me."

For the first time, his calm cracked. "No one will hear you out here," he said.

Her stomach turned, but somehow, she kept her voice even. "I'm not doing anything until I get answers."

His jaw flexed slightly. "You don't get to make terms. You're here. You'll cooperate. Or things will get… unpleasant." He picked up one of the glasses and handed it to her with a little flourish. "Drink."

She didn't move.

"Don't make this difficult," he said, lowering the glass a fraction. "We can do this the easy way. Or I can bring someone else in here to help me."

Dylan froze on that note. No. She didn't want that.

Slowly, she reached for the glass he held, wrapping her fingers around the glass. She didn't drink from it or say she wasn't going to. She just held it, keeping her gaze on the man in front of her.

"You said something about relaxing," she said, voice suddenly softer. "Maybe… maybe we just need to reset this."

The bastard's smile turned smug.

Taking a tiny step back, she went for trying to act shy. He hadn't been around her that long. Maybe she could pull it off. Glancing down at the glass, she just let the panic come on. Even embellished it a little. Acting like she tripped in her nervousness, she "accidentally" slung it straight at him. The drink and whatever it was laced with soaked his shirt and pants while ice slid across the floor around them.

"Shit," he barked, looking around for something to use to clean himself. "Are you fucking kidding me?"

"I'm sorry!" she gasped, backing away toward the far side of the room. "It slipped!"

He swore and turned toward the kitchen. "How did your clumsy ass ever make it as a fucking waitress?" he went on.

While he was doing that, Dylan moved quickly. Frantically, she looked around, looking for anything that she could use for a weapon. Anything that could buy her another minute.

With an ache in her chest, she couldn't help but wish she'd listened to Jason. She shouldn't have gone back. She should have known something like this would happen.

Jason would never find her, and she had no way to reach him in this hell. She just hoped she'd see him again.

* * *

Vendetta

The van fishtailed onto the gravel drive, headlights off. Vendetta killed the engine before the dust even settled, the door already swinging open. He was moving before his boots hit the ground.

The place was too quiet. The lights were on, wide open to the lake like a Goddamn catalog shoot. But there wasn't an event here. No music or laughter. There were no signs of a fucking party. Just polished silence and darkness beyond the front windows.

Vendetta didn't go in blind. He approached the front door quickly, moving fast because all of the fucking lights, and disabled the security system. It was the same model the Oak Grove compound used, and just as lazy on updates. Once the keypad was dark, he didn't linger.

Next, he rounded the house, moving low. His boots were silent on the flagstone path, his fingers brushing the handle of the knife tucked inside his jacket. The side entrance was locked, but that wasn't a problem. A few seconds and one hard shoulder check later, he pushed his way inside.

Inside, the air was warm and heavy. Keeping his eyes and ears open, he kept moving. That's when he heard the footfalls. Two men heading down the hall toward him. They were decent-sized, dressed casually. They were talking about liquor and women, even though he wasn't trying to hear their words.

Vendetta moved before they saw him. One guard went down fast with a sharp strike to the throat, cutting off any sound, a clean elbow to the temple putting him out cold. The second turned but he didn't move fast enough. Vendetta caught him by the collar and slammed his head into the wall hard enough to drop him. Catching the body, he eased it down.

His pulse ticking faster, he stepped over them. Approaching the living room, he heard a voice echoing in there. "… ruined my shirt. You think that was cute, you little cunt?"

Vendetta's blood went cold. Turning the corner, he saw Dylan. His girl was backed up to a marble counter, her hands curled into fists at her sides.

Some polished bastard stood there wiping his pants, towering over her, looking angry and entitled. Vendetta thought this might be the guy Eli had brought to *Ned*'s -- the one who gave her the creeps.

The man made a move in her direction. Vendetta didn't hesitate. In three steps, he crossed the room. The man turned just in time to catch the full weight of Vendetta's fist crashing into his jaw. Bone cracked against his knuckles. He went down hard, glass and ice scattering beneath him. The fucker tried to scramble up.

Vendetta kicked him square in the ribs, sending him crashing into the leg of the coffee table. "Touch her again," he growled, "and I'll cut off a hand."

The man wheezed, spit and blood painting his chin. "Who the hell are --"

Vendetta didn't answer. He just grabbed the guy by the collar and slammed his head once into the polished floor. Then it was done.

He turned, his chest still heaving, and found Dylan frozen in place. Her eyes were wide, her hands trembling.

"I…" she started, her voice cracking.

Vendetta crossed the room to her but approached carefully. "Are you okay?"

She nodded too quickly, too many times.

Opening his jacket, he handed her his backup knife. "Hold on to that," he said. "Just in case."

Dylan gripped the knife like it was the only thing anchoring her, staying close behind him. Vendetta threw open the side door, his gun drawn just in case. But the place stayed quiet. If anyone else had been there, they were gone or hiding. They sprinted to the van. The second the doors slammed shut behind them, Vendetta started the engine and peeled out of there, gravel spraying like shrapnel.

Only when they were halfway down the road did either of them speak.

"You came for me," she whispered, voice thick.

Vendetta's hands flexed tighter on the wheel. "Next time," he said, jaw like stone, "I won't be late."

Chapter Six

Dylan

She hadn't said much on the ride back. Her voice had barely worked, her entire body humming from fear and adrenaline. The silence in the dimly lit motel room felt louder than anything that had happened tonight. It made the thoughts racing through her mind feel like a scream. Her hands curled around a glass of water she hadn't yet taken a sip from as she fought for control.

Dylan sat on the edge of the bed in Jason's motel room, glaring at the jacket her uncle had made her wear tonight. Throwing it on the floor had been the first thing she'd done when Jason brought her here, watching it like a snake that could bite her. It had been a uniform, and a lie. Her uncle hadn't handed her a shift. He'd handed her off like a… She didn't even want to think the word right now. She was too close to spiraling as it was. And she'd gone along with it, suspecting the entire time that something wasn't right. She'd told herself it was just a job, just one more night. Now she couldn't decide if she felt more sick or stupid.

Jason sat in the worn chair between the door and the bed, like he was guarding her. He looked ready to protect her from everything outside, just like he had at the lake house earlier tonight. She could still hear the crack of Jason's fist breaking that man's jaw. She could still picture the look in his eyes, the cold precision of someone who'd been in too many fights that were less about winning, more about surviving.

Dylan's trust was frayed down to threads. Eli had handed her off like she was nothing, a favor to some twisted client. Tonight, she'd seen clearly what her uncle truly was. And now here she was, tucked away in a cheap motel room with the only man who'd fought to protect her. Jason had held her when she was shaking and looked at her like she was still a worthwhile person even after everything.

But Jason had tried to warn her, hadn't he? And somehow, he'd found her tonight. How had he found her? She had no phone to contact anyone. Eli had taken it. He'd told her about her "special shift" about three minutes before a car came to whisk her away.

And now, Dylan wasn't sure if she was searching for the truth or clinging to the man close to her now because he was the last thing that felt real. Maybe it was both. But she needed answers. Because whatever came next, she couldn't let herself be blinded again.

Jason simply sat there quietly, gorgeous and muscular. She loved every moment she'd spent with him. But there were unanswered questions even with her savior. He was a medical courier working temporarily in Oak Grove, of all the damn places. Why only temporarily? He'd never said. Every time she'd offered to go back to his for the night, he'd had an excuse ready as to why it wasn't a good time. And the way he always preferred to make love in the dark puzzled her, especially as gorgeous as he was.

What had caused that distinctive scar around his neck that she hadn't found the courage to ask him about?

Dylan shivered just thinking about how he'd burst into the lake house tonight like a Goddamn mercenary. One second, the creepy man her uncle had given her to had been looming over her, barking threats like he owned her. The next, Jason had hit him like a wrecking ball. All she'd seen then was violence delivered with the calm of a man who'd obviously done it before. It should've scared her. Maybe it did, a little. But what cut deeper was how focused he'd been on getting to her. Like nothing else mattered, not inflicting pain or vengeance. And at that moment, she hadn't been afraid of him. She'd never felt safer in her life. She still felt that way.

But she also knew Jason wasn't telling her everything.

She finally broke the silence. "Who are you?"

He didn't move. "Jason."

"That's not what I meant." Her voice shook, but she didn't look away. "You knew. You knew something like this could happen. That night when I told you about that rich fucker Eli brought to the bar, you tried to warn me."

Jason's dark-eyed gaze met hers. "It didn't take much insight, Dylan," he said carefully. "You were uncomfortable that night. You should always listen to your gut."

"But I didn't listen to my gut," she said, as tears of frustration stung her eyes. "And my uncle, my fucking uncle just… pimped me out tonight."

Jason's gaze didn't waver. Slowly, he rose from the chair and stepped closer to her.

"No," he said. "He *tried*. But you didn't let it happen." He sat next to her on the bed, carefully, like not wanting to scare away a frightened animal. "You fought him and bought yourself some time. And if I hadn't shown up tonight, I know you'd have found your own way out."

Dylan listened, still shaking and not caring if he saw it.

"And what your uncle did?" Jason continued, quieter now. "That's not on you. That's on *him*. The only thing you're guilty of is trusting someone who should've protected you." He paused, took a deep breath. "But you're not alone in this anymore, Dylan."

Her fingers tightened around the glass she still held. "So, what now?" Her voice cracked. "What am I supposed to do? Just… go back and act like this never happened? Apologize to my uncle? What do I do when that man shows up again at *Ned*'s, because he *will*."

"You *don't* go back," he said. "Not to your uncle or *Ned*'s. Not after this."

Her chest tightened at the forceful way he spoke. "But Eli's my family. He's the only family I really have left… I mean, maybe he didn't know what that guy's real intentions were."

Jason's gaze met hers, steady and calm. There was steel beneath it. "He *did* fucking know, Dylan. That man handed you over like you were inventory. Family doesn't do that."

Dylan didn't argue, but she blinked back tears. "I just moved back to Oak Grove. Now I have to leave again? And if I leave, won't he come looking for me?"

Jason nodded. "He will. That fucking guy he had you delivered to won't do business with him again until he fixes the situation with you. And if he can't fix it, well, they can't have you out there talking about any of it."

Shaking her head, she snorted, though it really wasn't funny. "Eli took my phone. Said I'd get it back later."

Jason didn't say anything, but she saw a shift in his expression.

"Now what happens?" she asked. "What's he going to do when I don't show up for my phone -- or my job?"

"He's got his club out looking for you," Jason explained. "Right now."

That froze her to the spot.

Jason's gaze pinned her in place. "Eli Crizer doesn't let things go. And he values his reputation more than most in our world."

"You talk like you know him," Dylan said. It wasn't the first time she'd thought that.

"I know the type," he said, staring at the floor.

No, it's more than that.

"That's not an answer." She stared at him, instinct driving her on. "Jason… how do *you* know what Eli's capable of?"

His gaze returned to her, and he didn't blink. "Because I used to wear the same patch."

Dylan just stared at him, her heart thudding, with every muscle in her body going still. Of all the things she expected to hear, she wasn't ready for that. "What did you just say?"

Jason didn't move, didn't try to soften it. "I used to be one of them, Dylan. A Cottonmouth. I came from the Abingdon chapter."

"No," she whispered, shaking her head like she could rewind the last ten seconds. "No, you can't be. That doesn't make any sense…"

"It makes perfect sense," he said slowly. "Doesn't it?"

She looked at him, *really* looked at him. Jason had never conducted himself like a man trying to prove something. He didn't try any false bravado while he was meeting her stare head-on. He just looked so tired, like each word cost him more than he'd expected.

Dylan's gaze immediately went to the scar at his neck, and he knew it. His fingers lifted, tracing it like it still burned after all this time. It was a deep wound that had healed physically. Emotionally? Maybe not. Jason lived with it every day, saw it in the mirror each morning. It made her realize something. For all Jason's strength, all his control, he was trying to figure out what to say to her, and it wasn't easy for him.

"I didn't know what was *really* going on when I came to Oak Grove last year," he said quietly. "The Oak Grove chapter said they needed help with expansion. New chapters, bigger ops. I believed them, and a couple of others from Abingdon came over with me."

Rising from the bed, he stood before her, grabbing the hem of his hoodie and pulling it off. After he dropped that to the floor, he pulled off the dim white T-shirt he wore beneath and turned his back to her.

There, tattooed across his back, bold and brutal, was the mark of the Cottonmouth MC. A coiled cottonmouth, its body thick and twisted in strike position, fangs bared, tongue extended like it was hissing at the world. The detail was vicious and every scale, every shadow was inked with a precision that felt more like a warning than a design. It stretched between his shoulders like a brand, set deep into skin marred by scars, some fresh, others older. Some had healed wrong. It wasn't art. It was history carved in ink and blood.

"I didn't come down here to be part of what they're actually doing," Jason said, pulling his T-shirt back on. "But once I saw… *really* saw it? The girls kept in warehouses like animals, the deals. All the fucking lies? Well, I pushed back." His voice dropped to a near whisper. "They called it betrayal when I told them I didn't want to be part of it. Said I was soft. I wasn't patched in to Oak Grove, just sent in to help… so they used me to send a message to anyone else getting cold feet."

He sat down next to her again, but a little farther

away this time. Slowly, Jason lifted his chin. The motion was quiet but deliberate, a man exposing the most vulnerable part of himself. And when the dim light hit it, Dylan saw all of it. The jagged, raised line that circled the front of his throat, uneven in places, discolored in others, the kind of mark that didn't come from an accident or a bar fight. It looked like a cord or rope caused it. Like some tried to choke him or hang him.

"Oh my God," Dylan whispered, her voice cracking. She felt her stomach turn, tears stinging her eyes. It wasn't pity, just realization of the raw horror of it. Jason hadn't just been betrayed. They'd tried to erase him entirely. She didn't realize she was moving until one hand reached out, hovering inches from his skin. Her voice trembled. "They did that to you."

"Yeah," he said, holding her gaze, so much emotion in his dark eyes. "I'll be honest, I've helped move guns. Drugs here and there, but I hate that shit, especially when dumb fucks try to sell it to kids. But human trafficking? I want no fucking part of that."

"Human trafficking?" Dylan's heart dropped. That's what her uncle was into these days? Her evening was making a little more sense now. "My uncle? Did he have anything to do with the..." She pointed to the scar encircling his neck.

"Eli gave the order," he said.

The tears came on. "And you came back here? Knowing what they would do to you?"

"I came back for revenge," he said quietly. "I came back to shut them down... And then I met you."

Dylan lowered her hand, blowing out a breath.

A darker thought crept in, like a splinter under her skin. Jason had come back for the ones who wronged him. But she was Eli's niece. Her hand dropped to her lap, fingers curling tightly. Had she been a pawn on the board all along? Was every moment, every kind word, every look, every time he held her in the dark… just part of the long game?

Dylan studied him as if she was seeing him for the first time. The warmth in his eyes, the exhaustion and pain. The way he watched her, like she was the only thing anchoring him. Still, the question festered. She had to ask.

"Is that why you talked to me?" she said, barely above a whisper. "Because I'm his niece?" she asked, trying to sound sarcastic, but sounding hurt instead.

He shook his head, raking a hand through his hair. "I didn't know at first. Not until the night you mentioned him," he said quietly. "When I left that next morning, I saw your birthday picture with him in the background."

"So, what was I then?" she asked, voice low but biting. "Just part of the job either way? I was useful as someone working at *Ned*'s, but then you figured out I was related to Eli and that was a bonus?"

Jason's expression shifted, something between regret and restraint.

"Was it all just intel?" she pressed, letting the tears fall. "Me, the bar, what I knew about Eli? Is that why you talked to me? Slept with me?"

So many emotions played across Jason's face. She saw guilt, yes, but it wasn't the dominant emotion there. It took a little of the wind out of her sails.

"God, I thought you were the only person who actually gave a damn about me," she whispered. "And the whole time, you were watching me like some undercover op. Like I was a way in." Her throat tightened. "Did any of this mean anything to you?"

More silence, thick and loaded. He dropped his

head, not moving next to her.

"No. You weren't just part of the job." His tone wasn't defensive, but honest. "You never really were."

Dylan crossed her arms. She'd been trying to get the emotions from a traumatic night under control, only to learn the man she fell for wasn't who she thought he was. Her eyes stayed on him, waiting. Daring him to go on.

Jason took a slow breath, like it would hurt him to say the next part out loud. "When I first saw you... it was at the bar. You were laughing with Peggy. I wasn't even supposed to be looking at you. I was watching Cottonmouths, watching movement, drop-ins, timing. But then, there you were." He shook his head, like it still didn't make sense. "You were confident and gorgeous."

Dylan's arms loosened a fraction as he continued. "I told myself not to get involved. That if I kept my distance, I could finish what I came to do and disappear. But I kept showing up. Finding excuses to be near you. To see if you were okay." He glanced away for just a second. "That's when I stopped being careful. And that's when it stopped being about the job."

The silence that followed was different this time, fragile.

"You weren't part of the plan, Dylan. But you became the reason."

Her heart clenched, her gaze dropped. Something in her wanted to believe him. Wanted it so badly it hurt. Staring down at the water glass still clutched in her hands, her grip had gone white-knuckled, her fingers aching. But she didn't let go. "You should've told me," she said softly.

"I know."

"I don't know what's real." Dylan looked up at him through frustrated tears. "You were the only person I thought I could trust. And now… I feel like I'm drowning in everything I didn't see coming."

He ran a hand through his hair, tension bleeding out of him like slow poison. "You were a bright light in a place that was nothing but shadows. And yeah, at first, maybe I thought getting close to you would help. That you might know something about Eli that could help me take him down. But it stopped being about that the minute I realized you had no idea who your uncle really was, and how close you were to getting hurt. I didn't tell you who I was because it would've put you in more danger. If you knew the truth, you would've reacted differently. They would have noticed. Eli would've noticed. I wasn't willing to risk that. Not with you."

"That's why you showed up tonight?" she asked. "You saved me when no one else even knew I was gone." She sat there for a moment, watching him like she didn't know if she should be angry or grateful. Or both.

Her voice was softer this time. "How did you know where I was tonight? How did you find me?"

Jason exhaled slowly, his gaze never left hers. "Peggy," he said. "She saw the car you climbed into. Took a picture of the plate before they drove off. She didn't know what to do with that information, so she waited for me to come looking."

Peggy *and* Jason saved her life tonight.

"I was already circling the block. Something didn't sit right," he continued. "You didn't message me, and… I just knew. I knew I was already too late the second she walked up to my van. I narrowed it down to a couple of different possible locations. And then I got lucky."

Dylan swallowed, her throat tight. "But you still found me." Her heart dropped just thinking about what might have happened if Jason hadn't shown up.

"I would have torn this town apart to find you," Jason admitted, conviction in his voice. "I didn't plan to meet you. I didn't plan to stay. I was just supposed to gather intel, figure out where the bodies were buried, and strike with enough evidence of why I was doing what I planned to do, just in case I got caught."

"You're not going through with it now?"

"I told you," he said. "I plan to shut them and their entire fucking operation down. But I could have lost you tonight, Dylan. And I realized… I need to keep you safe more than I need to deal with all of that right now. After what happened tonight, you're in danger from your uncle and the Cottonmouths. Do you understand? And the minute they figure out who I really am…"

"Who are you, *really*?" Dylan needed to know.

"My name is Josh Lawrence," he admitted. "Before they killed me, my brothers called me Tank."

Considering he was built like a brick wall, she could understand why he was called that.

A corner of his mouth curved up. "I was a Marine, a tank operator… But Tank died that night, under the tree they hung him from."

They hung him? *Your uncle gave the order.*

"The minute they figure out who I am and you're with me, you're as dead as I am," he added.

The sincerity of his words left Dylan scared. As much as she had reasons to doubt Jason… *Josh*'s intentions, she cared enough about him to hope he wouldn't go by himself to face Eli and his Cottonmouths. What if they actually killed him this time?

"Did you plan on facing them alone?" Dylan shook her head, her eyes wide with disbelief. "That's vigilantism, Josh. And you could die for real this time."

Shifting next to her on the edge of the bed, he folded his arms across his chest. His body language told her that he'd made peace with that risk long before tonight.

"I've been living on borrowed time since the night they hung me," he said, his voice low but even. "Every day after that's been a choice. And I've made mine." His gaze locked on her, unwavering. "I didn't come back to Oak Grove just to survive. I came to shut this shit down. What they're doing, what Eli's fucking enabling, it's not just club business. It's slavery. It's kids and women like you being traded like property. It's the dangerous drugs sold to ruin lives. If I don't stop them, who will?"

His tone was heavy with conviction. "I've been careful, Dylan. I've collected proof, stuck with my plan. This was never a suicide mission." He hesitated, adding, "And if I walk away now, after everything I've seen… after what almost happened to you? Then I don't deserve to still be breathing."

Josh blew out a breath. "Right now, I need to get you out of here. Out of Eli's reach."

"Where would I even go?" She had returned to Oak Grove because she had no other place to go.

"I've got friends in Mercy," Josh said. "Strong enough to keep you safe and hidden. Strong enough to help me when the time comes."

"Who?"

"The Hounds of Hell," Josh replied. "Yeah, another MC. But when this criminal network came to *their* town, they fought them off. They didn't just hand over the fucking keys like Eli did."

"I've heard of the Hounds," Dylan said. "They're enemies of the Cottonmouths, right?"

"Not always," he said. "They owe me."

"Even if I'm Eli Crizer's blood?" she asked.

Josh's gaze met hers squarely. "You're not your uncle, Dylan."

Dropping her head, Dylan's heart cracked in her chest. Her whole life had been upended in a single night.

Josh moved closer to her on the edge of the bed. "We'll wait until morning," he said quietly. "I'll call in to work, take care of it. I'll drive you to Mercy myself. They'll protect you."

Dylan traced the rim of the glass in her hands, the water inside untouched and shaking faintly with her movement. She set the glass aside. "I came back here to get my feet under me," she said, her voice low. "To prove I could build something for myself. And now… now I feel like I've got nothing but wreckage."

The silence between them carried the weight of the truth they both now knew.

After a long pause, Dylan said, "You said the Hounds owe you. But what about me? What if I don't want to run? What if I want to help you?"

His brow furrowed, he tilted his head slightly. "Dylan --"

"No, listen," she interrupted, finally turning to look at him. "I almost got trafficked tonight by my own fucking uncle. I had *you* to save me… I don't think I could live with myself if I just hid out while my uncle and his men are doing worse to other girls who don't have someone like you."

Josh exhaled slowly, his gaze steady on her but shadowed. "It's too dangerous, Dylan. And if your uncle managed to get his hands on you…" He studied her for a long moment. Maybe he heard the bruised pride in her voice or saw the pain she wasn't hiding anymore. Underneath it all, she had the quiet rage of someone who'd been wronged and was no longer willing to be a victim again.

Finally, he said, "If you stay, it gets darker. It gets harder. And if you get caught in the middle of it again, there's no guarantee I can pull you out next time."

"I understand," she said. "But if I go to Mercy right now, all I'll be thinking about is what I didn't do."

Josh nodded, slow and reluctant. "I get it," he said slowly. "But if anything happened to you… I was losing my mind tonight, Dylan. Would I find you? Would I find you in time? What if they found out I was alive, and you were with me? What if they made *you* pay the price? I just… I couldn't fucking live with it if you got hurt or worse because of me."

"But you saved me," she pointed out. "I'm *safe* because of you."

"That's all I want," Josh said, moving closer to her. "So please just let me take you to Mercy in the morning, okay?"

Dylan shook her head. "You can't live without knowing I'm safe," she said slowly. "But you expect me to do the same? Go to Mercy, hang out with the Hounds who I don't fucking know. And not be able to breathe because my evil fucking uncle could kill you at any time? No."

The muscles in his forearm twitched as he braced his elbows on his knees, staring down at the worn carpet like it might hold the right words for this impossible situation. "You think I haven't thought about that?" he said, voice low and tight. "You think I don't know exactly how dangerous this is?"

He stood abruptly, dragging a hand through his hair and pacing the cramped motel room like a caged animal. "You don't get it, Dylan. I've already died once. I've already lost everything. My club, my name, my life… it's all gone. I've been living like a ghost for months just trying to get here. Just trying to do one fucking thing that matters."

Josh stopped, facing her again. His expression was raw now with anger, fear, and love all tangled behind his eyes. "And now you're asking me to let you stand in the blast radius with me?"

She stood too, her eyes burning. "You don't get to make that call for me."

"Wanna bet?" His voice rose. "You don't get to throw yourself into a war zone and act like I'm just supposed to be okay with it either."

They stood facing each other in the motel room, a breath apart, fury and fear crackling in the air like a live wire.

"I want to protect you, Dylan. That's all." He made one last peace offering.

"I know," she whispered. "But if protecting me means sending me off to Mercy while you risk everything? That's not safety. That's prison."

Dylan didn't know if she kissed him first, or if he kissed her. It really didn't matter.

Josh deepened the kiss as she clutched his T-shirt, pulling him into her. When she tried to push him back onto the bed, his strong arms wrapped around her like steel bands. But he didn't comply with her wishes, rushing her backwards until she felt off balance. She broke the kiss as her back met the wall, enough to knock a little wind from her.

He didn't let her recover. His hands dove for the

front of her jeans while the rest of him held her pinned to the wall with his body. Dylan ripped at his shirt now, stitches popped until it gave way in her hands. He shoved down her jeans and panties. She hung on to him to avoid falling as he pulled them free, lifting her and throwing her leg over his shoulder. He sucked her clit into his mouth and she gasped, clutching the thick locks of his hair and holding on while he took her apart with his tongue and fingers.

Josh pushed her to the edge with dizzying speed. She'd just reached her release when he stopped. She wasn't proud of the whine he drew from her when he rose from the floor, but she did help him get his jeans open, pushed them down his slim hips until his cock was free. Like it was effortless, his hands clutched her ass and pushed her up the wall. Just far enough to slide fully into her with one demanding movement of his hips.

Her body didn't have time to adjust as he began thrusting up into her like a wild man, so she wrapped her legs around his hips and hung on for dear life. His thrusts were fast and deep, bringing a shade of pain she wanted at the moment. His lips blazed a trail over her face and neck, his heated breath a rush against her skin that made her shiver in his grasp.

He was hers. *Her* man. Holding her to the wall like he never intended to let go. Her cries filled the room and her toes curled from all the desire building in her body. She didn't care if he was Jason or Josh or Tank. The man dominating her against the wall was the one she wanted, and her heart clenched in her chest to realize his loving had always been the same. Rough and dominant, a fire made just to consume her.

Dylan came on his cock, thrashing in his hold until she ran out of breath. He held onto her, keeping her against the wall. His own movements only gained in speed and strength, his mouth claiming hers for a kiss that sent heat racing through her blood. All she could see, all she could feel was him, and when he dropped a hand to tease her clit, the first delicate touch made her come again. The world was fading to black at the edges of her vision as the orgasm shook her, had her squeezing him with her thighs and pulling his hair for all she was worth. "I can't," she panted against the damp skin of his neck. "I can't… again…"

Josh kept fucking her into the wall. His grip on her tightened, not enough to hurt, but enough to make her feel his relentless need. "Yes, you fucking can," he said roughly against her skin. "Again… With me. *Now.*"

As if her body was his to command, Dylan came screaming as he pumped desperately into her, finally reaching his own release. Their hearts pounded together even as their movements stopped, as they stayed tangled together against the motel room wall. "If something happens to you," he whispered against her lips, "I won't survive it, Dylan."

"It won't," she promised. "I don't care who you are. Nothing is going to take me away from you. I won't let it."

Something shifted in his dark eyes, had her heart clenching in her chest. He said, "I don't know who I am sometimes. I just know… I'm in love with you."

Dylan pulled back to look into his eyes, the emotion there leaving her breathless. "I love you too, Josh."

The kiss they shared was tender, gentle. For the moment, they were safe from the storm.

Chapter Seven

Vendetta

The sun hadn't even cracked the edge of the horizon when Vendetta pulled the van around. Dylan climbed in beside him, her hoodie zipped to her chin and a small duffel bag hugged tightly to her chest like armor. She hadn't said much, just nodded when he asked if she was ready, and closed the door behind her like she never planned to open it again.

Vendetta checked the side mirror before shifting into drive. He was already on edge, adrenaline surging through his veins. Every instinct in his body screamed that Eli wouldn't let this go. He'd lost a high-ranking buyer, and he knew Dylan hadn't pulled off that escape by herself. All he had to do was talk to Peggy or anyone else who worked at the bar. They all knew she had a guy. They'd seen his van. Eli and his crew might even be at the warehouse right now, trying to shake any witnesses down for information.

Let them. They wouldn't get a Goddamn thing except an address for an extended-stay motel room that he'd picked clean before they left.

He scanned the rearview mirror again. Still nothing. But driving away with her just seemed too easy. It unnerved him because he knew from experience that nothing ever was.

"You're doing the right thing," he said, his voice low. But he wasn't sure if he was trying to convince her or himself.

Dylan didn't look at him. "Doesn't feel like it."

His hands tightened on the steering wheel. "I'm sorry this happened, Dylan. I really am. But you'll figure out where you want to go from here." Get a fresh start. With him.

Dylan nodded but didn't say anything else. She was gripping the strap of her bag so tightly her knuckles were white.

Vendetta meant what he'd said last night. He *had* to know she was safe. He couldn't take on this fight if there was any risk she was in danger. God, he knew he shouldn't have fallen in love with her. It hadn't been the plan. He just hoped that wherever she ended up once he got her out of this, he could still be part of her life. He didn't want this to be just a rescue and goodbye. Maybe, once the smoke cleared and Eli was buried under the weight of his own sins, Dylan might still look at him the way she used to. Like he was her hero, someone worth loving. But he couldn't say that out loud. Not while her world was still shifting beneath her feet like quicksand. She needed to feel safe, not pressured.

So, Vendetta kept driving, the wheel steady in his grip, and didn't say a damn thing. Even though every part of him wanted to.

He had one eye on the road, the other on the rearview mirror. A black SUV had tailed them for two blocks back near 221 but turned off toward the main drag. Still, his gut was uneasy.

Reaching forward, he turned off the radio. "I'll take a detour through Dusty Mile before we hit the Mercy County line," he muttered. "Just in case."

"Do you think he's already looking for me?" Dylan's voice was quiet. He knew she was afraid of the answer.

"I'd bet my patch on it."

She flinched at his words. He didn't want to scare her more, but there was no use in sugarcoating it.

Eli Crizer didn't let go of anything, never had. And he'd made the mistake of thinking Dylan was his.

It wasn't about love or family. To Eli, people were assets. Some made him money. Some earned him loyalty. Others were used as leverage. Dylan had been all three, and now that she'd slipped his grasp, she was a big liability.

From what Dylan told him, Eli hadn't lifted a hand to raise her, hadn't even acknowledged her in public half the time. But the second she defied him, disappeared off the grid, and ran with a man whose identity he didn't know, she became something he had to punish. Not because he missed her or fucking cared. But because disobedience demanded consequences, and he couldn't have word get out that someone defied him and lived to talk about it.

Eli Crizer ruled through fear. And when fear didn't work, he turned to brute force. That's what made him dangerous, and why Vendetta was driving like every second counted. Men like Eli didn't just let go. They hunted and destroyed.

Vendetta glanced at her again. Dylan wasn't property. She was a Goddamn spark in a powder keg, and one more reason he was willing to blow the whole thing sky-high.

Dylan still stared out the window, her eyes fixed on the trees racing past as if they could answer the questions in her head. She hadn't looked his way since they crossed the county line. He didn't push, guessing she needed silence.

But then, out of nowhere, her voice broke through the hum of the tires. "Do you know what happened to Jared? My cousin? Wasn't he one of you?"

Vendetta's grip on the wheel faltered slightly. They'd talked about him once, Dylan believing he'd just run off to avoid his father and some gambling debts.

"Jared Crizer," she added, softer. "My cousin. They called him Baby Face."

The silence that followed wasn't the same as before. It was much heavier now.

Dylan finally turned to him. "You do know."

He blew out a breath. "Dylan…"

"Don't lie to me," she said. "Not about this."

It was the first time since last night that she'd referenced his deception. And it hit him hard, not because her voice was sharp or cruel. That would have made him feel better. Her voice was steady, and there was hurt there. She was asking for something real.

Gripping the wheel tighter, the ghost of her words echoed louder than the hum of the tires on pavement. He'd known this was coming. Now that the shock was wearing off, the questions would start. And this one…

He glanced at her out of the corner of his eyes, his heart clenching. What if, no matter how hard he fought to protect her, the way he came into her life had already poisoned whatever they had between them? Whatever they were becoming, he wanted it. At some point, she'd become more important than the revenge he wanted, the peace he needed. He just didn't know if they could survive the truth. "After everything you've been through, I really don't want to add to it."

"But you were one of them," she said. "Or close enough."

"Close enough to know the truth." His voice was low, careful. "Jared didn't run. Yeah, he had gambling debts, and from what I heard, he and Eli didn't get along."

She released a slow breath, already bracing for the answer.

Vendetta kept his eyes on the road. "Eli killed

him."

When he spared a glance at Dylan, she looked like she'd been slapped. She looked away, but her voice still held. "Why?"

"Jared crossed a line," Vendetta said quietly. "He wanted Eli to bail him out of debt. When Eli wouldn't, Jared tried something else. Razor is the president of the Mercy Hounds. His daughter came back to Mercy after her grandmother died, and Baby Face saw an opportunity. He always thought she was Eli's kid. He used that as an excuse."

Dylan's gaze dropped. Vendetta was pretty sure she didn't really want to hear the rest.

"Baby Face grabbed her off the street," Vendetta continued, voice flat with disgust. "Sold her to a Cottonmouth hangout. Tried to turn her out like she was nothing, but the Hounds got to her in time… Baby Face figured Eli would take notice, and he did. But the girl wasn't Eli's. And when Eli found out what he'd done, embarrassing him and causing trouble in his name with the Hounds, he didn't hesitate." He cut her another glance. "Eli shot him. Right there in the Hounds' clubhouse in Mercy. No trial or fight. Just a bullet."

Dylan stared at the dashboard, her voice cracking as she whispered, "He killed his own son."

It wasn't a question. And all he could do was nod in answer.

They still had a half hour to go, every minute building tension in his chest like storm pressure. Still, with every mile they put between Dylan and Oak Grove, he felt a sliver of relief.

Just a little longer. Mercy was waiting.

* * *

Dylan

"Welcome to Mercy," Josh said as they passed its city limits sign.

Dylan sat shaking in the passenger seat as the van turned off the main road and rolled through a gritty corner of Mercy. The streets were older than those in Oak Grove, narrower, and cracked. It was the kind of place where every brick had a story. Josh slowed the van in front of a corner building in a run-down strip mall. At first glance, it didn't look like much. But as they pulled up in a parking lot across the street, the storefront came into view.

Graffiti-style murals covered the outer wall. Dark, expressive artwork stretched across the brick like a tapestry of rebellion. Skulls, wings, serpents, and flames danced together in an eye-catching but chaotic symmetry. Its bold neon signage glowed above the door in fiery red and cool white: *No Mercy Ink,* the shop making its presence known against the overcast morning.

Tinted windows shielded whatever was inside, but the glass was lined with displays. Elegant tattoo designs of snakes coiled through roses, broken clocks, battle-worn angels. A wrought-iron bench sat beneath a rusty metal awning out front, with a beat-up bucket on the ground serving as a makeshift ashtray.

Dylan's eyes lingered on the sign. "This is it?"

Josh nodded, one hand resting on the steering wheel. "This is *No Mercy Ink*. Deva, Razor's old lady, runs it with Outcast, her brother. They know we're coming."

The van ticked as he shut it off. Outside, it was quiet, but it wasn't peace she was feeling. It was pressure, like the street held its breath whenever strangers arrived.

Josh glanced her way. She didn't miss the concern that had bled into his expression. "Just let me talk, all right?"

Dylan gave a slow nod. "Yeah, okay." But her eyes stayed fixed on the glowing sign as if it might blink out and leave her in the dark again.

Opening his door first, Josh scanned the street one last time before stepping out. Dylan slowly followed, but her anxiety was spiraling. The wind pulled at her jacket as they crossed the street toward the tattoo shop.

Josh opened the shop door and the sound of a motorcycle revving growled overhead. The smell of ink and antiseptic hung thick in the air. The walls were lined with black-framed tattoo designs, each piece more intense and expressive than the one before it. Dylan heard the low hum of a tattoo machine vibrating from the far corner where a gorgeous young woman with vivid purple hair worked over a client's arm, steady and focused.

She didn't look up. "We're not open yet unless you've got an appointment," she said coolly, not missing a beat with her needle.

But someone else stepped into view, tall and broad-shouldered with nearly black hair framing his face in loose waves. The man had calculating blue eyes and the unmistakable bearing of a man who'd led through fire.

Josh knew him, approaching him with a nod. "Outcast."

Recognition hit. A flicker of surprise crossed Outcast's face, followed immediately by suspicion as he turned those bright blue eyes on her.

"Vendetta," Outcast said, his voice low. "I knew you'd be calling sooner or later."

Vendetta? Was that Josh's club name now? Given what he'd been through, it was fitting.

Behind him, two more men stepped into view. One was tall and blond, handsome like the leading man in a movie. Dylan had to smile because his patch said "Hero." The other had long silver hair framing his face, the same silver streaking his beard, and the kind of stillness that demanded respect. His patch said "Razor," and she remembered Josh saying he was the club president.

Deva finally looked up, wiping her gloved hand on a rag. Her gaze moved from Outcast to Josh and then to Dylan. "He's not alone."

Josh stepped back so they could all see her, keeping his voice calm but firm. "She's the reason I'm here. This is Dylan Crizer. Eli's niece."

If the floor could have just swallowed her up right there, Dylan would have been just fine with it. Anything to escape the sudden pressure of being the center of attention in a room full of rough, dangerous-looking bikers. She felt the weight of their gazes, sizing her up, measuring risk. And she knew they saw Eli Crizer's blood. The niece of the man they had every reason to hate.

It was Hero who looked at her the longest, his blue eyes narrowed with open skepticism. Like he was trying to decide if she was a threat, or just another problem they didn't need. She couldn't blame him.

Dylan straightened her shoulders anyway, even though her stomach churned. She wasn't there to cause trouble. But part of her still wasn't sure she belonged.

Razor took a single step closer, his presence cutting through the room like a blade. "Why'd you bring her here?"

"She's in danger," Josh replied. "From her own

fucking uncle. Eli tried handing her off like she was property to one of those men from Sinister Skin. And I couldn't allow that. She's mine."

Dylan's breath caught. *She's mine.*

The words should've felt possessive or territorial, even. And maybe coming from someone else, they would have. But not from Josh. When he said it, his voice cracked slightly, like the claim came from a place of desperation, not the need to dominate. It felt like he'd been holding the words back too long, and the only way to protect her now was to make it clear to everyone, including himself, that she wasn't just a pawn.

Heat flushed her cheeks, but not from embarrassment. She glanced toward the Hounds, aware of the judgment in Hero's gaze, the way Outcast's jaw tensed, and the way Razor stood still as stone. But none of it mattered at that moment.

Josh had said *she's mine,* and she didn't feel owned. She felt chosen. And God help her, part of her needed that right now more than anything.

Then Razor spoke, his hazel-eyed gaze on her. "You vouch for her?"

Josh nodded. "With everything I've got."

Outcast didn't smile, but the tension in his shoulders eased.

From the far corner of the shop, Deva wiped her hands on a clean towel and stood, the purple locks of her hair catching the overhead light as she crossed the floor. The hum of the tattoo machine faded as her client leaned back, clearly understanding this moment wasn't about him. When Dylan looked closer, she realized the man in her chair was wearing a Hound cut too.

Deva glanced at Dylan with a quiet, assessing look. "Razor," she said gently, coming to stand beside him. "Look at her. She's scared to death."

Dylan felt her throat tighten. She wasn't *trying* to look scared. But her whole body was still humming with leftover adrenaline, fear, confusion, and heartbreak, so much that she couldn't hide if she tried.

Razor's sharp gaze moved back to Dylan. The man radiated power, but at Deva's words, his expression shifted just enough to feel like just maybe, she wasn't walking into the lion's den completely alone.

"You're safe here," Razor said to her.

Dylan's voice barely worked to answer, "Thank you."

Behind her, Josh exhaled loudly.

Razor nodded, his focus back on Josh. "We'll talk at the clubhouse. I want the full rundown. Everything you've seen. Everything you've got."

"You'll get it," Josh told him.

Razor turned toward the others. "Mount up. Let's move."

Outcast clapped Hero on the back, already headed for the door. Deva returned to her client with a pat on Dylan's shoulder as she passed.

Back in the van, Dylan waited quietly as Josh started the engine. Her nerves hadn't eased, but something about being around Deva, her calm and confidence, made her feel just a little less like an outsider. She still wasn't sure she belonged, but they hadn't shoved her out yet, either.

The drive to the clubhouse was mostly silent, save for the rumble of bikes ahead and behind them. Josh kept checking the mirrors, ever watchful. Dylan didn't ask where they were going. She figured she'd find out soon enough.

When they arrived, the building loomed in front

of them like a fortress dressed in weathered brick and quiet history. It didn't feel threatening. It felt… safe.

"This used to be Mercy's sheriff's station," Josh explained. "My grandmother lived over here when I was a kid. I remember it."

The building still looked the part from the outside. It was solid brick with reinforced windows and a front stoop that had once welcomed lawmen instead of outlaws. The Hounds hadn't bothered to strip the bones of the place. They'd just reshaped its purpose. The front desk was now a check-in point for club prospects and guests. The briefing room, where deputies once gathered for morning updates, looked like it now served as the club's meeting room, the Hounds' patch hanging on the wall where a county seal used to be.

Despite the rough edges, the space felt lived-in and secure. The kind of place you could hole up in when the world outside got ugly. And right now, that was exactly what Dylan needed.

Razor directed his men to the meeting room while Josh led Dylan down a quiet hallway. He opened the door to a simple but clean spare room with a bed, dresser, and lamp. Soft light filtered in from a nearby window.

"You'll be okay here," Josh said, his voice softer now. "Get some rest. I'll check on you in a bit."

"Thanks, *Vendetta*."

He started to close the door, then paused, smiling. "You don't like it?"

She gave the faintest smile. "It's perfect."

He closed the door behind him, and Dylan sat on the edge of the bed, finally letting out a slow breath. For the first time in days, maybe longer, the danger wasn't right outside the door. Maybe a nap was in order.

* * *

Vendetta

It was his first time in the Mercy Hounds' clubhouse, and the room smelled faintly of familiar things. Coffee, leather, sweat, and whiskey. They all sat at a long table with dusty blinds covering the windows. The crazy energy in the room was coming from all the Hounds.

He stood at one end of their table, his hands braced on the cold surface in front of him. Razor sat at the head of the table opposite him, quiet but watching with eyes that didn't miss a damn thing.

To his right, the VP leaned back in a chair, arms crossed, his gaze sharp. He had solid white hair, but he wasn't old; he couldn't have been out of his thirties. Identical twins, enforcers no doubt, sat together near the door, murmuring to each other in low voices until Razor shot them a look.

Vendetta tried not to make it obvious that he was reading patches, but the names made him feel like less of a stranger. Crash, Beast, Player… every man there was a brother forged by battle, betrayal, or blood. He could feel them sizing him up, because he doubted that most of them knew what he was really doing there in their midst.

Razor sat forward, resting his forearms on the table. His voice was low but carried like gravel on steel. "Most of you remember that this isn't the first time we've had bad blood with Sinister Skin."

A few heads nodded. Beast scowled. Outcast stared at the table like he was watching old blood dry.

"They tried to come through Mercy not too long ago," Razor continued. "They tried to push their filth under the radar here. Leaning on us to let 'em 'expand.' When that didn't work, they set their sights on the people around us. They tried to shut down *No Mercy Ink* and came after Deva and Outcast."

Razor wasn't trying to sway sympathy. He laid out facts.

"We pushed back," Razor said simply. "Took out their warehouse, freed those kids they were trafficking. We sent a message."

"And now," Snow added, his voice dry, "they've hit Oak Grove?"

Vendetta gave a short nod. "And Eli rolled out the welcome mat."

"They picked the wrong fucking side of the state," Player muttered. He was a big, broad-shouldered biker with tattooed knuckles and the kind of energy that said he'd rather solve problems with his fists than words. He leaned back in his chair, arms crossed over his chest, but his eyes burned with anticipation. Vendetta pegged him as one of their rabble-rousers, the kind who'd be the first in and the last out of a fight, grinning the whole damn time.

Razor didn't take his eyes off Vendetta. "Go on then," he said. "Tell 'em who you are. And why the hell you're standing in my clubhouse with Crizer's niece in tow."

The room fell silent, all eyes landing squarely on him. Vendetta straightened a little, feeling the weight of the moment. If he wanted their help, he had to earn it.

"Name's Josh," he said evenly. "I go by Vendetta now. Before you ran Sinister Skin out of here and they set up shop in Oak Grove, it was Tank. I was a member of the Abingdon chapter of the Cottonmouths. I patched in young, right after I got out of the Marine

Corps. I followed orders even when I didn't like 'em. Back in the fall, the Oak Grove chapter said they had some big ops coming and needed extra hands. Me and a couple of my Abingdon brothers came over. And that's when everything went to hell."

A few heads nodded around the table.

Vendetta didn't bother sugarcoating it. He laid it out plain. The ops started as muscle-for-hire gigs, backdoor security, and roughing up deadbeats for loan sharks. But that changed fast. The Cottonmouths began taking jobs directly from Sinister Skin. Jobs that involve moving people, not just product. Girls and teenagers, a few young men. All of them scared, drugged, and completely disposable to most of his Cottonmouth brothers.

He explained that he started asking questions and pushing back. When he wouldn't shut up and follow orders, they strung him up in the woods off a forgotten road and walked away like they had taken out the trash.

"Tried to hang you?" Player asked, looking genuinely curious, his usual smirk tempered by something sharper now. Respect, maybe.

"They did more than try," Vendetta replied, reaching behind his neck to tug the collar of his hoodie down even farther. He lifted his chin just enough to show them.

The scar was angry and jagged, a brutal, uneven loop of damaged skin wrapping around the base of his throat. No clean line, no surgical precision. Just the mark of something vicious and rushed, the kind of wound meant to silence.

A couple of the Hounds swore under their breath. One of them, one of the twins, sat back like he'd just been punched.

Vendetta let them have a long look. Then he pulled the hoodie back up and sat down. "I'm still here. They think I'm dead. They told the MC I ran off, went nomad."

Beast gave a low whistle. Snow slowly shook his head.

"I went dark. I hid out and tracked what I could. I waited. I didn't know how far it went, how deep Sinister Skin had their claws in the Cottonmouths."

He paused, his gaze flicking briefly toward Outcast, then back down to the table.

"And then I ran into him," Vendetta said, jerking his chin toward Outcast. "He was trying to get his old lady back from Louisville. And that kind of loyalty? That kind of grit to walk into the fire and drag someone out? That reminded me what I'd lost… and what I needed to do."

He looked around the table again, more steel in his voice now. "I stopped hiding after that. Figured if the Cottonmouths were too far gone to fix, maybe they could still be shut down."

Vendetta paused, glancing briefly in the direction of the spare room where Dylan was resting.

"I came back to Oak Grove under another name. And that's where I met Dylan working as a waitress at *Ned*'s. I didn't know who she was at first. But then I found out she was Eli Crizer's niece. And she was caught right in the middle of all this shit." He let out a breath, slow and deliberate. "I was gonna finish this job myself. Collect proof and try and break the network from the inside. But Eli? He offered his own fucking niece to one of those SS pricks like she was just another girl to sell."

A dark ripple moved through the room.

"I had to pull her out because she's a target now,

so I need her kept safe. And I need help taking Eli and these fuckers down and breaking whatever pipeline Sinister Skin's building in Oak Grove. Especially since all of you managed to shut that shit down in Mercy."

Vendetta looked Razor dead in the eye. "I came here because I knew you'd remember what they tried to do in Mercy. And I'm betting you'd rather end this on our terms than wait for the war to come back to your door."

Razor's gaze didn't leave Vendetta. "So, you're asking us to go to war with a rival chapter and a cartel-run operation. For a town we don't run and for a girl who carries their president's blood."

Vendetta didn't flinch. "I'm not asking you to fight my war. I'm asking you to help me finish the one they started. If you don't, this shit spreads. They'll come back to Mercy, and they'll hit you hard. But you already know that."

There was a beat of silence.

"We're still here after the shit they pulled here in Mercy," Outcast said slowly. "You're still here after what they did to you. We're patched in different clubs, sure, but it seems like we're on the same side of this."

Vendetta looked at him, surprised.

Snow nodded. "Hell, we ran the Mafia out of here. I sure as fuck don't want them back here again. Emily's just got the new bakery off the ground."

One of the twins nodded.

Player wore a wide grin. "Getting rid of Crizer and that bunch over there in Oak Grove? I'm game."

Vendetta wasn't surprised by that.

Razor gave a slight nod, then looked around the table. "Let's hear what Vendetta's got planned."

"I appreciate the time," Vendetta started, his voice steady.

"Start talking," Razor said.

"Sinister Skin's in Oak Grove. Deep. They're not just pushing product as hard as they're pushing people. They're trafficking, mostly teenage girls and younger women. They're slick, routing through temporary safe houses, hiding behind fake medical shipments. One of the hubs is a medical supply warehouse called *INeeda*," Vendetta said.

"I took a job there as a courier and started noticing things… deliveries that didn't make sense, shell routes, manifests with missing destinations. They were using it as a front to cover their tracks. Drugs, weapons, even medical sedatives were being funneled through. It gave me a window into how deep the operation ran, and how far they were willing to go to keep it quiet."

A couple of Hounds muttered curses. Beast cracked his knuckles.

Vendetta nodded grimly. "And Eli Crizer, he's in bed with them. Not just tolerating it. He and the Cottonmouths loyal to him are helping him run it. Half his table's turned. The other half's too scared or too paid off to stop it."

Outcast leaned forward. "How long?"

"A few months now," Vendetta said.

"And now you're here," Razor said, his voice unreadable.

"You already know I was going after Oak Grove for what they did to those girls. To me," Vendetta said. "And I'm sure as hell not letting them get away with what they did to Dylan."

Outcast nodded. "Vendetta got me and Anya back safe and helped us take out Sebastian Six. I can't speak for anyone else, but I'm definitely in."

A beat of silence followed Outcast's words,

heavy and meaningful.

Crash leaned forward, resting his tattooed forearms on the table. "Six was a bastard. After what you told me he did to you and Anya," he said, glancing at Outcast, then back at Vendetta. "You've got my vote."

Beast gave a grunt of approval, already looking to be itching for a fight. "They're moving girls like cargo. Anyone helps stop that, I'm down."

Axel exchanged a look with Ryder, then gave a sharp nod. "We all saw what Sinister Skin tried to do here. If it's spreading through Oak Grove, we've got a choice. Shut it down now or let it come knocking again."

"Margot's going to be pissed," Ryder said. "But yeah, I'm in."

Player tapped the table with a finger, his eyes flicking to Vendetta. "Just tell us where to hit."

The air shifted. Suspicion turned to solidarity. The kind forged in blood, not just patches.

Razor looked around the room, reading the temperature. Then his gaze returned to Josh. "Looks like you've got more than one in."

"I trust you," Vendetta said simply. "And I need backup. If I go back in alone, it's suicide. But if *we* go in right, we can burn their whole fucking operation to the ground."

Crash leaned forward. "What do you need from us?"

Vendetta looked around the room, meeting every set of eyes.

"Intel. Manpower. Leverage. If we cut off the supply lines, expose the connections, and turn a few of their guys against them, we can run Sinister Skin out of Oak Grove."

Silence held for a long beat.

Then Razor sat back in his chair. "We're listening."

Chapter Eight

Eli

The office reeked of cigar smoke and sweat. He had a horrible fucking headache that rage and panic had started building the minute Rick Earle called him last night.

He'd painstakingly set up that evening at the lake house for Earle, a higher-up in the organization he needed to keep happy. When he signed up to be part of their operations, he hadn't realized how often some of the Sinister Skin lieutenants would be coming around to "check on things." And on one such evening, the night he met Earle to begin with, he took him over to *Ned*'s and the man's eye fell on Dylan, his niece. Of course it had.

That was another sore subject all in itself. He hadn't wanted Dylan working at *Ned*'s. Eli had explained it wasn't the kind of place for her, not with the deals being made in the back and the kinds of men sliding into booths like they owned the damn place. But she was stubborn, just like her mother had been, and refused to take no for an answer. Dylan said she needed the money, and that she could handle herself.

Eli knew he should have shut it down right then. He should've found some strings to pull to make sure she didn't get the damn job. Then he could have kept her at arm's length like he'd originally intended. But she'd worn him down, and somewhere along the line, he started to believe maybe having her close was better. It would be easier to keep an eye on her at *Ned*'s, keep her out of trouble. It would also be easier to make sure she didn't start digging into things she didn't understand and didn't need to be a part of.

The choice blew up in his fucking face. Eli told

himself at the time when he made the arrangement that it was just business. Handing Dylan over to Earle wasn't personal, it was leverage. A show of loyalty to the network, and solid proof that Eli Crizer was still useful to them and dependable.

But deep down, he knew the truth. It had been about control.

Dylan's involvement in his world wasn't the best look for him. She'd come back to Oak Grove and turned a blind eye to how the town had changed. She'd insisted on working at the bar against his advice. She'd run her mouth about independence, like her blood wasn't soaked in Cottonmouth legacy.

Worst of all, *she reminded him of her mother*. She'd been a firebrand too. She'd been defiant and independent, always questioning club business, and pushing boundaries. She never quite bent the way women in their world were supposed to. She'd called him out, challenged his leadership. And when she got pregnant with Dylan, she'd walked away from the club entirely. *From him*. And she never came back.

He saw that same rebellious look in Dylan's eyes now. The quiet judgment, the stubborn pride, and worst of all, her refusal to fall in line and follow orders. It was like looking at a ghost. Maybe that made it easier to hand her over to Earle. Dylan wasn't just another mouthy girl trying to slip out from under his thumb, she was a reminder that the blood in his family had *always* rebelled.

Jared had been the same way. His only son had thought he knew better. After taking the name Baby Face in their MC, he'd thought he could game the system, cut corners, and make deals without Eli's approval. When he went too far and crossed a line that couldn't be uncrossed, Eli did what had to be done, family or not. Besides, putting a bullet in his son's brain put the fear of God into the rest of the Cottonmouths. Operations in his chapter had been smooth as glass until recently.

Dylan was walking the same path right now. Blood didn't make them loyal. If anything, it made the betrayal so much fucking worse.

Eli Crizer didn't tolerate betrayal. Not from outsiders, but especially not from his own fucking blood. When the offer came down, one night with Dylan in exchange for a seat at the table, he took it. Not because the approval he'd garner was worth that much to him. It was because she *wasn't*. Not anymore. She'd made her choice.

Now that choice had made him a liability. Dylan hadn't just walked away, she'd run. And the only thing he knew for certain right now was that she hadn't done it alone.

They'd torn through her apartment the same night she vanished and found nothing. No notes or burner phones. Hell, there was nothing to indicate she even packed a bag. Just the scent of her cheap perfume and the ghost of a girl who used to believe in him.

Ned's had been scrubbed too. He'd had his men go over every inch -- the freezer, staff room, and storage. His niece left no trail or clues behind. Dylan had vanished like smoke, and that wasn't an accident. Someone had fucking helped her, and that someone was strategic and fast. Eli was now the one scrambling to catch up.

Dylan was the fucking reason he was here now. His niece wasn't just a threat to the operation; she was a stain on his name. She'd betrayed him. He was choking on the rage that threatened to consume him. Rising from his seat in the corner of the room, he started pacing like a caged animal. The muscles in his neck were tight, his fingers itching for another smoke, but he didn't light one yet.

Across the room, Peggy slumped in the metal chair they'd tied her to. Her lip was split, and one eye was already swelling shut. Trucker, one of his enforcers, stood next to her, rolling his shoulders like he was ready for round two.

"She's not talking," Trucker muttered.

"She will," Eli said coldly.

Peggy lifted her head, shakily. Fat tears rolled down the older woman's face. "I swear I don't know who helped her…"

"Bullshit," Eli snapped, his voice low and dangerous. "You were the one always covering for her. Running drinks for her. Watching out for her."

"She's my friend," Peggy muttered.

"She's a fucking liability," Eli growled. "And someone helped her run. Someone helped her make me look *weak*. So, unless you want Trucker here to do permanent damage…"

"I don't know his name!" she shouted, wincing as Trucker stepped forward again, holding a pair of pliers. "I don't… I just heard her call him Jason. He's a delivery driver. He works at that medical place -- *INeeda*."

The room went silent. Eli paused, turned back to her. "Now we're getting somewhere. What's his fucking name?"

"Jason," Peggy cried as Trucker waved the pliers in her face.

"Last name?"

"I don't know," she said, her desperate gaze fixed on those pliers. "I never got a last name. I swear!"

"How do you know he works at the warehouse?"

Eli wanted to know.

"He made deliveries to *Ned*'s all the time," she said. "He always drives that white cargo van. I never saw him drive anything else."

"So, we need to talk to Freddie," Eli said more to Trucker than to Peggy. "See who Jason is."

Peggy exhaled in relief, thinking maybe her ordeal was over. But it wasn't.

"Describe him," Eli said, gaze snapping back to her. "Now."

Peggy licked her split lip. "Tall… six-four, maybe? Dark hair, dark eyes. Beard. Wore a cap sometimes. He's real quiet. He doesn't talk a lot."

Eli stared her down. "And how'd he find the lake house?" he asked, voice sharpening.

"I don't know."

He took a step closer. "How'd he find it? I took Dylan's phone so he couldn't have tracked her by GPS."

"I said I don't know!" Peggy cried, shrinking back.

Eli grabbed her face, his fingers digging into her cheeks. Trucker stepped forward, the pliers in his hand gleaming in the light.

"Last chance," Eli hissed. "How did he know where she was?"

"I told him she left in a black sedan. I -- I didn't know what was happening. I thought it was just a private party she was working. She looked scared, and I got a picture of the license plate, okay? I showed it to him."

Eli stilled. A license plate wouldn't lead someone to a lake house like that. Not without tracking experience or working knowledge of some things he shouldn't have known. His stomach turned. Something was deeply fucking off. Peggy's description of the man circled in his mind like a ghost. The physical appearance she gave sounded familiar. She'd described him as tall and quiet. The only other thing Eli knew about this mystery boyfriend of Dylan's was that he'd found her fast, without an address. Then he'd proceeded to take down Earle and his armed guards and leave with Dylan. Only a certain type of man could pull something like that off, and he matched her description.

Eli had known a man like that once.

Tank was supposed to be dead. They'd left him swinging from that tree, dead as a hammer. Eli had made sure of it. But the next day, uneasy and itching with something he couldn't shake, Eli went back to the spot alone, just to be sure.

The body was gone. The rope lay in the dirt, bloodied and frayed next to the crate, but the chains were missing. No Tank. No sign of animals dragging off the remains. Just empty woods and silence.

For weeks, Eli waited. For cops to ask questions. For a body to turn up. For someone to say something. But no word ever came, making the story they made up about him going nomad plausible.

Maybe Tank had died out there and someone stumbled across the body first -- some hunter, maybe, or a local kid sneaking through the woods. And maybe they didn't want to get dragged into a police investigation, didn't want to answer questions or explain what they saw.

That's what he'd told himself on a regular basis. No way Tank survived all that. Not the beating *and* the hanging.

But the longer the silence stretched, the more that seed of doubt in Eli's gut sank roots. What if he hadn't died? What if someone had helped him? What if Tank was still out there, hiding and planning?

Eli told himself it wasn't possible. But he'd checked his locks more often and slept with a gun closer to hand.

If Tank was still alive…

Eli stepped back, exhaling through his nose. "Get her out of my sight."

Trucker pulled a knife to cut the rope holding Peggy in the chair. She groaned in pain as he hauled her to her feet.

"She needs a hospital," Trucker muttered, almost reluctantly.

"Then drop her in one and make it look like a mugging," Eli said, heading back to his desk.

When the door shut behind them, Eli sat. Grabbing his phone, he entered a number. A voice on the other end answered. It was a network contact, mid-tier.

"We got a lead," Eli said. "One of the warehouse guys working at *INeeda* here in Oak Grove. 'Jason' is all we got right now. Dylan Crizer's been with him this whole time."

A pause. "You want it quiet?"

"No," Eli said, his voice ice. "I want it *done*. The bounty goes wide; every Cottonmouth, every affiliate. Dead or alive."

"What about the girl?"

Eli's hand clenched around his phone. "Bring her back alive and unharmed. She's mine."

He hung up. And for a long moment, he just sat there, the pressure in his temples squeezing like a vise. Earle had already called twice, threats hidden in every word the man said. Eli knew what happened to men who failed SS. He'd seen it. Now he lit a cigarette with shaking fingers, pulling in a deep drag and staring at the wall.

The name scratched at the back of his mind like a ghost clawing at a coffin lid. But that was impossible. Tank was dead.

Wasn't he?

* * *

Vendetta

Vendetta didn't look up right away when he heard the knock. He was sitting on the bed next to where Dylan slept, her breathing finally even. After everything she'd been through with her uncle, almost being trafficked at the lake house, and then learning the truth about the man she'd slept with and trusted, she must have crashed the minute her head hit the pillow. She looked so small now, vulnerable in a way he'd never seen when she was awake.

He watched her for a moment longer, wishing he could just stay there with her. And he swore to himself that if he failed at everything else, keeping her safe had to be the one thing he got right.

The knock came again, followed by Hero's voice on the other side of the door. "We've got company," Hero said. "Cottonmouths. They mentioned *Tank*."

Vendetta froze. Who the fuck could that be? He took one last look at Dylan, brushing a hand lightly over her blanket-covered leg, and rose silently from the bed. Stepping out into the hall, he closed the door behind him with careful quiet.

"Who?" he asked.

Hero gave him a grim look. "Come see for yourself."

"Did they ask for me? Or Tank?" Vendetta asked, thinking it sounded shady as hell.

Hero shook his head. "They sent a message through one of the low-level contacts we use out of Roanoke. Just said they needed to speak to anyone who had a problem with Eli Crizer." He paused. "Razor screened them himself. Said you'd want to hear it. Outcast was there too."

Vendetta's brows lifted. "And Razor trusts them?"

Hero snorted. "Razor doesn't trust anyone who shows up without warning and smells like Cottonmouth." Then his gaze steadied. "But Razor said if they were lying, he'd know it."

Vendetta exhaled through his nose and rolled his shoulders once. "Fine. Let's see what they've got."

Nervous energy ran through him like electrical current. He followed Hero down the hall, keeping calm. Whatever this visit was, it wasn't random. And Razor wouldn't have entertained it unless it was something worth hearing. He didn't know the Hound president well, but that much he knew.

As they stepped into the Hounds' common room, the first thing he saw were Razor and Outcast, standing off to the side. Then he spotted two other men waiting, both wearing Cottonmouth patches. Vendetta froze. He knew them.

Shade and Ripper. His brothers from the Abingdon chapter of Cottonmouth MC. They'd come with him to Oak Grove when Eli called in support months ago, before everything turned to rot. Shade looked the same as ever with his dirty blond hair just reaching his shoulders, his steady, green eyes sharp beneath a low brow. Ripper's blue-eyed gaze widened on Vendetta when he spotted him, then he ran a hand through his dark hair nervously.

He hadn't seen them since the day Tank died. All

three of them had asked questions back then about what was really going on with the Oak Grove MC. But no one gave them answers. He'd spoken with them after what he saw at the compound that last morning. But he never told them he was hitting the road that night. He hadn't decided that until later, until after they'd called to arrange a "meeting."

Ripper was the first to break the silence. "You're *alive*?"

Meeting his gaze, Vendetta said, "That's the rumor."

"What the fuck happened?" Ripper was astonished, color flooding his face. "Eli told us you couldn't handle the direction we were going in and abandoned your patch. I mean, we knew you had issues with the shit him and his bunch were doing. So do *we*. It made sense you'd hit the road, go nomad over it. But no one saw you at all after that and it never sat right with me."

Vendetta snorted. He'd allegedly abandoned his patch? It wasn't even a creative cover story.

His brothers from Abingdon looked at him like he was a ghost. Shade slowly shook his head. They knew Ripper wasn't letting this go.

"A lot of shit has gone down over the last couple of days," Ripper went on. "Eli's tearing everything apart trying to find his niece because she pissed off someone in Sinister Skin. He handed her off to one of theirs. Turns out he's some higher-up. He told us Dylan was cool with it. But she must not have been. A boyfriend she had that Eli didn't even know about busted her out, and that Sinister Skin guy had armed guards with him that night. Not just anyone could have done that. Eli's running scared and he's turning on his own to keep control and cover shit up. Things are bad in Oak Grove now, brother."

Vendetta listened, said nothing.

"We had a big fucking meeting this morning," Ripper explained. "Someone brought *you* up. What if it was Tank, coming back to fuck with us? Eli was fuming, told us it couldn't have been fucking Tank, because Tank was *dead*. He promised that anyone who turned against him would end up just like Tank."

Eli had admitted it then. Fury rose in him like bile, and it was hard to force it back down.

"All hell broke loose then," Ripper said. "Because a *lot* of us have been real uneasy about the shit that's been going down. Then we hear that Tank had been fucking *dead* this whole time. You could just look at him and know what he did. Shade and me put it together. That him and his little circle had to have been the ones to kill you, then cover it up."

Shade, who'd been listening as he had, stepped toward Vendetta, his assessing gaze on his throat. Vendetta held still for him, let him take it all in. After a moment, Shade's gaze met his. "What the fuck happened, brother? You didn't have that scar around your neck the last time we spoke."

Ripper was looking now too, so many emotions crossing his face it was impossible to miss. *Rage. Regret.* Something approaching to shame. He'd always been ruled by a hot temper and a big heart, always the first to swing, but never the first to walk away from a brother who needed him.

Shade, though, he was steady. Cool, the way he'd always been. The one who held the line when the rest of them cracked. But even now, Vendetta could see the shift in his expression, the anger he was holding onto. They were both waiting, watching him. Looking at the man standing in front of them like he was a ghost come back to life.

Vendetta exhaled slowly, peeling back the edge of his hoodie, just enough to give them a better look at his scar. He wanted them to see where the rope burn had torn through his skin.

"That night," he said in a low voice, "they told me we were meeting to talk. Just clear the air, and part ways like brothers."

Ripper's face twisted. "Bones?"

Vendetta nodded. "Called me personally and told me Eli didn't want bad blood between chapters." He paused, the words heavy in his chest. "The location was isolated, gave me a sick feeling in my gut. I decided to run, to leave that night. But they caught me before I could make it out of town."

The silence that followed hit hard. They listened as he told them everything that had happened that night. Shade's fists clenched at his sides.

Meeting Ripper's gaze, Vendetta felt the weight of his story in every word he spoke. "To this day, I don't know how I ended up on the ground. I buried Tank that night, what was left of him. I took a new name and came back to finish what I started."

"I didn't know what to believe," Shade told him. "The last time we talked was right before you disappeared, over at my apartment. Remember?"

He did remember. The three of them talked for a couple of hours about the state of things in the Oak Grove Cottonmouth chapter with the criminal organization they were getting tangled up with. His brothers had been just as upset about the trafficking and drugs as he was. They just didn't see things the same way. Shade thought it would be best to try and fade into the background, head back to Abingdon after a time. And Ripper was all about that idea. Maybe that's what they were doing now.

The problem was, Eli wouldn't have just let them leave no matter how slowly they tried to move. Not knowing what they knew. And Shade had done his damnedest to talk him out of confronting Eli and his inner circle that day at the compound. In hindsight, Shade had been right. Hitting things head on had always been Vendetta's way, but it sure as shit hadn't served him that day.

And now, here were his brothers. In Mercy.

Shade had been quiet through it all, but now his voice broke the silence. "Is it true?" he asked. "Are you the one who got Eli's niece out?"

Vendetta didn't blink. "Yeah. I got her out."

Shade's expression didn't change much, but something shifted. A flash of understanding.

"How long had you been back?" Ripper asked, incredulous but not judging. "Back in Oak Grove with that target on your back?"

"Not long." Vendetta nodded. "I didn't know Dylan was Eli's niece when I met her. But by the time I did, it didn't matter. She didn't know anything about what was going on. She was just trying to survive, same as anyone. Eli handed her off like property, and I couldn't let that stand."

Shade gave a slow exhale. "Damn."

"Yeah," Ripper muttered. "No wonder he put a bounty on your ass. You didn't just piss Eli off. You made him look weak to Sinister Skin, and now he's in deep shit with them."

Good. Vendetta arched a brow, sharp and steady. "What bounty?"

Shade answered, his voice grim. "Went out this morning through back channels tied to the network. Eli's calling in every favor, every affiliate still willing to do business with him. Five grand to bring in Dylan's boyfriend dead, ten if he's still breathing. Word is Dylan's worth even more if she's delivered alive."

The words hit like a hammer. He'd be dead before anyone put a hand on her.

"He's desperate," Shade went on. "Trying to fix this situation. Sinister Skin doesn't tolerate fuckups. So now he's got people out there looking to clean up his mess before someone higher up decides he's not worth protecting anymore."

Vendetta crossed his arms, his gaze narrowing. "He thinks it's me?"

Shade shrugged. "I don't think he knows for sure. I think he's hoping it's *not* you."

Ripper picked up from there. "Wishful thinking won't save him. He's not stupid. Paranoid as hell, sure, but not stupid. He knows somebody helped Dylan. And after she vanished, he started shaking the tree hard."

Shade nodded. "That's when Peggy got pulled in."

The mention of Peggy's name sent a chill down his spine.

"They worked her over," Ripper said quietly. "They didn't kill her, but she's going to be in the hospital for a while. From what we heard, they finally got her to tell them Dylan had a boyfriend. Some guy named Jason who worked for *INeeda*. She said he was quiet, drove a white cargo van."

Vendetta blew out a breath. *Thank God I got us out of Oak Grove when I did.*

"That was enough," Shade said. "We volunteered to go talk to Freddie at *INeeda* ourselves. Told Eli it was to keep things discreet, in-house. We ain't said shit to him though."

"Freddie didn't want to say much at first," Ripper added. "But I know his sister. When we pushed the right way, he gave up what he had. He described *you* to a T."

"But he mentioned Jason had a scar," Shade said, eyes on Vendetta now. "Said he always wore hoodies, like he didn't want people to see it. Barbed wire-looking, across his neck. It was the only thing that didn't fit. Until it did."

Ripper nodded slowly. "Even if it *was* you, we had no idea where to find you. We just up and left Oak Grove and planned to lay low for a while. The last we heard, Eli wasn't ruling out the Hounds over here in Mercy. He said maybe they had something to do with it. That was why we thought to get a message in, to try and warn the Hounds of what might be coming."

Silence settled again, heavier this time.

"He's not sure it's you yet," Shade said. "But once he confirms it? Every guy in Sinister Skin's gonna have your picture and a loaded mag." Shade hesitated, then added quietly, "We didn't know. About what happened that night. If we had… we should've looked harder. We should've known something was wrong."

Ripper looked down, jaw flexing like he couldn't decide whether to punch something or kick himself.

Vendetta kept his voice steady. "You weren't the ones who wrapped the chain around my wrists." He looked between them, two men who had once called him brother, and maybe still could. "You believed what you were told. I might've too, back then."

Shade's throat bobbed with a hard swallow. "Still doesn't make it right."

"No," Vendetta agreed. "But it makes *this* right. You're here now." And that was enough. For him, and for what came next.

Silence settled thick over the room, every man processing what Shade and Ripper just laid down. The threat wasn't abstract anymore. Sinister Skin was losing patience, and Eli was even trying to loop the Hounds into his latest fuck-up. The countdown was on.

Razor stood near the back wall, his arms crossed, his expression carved from stone. Outcast leaned beside him, quiet but watchful.

It was Razor who broke the silence, his voice low but sharp. "Sounds like Eli's finally crossed the line we can't ignore."

"He's desperate," Shade said. "That's when people start making bad moves."

Vendetta said, "And he's not gonna stop trying to cover his tracks."

Outcast pushed off the wall. "Then we don't give him time to."

Razor nodded once. "Exactly."

Stepping forward, Razor pulled a paper map that had seen better days from a small file cabinet by the wall. He spread it out on the table at the center of the room, glancing at different points on it as the others gathered round. "We don't solve this with just bullets. We need to bleed this thing from the inside. Quiet first, then loud."

Razor pointed to a red circle around Oak Grove. "We go in with a plan. We start by cutting off their logistics. Any safe houses, drop points, and runners. Anything we can dismantle before it blows back." He looked over at Vendetta. "You're at the center of this. You've been close to it longer than any of us."

"I've got names," Vendetta said. "And I've got eyes on two of Eli's men who are afraid but not loyal. We squeeze them right, they'll give us what we need."

"Good," Razor said. "Hero, Outcast -- you're with *him*. Shade, Ripper, you two know the town too. You help guide the second wave. I'll put Snow, Crash, and Player with you."

Razor looked around the room once more, his tone turning iron. "I'll call a meeting with the rest. Eli thinks he can drag Mercy back into this? He's about to learn otherwise."

"We going to keep someone here in town?" Outcast asked. "Just in case."

His president nodded. "Ryder will stay with a couple of Hounds. He also has Margot, and she can be ready to pitch in if shit goes down."

Razor caught the look Vendetta gave him and grinned. "Ryder's old lady is a local deputy."

All he could do was nod. It was the first he ever heard of a biker with a lady cop. But these days, with all he'd been through, not much surprised him anymore.

"Good," Razor said. "Then it's decided. We'll do some scouting today. And tomorrow..." His gaze darkened. "We send a message Eli won't walk away from."

* * *

Dylan

Dylan sat cross-legged on the bed when Josh returned to the room. She had pulled on one of his flannel shirts, sleeves rolled halfway up her forearms, to cover her tank since the air conditioning kept the room cold. She felt a little better after her nap. She still felt the danger looming beyond the walls of the Hounds' clubhouse, but not as sharply.

She looked up when Josh walked in, closing the door behind him and locking it. The grim look on his face made her stomach drop, and he hadn't said anything yet.

"What's happened?" she asked.

Josh took a seat on the edge of the bed, his shoulders tense beneath the weight of everything. "Two of my brothers showed up," he said quietly. "Shade and Ripper, who came over from the Abingdon chapter with me. Guys I rode with before everything went to hell."

Dylan's brow furrowed. "They knew you were here?"

He shook his head. "They figured it out. Put the pieces together. They talked to my boss at the warehouse, and he told them Jason was a quiet guy with a bad scar on his neck. They came to Mercy to warn the Hounds because Eli's pointing a finger at them too. Anyone but his fucking self. Turns out Shade and Ripper are also done with Eli. If I were a betting man, I'd say they aren't the only Cottonmouths in Oak Grove ready to abandon ship."

Her lips parted, absorbing the shift. "Do they know about *me*?"

Josh nodded. "They know what Eli's trying to do," he said. "They said there's a bounty out on both me and you. And that he wants *you* alive, probably to clean up his mess, or worse."

Dylan wasn't surprised, but she didn't look away either. "What else?"

Josh hesitated, then exhaled slowly. "Peggy's in the hospital. Eli's people worked her over. She didn't give much. Hell, she didn't have much to give them in the first fucking place. But it was enough for them to start connecting dots. And now Eli's panicking."

Dylan went still. "He's coming here?"

"He won't get the chance," Josh said. "We're

taking the fight to him in Oak Grove, where it belongs."

Staring down at her hands, Dylan sighed. It was bad enough Josh had been dragged into this. Now Peggy was in the hospital just for trying to help her. "I don't want to be the reason Mercy or the Hounds get pulled into this."

Josh reached out, gently took her hand in his. "You're not. You're not responsible for any of this, Dylan. Not Eli pointing a finger at Mercy. Not Peggy being put in the hospital. You can't blame yourself, okay?"

Dylan's heart sank. It sure felt like everything was her fault.

"One thing you need to understand about your uncle," Josh told her. "You escaped him, Dylan. And that's got him rattled. You made it out and that wasn't supposed to happen. Now he's spiraling. If he's paranoid enough to blame Mercy, he's scared. That means he's already cracking."

She swallowed hard, her voice barely above a whisper. "What happens now?"

Josh looked at her, *really* looked at her. For a moment, he didn't speak. Just brushed his thumb gently across the back of her hand like he was grounding both of them.

"Now," he said quietly, "we finish it. We bring the truth into the open. Expose everything he's built and burn it down before he can do to someone else what he tried to do to you."

Dylan sat back, her breath catching. Her voice came steadier this time. "For your revenge."

Josh blew out a breath and nodded. "Yes."

Dylan's gaze held his. "For every girl who comes after me. For *my* part."

There was a pause, then a mutual spark between them.

Josh gave a small, solemn nod. "We do it together."

Chapter Nine

Vendetta

The morning air was sharp, the perfect match for the mood, anticipation, and quiet resolve. Vendetta stood outside the Hounds' clubhouse with Tank's leather cut on his back, his hands flexing at his sides. The roar of engines echoed through Mercy as bikes lined up, headlights glaring through the thin veil of mist clinging to the road. It wasn't just the Hounds now. It was *his* brothers too, Ripper and Shade, suited up and ready to ride.

This wasn't just payback. This was the reckoning.

Outcast stood nearby, speaking low with Razor and Beast. Snow and Axel tightened the straps on their gear. Crash lit a cigarette with a glint in his eyes that said he hoped someone tried to stop them. Hero ran one last check on weapons from the bed of a truck, and Player leaned on his bike like he was itching for war.

Vendetta's eyes scanned them all. These weren't just men with patches; they were the line in the sand. The answer to what had been done in Oak Grove. *The last thing Eli Crizer and his crew would ever see coming*. He felt the weight of what was about to happen settle into his spine. Dylan was safe, and as long as that was true, he could do anything. Margot and Ryder were holding down Mercy.

But none of them would be safe, not for long, if Eli kept his grip on Oak Grove. Not after what he'd built.

When he looked up, he saw Dylan standing just beyond the line of bikes, her arms wrapped tightly around herself like she could hold all the fear in if she squeezed hard enough. The cut on his back didn't say Vendetta. It said *Tank*. And maybe that's what scared her the most: him going back as the man they tried to kill.

He was going back to *end* it.

Ryder stood beside her, quiet and watchful. Margot's hand rested gently on Dylan's back, grounding her. Margot wasn't in uniform at the moment, but Vendetta sure felt better knowing Dylan would be looked after by both sides of the law if anything happened.

Vendetta studied Dylan's face, memorizing every flash of emotion like it might be the last time he saw her. Her jaw was set. He knew she was trying to be strong for him, but her eyes betrayed her. They were shiny and brimming with fear she didn't speak aloud. He knew she wasn't just scared for herself. She was scared for him. Her fingers curled tightly into the hem of her hoodie like she was holding herself together by a thread. Her shoulders were tense, but she didn't cry or beg him not to go. That wasn't who she was.

His Dylan stood there, rooted by loyalty and terror both, and he saw it in the way her eyes kept drifting to his throat. To the scar. Like she was still haunted by how close the world had come to losing him once already. She was terrified he wouldn't make it back this time, and he felt that fear like a weight in his own chest.

"They'll bring him home," Margot said softly.

But Dylan didn't answer. Her eyes were locked on Vendetta as he crossed the lot toward her, heavy boots crunching gravel. Every step appeared to tug something loose in her chest. He stopped in front of her, close enough to notice that she was shaking. So much emotion in her big, beautiful eyes including just how much she cared about him. While Tank had had his share of one-night stands and short-lived old ladies, he'd never had anything like what he had with her.

"You don't have to say it," he said quietly, even as he saw it in her eyes. In her entire being.

"I might not get another chance," she whispered, tears welling up in her eyes.

Vendetta cupped her cheek gently. "You *will.*"

"I'm scared," Dylan admitted.

"Don't be." Vendetta said it as much for himself as for her. He kissed her forehead, lingered there. "No matter what happens today, I'm coming back for you," he vowed. "Believe it. And then we can start over, build a life together. You and me. I love you, Dylan."

Throwing herself into his arms, the tears did come then. "I love you," she said against his chest, tears soaking into his shirt.

Vendetta hated leaving her this way, but the sooner they returned, the sooner he could keep his promises to her. Easing back, he tipped her chin up with his fingers, making her meet his gaze.

"I'm finishing this today," he whispered. "And when I get back, I'll know that you're safe. I'll know he can never hurt you again."

Tears still sliding from her eyes, she nodded. When he pulled away, he smiled. "We won't be long." Vendetta looked at Ryder next. "She's under *your* watch."

"You have my word, brother," Ryder said, clasping Vendetta's hand when it was offered.

Margot nodded, her presence calm and steady. But it was the woman who stepped up beside her that drew Vendetta's attention next. Deva, Razor's old lady and Outcast's sister, was petite. But she carried herself like she could take on a storm and walk away dry. Her purple hair was pulled back in a loose braid, and her eyes, fierce and intelligent, missed nothing.

"Go on now," she said, her gaze moving from Razor to him. "Fuck 'em up and get your asses back here."

"Yes, ma'am," he replied.

He took a final look at Dylan, every part of him wanting to stay with her but knowing he couldn't. Not until he made her life safe again. Turning, he walked back to his bike.

"That's Eli Crizer's *niece*?" Player eyed her, his skepticism obvious. "How?"

Crash smacked the back of his head, but it was the look Razor cut him that ended it.

Engines thundered to life, the war drums of men with nothing left to lose and everything to fight for.

With a nod from Razor, they rolled out, heading for Oak Grove. *Into the fire.*

* * *

Eli

The blinds were half-drawn, casting hard lines of light across the battered table where Eli Crizer leaned, hands fisted, knuckles white. Despite the morning chill seeping through the windows of the compound, sweat clung to his skin. His thoughts were pure chaos, but the picture was finally clear.

Now he knew the truth about *Jason,* the quiet delivery driver with a wicked scar around his neck. He was the boyfriend Dylan hid from him. The one Peggy mentioned before they put her in the hospital. And funny enough, Jason disappeared the same night as Dylan. Freddie, Jason's boss at *INeeda* confirmed it. Jason hadn't shown up the next morning for his shift and they hadn't heard from him since.

Eli didn't believe in coincidence.

Now, he *could* believe this boyfriend wanted to

protect Dylan, to get her out of Oak Grove and away to safety. Most decent men would consider doing that. It was the rest of the story that didn't add up.

Dylan didn't know when she showed up for her last shift at *Ned*'s that her uncle was handing her off to Earle for the night. The only people who knew were him and Earle. Eli had taken her phone, told her it was a private shift where she'd just serve drinks, and then watched her get into the car Earle had sent for her. No one else knew what was really happening or where they were going. Not even Peggy, though she'd sure as shit tried to interfere.

But all Peggy had was a picture on her phone of the license plate. That was all. No address, nothing. And during the beating she'd taken, Peggy confessed that the minute Jason showed up behind *Ned*'s, she told him Dylan had been driven off, sent him the picture of the license plate. That's where her story ended. That was where the entire fucking story of Dylan ended.

Since then, he'd been dealing with a very pissed off Earle who had a broken jaw and broken ribs. And he'd set off a shitstorm at Sinister Skin that had been raining down on him since. The agreement his MC had with the organization was hanging on by a thread. They'd made it clear that to earn his way back into their good graces, Eli needed to present them with two bodies: Jason's and Dylan's.

Earle had described what happened in the lake house with Dylan. A man had broken in, took his guards down, took *him* down, then left with her. The man's description of Jason matched everyone else's. Tall and muscular with dark hair and nearly black eyes. Earle hadn't mentioned seeing a scar, but everything else tracked.

While most boyfriends would want to protect their girl, how many would even be capable of doing what was done that night? How many would be able to track down their girlfriend to a remote location with nothing more than a description of the car she rode in and a picture of its fucking license plate? For that to even be possible, the man would have to had experience with tracking people down and at least a basic knowledge of the operation that captured her. Most men wouldn't have that kind of experience. It was more likely Jason would have learned it working for the law or in the military.

But then for a man alone to break into the house once he found it and rip through the guards, through Earle, and leave with Dylan? Yeah, a couple of his Cottonmouths had the skill set to pull that off. One of them was dead. Well, he was *supposed* to be dead…

The scar around "Jason's" neck? All the brave, incredible shit "Jason" had pulled off? The quiet demeanor, the nerve it must've taken to accomplish what he had? Eli hadn't wanted to believe it at first. Hadn't wanted to see what was staring him in the face. But his gut, every instinct he had, told him Jason almost had to be *Tank*. Tank had survived. Somehow, he'd fucking survived hanging at the end of a noose and made it back. According to Freddie, he'd been working for him for weeks while Eli had been completely unaware. If it was Tank, he'd changed his name and slipped back into Oak Grove like a ghost. And during that time, he took up with Dylan. The fucker had Dylan right now.

A sick heat bloomed in Eli's chest, filling him with rage. He gazed at the men still in his club who were loyal to him. There were only a handful of them left. The rest lingered at a distance, and their silence spoke volumes. No one had said anything yet, but the looks they cut him told him that nerves were on edge. The lies about Tank had left a crack in their loyalty, and now that crack was starting to split wide open.

While most of his Cottonmouths had initially been told that Tank hit the road like a cowardly piece of shit, the men before him knew what really happened to him, the one he'd made an example of. The one they'd *hung*.

And now he was alive. Back with a vengeance and he had Dylan. His blood. His *family*.

Word had gotten out, too, fast and ugly. Not just about Dylan running or who her boyfriend might be. But the truth about *Tank*. They knew now that their brother hadn't walked away. Eli had given the order to kill him. That kind of truth wouldn't stay buried, no matter how deep you shoved it. It slithered through the ranks, whispered over beers and barked across backrooms. Eli could feel the trust bleeding out of his club like an open wound. He hadn't wanted to believe it would matter. He was president, damn it. His word was *law*.

Now he wasn't so sure. He saw it in the way some of the younger guys looked at him, like maybe they were wondering what line they had to cross before ending up on the wrong end of a noose. Eli never would have guessed how much one ghost could shake a club until that ghost came back swinging. And he had no Goddamn idea just how bad the fallout would ultimately be. But deep down, he knew the answer was coming, and it wouldn't be pretty.

"Son of a bitch," Eli muttered, pushing away from the table. "He's been inside our walls, watching and listening, while we sat here with our dicks in our hands."

No one spoke. They just waited while his mind cracked like glass beneath a hammer.

"Freddie should've said something," Eli said. "That scar alone -- hell, *I* should've seen it."

Grudge finally spoke, voice low. "Freddie didn't know. The man barely leaves his damn warehouse."

Eli pointed at him, eyes burning. "Don't start. *None* of you figured it out either." He took a deep breath, trying to force his fury down. But it just sat under his skin like a live wire. "He's not just after me. He had a bug up his ass about Sinister Skin the entire time he was here." His voice dropped lower when he said, "He wants a fucking war? He's getting one."

Trucker shifted in his seat, his gaze sharp beneath his ball cap. "Our scout said he's got an MC riding in behind him, a couple of them Cottonmouths. Most of 'em, he said, were Hounds out of Mercy."

Eli's blood ran cold. "The Hounds?" he said, like the word tasted foul.

Trucker nodded. "That's what he said. Rolling deep."

Eli's jaw clenched. "A couple of Cottonmouths…" He leaned forward. "Shade and Ripper?"

Grudge looked up from where he'd been oiling a rifle. "Last time I saw 'em was yesterday morning. Figured they'd skipped town, kept their heads down."

Eli's stomach turned. "Should've clipped them when I had the chance." Pushing away from the table, he started pacing. "Those two came over from Abingdon with Tank. I should've known they'd come sniffing around once word got out."

Bones muttered from the corner, "Didn't know there was any word."

Eli stopped in his tracks, his glare cutting

through the room. "There always is. You kill a brother and bury the truth, the ground remembers. Eventually, somebody always digs it up."

Grabbing the coffee mug in front of him, he smashed it against the floor just to hear it break like his last thread of control.

"So now he's bought himself some Hounds?" Eli muttered, his gaze moving over each of his men.

"Well," said Grudge, leaning forward. "Hounds don't ride for cash. They ride for cause. And I'd be willing to bet they're backing him because of Sinister Skin."

Eli stilled, feeling the sting. He was losing fucking control of his chapter. And now another club, the fucking Hounds out of Mercy, no less, was rolling in like executioners. He glanced around the room again, at what was left of his inner circle.

"You all with me?" he asked, voice cold.

There was a beat of silence. He knew Trucker, Creep, and Bones were in. Eagle and Grudge? He wasn't so sure.

Trucker gave a stiff nod. "We're in."

"Then dig in," Eli said, turning toward the door. "This place is going to be a fucking fortress by nightfall."

But even as he marched out, barking orders and rallying his men, a dark thought gnawed at the back of his mind. Tank hadn't merely run away from them. He'd risen from the grave. And a man who came back from the dead didn't have limits, didn't know fear. He wouldn't care about rules or consequences. No, he was looking for more than payback. Tank was coming to end everything Eli had built from the inside out. You couldn't outplay a ghost no matter how loud you shouted or how many guns you stacked at the door.

That meant he had nothing left to lose -- except Dylan.

That gave Eli an idea. If Tank was coming for him, it wasn't just vengeance driving him anymore. It was *her*. Dylan had to be in Mercy, especially since he'd buddied up to the Hounds.

Eli didn't know how the showdown would end when Tank rolled into Oak Grove… but he had one last card to play. If he couldn't stop the ghost head-on, he'd hit him where it hurt most.

He'd take out Dylan.

* * *

Vendetta

The roar of their bikes faded when they stopped and dismounted in the dense tree line just outside Oak Grove. They weren't far from the Cottonmouth compound now. The sun cast long shadows across the abandoned logging road Razor had suggested they use as cover. Vendetta crouched beside Shade and Outcast as they gathered around the map they'd brought, his gaze scanning the ridgeline.

Vendetta felt calm in that moment, the kind of calm earned by surviving the worst. His heartbeat was steady, his breathing even. Beneath the surface, every nerve he had was lit with purpose. He wasn't just after revenge anymore. Now he was chasing justice, reckoning, and elusive closure, all of it wrapped in one cold, focused mission. The weight of the cut on his back -- *Tank*'s cut -- reminded him what had been taken. His brothers beside him reminded him of what he still had.

He was ready to finish this.

"This is it," Razor said, voice low and even. "We go quiet until it's time."

"The compound is about a mile out," Ripper added, adjusting the scope on his rifle. "They have spotters on the roof."

Vendetta nodded. "Then we don't walk in the front door. Shade, you still remember the drainage tunnel?"

"Yeah," he said grimly. "Runs up behind the equipment shed. Low tech, low visibility."

Vendetta looked toward the fading sun, thinking about the best ways to hit the Cottonmouths. "We take two teams. One goes in quiet through that tunnel. The other circles and keeps them busy once we're in. We hit hard and fast. No hesitation."

"What about Eli?" Crash asked from behind, shotgun resting on his shoulder.

Crash's question lingered in the quiet, and all eyes turned to Vendetta. His gaze swept the horizon like he could already see the fire coming. His gaze cut to Razor and Outcast, wanting their take because they knew what it meant to take back what had been stolen.

Razor gave a short nod, his hazel eyes sharp. "We'll split the crews. My team will circle east with Crash, Beast, and Player. We'll raise hell, draw eyes. You take the tunnel team with Shade and Ripper and a few of ours."

Shade adjusted the strap of his rifle, glancing at Vendetta. "Once we breach, I'll lead right. You take left with Ripper. We clear the main floor, then converge in the center."

Vendetta nodded. "That will work." He blew out a breath. "Leave Eli to me. I want him alive long enough to look me in the fucking eye."

Crash gave a dark grin. "Copy that. We'll bring the fireworks."

Razor stepped closer, his voice low but steady.

"This ends tonight, brother. No more girls disappearing. No more needles on our streets. No more cowards wearing cuts they didn't earn, selling out kids to line their pockets."

His gaze swept across the men gathered around him and every one of them was ready to bleed for the patch on their back. "I want Sinister Skin out of our Goddamn territory for good. We're shutting down what they never should've gotten away with in the first place."

Clapping Vendetta on the shoulder, Razor's voice was firm and final. "Let's burn it all down."

* * *

Dylan

The sun dipped low behind the hills of Mercy, painting the sky in streaks of crimson and gold. The Hounds' compound was almost too quiet. Dylan sat near the window, watching the dusky horizon with restless eyes, her knees drawn up beneath one of Deva's old quilts. It was peaceful, but that peace felt borrowed. *Fragile.*

Margot double-checked the locks on the front and back doors, her deputy's badge tucked away but her sidearm visible. Deva moved with her usual calm, but even she had ditched her sandals for boots and kept a knife clipped to her belt.

Jade lounged with her phone, pretending not to glance out the windows every five minutes. This was the first time Dylan had met her; Hero's old lady and Razor's daughter. Somehow, that combination should've been intimidating. But it wasn't. Jade had long dark hair that spilled over her shoulders in loose waves, and eyes sharp and cool like her father's. But her easy manner made her feel instantly approachable.

There was a quiet confidence about her, like she'd grown up around danger and decided to smile through it anyway. Dylan liked her immediately.

Ryder stood in the center of it all, arms crossed, calm as a man watching a storm he knew wouldn't touch down.

"They'll be fine," he said, mostly to Dylan. "Vendetta's got half the damn Hounds with him. Razor, Axel, Outcast? That place will be ashes before they're touched."

Dylan tried to smile. "I know. I just --"

A low rumble cut her off. Not the familiar roar of bikes. What she heard was something else.

The sound was the slower, steadier cadence of a car engine, idling just beyond the tree line.

Jade sat up straight from the couch, phone forgotten in her lap. "Anyone expecting company?"

Ryder's posture shifted just slightly. "Nope," he said, on high alert now.

Deva was already moving toward the back hallway, hand going to the pistol tucked at her hip. Margot stood, eyes narrowing toward the front windows. "Could be nothing," she said. "It could be someone checking gates. But let's check it out."

Ryder nodded to one of the Hounds. "You and Hopper take a walk. Eyes open. Don't engage unless they do."

Dylan stood near the hallway, arms crossed, trying to quiet the nervous drum in her chest. The quiet around her felt… wrong. It was too still.

And then she heard it. Just the faintest sound, like a floorboard giving beneath cautious weight. A whisper of movement from the side of the house. She turned, pulse spiking, and stepped back into the living room.

Margot glanced up, sharp. "What?"

Dylan didn't speak. Just pointed a finger toward the hallway.

That was enough. Margot was up in an instant, gun in hand, her gaze darting toward the shadows. Deva followed suit, silent but focused. Jade set her phone down carefully, motioning Dylan to walk in her direction.

A man burst from the hallway, fast and terrifying like a vision from a nightmare. She recognized him from *Ned*'s as one of his uncle's men. He had a footlong blade in his hand. His hard, dark eyes were on *her*. Of course. Eli had sent men to kill her.

Jade grabbed Dylan by the arm, hauling her in the direction of the kitchen.

Behind them, Margot fired. The shot rang through the house. Dylan whipped around to watch the injured biker stumble, gripping his bleeding side. But he didn't go down.

A second crash had Dylan jumping where she stood. She was close enough to the kitchen to see the back door explode inward and a larger biker, who she also recognized from her uncle's MC, roared in. Fear rooted Dylan to the spot until Ryder slammed into the man mid-charge, the two men crashing into the counter hard. A bottle shattered as Ryder drew his knife. The brawl exploded into fists and fury, flashes of silver.

"Deva!" Margot shouted, but it was already too late. The man bleeding all over the floor slammed into Deva hard as she tried to block him. The impact sent her crashing into the pool table, hitting the floor so loudly Dylan winced.

"Dylan -- the drawer!" Margot barked, snapping off another shot that grazed the biker's shoulder but didn't stop him.

Dylan yanked open the drawer at the side of the pool table, and there it was. Margot's backup Glock, just where she said it would be earlier. Gripping it with both hands, Dylan aimed it at the man's head. Her heart was racing, her arms trembling, but she held it steady. Her gaze locked with his, just as she'd seen her uncle do a hundred times.

The biker scoffed from where he'd landed on the floor. "Safety's on," he said as he started pulling himself up from the floor.

"There's no safety on that gun," Margot told her calmly, her own firearm trained on him.

He made it to his feet, staggered toward her. Blood seeped through his shirt, fury burning in his eyes.

Dylan aimed the gun at his face, not moving otherwise. Fear battled with the anger swelling with her, and fear was losing. Her fucking uncle had tried to traffic her, and when that hadn't worked out for him, he'd sent these men to kill her.

"Don't," Dylan said, voice low and even.

He stood on unsteady feet, losing a lot of blood. His gaze still locked with hers before flicking to the Glock in her hands and back.

The fight wasn't this random Cottonmouth's anymore. It never had been.

Dylan's hands tightened on the grip, the adrenaline burning off just enough for her fury to rise. "He sent you to kill *me*?" she asked, her voice trembling, but not from fear.

The biker didn't answer at first. His lips parted like he was thinking about denying it, might spin some story. Slowly, he sneered instead. "You ratted him out," he spat. "You ran to the wrong side." His breath was ragged. "That delivery guy. What the hell did you think *he* was gonna do? Save you? What'd you *think* would happen?"

Margot stepped in behind him, her gun raised. "You're about two seconds from finding out what happens when you threaten someone in Mercy."

"He was one of *you,*" Dylan snapped. "You called him Tank."

The biker hadn't expected that. The name stunned him, halted the bravado in his eyes for just a second.

"My uncle betrayed him," she went on, every word deliberate. "Hung him in the woods for daring to speak out. Left him to die."

"That's not…" he started, shaking his head. "That's not what happened. I heard that shit. Tank ran off like a fucking coward."

"No," Dylan said, her voice low but unwavering. "He didn't go anywhere. He crawled out of his grave, still wearing the scar the rope gave him. He took a new name. He's Vendetta now."

The biker's mouth opened, but nothing came out.

Dylan didn't move, even with all the adrenaline running through her. "And he'll be talking to Eli very soon."

A low voice cut through the tension behind her. "The guy I just dropped in the kitchen won't," Ryder said, stepping into view, calm and deadly.

The biker Dylan had a gun on, whipped around to look at Ryder. "You fucking killed him?"

Ryder gave a humorless grin as he closed the distance. "Nah. Not yet." He leaned in, his shadow falling long across the man's face. "But don't worry, he won't be the only Cottonmouth taking a dirt nap by the end of the night."

The man tried and failed to keep the emotion off his face. It looked like the truth was finally seeping in.

Ryder nodded toward the door. "Let's get them both out of here. This one's leaking on the damn rug."

Chapter Ten

Vendetta

The moon was a dull blade scraping the edge of the sky. Vendetta crouched low behind the rusted frame of a logging trailer, his breath misting in the cooling air, his ears tuned to every creak and rustle in the woods. The entrance to the drainage tunnel loomed just ahead, half-choked with overgrowth and moss, like the earth itself was trying to swallow it.

It reminded him of Fallujah, dusk patrols with his unit moving low and tight through alleys choked with dust and tension. It was different soil, but he felt the same charged silence before the coming storm.

Behind him, Shade tapped twice on the butt of his rifle. *Ready*. Ripper and Axel ghosted into position at his flanks. Outcast scanned their rear, calm as ever, while Snow adjusted the strap on his gear bag and gave a nod. Snow, the Hounds' VP, was a late arrival. The man had a deadly look in his eyes. As Vendetta watched, he pulled a balaclava from his pocket, covering his solid white hair so he wouldn't give away their position. *They were in it now.*

A half mile to the front, Razor, Crash, Beast, and Player were already raising hell. Bike engines roared, the sound of gunfire ripped open the quiet evening. Smoke bombs bloomed like thunderheads at the front edge of the compound. The commotion would keep most of the Cottonmouths' attention on the diversion team. That was the plan.

But the plan didn't account for the eerie lack of response.

Vendetta's gut twisted. There were no return shots, and he didn't see a flood of Cottonmouths charging out to defend their gate. Just a couple of scouts moved along the rooftops, their silhouettes pacing and twitchy. There weren't enough of them up there. Not by a long shot.

"It's too quiet," Ripper muttered, echoing his thoughts.

Vendetta's gaze studied the compound walls beyond the tunnel's edge. "Maybe word got out…"

"Or maybe it's a trap," Snow said flatly.

Snow could be right. But Vendetta had lived too long, fought through too much, to assume hesitation meant surrender. Were there cracks forming in what used to be loyalty? Or was this a setup?

"Shade, you and Hero take your half right when we breach," Vendetta said quietly. "Find the control room. Knock out their comms if you can. I want Eli deaf and blind."

Shade nodded. "Copy that."

Vendetta looked at the others. "We go left. We hit the barracks first, clear it. Then we move on Eli."

His pulse pounded like war drums in his ears as he moved toward the tunnel entrance. The air was cooler inside, thick with damp stone and rot. They moved in single file, with their rifles raised and their boots silent against the concrete.

Every footstep forward brought him closer to the reckoning he'd craved for months. And it wasn't just about revenge anymore. It was about carving out the infection Eli had allowed to spread when he allowed Sinister Skin and their corruption into Oak Grove.

Vendetta felt ghosts walking with them. Tank, every girl who never escaped, and every brother twisted by fear or guilt.

He swore he wasn't going to relent until it all fucking burned down.

The metal grate gave way with a low groan, the

sound dampened by the tunnel walls. Vendetta led the way, his boots sinking into wet leaves and sludge, his rifle tight against his shoulder. Behind him, Outcast and Snow followed like shadows. Ripper and Axel closed the line. The stink in the drainage tunnel was sharp. The smell of combined old water, rust, and mildew rose, and it was still way too quiet on the Cottonmouths' side of things. Vendetta's breath slowed as he counted the seconds between steps, his instincts sharpening. It reminded him of crawling through irrigation ditches outside the wire, waiting for a trigger man to make his move. This was a different mission on the other side of the world, but he felt that same edge-of-your-soul anticipation.

When they emerged behind the equipment shed, moonlight cut hard across the gravel. It was quiet now out front. But he knew they would have heard a counter offensive if one had been launched. Was Razor and his group, whose job was to keep Eli's eye on *them*, just waiting them out now?

The compound spread out in front of them in long rows of metal buildings with floodlights washing over bare ground and fences. Now, there were just two spotters on the roof.

"Ripper," Vendetta whispered, pointing upward. "Roof left. Quiet."

Ripper nodded, disappearing into the shadows like smoke.

"Outcast, Snow, cover him. Axel, on me."

They moved slowly, in silence. Every step was a test of nerve. Until a shout cracked the quiet. Then a shot. Ripper's suppressed rifle barked once, and the spotter folded, gone before he hit the tin.

That was when all hell broke loose.

From the front gate, the roar of engines shattered

the stillness, and he knew it was Razor's team.

"Showtime," Vendetta muttered, keeping low as he sprinted to the next structure as alarms began to wail.

This was the breach. This was Baghdad, building by building. The muscle memory surged -- angles, cover, communication without a word. Fire and chaos to the front. Precision at the core.

"Split," Vendetta ordered, panting now. "Shade goes right. We go left."

Catching Shade's gaze across the yard, he saw no hesitation. His friend peeled off into the smoke and floodlight glare with Hero and three more Hound soldiers. Gunfire broke out near the gate. Razor and Crash were drawing attention away from them, exactly as they'd planned.

Ripper fell in behind him with Axel, Outcast, and Snow, pressing into the flank. A figure bolted from a warehouse; Vendetta raised his weapon but held fire. The Cottonmouth was unarmed and running.

But there was more movement from the barracks.

"Eli's close," Vendetta said, voice tight. "You feel that?"

Outcast grinned, teeth white in the dark. "Yeah. It's the stink of fear."

They crept forward, sweeping corners and clearing structures as chaos broke out across the yard. Voices shouted orders. A few Cottonmouths fired wildly into the trees, probably not even sure what they were shooting at. That was the problem with half-loyal men. They stopped fighting when the cause didn't mean shit to them.

Vendetta took a deep, steady breath. He hadn't come here for noise. He'd come for *justice*. For Dylan. For Tank and every piece of himself left bleeding in those woods. And he was going to fucking take it. *Tonight*.

Gunfire ripped through the night, closer now. Vendetta crouched low beside a rusted-out barrel as bullets kicked gravel at his boots. Across the yard, Axel returned fire in tight bursts, driving back two Cottonmouths pinned near a loading dock.

"They're already folding," Snow muttered, ejecting a spent mag. "They didn't even commit to the line."

Vendetta's gaze tracked movement. He saw two more bolting from the barracks with weapons half-raised, looking confused and scattered.

"Because they know it's over," Vendetta said. He surged forward, cutting across the gap, Outcast and Ripper flanking left and right. Axel hit the outer wall of the main building first and dropped to one knee.

"Door's locked," he hissed.

Vendetta didn't stop. He turned his shoulder, braced, and slammed into it. The old hinges groaned. On the third impact, the door gave, swinging inward with a screech. Nothing but smoke and shadows greeted them. They made it inside, into a narrow hallway lined with storage doors. Red exit lights flickered like failing pulse monitors.

Vendetta stepped in first, rifle raised, sweeping left. Ripper slipped past him, clearing right. A shot rang out from upstairs, close. The Cottonmouths were still here.

Outcast reached for his comm. "Shade, we're in the main structure. Watch the upper floor."

A pause. "Copy. Already clearing the south wing. They're scattering. Trucker's down. Creep's bleeding. Eli's running for it."

Vendetta's heart slammed. "He's here," he

growled. "He's still fucking here."

Ripper jerked his chin toward the stairwell. "End of the hallway."

"Then let's fucking finish this," Vendetta said, his voice low and sharp as a knife.

They pushed forward in formation, a team forged in blood. Two Cottonmouths burst out from a side door, Axel fired point-blank, dropping one. The other lunged with a blade, barely missing Outcast's arm before Vendetta laid him out with the butt of his rifle. They reached the stairwell with its narrow concrete steps. Old lights flickered above them.

Vendetta turned to them all. "Anyone not ready to see this through, say it now."

No one moved.

"You helped me get Anya home to Mercy." Outcast rolled his shoulders and shrugged. "I'm keeping my end of this."

Ripper smirked. "Let's go put the bastard in the dirt."

Vendetta nodded without a smile. "Eli dies tonight."

He took the stairs two at a time. And at the top, he saw blood on the wall, boot prints smeared down the hallway. A door slammed ahead of them.

"That one," Vendetta said, already moving.

It was time for the reckoning.

The door gave way on the second hit, splintering beneath Vendetta's boot like brittle bone. Wood cracked and hinges screamed, but none of it mattered, not compared to the man inside.

Eli Crizer. There he stood, pistol in hand, like it meant something. Like it could change what was already written.

Vendetta stepped through the haze of busted

wood and plaster, the hall light casting a long shadow across the floor. Tank's old cut clung to his back like a second skin, soaked in ash and blood, stitched by ghosts.

"You gonna shoot me this time?" he said, voice steady despite the fire in his chest. "Fucking do it. But you better not miss."

Eli's hands shook. Vendetta could see his fear. Denial and disbelief were stamped across his face.

Vendetta took another step. Then another. Only then did Eli raise the gun, but it was too late. Vendetta was already on him, slamming into him with months of rage and pain packed into one hit. Eli's gun clattered to the floor as their fists started flying. They crashed into the desk at the center of the room, papers flying, furniture cracking beneath the weight of unfinished business. Vendetta didn't stop. Fury had him using his fists and elbows to do damage, to release the fear and betrayal he'd suffered with a noose around his neck.

He was so lost to his rage he barely heard Eli yell. Barely felt the sting of his knuckles. Grabbing Eli by the collar, he drove him into the wall.

"You left me in the woods to die," Vendetta growled, nose to nose with him. "You hung me like a fucking traitor. For what? For telling the truth?"

"You were tearing us apart!" Eli yelled, dazed and bleeding. "You were gonna tear the club fucking apart."

"No." Vendetta's voice broke, low and raw. "I was trying to stop you from selling kids to fucking perverts. That's all I ever tried to do. You're the one who made it about power."

Eli pushed off the wall and swung. Vendetta caught it midair and dropped him to the floor with one brutal punch. Eli didn't move after that, and the world started slowing down.

Vendetta stood over him, breathing hard, fists still clenched. Every nerve in his body screamed for closure. For justice and blood.

He heard footsteps coming up behind him. Ripper with Axel, Outcast, and Snow. Eli's breathing was ragged, the way his hand pressed into his ribcage told Vendetta he'd broken some ribs. *Fucking good.*

Vendetta stared down at the man who'd destroyed him. The man who'd named him traitor. The man who'd killed Tank. Raising his booted foot, he was ready to finish it, end it all. But something in him paused. It wasn't weakness, and it sure as fuck wasn't mercy.

"I *should* kill you," he said. "I really want to fucking kill you for what you've done… But I won't."

Eli coughed up blood, looked up, confused. "Why?"

Vendetta leaned in, voice low and sharp as a blade. "Dylan may not be here with us, but I'm here for her just as much as I am for Tank."

He grabbed Eli by the collar again, dragging him upright just enough so their eyes locked.

"You don't even honor your own blood," Vendetta snarled. "You killed your son. I didn't give a damn about Baby Face myself. But deep down, you knew what he was. A fucking monster in the making. Just like you. Maybe worse. And you were fine with it, as long as he followed orders and kept your hands clean."

His voice dropped, guttural now. "But Dylan? Turning out your own fucking niece? You let men fucking circle her like dogs. You sold her off like a piece of meat because she was inconvenient and some middle-aged fucker from Sinister Skin wanted to get his dick wet. But she wouldn't bend the knee." Vendetta shoved him back in disgust. "You betrayed her. You betrayed *me*. And you betrayed this whole damn club."

Ripper came up beside him, holding the pistol Eli had dropped. He offered it to Vendetta grip first.

Vendetta took it, feeling the weight of cold metal in his palm. But he didn't lift it. Instead, he stepped back. He didn't want to explain to Dylan why he had her uncle's blood on his hands, no matter how much the fucker had it coming.

"He's done," Vendetta said. "Drag him out of here. I want the whole town to know he fell on his knees --"

CRACK.

When the single gunshot ripped through the room, Vendetta turned.

Shade lowered his rifle, calm and unflinching, his eyes fixed on Eli's now dead body.

"I respect your choice, brother," Shade said. "But that was for the Cottonmouths. He betrayed this club. He left you hanging in the woods like garbage and told us you ran." Shade's tone never rose, but it was heavy with judgment. "And there's only one punishment for a brother who breaks that deep. That's our law. He made his choice the second he tried to bury you and burn everything we stood for."

Vendetta didn't move and couldn't speak for a second. What Shade said was right, and he nodded his understanding while he tried to ignore the part of himself that was glad the fucker was dead.

"Let's wrap this up," Vendetta said finally.

* * *

Vendetta

The compound's main room still smelled like gunpowder and sweat. Blood stained the concrete in two places. Eli lay under a tarp in the corner, along with Trucker, Nate, and one other of the Cottonmouth loyalists. Their deaths had shaken the foundation of an MC already in turmoil. But the club wasn't broken.

The remaining Cottonmouths stood silent, clustered around the space like men waking from a long, hard nightmare. Some had blood on their knuckles. Some had tears in their eyes. All of them stared at the man standing before them with a scar around his neck that permanently marked the damage Eli Crizer had done.

Vendetta stood tall in the center of that gathering, Razor, Shade, and Ripper flanking him. The Hounds loomed at the edge, all quiet but watching. He saw respect in their eyes, loyalty earned.

"You see the scar," Vendetta said, pulling down the collar of his shirt slightly. "So now you know the story's real. Eli and those loyal to him hung me for disagreeing with him. For saying we were better than what he'd turned this club into." He looked around the room, locking gaze for a long moment with each man. "Four of your brothers are dead, maybe more, because they backed a snake who sold women and kids. If any of you are still loyal to Sinister Skin or think selling girls is a justifiable hustle, I want you gone. *Now*. Don't fucking wait for another war."

Silence. A few of the Cottonmouths exchanged heavy glances, but no one left.

Vendetta gave a small nod. "Then let's be clear. The Oak Grove chapter of the Cottonmouth MC is done with trafficking. We're shutting that shit down, starting here. Starting now."

Razor stepped forward, arms folded. "If that's

your mission, then the Hounds in Mercy have your backs."

Vendetta nodded. "We wouldn't have made it through that gate without you," he said, meeting Razor's gaze. "You didn't owe me a damn thing, but you showed up anyway -- and not just for me. For something bigger. Something you kept out of your town." He looked around at the Hounds gathered there. Men he'd bled beside and who hadn't run when things got ugly.

"Mercy's got some of the toughest bastards I've ever known," Vendetta continued. "And I'll tell you this right now, we're not looking to build empires here. But we are looking to burn down the ones built on blood and fear. If that's the kind of war you're willing to fight…" He paused, then offered Razor his hand. "… then we're brothers now too."

Razor stepped forward without hesitation and gripped his hand hard. "Welcome to the war."

Ripper exhaled and stepped up beside Vendetta, glancing toward Eli's covered body. "He had it coming. We all knew it. We just didn't want to be the ones to say it."

Shade stepped into the center, scanning the remaining Cottonmouths with his usual quiet dominance. "Our club needs new leadership," he said. "And not just a patch and a name. We need someone who already bled for it. Someone who already *died* for it."

He looked at Vendetta. "Tank's dead. But you, Vendetta, you came back to finish the fight. I nominate you to be our new president. If anyone's got a problem with that, speak now."

Nobody did. Not one man stepped forward. Not one voice rose in protest. The silence rang louder than a gunshot.

Shade took a slow breath, then turned toward the group like a judge passing sentence. "Vote. Vendetta for president. Show of hands."

The response came without hesitation, raw and unanimous. Every Cottonmouth hand went up with yells of "Vendetta for president!" and a couple of "Hell yeahs." One man thumped his chest. Another tilted his chin in a silent nod, eyes locked on the scar around Vendetta's throat like it was a badge of honor.

It was done, the shift rolling through the room. A corrupt legacy had been buried under gunfire and truth. What remained was rough-edged hope, but it was enough for a new start.

Vendetta looked around the room, at the faces of men who'd been twisted by Eli's lies and finally pulled back from the edge. They were tired and bloodied, but still dangerous men who stayed for the right reasons. And they had chosen him.

Giving a slow nod, Vendetta let the weight settle on his shoulders like the cut on his back. It felt heavier than it used to… but it still fit.

"Tank died out in those woods," he said. "Alone. Betrayed. Strung up for speaking out against what this club was becoming." His gaze swept across them. "But I didn't stay dead. I crawled out of that hole with a promise to myself. If I made it back, I wouldn't let that shit stand. Not in my name. Not in yours."

He paused, carefully considering his words.

"I'm Vendetta now. And this club? This patch? It's getting a second chance in Oak Grove. If you stay, you're going to bleed for it. There are some dark days coming, brothers, while we get this shit out of our town. It's going to be a fight every day. No more selling people. No more letting predators call the shots.

This is your last fucking chance. If I catch any of you still doing that shit from this moment on, you'll end up like Eli."

Still, no one moved.

"Good," Vendetta said, jaw tight. "Then let's rebuild this MC."

Ripper clapped him on the back. "Cottonmouths, reborn," he said with a grin.

And from the corners of the room, an older Cottonmouth spoke, low but certain. "Never thought I'd be proud to wear this patch again."

A new era for the Cottonmouths of Oak Grove began.

* * *

Dylan

Dylan stood on the front porch of the Hound clubhouse sometime after midnight. Her arms were crossed over her chest as she waited each painful minute for the outcome. Margot stood nearby, feeling obliged to protect her if she was going to insist on waiting on the porch. Jade waited just inside the door, pretending she wasn't watching out the window. Ryder had gone quiet an hour ago, and Dylan hoped that wasn't a bad sign.

Deva walked back out with a fresh glass of water, moving like the entire affair was over and her side had won. Dylan wished she had that kind of confidence tonight instead of standing there saying every prayer she ever knew that Vendetta and everyone else came back in one piece.

The roar of bikes signaled their return before she saw them. And then in the darkness, headlights broke through the trees. One after another, the Hounds rolled in, all bruised, bloodied, but victorious. Frantically, she watched for him to roll in with them. Her breath caught when she finally spotted him.

Josh.

He pulled off his helmet and parked his bike, and her world narrowed. Everything else fell away. Josh was alive. He'd come back for her.

Josh moved straight toward her with no hesitation. She launched off the porch steps and into his arms before he could say a word. He caught her with a grunt and held on like she was the only thing anchoring him to the earth.

"You're back," she whispered against his neck, feeling the tears falling but not caring.

"I told you I would be."

She pulled back just enough to look at him. "Are you okay?"

His dark-eyed gaze searched hers. "I am now."

She looked him over for wounds, noting the fresh scrape across his temple, the dried blood on the knuckles of his hands. "You don't look okay."

"I'm not gonna lie," Josh said, brushing a thumb across her cheek. "It got ugly. But we won, Dylan. Eli's gone. The Cottonmouths aren't his anymore."

She wasn't sure she'd heard right. Dead? How much did she want to know? She asked, carefully, "Gone?"

"Eli's not gonna hurt you again," he said gently. "Or anyone else. It's over."

She let out a shaky breath and leaned her forehead against his. "Thank God."

Dylan wasn't happy that Eli was dead. She hated that it had come to that, hated that blood had to be spilled for her to finally be free. But the truth settled over her, a heavy, quiet relief. She didn't have to be afraid anymore. No more running.

And no more girls would be passed around like property. No more secret shipments, or silenced cries in the dark. The pipeline Eli helped build had been severed. Shut down. Maybe now, someone else would be free too.

For the first time in days, Dylan could breathe. And she was breathing him in.

"Don't breathe too easy just yet, sweetheart."

Her brows knit. "Why?"

"Eli's gone," Josh said, voice low and steady, "but Sinister Skin's still out there. And they've got long memories. If they think you're a liability, they'll come looking."

Her heart stumbled in her chest. "So what now?"

"Now," he said, wrapping an arm around her and pulling her close, "you let me worry about that. You're not running anymore, Dylan. You're coming home with me."

"Home?" She honestly didn't care where. She just heard the words "with me."

Josh stopped to cradle her face in both hands. "Wherever I am, that's where you belong now. And for a while, we're going to be living at the compound until I can be sure you're safe."

"The what?"

He smiled. "Yeah, it's like the Hounds' clubhouse, only more like a fortress."

She nodded. "Okay."

He pressed his forehead to hers. "I didn't fight my way back just to lose you again."

Behind them, engines cooled, and voices carried, but for a moment, there was nothing but the two of them.

It was over.

The door creaked open, and the warmth of the

clubhouse wrapped around them like a worn leather jacket, smoke-tinged, familiar, and alive with murmured voices. Dylan walked beside Josh, his hand on the small of her back. She didn't say anything until they reached the room she'd been staying in. Once the door closed behind them, she glanced up at him.

"The compound," she said quietly. "Does that mean you're… a Cottonmouth again?"

He looked down at her, lips twitching into something between a smirk and a sigh. "Not just a Cottonmouth," he said. "They voted me in as the new president."

Her eyes widened. "Wow."

"Yeah," he nodded. "Ripper's my VP. And Shade… You'll meet them. Several of the Cottonmouths sided with us. It's a good place to start. But we've got a lot of rebuilding to do."

"Good," she said. "And I'm *glad* you're taking his place. You can make sure nothing like this ever happens again."

"Yes, ma'am."

"But, Josh… doesn't that put an even bigger target on your back?" Dylan folded her arms, concern clouding her expression.

He leaned in, pressing a kiss to her temple. "Probably."

Dylan cut him a look.

"But," he added with a grin, "I'm not planning on dying again anytime soon."

She wanted to laugh, to cry, maybe both. Instead, she looped her arms around his waist and leaned into his chest. "Good. Because I just got you back. I'm not letting you go this time."

Josh held her close, voice low and sure. "You won't have to."

They hadn't stood there for long when his hands started wandering, over her back, her ass. When she gazed up at him, he claimed her mouth in a heated kiss that had her heart flying. His grip tightened on her, pressing her close enough to feel every hard line of his body. The heated length of him under the rough denim of his jeans let her know that he wasn't ready to sleep just yet.

When she finally broke the kiss, her breath came in a rush. "Don't you want to wash up first?"

"No, I want you first," Josh whispered hotly.

Dylan thought he meant to shove her back onto the bed, but her back met the wall next to it. Then Josh was all over her. While his heated kisses scorched her lips, his hands moved roughly over her breasts, down to her hips. He wasn't gentle when he pulled open the front of her jeans, yanking them down her legs. Her sandals came off too as he pulled each ankle free of denim. Her panties came off with a quiet rip just a beat before he pulled one of her legs over his shoulder.

Josh buried his face between her legs after that, working her with lips and tongue. Not that he needed to. She wanted to feel him close, inside her. Her thighs trembled around his face as she grabbed handfuls of his dark hair, clutching at it as his tongue twisting in her folds made her senseless. When the tip of his tongue zeroed in on her clit, Dylan wasn't sure how long she could remain upright. Sensual pressure built in her body, driving her insane.

When he slid one finger inside her, Dylan gasped. When he slid the second one in, she was right there on the edge of release…

Josh grinned at the low whine that escaped her lips when he stopped. The bastard winked at her as he rose then, allowing her leg to slide down so he could work his belt open and pushed his own jeans down just enough to free his cock. She watched it bob as he moved back to her. It was easy enough for him to grab her hips, push her up the wall. His powerful body pinned hers to its surface as he slid his cock inside her in one quick thrust that took her breath away.

Dylan's heart was racing when he started moving inside her. Josh dropped kisses over her face and chest, then caught her lips in a dirty kiss that was all teeth and tongue as he rocked her. All Dylan could do was hang on, grabbing at his shoulders and his hair as he fucked her hard and fast. Her legs were wrapped around his waist, encouraging him. Letting him know she needed more.

"You're all mine," he whispered against her lips. "My Dylan."

"Yours," she managed weakly. But it wasn't just her body he'd claimed. Dylan had never had any man make her feel like she was more than a fun time here and there. Josh kissed her like he needed it to live, loved her like it was his life's mission. There, trapped between his driving body and the wall, she didn't need anyone or anything else. Just him, to be loved by him.

In no time, he had her body fighting for its release. Lust like lava ran through her veins as he fucked her against the wall, his movements faster and harder. When she came, her pussy clamped around him and she buried her cries in his shoulder. The rest of the world was lost to her as she mindlessly hung on, letting the orgasm shake her fiercely.

His hold on her tightened, almost painfully. He pumped into her wildly, dragging out her release as he came. Josh shook as he fucked her, Dylan entirely wrapped around him, their hearts pounding furiously. Seeming to be in no hurry to move, he kissed her, slow and sweet. "I doubt the tub in the bathroom is big enough for two," he said. "But I'll bet we can make the shower work."

Dylan smiled. "Round two then?"

"Round two," he said, pulling her into his arms like it was nothing, and carrying her into the bathroom. Tomorrow would be soon enough to figure out their future.

Shade (Cottonmouth MC 2)
A Hounds of Hell MC Romance
Jamie Targaet

The moment I see Jazz, I know I can't let her walk away.

Jazz: My sister Claire disappeared three weeks ago. The police are calling the case a runaway, but I know better. Rumor has it the Cottonmouths and Sinister Skin are behind the girls going missing in Oak Grove -- the reason no one asks too many questions. So I go looking for her myself.

I never expected to find the answers waiting behind the doors of a biker compound -- or in the green eyes of the quiet enforcer who looks at me like I already belong to him. Shade says he will find Claire. But men like him don't do favors. They make promises. And the way he says *mine* sounds an awful lot like forever.

Shade: Oak Grove is supposed to belong to the Cottonmouths again. We bled to take it back. But the men we drove out didn't disappear. They just got smarter, quieter, and more dangerous. Then Jazz walks into my life. And I know I can't let her go.

I know the men who took Claire are tied to the same rot we just carved out of this town. And they've made one fatal mistake. They turned this into my fight. I won't stop until the threat is buried. The Cottonmouths protect their own. The war they started is about to end in blood.

Prologue

Shade

A few months earlier...

When Creep texted us that evening to roll out to *Ned's Sundown Lounge*, we should've fucking known it was gonna be some kind of bullshit.

He had said Eli wanted to clear the air. That there'd been talk in the club, and we deserved to hear things straight about a "sensitive topic." The timing was too damn convenient. Me and Ripper had been tearing up every road between Oak Ridge and the Kentucky line looking for our brother Tank. And now suddenly Eli wanted a sit-down? Either it was about Tank, or it was one hell of a coincidence that they had some big revelation to drop right when our brother was missing.

The last time I talked to Tank had been the day he apparently "disappeared." He'd come over to my apartment and had Ripper meet us there. I remember him lighting a cigarette like it might keep his hands steady. He told us straight up that he didn't like where things were heading in the Oak Grove chapter of Cottonmouth MC. Said the club's president, Eli, was making promises to people you didn't want to owe favors to. Running guns was one thing. Hell, even drugs. There's a code for that. But selling drugs to kids? Selling the kids *themselves*?

Human trafficking was a line Tank just couldn't cross. And I got it. So did Ripper. We'd all done dirt, but this was rot. Real, soul-deep shit that blackened whatever was left of the Cottonmouth name in Oak Grove.

Tank had been ready to storm the compound and tell them what's what. Sure, we all *wanted* to do that.

But there was only one way it was going to go with that corrupt bunch of assholes. They were making a shit ton of money, and they didn't feel any pain from the activities Sinister Skin brought to Oak Grove. Of course, they weren't going to listen. No, they protected their gig.

I all but begged Tank not to confront them. I told him all we had to do was lay low for a while, fade into the background. When the time was right, we'd just quietly head back to Abingdon or some other chapter. In my head, we could take the path of least resistance and be rid of it all in time.

Tank? He was adamant that my approach wouldn't work. He kept saying that with everything we knew, Eli wouldn't just let us slip away.

Me and Ripper had grown up with Tank, and we knew him better than anyone. The three of us had come over to the Oak Grove chapter from Abingdon just a few weeks back. We'd heard they needed muscle, and extra hands for some well-paying "special projects" that were hush-hush even by Cottonmouth standards. There wasn't a lot going on in our neck of the woods, and the promise of money sounded good. We rode in together, loyal to the patch and each other.

The first couple of weeks were quiet. Maybe a little uneasy, but quiet. Then the tone shifted. Shit started feeling off. Secrets were spread behind closed doors. The side glances lasted too long, and way too many questions were answered with silence.

Then Tank disappeared. There were no goodbyes, no warning.

I've never believed in coincidences. Not in this club, and not with those men.

Tank had been missing for three days now. There'd been no word. He wasn't answering our calls or texts. I even drove over to his place. Tank wasn't there. There was no way to tell if his shit was gone too. But Tank wasn't the type to just vanish. If he was off the radar, it meant something bad had gone down.

And now Creep was calling us into *Ned's* like everything was fine.

Things were far from fucking fine.

Somehow, I knew. Deep down, I fucking knew Eli and his goons had something to do with Tank's disappearance. I also knew that whatever Creep was going to say wasn't gonna be the truth. But there was gonna be a story.

With Ripper at my side, I stepped through the door of *Ned's* that night like I owned the damn place. Truth was, none of us owned it. Not anymore. Not since a certain criminal group that went by the name Sinister Skin started sniffing around and Eli started making deals with the devil. The bar had been Cottonmouth territory for years, a place to unwind, drink, brawl, or blow off steam. That was before our time in the Oak Grove chapter.

So yeah, I noticed real quick when most of the bar, half of them Cottonmouths, stiffened like they'd just seen a fucking ghost.

The air reeked of cowardice and cheap whiskey. Conversations stopped mid-sentence. People shifted in their seats, glancing down into their glasses, pretending they didn't see us. And these weren't strangers. These were our brothers and fellow Cottonmouths. Now they barely had the balls to look at me.

Ripper leaned toward me, his voice low. "Why does it feel like we just walked into a fuckin' wake?"

Maybe we had. They just hadn't buried the body yet.

Creep was part of Eli's inner circle. He was posted up at the bar like a smug little king, his lips curled in a smile that made me want to smash his face straight through the counter. His cut was unzipped, hanging loose. Clearly he didn't give a damn about club pride anymore. He was tall and gangly, looking like he'd crawled out of some gutter and forgot how to get back. Pasty, gaunt skin clung to sharp cheekbones. His teeth, what few he had left, were yellow and rotting. The stringy mess of dark hair hanging around his face didn't help.

The name *Creep* was fucking accurate. He looked like the kind of guy who stared too long at girls half his age and laughed when no one else was joking. And he was smiling when he spotted me, like he thought he was the smartest bastard in the room.

He raised his glass as we approached. "Shade. Ripper. Glad you came."

I didn't answer. I just stood there, letting the tension between us play out. I wanted the little bastard to feel it.

He took a sip of his drink, ignoring the fact that he'd summoned us to a graveyard in disguise. "Figured you'd want to hear it from me."

I kept my voice calm. "Hear what?"

He was dragging it out. The fucker was enjoying this while that dumb kid -- what was his name? Nate? -- watched on with the stupid grin he always seemed to be wearing.

"Tank," he said finally. "He's gone."

Gone. That was how he said it. Like Tank had just wandered off.

Ripper straightened beside me. "Gone where?"

"Nomad." Creep shrugged. "Couldn't stomach the direction Eli's takin' us in. Said it was gettin' too heavy. So, he packed his shit and bailed. Didn't even say goodbye to anybody."

There it was. The lie I expected. Tank went nomad? They expected us to believe that one of the bravest sumbitches I'd ever known couldn't handle the business or the pressure? No fucking way.

Tank didn't bail. And he sure as hell didn't run.

I stepped closer, slow and deliberate, until I could smell the rot on Creep's breath over the liquor-soaked air. The whole damn bar had gone quiet. Every eye in the place was locked on us now. Ripper didn't say a word. But he was ready behind me, just in case.

"You really expect me to believe that?" I asked, keeping my voice low. "That Tank, the same brother who we've bled with, spilled blood for, ran off without a word 'cause things got *heavy*?"

Creep's smirk slipped just a fraction. "Look, I'm just tellin' you what I heard --"

"From who?" I cut in, my hand finding the blade inside my cut. "Tank himself? You and I both know better than that."

The fucker tried to act confused, but I saw the flash of fear in his dark eyes. "Man, I ain't got nothin' to do with --"

I moved fast. One hand slammed him back against the bar, the other drawing steel. The tip of my blade pressed right up under his chin, catching that patchy beard of his as I leaned in.

"Lie one more Goddamn time," I growled, "and I'll gut you right here in front of all these weak-ass cowards you drink with."

Creep swallowed hard. "Shade --"

"You think I won't?" I pushed my blade deeper into his skin, making him wince. "You think I'm just going to listen to you lie about my brother? Tell me what *really* happened, Creep. What did Eli and the rest of you fucks do?"

His beady little eyes went wider. The man was literally trembling against the edge of my blade. One wrong twitch, and I'd open him from throat to belly.

It got quiet. Even the bawdy country music playing on the jukebox seemed muted. The entire bar was on edge, and no one dared to step between us. Ripper stayed ready at my back.

"I don't know shit," Creep finally whispered.

"Wrong answer." I dragged the blade down his chest just enough to split his T-shirt, to carve into the leather of his cut, and draw a hot line of red beneath all of it. I didn't cut *too* deep. Just enough to make him squeal in front of his cowardly little buddies. They all got to see that Shade wasn't someone you fucking crossed, and Tank wasn't someone you lied about.

Creep howled and shoved back, stumbling off the barstool and crashing into a table behind him.

"That will leave a nice scar," I said, turning to the rest of them and pointing at Creep with my blade. "Let it remind all of you what happens when you fucking lie to me."

And then, to Creep directly, I said, "If I ever find out that something happened to Tank and you had a hand in it, you're fucking dead."

Creep clutched his chest, blood leaking between his bony fingers. The man's eyes were wild with fury and shame. I folded up my knife and turned to go when he barked out a sound halfway between a laugh and a snarl.

"You think you're untouchable, Shade?" he spat in a ragged voice. "You better watch your back. It ain't just Eli you need to worry about anymore."

I turned slow, just enough to glance over my

shoulder. "You mean those snakes Eli let crawl in here while we weren't lookin'? The ones sellin' girls and fucking poison out the back doors of our town?"

Creep didn't answer. I think he knew better.

I took a step closer, staring him down. "I ain't afraid of criminals playin' club. And I sure as hell ain't afraid of *you*."

Creep glared at me, but his hand was still pressed tight to his ribs. He wouldn't be making a move tonight, and he knew it.

Ripper moved past him on the way out, moving slowly, like a warning wrapped in leather and steel. "You best be careful what you say about your brothers," he said as he stared Creep down. "'Sometimes it comes back to bite you in the ass."

Creep muttered something. I thought I heard him say something to the effect of "this one ain't coming back." But when I turned back to glare at him, he wisely shut up.

The man's parting words didn't sit well with me. Was Tank dead? Had they gone that fucking far?

We walked out like we'd set fire to the place, and just maybe we had. *Ned's* would remember. Creep sure as hell would.

And next time? I would cut him the fuck in half.

Chapter One

Shade

The compound was quiet, and the yard was littered with toolboxes, paint cans, and various other supplies we were using to patch everything up after the club's civil war a few weeks ago.

Our place had been torn to hell in the shootout that took place when we took Eli and his slimy inner circle down, getting them the fuck out of our chapter and compound. Vendetta, the man who'd once been Tank but who had survived the hanging meant to kill him, had led us back to reclaim the Oak Grove chapter for the loyal Cottonmouths. We'd won with a little help from the Hounds of Hell in Mercy. After the celebration, our compound was left with bullet holes, splintered frames, and busted glass. It had been a hell of a mess to clean up, and we weren't done yet.

I was out back, replacing the siding on the last barrack that needed outside repairs. I had a hammer in one hand, and a headache that had been riding me since dawn. Still, I couldn't shake the thought that we just might be wasting our damn time. We'd fix this place up, sure, but for how long? Yeah, Eli was dead and some of his crew were gone with him. But not all of them. Creep had been shot but he'd somehow survived that night. That fucker could still be running around. A few others loyal to Eli had made it out too.

Sinister Skin wasn't going anywhere. Of that I was sure. And until we flushed out the rest of that rot, the repairs we made almost felt like a Band-Aid over a bullet wound.

"Guess it's time to start on indoor repairs," Ripper muttered, strolling out with a cold beer and no shame.

Vendetta followed him out, looking a little rougher than he usually did. But that was our friend's new normal these days. The patch on his chest said *president,* and he wore it like it had its claws dug into him. Dylan had finally got him to sleep a full night last week. Ripper and I damn near threw a party. Vendetta was a good man but he's a grouchy asshole on no rest.

"Got word from Mercy this morning," Vendetta said, cracking his neck. "Snow says there's no sign of the cartel left over there. At least not so far. Guess threatening Player's girl wasn't the brilliant move El Cuervo thought it was."

Ripper snorted. "You mean right before she pulled a gun on him? Shit, I'll never forget the look on Player's face. Like he was about to pass out and propose all at the same time."

Vendetta smirked. "Yeah, the cartel folded faster than I thought they would, honestly. If I had to guess, the Hounds haven't seen the last of them."

"If they come back, are we helping out?" Ripper said.

Vendetta nodded. "Most likely. Locked and loaded."

I didn't disagree, but I didn't join in either. Cartel trouble made for good stories now that the business was done. But we were still knee-deep in our own brand of hell here in Oak Grove dealing with the remnants of Sinister Skin. The Hounds in Mercy had booted them out of their territory. It looked like we still needed to do the same.

"I'm glad we helped them out." Shaking his head, Vendetta said, "It's the least we could do. We couldn't have taken this place back with just half the club. They helped us pull it through."

Before any of us could say more, I heard

footsteps coming closer. Two of our prospects, Cowboy and JJ, came running in like their asses were on fire. Both were out of breath, wide-eyed, and wired.

"Boss," Cowboy gasped. "You're gonna want to hear this."

Vendetta straightened up instantly. I set down my tools and wiped my hands.

"We just saw Creep," JJ said. "He ain't dead."

Silence fell like a Goddamn hammer. I fucking knew it. *Creep*. That scrawny piece of shit had a face I wish I could forget and a scar down the middle of his chest that I'd personally gifted him. The bastard was supposed to be out of Oak Grove. Gone and smart enough to stay gone. I'd *known* he wasn't dead.

Vendetta's voice dropped low. "Where?"

JJ swallowed hard. "Here, on the edge of our own fucking property."

My head snapped up. "You're kidding me. He came here?"

"And he wasn't alone," JJ said. "Eagle was with him."

I had to laugh at that. "Eagle? That prick's still walking?"

JJ nodded. "And get this. They had a couple of guys with them we didn't recognize. They weren't from around here, but they looked like muscle."

"They approach you?" Vendetta asked.

Cowboy shook his head. "Nah. They saw us coming and bolted. Didn't say a damn word."

"Vehicle?" Vendetta asked.

"Black SUV. Nice one," Cowboy answered. "Tinted windows. Couldn't see plates."

Of course, it was a nice SUV. Sinister Skin loved riding on money they didn't earn. Vendetta stepped in closer. "Where exactly did you see them?"

"At the old south gate," Cowboy replied. "Right where the fence line dips."

I shook my head. Fifty acres of land surrounded the compound, most of it wild and untouched. The woods were thick enough that a man could ghost through them without ever being spotted. We had cameras and sensors up at the main gates, but out there? A couple of wrong turns and someone could camp out on us for days before we ever knew.

Vendetta must've been thinking the same thing, because his eyes narrowed in that calculating way of his.

Vendetta's gaze met mine. "You thinking what I'm thinking?"

"If I had to guess, they're trying to rebuild," I said. "Trying to keep Sinister Skin's shit alive under a new flag."

"Or a temporary one," Ripper added.

Vendetta gave the two younger Cottonmouths a nod. "Good work. Now I want you two to stay on the perimeter today. Keep eyes on it. No contact, no hero shit. Just eyes."

JJ's spine straightened like he'd just won an award. "Yes, sir."

"You see anyone besides Creep and Eagle, you let us know right away," Vendetta added.

The prospects headed back the way they came. As soon as they were out of earshot, Vendetta turned toward me.

Creep. Eagle. Unknown muscle. Icons of every problem we hadn't finished burning out of Oak Ridge.

"They're scouting us," Vendetta muttered.

"Yeah," I said, rolling my shoulders, muscles humming for a fight. "And they're stupid enough to do it on our land."

Ripper shook his head. "The fuckers are still here and still working with Sinister Skin. Jesus."

"I'd bet on it," I muttered. It was already leaving a bad taste in my mouth. "Sinister Skin doesn't give a shit who the club president is. They made a deal with Eli, not the patch. They're still going to expect the Cottonmouths to hold up our end of the bargain."

Vendetta nodded grimly. "Not *these* Cottonmouths. We didn't agree to any of it, and I'll go to war over that. That's Creep and Eagle's problem now. That group will expect business to keep moving. And if it doesn't --"

"They're dead," I finished for him.

All three of us stood there letting that sink in. We weren't just talking about traitors. We were talking about assholes left from Eli's regime, caught in a trap of their own making. Hell, we could still be implicated because of Eli and his bunch before it was all over with.

Vendetta exhaled frustration, the half-empty beer bottle in his hand forgotten. "All right. Let's lock it down."

Now we're talking. I was already keyed up.

"I want double coverage on both gates," Vendetta went on, his voice cool and clipped in that way that always meant shit was about to get serious. "No one gets in or out without us knowing."

Ripper tossed his empty bottle into the trash. "You think they're close?"

"They're testing the fence," Vendetta muttered. "Probably trying to figure out where we're soft." He turned to Ripper. "Go call Snow. See if he can hook us up with a surveillance system around the south gate. Sounds like we need it."

Ripper nodded, already moving. Snow, the

Hounds' VP, ran an electronic security system in Mercy, which was handy right now. But I knew he really wanted Ripper out of earshot to talk to me in private.

Vendetta looked at me. "Shade --"

"I'm going," I cut in, letting him know there was no way I wasn't.

He studied me for a second. "I need eyes, not a body count."

I didn't say anything. Vendetta had been watching me ever since that night when we took back the club, since I put a bullet in Eli without blinking. No hesitation. No second thoughts. Just the right thing done fast.

Vendetta respected restraint. Hell, I respected him that night. Dylan's uncle or not, Vendetta held the line and kept his cool, even when Eli spat on everything this club ever stood for.

But me? I didn't have that kind of patience. Eli had tried to take down the entire chapter. He was a stain on the Cottonmouth name. He'd had it coming, and somebody needed to do what everyone else was too damn careful to do.

And Vendetta knew it. At times, he watched me like he was waiting to see which version of me he's going to get: the one who listens, or the one who pulls the trigger and deals with the consequences later.

Either way, I decided maybe I'd be going.

I gave a sharp nod. "You'll get what you need."

He didn't say anything for a long minute, just stared me down. Just when I thought I was getting a lecture, he decided to move on.

"Shade," he said, voice low. "What's the one place they'd go where Sinister Skin still has leverage and where two assholes like Creep and Eagle can walk in without raising suspicion?"

I didn't even have to think. My stomach dropped. "*Ned's.*"

Vendetta's expression darkened. "We burned Eli out of here. But we didn't burn out the cancer."

No, we hadn't. We'd been too busy fixing up the joint and helping the Hounds to pay much attention to what was happening outside our walls.

Was *Ned's* still running girls through the back? Were they still funneling cash to the same bastards Eli crawled to? Were they still poisoning our town with the kind of business Tank fucking died opposing?

"Hold up," I said. "Eli co-owned the place with Ned. With him gone, who's running it now?" Everyone knew Ned was a barely functioning alcoholic who was terrible at managing money.

"We need to find out." Vendetta hooked a thumb in the direction of the front gate. "Gear up. We're taking a ride."

A slow, vicious smile curved up my mouth.

"Let's do it," I said.

And just like that, we were hunting again.

* * *

Jazz

The whole vibe inside *Ned's Sundown Lounge* had been off tonight from the second I showed up for work. The bar's usual low buzz felt wrong. It was too quiet in some corners, where men I'd never seen before talked low at cluttered tables. It was too loud everywhere else, like the regulars were pretending it was a normal Friday night when everyone could feel it wasn't. People, mostly men, from both groups kept glancing at the door like they expected trouble.

And then trouble walked in. Two of them. The

men, both tall and hard, were covered in ink and shadows. My stomach dropped the moment I saw the patches on their cuts -- the familiar coiled serpents stitched in black and bone-white thread on black.

Cottonmouths.

I'd heard stories about the notorious motorcycle club since I was a child. Mostly whispered ones from my Aunt Susan, who tried to keep her fear-shaped memories from me and Claire. We heard them anyway.

The night Cottonmouths came to our house was burned into my memory. Three bikers showed up after our mother died and our father had been too high to be scared but not sober enough to protect us. When he wouldn't hand over the money they claimed he owed them, the leader grabbed me by the jaw and dragged a knife along my cheek. He didn't cut me, but I remember how threatening that cold steel felt gliding down my face. He told my father all the ways he could make a little girl scream in words I'd never forget.

The neighbors called the cops, who showed up in time to save me and Claire from whatever would've come next. But I still remembered the man who held that knife, could still clearly picture him in my head. I remembered thinking how wrong it felt that someone so handsome could be that cruel. *Baby Face*. That was the name stitched on his jacket.

Taking a job at *Ned's Sundown Lounge* has been scary enough. *Ned's* is a known Cottonmouth hangout, and the mission I was on to find my sister was exactly why I chose it. But the fear of seeing Baby Face again lingered in my mind every single night I worked at the bar. I prayed I'd never see him again, which was ridiculous. He wouldn't remember the child he threatened that night. He might have laughed at that memory if I ever tried to pass it to him.

The two Cottonmouths who just walked in were just as scary, and in some ways, worse. Hell, the whole town of Oak Grove was scary itself with all the drugs and guns in its poor neighborhoods. Now people were vanishing. Specifically, girls and young women were vanishing. Girls like my seventeen-year-old sister, Claire.

I froze halfway to my next table, a tray balanced on my palm, and my heart pounding away in my chest. The bigger of the two newcomers was Vendetta. A friend had pointed him out to me once from across the parking lot, whispering the way people did around a campfire telling stories they weren't supposed to repeat.

He used to be Tank, she'd said. *Before they tried to kill him.*

I'd laughed it off back then. Sounded like one of those exaggerated Oak Grove legends. The Cottonmouths loved their tall tales and stories of revenge, and local people passed them around after too many beers. I remembered something about a disagreement inside the club, how a few of his own pissed-off members dragged him out into the woods and left him hanging like a warning. But he didn't die. Apparently, he dragged himself out of the forest and got his revenge.

I'd thought it was just a story… until he moved. Just a subtle turn of his head and I saw it. The twisted ring of scar tissue circling his throat like a macabre necklace.

My blood went cold.

People in Oak Grove said he shouldn't have been able to come back from that. But he did, then tracked down the club president who gave the order and every friend who stood with him. They said that when he was done, he took the whole damn club for himself.

That's when Tank died and Vendetta was born. With his tall, muscular build, his long hair brushing his shoulders, and that intense, unblinking stare, he *was* terrifying. Some folks had told the story in *Ned's*, believing he really came back from the dead. I didn't believe that. But with each telling of that tale, the man's legend grew. No one got too close or looked for too long, not unless they were looking for trouble.

And now Vendetta was standing ten feet from me in *Ned's*, on a night that already felt wrong. And trouble was standing right next to him.

He was leaner, blond and quiet. One of the other waitresses told me he was called Shade. The man didn't just look around the bar the way most men did. He surveyed the bar, his eyes cold and predatory, taking in faces, threats, and exits. He may not have survived a hanging like his friend, but he looked even more dangerous than Vendetta to me.

And then he found me. It was just one second, one flash of his green eyes, but it felt like someone had reached into my chest and squeezed. I immediately looked away and focused on my next table, my anxiety climbing higher by the second.

Something bad was going down tonight, and the arrival of those two Cottonmouths just confirmed my gut feeling. Every instinct in me screamed to get out. I wanted to walk to the back, grab my bag, and make up some excuse about feeling sick or needing to check on my aunt. Anything to leave the bar *right now* before whatever was building finally snapped.

But guilt held me in place like a hand around my throat. Claire was still missing. If I left… what if tonight was the night someone slipped up? What if I overheard something, one hint, one name, one rumor, that could lead me to her? Every hour I stayed felt like I was standing inside a nightmare, but leaving would be abandoning my sister all over again.

So, I stayed, even though every fiber of my being wanted me to run.

My aunt's warning from last week ran through my head again. *Girls go missing in Oak Grove, Jazz. The Cottonmouths are part of the reason why. Don't tangle with them. I don't want to lose you too.*

Tonight, the bar was filled with Cottonmouths, and the latest arrivals' very presence seemed to be feeding the fear of everyone who was paying attention. Ned, my boss, spotted them from a side table where he was visiting. When he glanced over at them, his eyes widened comically.

Good. It isn't just me. I took orders and scrambled back to the counter, ducking behind it. I wanted to disappear long enough to breathe, but no luck. Ned was already shuffling in my direction, toward the back hallway with the urgency of a man trying to escape his own execution.

I shouldn't have stared at him. I knew better. I shouldn't have tried to read the man's cold expression. When his gaze tracked the room again, I realized something he hadn't yet. One of the offices in the back hallway had a light on, its door not fully shut. A shadow moved. Someone was in there. We were all told to never go back there. Ned was out front in the bar. So, who was back there? Someone hiding from Vendetta and Shade? Or was it someone Ned feared even more than the bikers holding him?

Was it them? *Sinister Skin.*

I knew that name just like every girl in Oak Grove did. Sinister Skin had showed up last year with a shady tattoo shop on the edge of town. No one thought anything of the grimy little hole-in-the-wall shop at first. Then their presence spread fast, like a cancer. The shop turned into a meeting place. Then the meeting place turned into trafficking rumors. And soon enough, girls started disappearing in patterns nobody wanted to admit were actual patterns.

My Aunt Susan was convinced Claire's disappearance had something to do with the Cottonmouths. Call it old prejudice or fear from my father's run-ins with them. But I wasn't so sure. Sinister Skin was newer and bolder.

And *Ned's* was one of the only places in Oak Grove where both groups drifted through after dark. That was why I took the job here in the first place. Not for the tips and certainly not for the company. If anyone in this town full of scumbags knew what had happened to my sister, be it the Cottonmouths or Sinister Skin, the bar would be where I'd find the information I was looking for.

My fingers tightened around my tray until they hurt.

Shade's attention shifted to me again, and every instinct in me screamed. *Don't look at him. Don't you dare.* But I did. They were here for a reason, and my gut told me Ned was only part of it. Were they looking for whoever was in that back office? I couldn't shout a warning. If I did, whoever was hiding back there would know I noticed.

So, I did the smallest, riskiest thing I could manage. I moved my eyes. One shift, slow in the direction of the hallway, the door.

Shade stilled, like a wolf scenting blood. He didn't look away from me. Hell, he didn't even blink.

I froze, terrified and horrified all at once. Why

was I trying to help *them*? For all I knew, they had taken my sister or knew what happened to her.

Before I could think another thing about it, the door in question swung open and a man in a tailored shirt stepped out, smiling like a shark.

Fuck. It was Rick Earle. The man was Sinister Skin royalty, and he'd been here at least once a day since I started working here. His gaze drifted lazily across the bar, landing on me first. The man's smile widened slowly, as he looked me up and down. Everything about him gave me the creeps.

Fear rooted me to the spot. From the corner of my eye, I saw Shade move. It wasn't much. He shifted his weight, taking an intentional step into Earle's line of sight like a wolf stepping out of the shadows. It sent a message. *Look at me, not her.*

Earle's focus moved to him, and irritation bled into the man's expression. He clocked the cut, the patch, and the man wearing it.

Shade didn't step forward toward him. No, he just tilted his head, the way a predator would when it's decided how the kill will go. One corner of his mouth curled up as he studied Earle like a line had been crossed.

What the tipping point was, I couldn't have said. Maybe it was the way Earle's stare lingered on me too long, or the way Ned flinched behind Vendetta. And while it was generally believed that the Cottonmouths and Sinister Skin were in business together, it looked like these two Cottonmouths and Sinister Skin being in the same room were going to end with blood on the floor.

But I watched. For one breath, Shade was still.

The next, his spine straightened, and his shoulders angled in a way that framed Earle as a target. It was quiet, the silent kind of readiness that came from a man who didn't bluff.

And Rick Earle felt it. I saw the exact moment he did. His smile faltered as some realization hit him. The second Earle understood Shade and Vendetta weren't there by accident, I knew with bone-deep certainty that whatever happened next wouldn't be a bar fight.

It was the opening shot of a war.

And I was standing dead center inside it.

* * *

Shade

Ned's Sundown Lounge smelled like stale beer, cheap perfume, and the scent of unease that people tried to cover with laughter. It was half bar, half diner, and all trouble, the kind of place where the lights buzzed, your boots stuck to the floor, and every bad decision in Oak Grove passed through at least once. The jukebox played the same tired music low over the speakers. Mostly men clustered at corner tables, with some trying not to draw attention and regulars who looked tight, wary, ready to strike.

We were here to find Ned and get some answers. We needed to make sure the shit Eli left behind didn't choke the rest of the chapter.

Who owned *Ned's* now that Eli, who had co-owned it with Ned, was gone? Was product still being run through it? Did Sinister Skin still have its hooks in the place?

Vendetta wanted clarity, but I wanted confirmation. And both of us wanted the truth before someone tried to bury it.

That's when I saw her. Behind the bar, she was sliding a tray onto the counter like she'd done it a thousand times. Hell, maybe she had. But why the hell would a woman who looked like *her* be working in a place like this? Did she have a damn death wish? Her long, dark hair was pulled back into a messy braid, and a couple of loose strands brushed against her pale skin as she moved.

When she walked out from behind the bar, her body was all soft curves and long limbs. Her black tank top was too small, and her jeans fit like a second skin. *Holy hell.*

She must've felt the weight of my stare, because she stopped mid-step and looked up. Her wide eyes were the color of good bourbon. *Damn.*

But the look she gave me wasn't curiosity. No, it was *fear*. Not the kind women usually showed, with interest first, then nerves. No, that look told me she already built a story in mind about who I was.

A Cottonmouth. One of the men who not only ran *Ned's* but Oak Grove. For all she knew, I was one of the monsters behind everything wrong in Oak Grove right now. The chapter under Eli's leadership had really fucked things up.

She tore her gaze away fast, like looking at me too long might get her hurt. She approached a table of younger Cottonmouths, prospects and half-drunk idiots leering at her like a damn buffet. She forced a smile, but it was thin and brittle.

It was obvious that she hated being here. And the minute she saw me, she hated *me* too. Whoever she was, she didn't belong in *Ned's*. Especially not with Sinister Skin poking its claws back into Oak Grove.

Just one word came to mind as I watched her. *Mine*. It was instinct, the kind that didn't miss and wouldn't fade.

Ned spotted us the moment we walked in. I watched recognition hit him like a punch to the gut.

His face went pale first, then his shoulders curled in, like he was trying to make himself small enough to disappear behind the bar taps. His focus darted from Vendetta to me and back again, wide and frantic. It was the look of a man who *knew* he'd been living on borrowed time and had just found the collectors at his door.

He fumbled a glass, nearly dropped it, muttered something to a customer, then backed away, like he could sneak out of his own bar without us noticing.

Coward. Or maybe just smart enough to know the shit Eli left behind was finally circling back.

Vendetta snapped my attention back with a jerk of his chin toward the hallway. Ned was slinking off like a weasel caught stealing chickens. "Let's go," he murmured.

I followed, but not before checking on the girl again, and that's when she looked at me. *Really* looked. Yeah, she was still scared of me, but also scared of something else. Her gaze shifted sideways, once. The movement was quick and sharp.

I caught the message instantly. Vendetta did too. We stepped in closer, cutting off Ned's retreat. Vendetta grabbed him by the shirt and slammed him against the wall. The man looked terrified. "Thought we said you were done with surprises," Vendetta said, voice low.

Ned choked on air. "I didn't --"

From the back hallway, Rick Earle stepped out like he owned the place. The man was a higher-up in Sinister Skin. He had a smile like a shark, and his eyes were dark and cold. His suit was expensive, tailored, and he had a watch that looked like it cost more than my bike.

He looked at the girl first. That was his *first*

mistake. The bastard stared a little too long, his mouth curling like he had plans for her. Then he spotted Vendetta. His whole expression changed then, flashing recognition, fury, and fear. Earle had good reason for that.

Vendetta was the man who had broken into a lake house at the edge of Oak Grove one night where Earle had Eli Crizer's niece, Dylan, right where he wanted her. He'd put Earle in a hospital bed for weeks. It was generous that Vendetta left him alive considering what the fucker could have done to Dylan, who was now Vendetta's old lady.

But now fate had brought Earle back to the man who'd ripped out the Oak Grove chapter of the Cottonmouths by the roots after they'd crawled into bed with Sinister Skin.

Vendetta stood ten feet from Earle, calm as ever, with Ned still in his clutches. He shoved Ned behind him, turning his full attention to the other man.

"Well," Earle said, sounding more confident than he looked. "Didn't expect to see *you* back here."

Vendetta's smile was lazy and lethal. "We're full of surprises."

The new tension in the bar drew more than a few eyes. Some of the conversation and noise died down.

Earle cut me a look before returning his attention to Vendetta, calculating fast. He wasn't stupid. He knew he couldn't win a stand-off with both of us. Not here, in public. Not without bodies hitting the floor before he ever reached the door.

Still, the sumbitch was proud. And men like him got dangerous when pride and fear collided.

"You're trespassing," Earle said, trying to stare Vendetta down. "This is Sinister Skin territory."

Vendetta let his intense stare drift around the bar

like he was taking inventory. "Funny," he drawled. Vendetta tapped his own patch with two fingers, slow and mocking. "I see several Cottonmouths in here."

I did too. And it pissed me off.

The fact that *any* of our boys were still drinking in this place was a fucking problem. Eli's poison should've cleared the second we burned his name off the roster. But there they were, three of them at a back table, hunched over beers like they didn't notice the snakes coiled in the shadows around them. Two older members were at the bar.

Why were they here? What deals were they turning a blind eye to?

And more importantly, who were they loyal to *now*?

My stare cut across them one by one, burning their faces into my memory. They'd be having conversations with me later. And they weren't going to enjoy a single second of them.

"And last I checked," Vendetta said, "Eli co-owned this place with Ned."

Earle shook his head. "Not anymore."

Vendetta arched a brow. "Is that right?"

"We bought Ned out," Earle said. "Paperwork's done. The keys are in our hands. You're standing in a Sinister Skin operation."

The words hit exactly where I expected them to. It was what I'd come here to confirm.

Eli's rot hadn't just infected the club. It had rooted itself into the damn town, right under everyone's noses. And Ned had sold out the second Eli's body hit the dirt.

I felt the shift roll through me. We weren't just cleaning up loose ends. We were taking back territory.

Earle, like an idiot, kept talking, trying to fill the

silence. "And *you* are still on the line for what Eli promised us."

Vendetta cut him off with a smile that wasn't a smile at all. "You had a deal with Eli. Eli's dead. So is your deal."

Earle smirked then but it didn't reach his eyes. "Oh, is *that* how this works? Eli gets dead and suddenly you boys think everything he promised just… disappears?" He took a slow, deliberate step forward. "You think killing him makes it all go away?"

Vendetta didn't answer.

The man just laughed, amused in a way that made every hair on the back of my neck rise. Like he was genuinely fucking entertained by the idea.

Vendetta shook his head. "I didn't kill Eli."

Earle froze.

I stepped forward just enough for the man to feel it. "I did."

His focus flashed to me, and he was smart enough to look worried then. But he kept talking, like a man trying to convince himself he still had leverage.

"Eli put the club on the line for the agreement," Earle hissed. "What he owed, *you* owe. His death doesn't change shit. You can't just walk in here and erase it."

Vendetta tilted his head, the faintest smile touching his mouth. "Watch me."

Earle swallowed hard. He knew exactly what that meant, just like he knew exactly what kind of men he was dealing with.

Neither Vendetta nor I moved. The girl stood frozen behind the counter, taking all of it in with wide eyes and shaking hands. Hell, the bar itself seemed to hold its breath.

Finally, Rick Earle lifted his hands, a mockery of

surrender. His hands weren't all that steady either. "This isn't the night, fellas," he said nervously. "But it's coming. All of you Cottonmouth motherfuckers owe a debt. And we *will* come to collect sooner or later."

Vendetta smiled like he couldn't wait.

Earle stepped backward, never turning his back, his eyes cutting from Vendetta to me to the girl one last time, longer than I liked. Then he slipped out the back door, a couple of his men trailing after him like rats abandoning a kitchen.

Ned still stood behind Vendetta, looking like he just might pass out.

I looked at the girl again. She was still staring at us in shock, maybe relief. I still wanted to know why the hell she was even in *Ned's*.

Vendetta moved closer, clapped my shoulder. "You see the way Earle looked at her?"

"I saw everything," I said. And I did. Earle's interest and the threat it posed to her.

Vendetta's look sharpened. "We're taking her home."

I didn't argue or question him. The way Earle looked at her? She'd be gone by morning, caught in their nets. I'd already made up my mind the moment I saw her.

Mine.

Chapter Two

Jazz

"We're taking her home."

Vendetta said it, tipping his head in my direction. It only took a second before shock took over. I was shaking so badly that I knew they had to see it.

Before I could stop myself, I blurted, "No. No, I'm not. I'm *not* going anywhere with you."

Vendetta jerked his chin toward the door, like I hadn't said a damn thing. It was a silent order Shade seemed to understand.

Shade moved in my direction, his movements deliberate. I backed up until the counter behind me dug into my spine. "This isn't happening," I said, holding my hands up. "I'm not going with you. I need this job, and my aunt will freak out if I just disappear --"

Shade cut me off with a look. "You can walk out," he said, "or you can be carried out."

My stomach dropped at those well-chosen words. "You wouldn't," I whispered.

Shade lifted a brow. "Try me."

Panic sparked hard and bright in my chest. "That's kidnapping!"

"No one's kidnapping you," Vendetta said, before walking toward the exit. "We're keeping you alive."

Shade angled his body toward me, giving me enough space to walk, but not enough to cut and run. "Move," he said.

I didn't. *I couldn't.*

My fists clenched at my sides. Fear and anger blended, making my voice shake. "I don't understand… Why *me*? You don't know me."

Shade's gaze raked over me again. "This isn't the time or place to be having this conversation. Not with Earle in play."

I swallowed hard, the memory of Earle's stare causing my anxiety to escalate.

"You stay here," Shade added, "you might be gone by sunrise."

Gone? What?

Something whispered over the fear in my head. What if they knew something about girls disappearing, like Claire?

Shade gestured once, a subtle tilt of his head that told me he would have no problem carrying me out like a sack of flour if I pushed this any further.

My mouth was dry, and I was dangerously close to tears. "My aunt… she'll worry."

Shade was unfazed. "She can worry from a distance."

"And what if I don't want to go?" I asked.

He stepped closer. Close enough that I had to tip my head back to keep looking at him. His voice dropped to a quiet warning. "Then you've already made your choice."

I felt the heat rolling off him. Shade had the kind of certainty that made me truly understand, that if I didn't start moving on my own two feet, he would pick me up and I wouldn't be able to stop him.

His next words were quiet and final. "Walking or carried, sweetheart. Decide."

The last piece of fight bled out of me on a shaky breath. I stepped forward.

Shade's focus followed my movements, but I could feel the shift in him. Several pairs of eyes were on me as I headed for the door with Shade at my back.

Vendetta stood at the open front door, waiting

for us.

And just like that, I followed two of the most dangerous men I'd ever seen into the night. There was no turning back, and maybe even a good chance I could end up missing like Claire. Or worse.

The night air hit me like a slap, cold and sobering. I should've felt safer outside *Ned's*, away from Rick Earle's dead-eyed stare. But walking between Shade and Vendetta felt like walking with two wolves who'd decided I was their evening meal.

We made it three steps before I found my voice again. "I need my things." I stopped short of the curb.

Shade's footsteps slowed behind me. "What things?"

"My purse. It has my wallet and my ID." I swallowed. "They're in my locker."

Vendetta muttered under his breath. "Jesus Christ."

"The employee lockers," I added quickly. "In the back. That's where Ned makes us keep everything."

Shade didn't say anything at first. His attention settled on me, heavy and assessing. Being his focus was unsettling in a way that made my shoulders tense. "Locker number," he said at last.

"Twenty-seven."

"And the key?"

I hesitated for a second too long.

Shade held out his hand. His movement wasn't aggressive or rushed. It had a certain inevitability to it. I pulled my small key ring out of my jeans pocket and dropped it into his palm. "I can go get it," I offered. "It's just --"

"No," he said. "You stay here."

Vendetta shifted closer, effectively cutting off my view of

+the lot without even trying. I caught the message loud and clear. I wasn't doing anything stupid with *him* watching.

Shade turned toward the back of *Ned's* without another word, shoulders squared like he was walking into enemy territory. As I watched him march off, I realized with a twist of dread, he absolutely was. My heart raced in my chest.

"What if they do something to him?" I blurted.

Vendetta snorted softly. "He would *love* that."

That did *not* help. I waited with my arms wrapped around myself, staring at the bar's dark back entrance with fear curling tight in my stomach.

Shade disappeared inside. The minutes stretched thin and sharp for me as we waited. I replayed the look Rick Earle had given me. The way his eyes lingered. The way the bar had felt like a trap I'd been standing in without realizing it.

Then the door opened. Shade came out carrying my purse clutched in his hands. One end of my phone charger cord swung from the small bag, showing he'd taken the time to make sure nothing got left behind.

My key ring dangled from his fingers. He handed the purse to me when he reached us. "You got everything?" he asked.

I nodded, swallowing hard.

He stepped in closer, not touching me, but close enough that his presence crowded out everything else.

"I'm protecting you, sweetheart," he said. "So don't play coy." His eyes locked onto mine, unblinking. "The men watching you tonight don't leave girls alive."

And for the first time since this whole nightmare started, I didn't argue. They seemed to know something about girls disappearing. *Do they know what happened to Claire*?

I tried to shove the fear down as his huge hand wrapped around my upper arm. "I'm not your problem," I said, though it landed weaker than I meant to say it.

His gaze dragged over my face like he could read every lie I'd told myself for the past week. "The hell you aren't."

Vendetta's voice cut through the tension. "Shade. Bring her on."

Shade held my stare for about three more seconds, daring me to run. Daring me to argue or fight back.

Pocketing my keys, he said, "Let's go, sweetheart."

Under the humming streetlight of a bar that posed a threat to women like me, I realized a couple of things. First, no one from the bar, my *job,* was coming to save my ass.

And I wasn't escaping anything tonight. I was being claimed.

* * *

Shade

She froze when Vendetta pointed to our bikes, parked at the edge of the lot. I grinned, watching her look over the bikes like that was somehow the line she couldn't cross. I didn't give her time to think about it as I grabbed my helmet, then set it carefully on her head.

She jerked back. "I don't need --"

"Yeah," I said, tightening the strap beneath her chin while her hands swatted at mine, "you do."

The way she huffed was adorable with indignation sparking bright underneath her fear.

I didn't even know her name yet. What I *did* know? She was too mouthy to be truly scared, and too brave for her own damn good. It grabbed my attention more than it should have. And it backed up my opinion that she had no fucking business in *Ned's*. She didn't know it yet, but we were doing her a favor in getting her out now.

Walking around her, I swung onto my bike and jerked my chin. "On."

She hesitated long enough to annoy me, then climbed on behind me. Her hands fluttered awkwardly before she finally, reluctantly, wrapped her arms around my waist.

And then I felt her tremble. She was trying to control it. Yeah, she'd probably never been on a bike in her damn life, and she was scared. But she refused to act like it.

When I revved the engine, she gasped and tightened her hold instinctively. It told me she trusted me at least a little without meaning to.

Vendetta took the lead. I followed, pulling out of *Ned's* lot with the girl pressed against my back. Her hold was tight, and she was still shaking. But her breasts felt nice plastered into me, her little body like soft fire behind mine, even through the leather.

The memory of Earle staring at her replayed in my head as we rode. The slick bastard's interest in her, the way his gaze lingered on her for too long. The threat that him and his entire fucking organization posed to her.

I fucking hated it. I hated the idea of Sinister Skin hands on her, that she'd even worked in a place they now owned. More than anything, I hated that she was now on their radar.

When we hit the highway, the night air ripped

past us, cold and sharp. She clung to me like she was aware that falling was death. And she barely had a top on. She had to be cold, but I hadn't brought a jacket to offer her. By the time we turned down the long dirt road leading to the compound, my mind was already made up about too many things.

Instinct had turned to resolve. She wasn't going back to *Ned's*. Ever. She wouldn't be going anywhere near Sinister Skin territory. In fact, she wasn't leaving my fucking sight until all of this was handled. And even then, we'd see how things went.

Vendetta cut his engine first when we reached the lot, and I pulled in beside him. Slowly, she let go of me, but her hands were shaking as she slid off the seat.

I took the helmet back from her, studying her face for the first time in decent light as she raked her fingers through her hair. If I thought she was gorgeous at the bar, it wasn't anything compared to her now with those amber eyes and flushed cheeks.

"What's your name?" I asked as I climbed off my bike.

She hesitated. "I go by Jazz."

"Is that short for Jasmine?" I asked as I got an eyeful of the rest of her. "Or do you have one of those old-fashioned family names that got handed down, but you couldn't live with it, so you shortened it to Jazz?"

The look that earned me… She was trying to figure out whether she could trust me.

After a moment, she sighed. "Yeah, it's short for Jasmine."

"Is there a last name?"

"Why do you need to know?" she asked.

I couldn't blame her for asking questions. She didn't know us, and she had no idea of the danger surrounding her.

Crossing her arms, she tried to look taller. "Why am I here? What do you want from me?"

I wasn't about to sugarcoat it. "You walked into the middle of a war," I said. "And Sinister Skin just put their sights on you."

She flinched.

Vendetta didn't have anything to add as he dismounted, and I could tell his mind was already running a mile a minute, piecing together what we'd learned tonight.

Ned had sold out. Sinister Skin had bought the bar outright. That meant funding, expansion, and connections in Oak Grove were resuming. They were running a quiet operation again with girls, drugs, or both. A bold move to plant themselves right back into our town after Eli died and his chapter was reclaimed by those of us who wanted Sinister Skin *gone*.

But, worse than that, some of our Cottonmouths were drinking in the bar tonight. The fuckers were disloyal at best, cowards at worst. I had their faces memorized, every damn one of them. Any of them colluding with Sinister Skin behind our backs would be dealt with severely. Especially considering that every one of them that stayed on the day we took the Oak Grove chapter back and put it under Vendetta's leadership swore loyalty to him, to the Cottonmouths.

Not Sinister Skin.

Jazz stood quietly, taking in the outer wall and front gate of the compound without shrinking. Well, she was trying to act like she wasn't afraid. But beneath that beautiful surface, I could tell she was.

"Take her to Dylan," Vendetta said, nudging my arm. "We need to call a meeting. *Now*."

I nodded, then jerked my chin toward the gate that Dylan had walked through, watching us with sharp, blue eyes. She was Vendetta's old lady these days, but she'd also worked at *Ned's* for a time. She had firsthand knowledge of exactly what Sinister Skin was and what it did to women and girls.

Jazz relaxed a fraction on seeing the other woman. Vendetta was smart. Leaving her in Dylan's hands was the best-case scenario.

"Go with her," I said. "Stay there until I come get you."

Jazz stiffened, her wary gaze back on me. "Are you… are you keeping me *here*?"

I stared her down. I needed her to know this was serious. "We're keeping you alive."

"That's not an answer," she said.

She didn't trust us and had no reason to. But right now, I needed her to listen to me. I stepped in closer, close enough she had to tilt her chin up to keep her eyes on mine.

"Yes, you're staying here right now," I said. "That's the only answer I've got to give you."

Jazz stared up at me, fear, anger, and confusion all swirled together in those deep amber eyes. She didn't look away, though. She didn't fold. Damn girl was braver than I gave her credit for.

I blew out a sigh. The least I could do after dragging her here into the dark heart of the Cottonmouth compound was not leave her standing by herself in the den of unfamiliar wolves.

"Come on," I muttered, nodding toward the gate where Dylan waited expectantly.

Jazz hesitated then followed beside me with steps that were small but steady across the gravel. I slowed my pace to match hers.

Dylan watched us approach with her arms crossed and a look sharp enough to slice. She'd survived *Ned's* and all the ugly truths behind it. If anyone here could handle Jazz right now, she could.

"Dylan," I said when we reached her. "This is…" I glanced at the girl. "Jazz."

Jazz swallowed, eyeing Dylan warily. "Hi."

Dylan gave her a slow once-over. "Let's find you a sweater. It's chilly tonight."

Jazz nodded. *Good.* She'd be safe with Dylan. More importantly, she'd *feel* safe.

Dylan pulled open the gate, and I waited until Jazz was on the other side beside her, until Dylan placed a steadying hand on her arm. I didn't make a move until the knot in my gut loosened a little.

Only then did I turn. We had an emergency meeting to call and plans to make. The rot of Sinister Skin had resurfaced like a herpes outbreak, and we needed to deal with it. *Right now.*

I spared one last glance over my shoulder, catching Jazz's gaze, her hands twisting nervously in front of her as I walked away. Dylan murmured something to calm her as she closed the gate and secured it, to draw her attention away from us and what we needed to do.

Jazz was safe for now. Sinister Skin wasn't taking her. Not while I was breathing.

We had work to do, and I followed Vendetta into the office building. It was time to gather the Cottonmouths, to find out who still remembered where their loyalty sat.

We needed to finish what Vendetta started and erase Sinister Skin from Oak Grove forever.

* * *

Jazz

Once the men had dashed off to their meeting

and Shade was out of view, Dylan caught my attention. "Come on," she said, motioning to the gate behind us with a tilt of her head.

The quiet gesture was enough for me to follow her. The compound door creaked open softly and warm light spilled over us as I followed her. It smelled like leather, paint, and something faintly sharp and clean beneath it.

The other woman's gaze moved over me slowly, and curiosity blended with concern in her wide, blue eyes. "I didn't know they were bringing someone back," she said in a careful tone. "Where did they get *you* from?"

"*Ned's*." It was the truth. I just hoped she didn't ask why because I had no idea.

Apparently, the mention of *Ned's* was enough to get a response I didn't know how to read when her expression darkened.

"Take a deep breath," Dylan said as she led me inside. "You're safe now."

Safe. The word felt too big for my chest right now.

I followed her into the first building but noticed that all the buildings looked the same. "Was this an army base or something?" I asked.

"Something like that," she said. "I think Vendetta told me there was a munitions plant nearby, years ago. The officers who ran the place stayed here, I think."

We walked into the first building, and it reminded me of the entrance to a museum. Framed photos hung on the walls, some of which appeared to be pretty old. A couple of glass display cases were hung up, filled with different types of memorabilia from their biker gang. An old-fashioned leather couch and a couple of matching chairs were situated in the corner of the room with a glass coffee table. The ashtrays on it were shiny and clean.

Dylan led me down a narrow hallway, with more old wood and framed photos. She navigated it like she'd lived here forever, confident and steady. We walked past a small kitchen, past a half-open doorway where I heard quiet voices, and down another hall.

"These rooms are ours," she said, nodding toward a door with a worn-out seven painted on it. "Vendetta and mine. Across from us is eight; that's Ripper's. Shade's next to him in nine."

I stumbled a step, staring at her. "I'm staying *here*?"

"Don't worry," she said with a small smile. "You'll be in the spare if you're staying. And it kind of seems like you are. The spare's on the other side of Shade's room. Number ten."

As lost as I was with the entire situation, I appreciated her patience and kindness.

Dylan led me into a simple room. It had a neatly made bed with folded blankets on the end of it. The dresser matched the bedside table, and a small lamp glowed a soft yellow. The room was plain enough but seemed safe. I noticed a lock on the inside of the door. Why was *that* necessary?

"If you want to leave your things here," she said, "we can go to the kitchen, have a beer?"

I nodded, placing my purse on the bed and following her back into the hallway. She darted quickly into her room, coming back with a simple black sweater she held out to me. With a quick thanks, I pulled it on and followed her to the kitchen.

I took a seat on one of the stools at the island in the kitchen. My hands were shaking so badly now that I tried to hide them in my lap.

Dylan pulled a couple of bottles of beer from the ancient refrigerator next to her. Twisting the cap off one, she handed it to me. She twisted the cap off the other beer before leaning on the other side of the island, looking directly at me.

She looked like she was around my age, maybe a little older. If I'd seen her on the street, I would *never* have guessed she was with a biker. Dylan's features were soft, her pretty face framed by soft blonde hair. Her blue eyes were warm as she waited patiently to see what I'd say.

But I had no idea what to say. She had no idea why I was here. Hell, I wasn't entirely sure I knew.

"You look like you've had a rough night," she said.

The words almost broke me. My throat tightened as I thought about where to even start. "Yeah." I swallowed. "I guess I have."

"Hey, it's okay." Dylan drank from her beer. "Coming here is a lot for anyone. Hell, it was a lot for me."

I studied her then. Dylan seemed like someone who had learned the hard way to be steady. "I… I wouldn't expect to see you here. I mean, this is where the gang lives, right? The Cottonmouths?" I said their name quietly, earning a look from her.

"Well, they don't consider themselves to be a biker gang," she explained. "It's a motorcycle club. And believe it or not, the Cottonmouths have always been a part of my life. My Uncle Eli was the chapter president for years."

I hadn't expected that. But it made sense with the way she moved through the compound like she belonged, the way the Shade regarded her with respect.

Something dark and guarded flashed behind Dylan's blue eyes.

Then it hit me. "Wait." It just occurred to me. "Eli Crizer? Is he your uncle?"

"He *was*." She gave a humorless smile. "You won't be meeting him. Vendetta made sure of that."

The words echoed, but they didn't sit right. "What?" I asked, my pulse picking up. Earlier during the confrontation at the bar, I remembered the moment Rick Earle sneered about Eli's death. I clearly remembered Vendetta's calm denial. *I didn't kill Eli.*

And then… my stomach dropped. "It wasn't Vendetta," I said, the realization sliding cold and sharp into place. "At the bar… he said he didn't kill him."

Dylan's focus didn't waver.

"It was Shade," I whispered.

She didn't correct me or even try to soften it. With a nod, she said, "Yes."

My chest tightened. I'd been standing ten feet from the man who killed the most powerful person in this town. I'd ridden on the back of his bike and argued with him like I was someone who mattered.

"And Eli --" My voice wobbled. "He was…"

Dylan's expression shifted. It wasn't with grief, but regret. "He was honestly a terrible fucking person. It's okay to say it."

Silence settled between us, thick and uneasy. The evening became more surreal if that was even possible. I was sitting in the hangout of a motorcycle club, talking to a woman about the death of her uncle like it was something normal. Nothing seemed quite real. But honestly, nothing had felt real since Claire hadn't come home that night.

"I'm grateful Shade was the one who did it," Dylan admitted. "Vendetta didn't want to be the one to do it… because of me."

I nodded. That made sense. It was chilling to remember the way Shade pointed out to Earle that he was the one who'd ended Eli. Like he relished the memory and would have no problem ending him the same way.

He was the same man claiming he brought me here to keep me safe. After talking with Dylan, I had to wonder, not just if I was safe here, but what kind of man I was trusting to keep me that way.

Dylan searched my face, like she was reading me the way Shade had earlier. "I'll bet you thought we were all monsters when you saw those patches, didn't you?"

Heat crept up my neck. "Honestly, yes. But this wasn't my first run-in with the Cottonmouths."

"Good," Dylan said without hesitation. "You're smart."

A shaky laugh escaped me, unexpected, but welcome.

"But," she went on, "you need to understand something. The Cottonmouths you knew growing up? They're not the Cottonmouths you're standing with now."

I pressed my lips together, uncertain. The Cottonmouths I knew growing up were terrifying. Was that a good thing or a bad thing? The memory hit me then, sharp and visceral. "Three of them came to my house," I whispered before I could stop myself.

Dylan's head tilted. "Go on."

"When I was a kid," I explained, "they showed up at our house after my mom died. They wanted money my father owed. When he didn't have it, the leader grabbed me. He had a knife…" I stopped, breath shuddering. "He traced it along my cheek. Told my dad all the ways he could hurt me."

Dylan's expression darkened, a cold fury settling into her eyes. "Then I'm surprised you didn't run away screaming the minute Vendetta and Shade walked in."

"It took some getting used to," I admitted, "working at *Ned's*. There are a lot of Cottonmouths there."

"The one with the knife sounds like Baby Face," she said after a minute. "Was he nice looking?"

I froze. "Yes. How did you --"

"He was my cousin." Dylan took a slow breath. "Eli killed him a couple of years ago. His own son."

I stared. "Why?"

"For embarrassing him, as I understand it," Dylan said.

My head spun. What a violent world Dylan lived in, though she seemed normal enough. Still, I couldn't help the small measure of relief that came with learning that the man behind that terrifying memory from my childhood was dead.

"So Baby Face is gone," Dylan added. "It's okay. You're not the only one he terrorized. But that's not why you're here tonight, is it, Jazz?"

Hearing my name grounded me.

"Why were *you* working at *Ned's*?" Dylan asked. The intensity of her expression told me how much my answer mattered to her.

I blinked back tears I didn't want to shed, trying to put it all together. The horror I'd been living through for the last couple of weeks, trying to find my sister or find out where she could be. And tonight, being pulled out of my job by two bikers I didn't know…

Dylan gave me a small nod. "Take your time."

My breath caught. "My sister. Claire. She, ah…

she disappeared almost three weeks ago." The tears started then, but I forced myself to go on. "She went out with her friend Scarlett one night to the lake festival -- they go every year -- and she didn't come home. Neither of them did."

Dylan's expression softened but his focus didn't leave me as she reached behind her to grab a small cardboard tissue box from the counter behind her. Placing it in front of me, she whispered, "I'm so sorry."

"It wasn't the first time girls that age have gone missing lately," I managed to continue, grabbing tissues and trying in vain to catch my tears as they fell. "We all know that. And I don't mean any offense, but we've all heard the stories. That the Cottonmouths and Sinister Skin were... trafficking girls and..."

She nodded then, her own eyes shining as she listened to me. But one thing that struck me at that moment was that she didn't seem surprised.

"The only reason I took a job at *Ned's* was because that's where they all hang out," I told her. "I thought if I worked there, I'd hear something. See someone. Anything."

"How old is your sister?" Dylan asked.

Is. Finally, someone was talking about Claire in the present tense. Still here and alive. Like there was still a chance I could find her.

"Seventeen," I said.

Dylan's voice didn't lose its edge. "I understand what you were trying to do. Really. I get it. But you're lucky the guys got you out of there tonight. Do you know that? You don't look like you're much older than your sister."

"I'm twenty-five," I said, sniffling and trying to stay upright.

"They don't care," she assured me. "I'm not

much older than you, and my own uncle tried to pass me off to a man named Rick Earle one night back when I was working at *Ned's*. My *uncle*. That's who these people are. That's why Vendetta took the chapter back. None of the Cottonmouths here now are saints, but they don't support trafficking girls and women. They don't agree with all the drugs Sinister Skin's been pushing out into our streets either."

Rick Earle. The man leered at me every day I worked at the bar.

She spoke with such conviction that it gave me a moment of hope. Like maybe I hadn't jumped from the frying pan into the fire tonight.

"The problem is," Dylan went on, "Vendetta got the corruption out of the Cottonmouths, but it's still in Oak Grove. Sinister Skin is still here. And until those assholes are run out of our town, no one is safe."

I nodded, agreeing with her. But the hole in my heart widened because Shade told me they were keeping me alive. They were keeping me *here*.

"If I'm stuck here," I said, "then I'm not out there trying to find my sister. If there's even a chance that she's…" I took a deep breath. "And my aunt, Susan. She's scared enough. She can't think she's lost me too. She…"

"Hey," Dylan wrapped a steady arm around my shoulders. "It's okay. I know you're terrified. But maybe ending up here isn't the worst thing that could have happened to you. You know?"

"How?" The word came out way more desperate than I meant for it to.

"You can call your aunt," Dylan said. "Tell her where you are. That you're safe."

Shade has taken your keys but not your phone.

"And my sister?"

It was all I could do not to let despair in. The police were overwhelmed with cases. Yeah, we'd been told they were "doing all they could do." But not in any way that inspired hope or made it sound like Claire had even the smallest chance of survival. "If anyone can get Claire back," she told me, "It's the Cottonmouths."

Chapter Three

Shade

The call went out fast. No delays or excuses would be tolerated. Each and every patched Cottonmouth in Oak Grove understood what an emergency meeting meant. You didn't finish your drink. You didn't take your time. You showed up really fucking fast or you marked yourself as a problem before the first word was ever spoken.

It was the first emergency meeting of Vendetta's presidency, which added another level of importance. No one yet knew how Vendetta would manage his first one. What were the stakes? The consequences?

The Cottonmouth compound was a repurposed government property, taken the way men like us took things. By force, by blood, and by refusing to fucking leave.

Before it belonged to us, it had been base camp for the Army personnel assigned to the local munitions plant. You could still feel that history in the bones of the place. The layout was what you'd expect. Every building had the same exact shape with the same dull gray siding. The windows were all the same, small and narrow, which I wasn't particularly fond of. It was designed to hold bodies, but not actual lives.

The compound was a collection of barracks. It had a mess hall, an admin building, and motor pool bays. There were several storage sheds with heavy doors and stronger locks. A few structures in the very back still had faded stencil numbers on the sides, like the Army thought they'd wander back in someday and pick up where they left off.

Now the place was ours.

The yard between the buildings was wide and

open. The gravel was packed down hard from decades of boots and tires before we ever walked in. Floodlights were positioned on tall posts along the perimeter, throwing hard white light across the compound leaving no shadows big enough to hide in. Even the darkness here was controlled, and it suited us just fine.

Tonight, we had the floodlights blazing.

Parked bikes were forming long, clean rows as they arrived. This wasn't a casual hangout or a social call. Men moved in and around the largest building, cigarettes lit and voices low. The air smelled like cold metal and pine from the tree line beyond the fence. In the distance, a generator hummed, making it sound like the compound itself had a pulse.

The main meeting bay sat inside what probably had been an armory. Its concrete floors and walls were thick enough to stop a bullet. The exposed beams high overhead carried sound well. The building had no stage or podium. Still, it was an ideal setting for Vendetta's first official meeting.

Cottonmouths packed in shoulder to shoulder with their cuts on and their eyes sharp. No weapons were drawn, but they were indeed there. I clocked a lot of them as they walked in. I saw holsters at hips, knives clipped inside boots, the occasional rifle propped within reach like a reminder that peace was a choice here, but not a guarantee.

Ripper, our new vice president, was already in position when I walked in. He stood near the front with his arms crossed over his chest. His focus was sharp as he watched each one of them file in. My good friend was the type of man you didn't have to announce to everyone. He carried his authority the way a hammer carries weight… really quiet until it hits.

Vendetta, the man we named president when we took the chapter back, stood a few feet ahead of him, waiting until everyone settled. He wasn't elevated or above everyone one. He sure as hell didn't strike a pose. My other best friend was just present.

That was the thing about Vendetta. He wore leadership like a second skin. It was like the title of president had been carved into him the same way that ring of scarred flesh had been carved into his throat. His cold gaze swept the room, slow and controlled. The low din of conversation died quickly without him having to ask.

I took my place slightly behind him and to the right, where an enforcer belonged. I stayed close enough to move fast if I needed to, but I was far enough back that nobody mistook who held the gavel.

The room finished settling. Boots stopped shifting, and arms were uncrossed. All eyes were on the front.

We'd gathered a lot of intel today. Still, I had to wonder how many of them knew why we were there or what was so urgent. That *Ned's* had been bought out by Sinister Skin, the cancer that almost caused our chapter to flatline. The fuckers were back, led by Rick Earle, who was strutting around our town like he owned it. Creep and Eagle had been spotted on our own property, like they had a fucking death wish.

And I'd seen five of our own sitting in the bar, drinking under Sinister Skin's roof, like their loyalty meant *nothing*.

Vendetta didn't start loud. "Here's how this goes," he said, his voice carrying clean through the room. "I'm not here to debate. I'm here to inform."

You could feel the air shift.

"*Ned's Sundown Lounge* has been bought outright by Sinister Skin," Vendetta announced.

The statement hit the room like a slug, only a few murmurs and a low curse disrupting the silence it left.

Vendetta scanned the room, and the sound died again. "Rick Earle was there tonight," he continued. "In *our* town. In a bar that used to belong to *this* chapter."

Ripper shifted his weight, taking a single step forward, and the men closest to him instinctively made space.

"We don't have proof yet," Vendetta said, "but if I were a betting man, I'd say that means the rot is all back with them. Trafficking. Guns. Drugs. Women. Kids. We've had this talk recently. Anyone who thinks that shit's acceptable under this patch is in the wrong fucking room."

That was when the faces changed in front of us. I saw anger. Disgust. *Fear.*

The old chapter had rotted the club from the inside by pretending Sinister Skin was "business." They'd convinced themselves that selling poison and bodies didn't count as betrayal as long as the cash came in. And there'd been plenty of it. It was the reason Eli and a handful of his loyalists had died when we took control of the chapter.

And now the corruption was trying to crawl back.

Ripper's voice came low and steady, built to carry in rooms like this. "This chapter does *not* sell women or children. And it sure as hell doesn't take money from people who fucking do." He looked across the crowd, slowly. "Anybody who's forgotten that can leave right fucking now."

No one moved. Yet. *Good.*

I stepped forward then. "I saw five of you at *Ned's* tonight."

And I started naming names, one by one. Each name sent a ripple of fear through the room. Heads turned and shoulders stiffened. One brother's jaw started grinding like he could chew his guilt into pure dust.

"I saw you drinking in *Ned's*." I made eye contact with each one of them, letting my words fall flat and cold. "After Sinister Skin bought it. After Rick Earle walked in." I paused. "You didn't leave."

That was the sin. Not being curious. Not being fucking stupid. *Choosing* to stay.

Vendetta didn't look at them yet. He let the silence do the heavy lifting for him. He allowed every man in the barracks to feel what it meant to have the president stand silent and consider what happened next.

When Ripper stepped forward again, his presence was unavoidable. "One chance," Ripper said. "If you took their money, if you made their deals, if you've been feeding them information… you speak up now."

The room held its breath for a long second. Finally, one of them cracked.

"I was just keeping an eye on 'em," Scutter said in a rough voice, scratching at his shaggy beard nervously. "I didn't --"

"You took money?" Ripper cut in.

The man swallowed hard. "Yeah."

Vendetta finally turned his head. If looks could kill, the man would be dead in a pool of his own blood.

"You're *done* here," Vendetta said.

Ripper moved first, marching to where Scutter stood at the center of the gathering. He grabbed the front of the man's cut and tore. The patch came off in a clean, vicious rip that echoed against the concrete walls. There was no ceremony in it. Just removal.

But patches weren't the only thing that made a Cottonmouth. Scutter knew it too. His eyes widened as I motioned to Grim and Butcher, standing off to the side of the gathering.

"No," Scutter said. "Wait --"

The fact that Vendetta's voice stayed even only made it worse. "The ink stays only if the loyalty does. Grab him."

Someone from the back fetched the torch. Scutter started thrashing wildly in their hold when he spotted it.

The hiss of fuel filled the bay, sharp and unmistakable. Every one of them knew what happened next. A few men looked away. Most didn't. You didn't look away from consequences, especially not in a club trying to survive.

Grim and Butcher dragged Scutter to the front of the room, then took him down. He fought, though his attempt was panicked and useless. I pulled my knife from my cut, sliced through his cut, through the back of his stained T-shirt. Scar came forward with the torch at the ready.

When the torch kissed his flesh, the scream echoed through the barracks like a demon's howl. The smell came next, the unforgettable stench of burning flesh and blistering ink. The serpent tattooed on Scutter's back warped and blackened, a traitor snake dying under the flame. Loyalty turned to scorched flesh.

When it was done, the guys hauled him up and marched him out to the gate. If he tried to walk back, he'd be killed. Scutter would live, but he was no longer one of us.

Vendetta didn't speak again until Scutter had been dragged away.

"That's the line," he said to the room in front of us. "Anyone crosses it again won't walk away." That's when he turned on the other four men I named, the others who had been at *Ned's* earlier. "If I find out any of you took money like that fuck did, you're dead."

Every Cottonmouth standing there understood exactly what kind of war we were in now. Not the kind fought with fists.

No, it was the kind of war fought with fire.

* * *

Jazz

My hands were still shaking when I pulled my phone from my purse in the small room Dylan had given me. The screen lit up immediately. I had four missed calls. All from Aunt Susan.

Taking a deep breath, I stared at her name for a long, silent minute, while my thumb hovered uselessly over the call button. She'd been calling while I was talking to Dylan, trying to wrap my head around everything that had happened tonight. She was probably worried sick.

As soon as I called her, this all became real. No more processing or breathing room. If I didn't call her, if I ignored those missed calls and stayed silent, I wasn't the strong woman she'd raised me to be.

I took a deep breath, and I tapped her name with my finger. She answered on the second ring.

"Jazz?" Her voice was already tight. "Where are you? Ned called and I --"

"I'm okay," I said too quickly. "I'm safe."

There was a pause on the line. I knew my aunt

well enough to know it wasn't relief. I should have thought about calling her before now. Of course, Ned called her when I left the way I did. With so many girls going missing lately in our town, including Claire, Ned didn't want to be implicated. While I was talking to Dylan here at the compound over a beer, she must have been losing her mind. My sister had been missing for nearly three weeks, and now she had no idea where I was or what could have happened to me.

"Where are you?" Susan asked again.

I swallowed. "Not at work anymore."

Another pause. Longer this time.

"Jasmine." She only used my full name when she was scared or angry. And right now, she was clearly both. "You don't leave work without telling me. Especially not *now*."

"I know," I said. "I didn't plan to. It just... happened."

"What do you mean it just *happened*?" Susan demanded. "Ned said there was an incident and you left. What incident? Are you okay? Were you hurt?"

I hesitated.

"I'm okay. And I'm not hurt. I swear."

Her breath came out sharp. "Then why aren't you *here*? Why didn't you come home?"

My stomach dropped. "Susan --"

"Does this have anything to do with those bikers?" she asked fearfully. "The Cottonmouths? They crawl all over that bar. Did they have something to do with this?"

"Please, just --"

"I told you to stay away from them." Fear bled into Susan's words now. "I told you what they did. I told you what your father --"

"I remember," I said, my voice cracking. "I

remember all of it. But please… please, just listen to me for one minute."

It was silent then.

"Okay."

"I'm with people who think… they can help us find Claire," I said. "People who know things the police don't. Or won't say."

At my sister's name, I heard her small gasp.

"That's a lie, honey. Whoever they are, if they *really* knew something, they would've gone to the police. They would have done the right thing, and --"

"You don't *know* that," I said, unable to keep the tears out of my voice. "And neither do I. But we're running out of time. And I couldn't keep doing nothing."

"You don't find one missing girl by risking another," Susan snapped. "You can't trade yourself for her."

"I'm not." And this time I meant it. "I promise. I'm not in danger. I just… I need a little time."

Aunt Susan didn't answer right away. I could hear her breathing unevenly, like she was pacing the kitchen the way she always did when she was trying not to panic.

"Are you telling me *not* to call the police?" she asked finally.

My chest tightened. This was the moment. It felt like my heart was cracking down the middle. While I liked Dylan, how did I know the Cottonmouths could help at all? What if they were lying to me? What if they couldn't help? Or worse, what if I were in very real danger and I didn't know it yet? What if Susan was about to lose both of her nieces?

Either way, I didn't have it in me to break her heart worse than it already was.

"Yes," I said. "For now. If you call them, it could make things worse. For Claire."

I heard the sound of her sitting down. Her deep sigh whispered through the phone.

"Do I know these people?" she asked.

Yes. But I couldn't do that to her. And technically, she didn't know Vendetta, Shade, or Dylan. It wasn't a total lie.

"No."

"You're asking me to trust people I don't know with your safety?" she asked.

"I wouldn't ask if I had any other choice."

Another long silence.

"You call me tomorrow," she said, her tone more acquiescent than defeat.

"Yes, I will."

"Not a text. A *call*."

"I will," I told her.

"And if I don't hear from you, if *you* disappear…" Her voice broke a little. "I don't care what you say. I will go to the police. I will go to the news stations. I will go to anyone who will listen."

"I understand." And I did.

"Do you?" Susan asked softly. "I already lost your mother. We have no idea if Claire is out there still or… I will *not* lose you too."

Tears stung the backs of my eyes. The last thing I wanted to do was to inflict any more pain on the woman who'd pretty much raised me and Claire, who had been everything to us.

"I'm still here." I hoped on my soul that it was the truth. "I'm not going anywhere."

She exhaled slowly, but I could hear the tears coming. "All right. Tomorrow."

"Tomorrow," I echoed.

"Jazz?" she added before hanging up.

"Yes?"

"I don't like this," she said. "I don't like it at all."

"I know."

"I love you," she said.

"I love you too."

The line went dead. I lowered the phone into my lap and stared at the wall, my heartbeat thundering in my ears.

Tomorrow.

Now, it was a deadline.

But what was I even doing? I was sitting here in the middle of a biker compound with concrete and floodlights and men with patches, with everything stripped down to raw truth. Nothing was dressed up or promised.

And I knew one thing with terrifying clarity. They hadn't touched me so far or lied to me that I was aware of. They hadn't taken my voice or my phone. What they had done was remove me from a bar where Rick Earle just might have been deciding what to do with me next. Shade said they were keeping me alive. I was willing to go on a little faith here, especially after talking to Dylan.

Maybe the men who brought me here *could* help find my sister.

* * *

Shade

Most of the chapter had already cleared out, those who didn't live here. The sound of boots across concrete faded as engines started in the yard. The stench of burnt flesh still lingered in the air.

The ones who remained were the ones who mattered. Vendetta stood near the table in the side office with his hands braced against the scarred wood. Ripper leaned back against a support beam with his arms crossed and a hard look in his eyes. Grim and Butcher hovered nearby. Both were ideal for quiet muscle, and both were sharp in different ways. Grim watched everything while Butcher seemed to enjoy what came next a little too much. Cain stood a little apart from the others, quiet as always, but he was dependable. Riot and Crowe lingered near the door, both watching the room the way men do when they're ready for trouble.

And there was me.

"The other four," Vendetta said. "The ones we saw at *Ned's* tonight? We're not done talking about them."

Ripper snorted. "No shit."

I nodded once. "They were still there even after Earle marched his happy ass out onto the floor."

Grim frowned. "Stupidity or loyalty?"

"Neither," I said. "It was comfort."

That got their attention.

"Comfort?" Butcher echoed, shooting me a look.

"They didn't look surprised to see Earle," I went on. "Hell, none of them reacted when *we* walked in. From where I was standing, the bar felt pretty fucking normal to them."

Ripper pushed off the beam. "Meaning?"

"Meaning they didn't think they were doing anything wrong," I clarified. "Which makes it even worse."

Vendetta exhaled slowly. "Who breaks first?"

"One of them," I said. "Not all."

Grim tilted his head. "You sure?"

"Yeah," I said. "Four stayed quiet tonight because they were watching the fifth. That's not solidarity. That's fear."

Butcher grinned. "I can work with that."

Ripper shot him a look. "You'll wait."

Butcher's grin didn't fade. "I always do."

We needed to keep Butcher back for a little while longer.

Vendetta straightened. "We don't burn them all. Not yet."

"No," I agreed. "We pull them apart."

Grim nodded immediately, already on the same page. "Separate rides. Separate rooms."

He meant logistics first. First, we'd strip away the comfort of familiarity. Isolation. No riding in pairs. No assignments together where they could line up their stories or bolster each other's nerves.

Ripper picked it up without missing a beat. "And separate stories."

I glanced at him, then back at the others. "You get four men telling the same lie, it holds. You isolate them, make them think they're the only one talking?" I shook my head. "The cracks start to show."

Grim leaned forward. "Especially if one of them thinks the others already sold him out."

"Exactly," I said. "We don't even need to accuse or threaten any of them. We'll let silence do the work for us."

Butcher grunted, unimpressed. "And if silence doesn't?"

"Oh, it will," I assured him. "Not one of them stayed quiet out of loyalty. You understand?"

Vendetta stood with his arms folded, letting it play out. "Walk me through it."

"We move them off their routines," I said. "Different shifts. Different errands. No chance to compare notes. We feed each one a slightly different version of what we 'know.'"

Grim smiled thinly. "See which one tries to correct the record."

"Or panics," Ripper added. "Or runs."

Vendetta nodded. "Right. No one moves until we're sure."

"Agreed," I said. "Right now, information's worth more than blood."

The room settled into the quiet that only comes when a plan locks into place.

I glanced at Vendetta. "We start with the other four at the bar tonight."

Vendetta nodded. "I agree."

"Poppy knows about Creep and Eagle." My gut told me he did. "And he knows more than he's said."

I thought of Jazz who was safe with Dylan. Of the way Rick Earle had looked at her tonight, and how close she'd been to becoming inventory.

"The longer Sinister Skin breathes in our town," I said, "the more girls disappear."

Vendetta's voice hardened. "Then we don't give them any more time."

Grim pushed off the wall. "I'll have eyes on the four by morning."

Ripper nodded. "I'll lock down the yard."

Butcher smiled. "And I'll stay ready to do what I do best."

Vendetta nodded, satisfied. "Meeting's done."

Grim peeled off first, pulling his phone from his pocket. His mind was already shifting to routes and schedules. Butcher lingered a second longer, grinning like he might get dessert later, before following Grim and the rest out into the yard.

Vendetta, Ripper, and I stepped out of the meeting bay into the open compound, floodlights still cutting the night into clean, controlled slices. The barracks loomed ahead of us as we headed toward the one sitting closest to the fence line.

Someone had stenciled a name over the door years ago in block letters that hadn't quite faded: MISSION CONTROL.

Fitting.

Ripper cracked his neck as we walked. "This is going to get bad, huh?"

Vendetta didn't look at him. "Yeah."

"The rot didn't leave," Ripper said. "It just fucking waited."

I stayed quiet. My head was already elsewhere, to the pretty thing we took from under Earle's nose tonight. And she was waiting with Dylan for me.

Jazz.

Vendetta slowed as we hit the steps, then stopped completely when he saw Dylan coming toward us from the side entrance. She looked calm enough, focused. I knew whatever she came to talk to us about had to do with the girl.

"Ripper," Vendetta said without turning. "Give us a minute."

Ripper glanced between us, then nodded once and kept going inside.

Dylan didn't waste any time. She stopped right in front of me, her blue eyes sharp. "I talked to her."

I didn't say anything. Just listened.

"She's holding it together," Dylan continued. "Barely."

Vendetta leaned against the railing, while he crossed his arms.

"She's got a sister named Claire," Dylan said. "The girl has been missing for almost three weeks. She just graduated from high school. Apparently, Jazz thought she might hear something at *Ned's*, so she took a job there."

So *that* was it. Otherwise, a girl like her in a place like *Ned's* was nothing more than a suicide mission. If we hadn't cut her off, it might have been exactly that. Still, it gave me insight into the young woman I picked out for myself. It told me she wasn't stupidly curious. Just desperate. And desperation got girls killed in Oak Grove these days.

"She's looking for answers," Dylan went on.

It settled something in my chest.

"What about the aunt she mentioned?" Vendetta asked.

"Well, the aunt knows something's wrong." Dylan's focus shifted back to me. "She doesn't know where Jazz is, just that she's safe. Jazz promised to call tomorrow."

Tomorrow, huh?

Dylan studied my face carefully. "The girl's scared, Shade. She's trying not to show it, but she is."

"I'm aware," I said.

"It doesn't help that she's already afraid of us," Dylan pressed. "Well, the Cottonmouths."

That got my attention.

"Her dad owed money," Dylan said. "Back when she was a kid. One of ours came looking for it. He put a knife to her face and threatened her when her father couldn't pay."

The name came next.

"Baby Face," Dylan said, like the name was distasteful. And it was. Eli's sadistic asshole son, like his father, was thankfully deceased.

It felt like an icy weight on my chest. I kept my expression flat, but it wasn't without effort. I remembered Baby Face, and the pathetic kind of man he was. Eli had only kept him around because fear was useful currency back then.

"I caught her up on everything," Dylan went on. "I told her Eli killed him, and Eli was dead. But she really doesn't know the difference between the men he protected and the men who came after."

No. She wouldn't. To Jazz, a patch was a patch.

I exhaled slowly through my nose.

"So yeah," Dylan finished. "She's sitting in the middle of a place that represents the worst moment of her childhood, and her sister is still missing. But... she's still standing."

And that mattered.

Dylan's brows pulled together. "I'm serious, Shade. Take it easy on her."

I finally looked at Dylan. "She's not weak," I told her. "She's just learned the wrong lesson from the wrong men."

"And what lesson is that?" Dylan asked, a hand on her hip now in challenge.

I didn't miss the way Vendetta smirked next to her.

"Fear is permanent," I explained. "Safety is temporary."

Dylan searched my face, and she shook her head. "You always treat your potential old ladies like this?"

"Who said anything about an old lady?" I asked.

She wasn't backing down. "I saw how you looked at her."

Vendetta leaned against the railing beside us. "He's never taken one."

It earned a quiet huff of laughter from Dylan, but I heard concern underneath it. "Then don't make *her* pay for that."

I met Dylan's stare. "I won't."

Whatever Baby Face had done to her as a child, whatever Eli had allowed during his time, was finished. Jazz wasn't standing in enemy territory anymore. She was standing in *mine*. And nothing wearing my patch was ever going to make her afraid again.

Dylan watched me for another minute, then nodded. "She's in ten, next to you. I told her she could stay there."

No, she *wasn't* staying there, but I nodded just the same. Dylan turned and headed back inside. Vendetta pushed off the railing and fell into step beside me as we climbed the stairs. "You believe her?"

I met his look squarely. "Yeah, I do."

"Good," he said. "Because if the sister disappeared because of Sinister Skin…"

If that were true, my girl's sister wasn't a missing-girl problem anymore. She'd be collateral in the war we only thought we'd ended.

We reached the door to Mission Control, and for the first time tonight, I realized something important. Jazz hadn't accidentally wandered into danger. She'd walked straight into it alone. Now I was going to finish what she started.

Chapter Four

Jazz

When I heard the knock on the door to the room Dylan had given me, I somehow knew it was Shade. The door opened quietly, but the air in the room shifted the second he stepped inside it. I looked up from where I sat at the edge of the bed, and my heart started racing.

Shade filled the doorway with his black T-shirt stretched across his broad shoulders, his cut unzipped, and dark ink climbing his muscular arms. The dark gold locks of his hair were smoothed back from his face, and his cool green eyes were sharp and unreadable. He surveyed the room around me, like he was taking stock and finding it lacking. Did he find me lacking too?

"You getting settled in?" he asked like the situation was nothing new.

I bristled instantly. "Why would I need to settle in?" I asked. "I was hoping I wouldn't be here long."

His focus shifted to my purse on the bed, then back to me. "You got what you need?"

It was like I hadn't spoken. "Yes," I said stiffly. "For now."

With a satisfied nod, Shade stepped fully into the room and shut the door behind him. The sound of the latch clicking into place sent a spike of awareness straight through my chest. The guy was twice my size and intimidating without trying. The fact that he was drop-dread fucking gorgeous didn't make it better.

"This is *not* where you're sleeping," he said without preamble.

I just stared at him. "Excuse me?"

"You're sleeping in *my* room." His words landed

heavy and final.

"And where are *you* sleeping?" I asked.

"Same bed as you," he replied.

I didn't miss the challenge there. My spine straightened, the temporary calm from my talk with Dylan earlier faltering. "No, you're *not*."

"Yes, I am," Shade insisted.

I stood up, my breath fast and shallow. "You don't get to decide that," I told him, though it sounded a lot more forceful in my head.

"I already did."

My anger flared. "You can't just --"

"I can," he interrupted, stepping closer. So close that I had to look up to keep eye contact. "Some of the older members of this club still have keys to rooms in these buildings and some of them don't belong here anymore. Right now, I don't know who. But we'll be sorting it out here very soon."

My mouth opened, then shut as I listened.

"My room has one door," he continued. "It has a new lock. Vendetta and I are the only ones with keys to it. And if someone still tries to come through it, I'm already between you and them."

"That doesn't make this okay," I said, hating the way my voice wavered despite my best efforts to sound calm.

"I didn't say it would," he replied. "But it will keep you alive."

"Then I'll sleep in your room," I said quickly. "You can take this one."

Shade didn't pause. "No."

"Why not?" I wasn't ready to give up yet. "Why can't we put a new lock on the door to *this* room? You could be the only one with a key."

"If someone comes through that door," he said,

"they're coming for *you*. I can't protect you from another room."

His words hit harder than I expected.

"I need to wake up between you and the problem," Shade continued. "Not through another locked door. Not half a second too late."

I had no answer to that. And the intensity of his look didn't let up.

"Same room," he said. "That's how this works."

And just like that, the compromise I'd offered dissolved into something uncomfortably final. I hated how much sense it made.

"And the bed?" I asked tightly. "That part of the plan too?"

"Yes." His cool, unaffected stare stayed on me.

Heat crept up my neck. "You think I'm just going to, what, crawl into bed with you and pretend this is normal?"

"I don't have expectations right now," he said. "If you're offering, we can talk."

"What?" That one word sounded so quick and nervous as it came from my lips. I was picturing that, a night in his bed. I didn't care for the way parts of my body lit up thinking about it.

"Or you can sleep," he continued. "You look like you haven't had any in a while."

Yeah, I knew I looked like hammered shit. He was right. I wanted to point out that he wouldn't have slept either if someone he loved was missing. But arguing with the man seemed pointless so I dropped it for now.

"You don't touch me." I crossed my arms, thinking there wasn't a lot I could do if he decided he wanted to.

He didn't respond to that. "Now," he insisted.

"Your phone."

He can't be serious. "No."

Shade held out his hand.

"I'm not giving you my phone," I said, backing up half a step. "That's not negotiable. I need to call my aunt tomorrow. I promised."

"You can call her tomorrow," he said. "On speaker."

The room went very still.

I stared at him, reeling not just from his words, but from the difference between this and the conversation I'd just had with Dylan.

She'd been patient and careful with me. She explained how things went in this terrifying place, the home base of a group of men I'd been scared of most of my life. Dylan had given me space to breathe and made me feel like I still had a say in what happened next.

The man who stood in front of me wasn't explaining anything, nor did he ask what I wanted. Shade laid out facts and expected the world to arrange itself around them. And the worst part was that I could see the logic under it. It was cold and brutal, and impossible to argue with. Still, it made the anger in my chest burn hotter.

"You don't get to listen to my conversations," I told him, clinging to the one line I can still draw.

"I don't *want* to," he replied. "But I need to. For everyone's safety I need to know exactly what's being said."

"You're pretty much demanding I trust you," I said, not hiding my frustration.

"I don't need to demand anything," he said, his eyes narrowing. "I'm just telling you how things will go. I'm keeping you safe."

I understood that. I just hated the heavy-handed way he was going about it.

"What if I say no?" I asked. I had to try.

Shade studied me for a long moment, assessing me. "If you say no, you're *still* sleeping in my bed," he said. "And I'm still taking your phone."

The air around me felt thin, and my chest tightened. I didn't want to give this man my phone. *What if he didn't give it back to me? What if he decided I was not going to call my aunt tomorrow? What if she called the cops*? Turning back to the bed, I pulled my phone from my purse. I took my time turning back to him, then slapped it into his palm. "You're unbelievable."

He closed his fingers around it. "But you're still breathing."

I turned away before he saw how close I was to angry tears. Maybe the Cottonmouths *were* protecting me. But he didn't have to be a complete ass about it.

"Get your things," he said. "We're moving to my room. Now."

I grabbed my purse and followed him out of Room Ten and into the room next door without another word. His room was much larger -- and darker, with just one window. A king-sized bed dominated the space, and everything was clean and orderly, like some military officer still lived there. There were no photos or decorations of any kind, and there wasn't a speck of dust on anything.

As I watched, Shade set my phone on the bedside table, placing his keys beside it. Next to those he placed a wicked looking knife he pulled from his cut, then a handgun he drew from the holster on his hip. "You can sleep on that side," he said, pointing to the other side of the bed. "The door stays locked. Bathroom's there. If you need something, you wake me. I'll go ahead and warn you now, I'm a pretty light sleeper."

"And if I don't want to?" I asked, standing at the foot of that massive bed like I was going to do something about it.

There was no softness in his green eyes. But a corner of his mouth curved up into the slightest smirk.

I stood there with my arms wrapped around myself, my pulse loud in my ears. The entire situation wasn't my idea of safety. My aunt would be horrified if she knew I was sleeping in a biker's bed with him to keep safe tonight, much less in the bed of a Cottonmouth.

But Shade was solid and unyielding. I certainly wouldn't mess with him. He stood by the bed, shrugging out of his cut before he tugged it free and draped it over the chair by the window. Then he grabbed the hem of his T-shirt and pulled it up and off in one smooth motion.

I looked before I could stop myself. What red-blooded girl wouldn't?

Ink covered his muscular torso, layered and deliberate. Black and green lines wrapped around thick muscle and old scars, some jagged and others faded with time. Marks of violence somehow always survived. His body looked like a record of every fight he had ever walked into and back out of.

When Shade turned, the breath left my lungs. The Cottonmouth from the club's patch dominated his back. It was huge and coiled with its fangs bared, the serpent's body spanning shoulder to shoulder in intricate detail. Its scales followed the lines of his wide, powerful frame like it had always belonged there. But, the ink on him wasn't merely decorative. It was a declaration of territory, of ownership burned into his skin.

That's when it occurred to me. He wasn't a man wearing a patch. Shade *was* the patch.

He caught me staring, eyeing me with quiet awareness. It was almost like he expected it and knew exactly what effect that image had on me.

"Eyes up," he said.

My focus snapped back to his face, and I felt heat creeping into my face.

Shade was a man dangerous in ways I could barely imagine. And as much as I hated admitting it, even to myself, lying in that bed with the man who had decided nothing was getting past him to reach me felt terrifying. To a lesser extent, there was excitement and admiration I wasn't willing to admit.

I walked around to the other side of the bed before slowly sitting on the edge of the mattress. At least there was a bathroom in the room. I wouldn't have to ask permission when I needed to go. And my side of the bed was closest to the bathroom, so I was thankful for small favors. I always carried a small toothbrush and a little makeup in my purse.

I pulled off my shoes then went to the bathroom to get ready for bed.

Shade had turned off the light by the time I'd returned, and I saw him stretched out on the other side of the bed from the compound lights filtering through the window. His back was to me and his breathing was slow. I hoped he was asleep already. His presence felt like a wall of heat and restraint.

I pulled the covers back and stretched out close to the edge on my side of the mattress. Just as I thought maybe I could doze off, his voice startled me awake.

"Remember what I said," he said into the darkness.

Staring at the ceiling, every nerve was awake, and anger tangled with the safety I didn't want to need. Beneath it all, somewhere in the quiet, I realized something that scared me more than any rule he had laid down so far.

I wasn't trying to get away anymore.

* * *

I woke up warm the next morning with the steady sound of a heartbeat beneath my ear. In those first few moments before awareness seeped in, it didn't occur to me to mind. It felt nice.

It was still dark, and the bedroom was wrapped in that early morning silence before dawn. For one hazy, dangerous second, I stayed still. I laid there, tucked against something solid and alive, breathing in the faint scent of soap and leather.

Awareness set in. Shade's arm was heavy around me. His hold wasn't tight, but it was oddly familiar. My cheek was pressed to his chest, my leg thrown halfway over his muscular thigh, and my fingers were curled against his bare skin like I'd done it a hundred times before.

I froze. Embarrassment didn't begin to cover my dawning emotions.

His chest rose and fell with his breath, the slow, steady thump of his heart beneath my ear. I felt his heat, his sheer size, anchoring me in place. At some point in the night, I must have shifted over to his side and made myself comfortable. I'd taken advantage of the man's warmth without permission or pride.

And he'd let me. Worse, he apparently had made no effort to move away.

My first instinct was to scramble back, put distance between us, and pretend with everything in me that this didn't happen. My second was to lie there and act like I was still asleep. Both courses of action feel pretty humiliating.

I stayed still, held my breath, and listened.

Shade was awake. I'm not sure how I knew that, but I did. His arm tightened just enough, a reminder. *You're here. I know it.*

I closed my eyes and felt my cheeks burning in the darkness. Yeah, I was painfully aware of how safe I felt where I was and how much that idea terrified me. This wasn't how I was supposed to wake up. It wasn't how I *wanted* to wake up. And yet, there I was, draped over the man who decided I wasn't leaving his sight.

I laid there for one more second, pretending I was still asleep, like that would magically undo the fact that I was snuggling with a man I met twelve hours ago. His arm stayed around me, heavy and warm. It felt like a boundary and a cage all at once.

His voice came out of the dark, low and calm, like he'd been awake the entire time. "You done playing dead?"

My eyes popped open. "I wasn't playing --"

"*Mmm.*" He shifted slightly, and the movement pulled me closer before he let me go again. Oh, it wasn't an accident. "You breathe different when you're awake."

I wondered what shade of red I was in that moment, and sighed. "Congratulations. You can make out breathing patterns."

A quiet sound rumbled in his chest. It could have been a laugh.

I tried to scoot back, to reclaim my space and dignity at the same time. The second I moved, his hand flattened against my waist. His touch wasn't rough, but it wasn't gentle either.

"Don't," Shade said.

I froze. "Excuse me?"

"Stay." One word. No explanation.

I blew out a frustrated exhale. "You can't just tell me --"

"I can," he cut in. "And you're going to listen. Last night proved you don't know how to keep yourself alive in my world."

My chest flashed hot with anger. "I've kept myself alive for years before you showed up."

"And then you walked into *Ned's*," he said, like that settled it.

I glared at the ceiling because looking at him felt like losing ground. "I walked into my job."

"You walked into a trap," he corrected.

I finally turned my head to look at him. His other arm was under his pillow, his hair was a mess of dark gold curls, and his eyes were sharp in the dim light, like sleep hadn't touched him at all. His focus moved over my face, my mouth. I swallowed then and he tracked that movement too.

I wanted to punch him even as I ignored the stupid butterflies dancing in my stomach.

"Are you always this charming in the morning?" I asked. If I didn't mouth off, I was afraid I'd actually say something honest.

His hand slid slowly up my side until his thumb brushed just under my ribs. The movement was deliberate, almost possessive.

"I'm always like this," he said. "You're the one who crawled over *me*."

"I did not." Even though I knew good and damn well he might be right. I had no idea.

Shade lifted a brow. In the dark, it looked like arrogance made flesh. "Your leg," he said. "Your arm. Your face on my chest."

I wanted the mattress to swallow me whole.

"I was cold," I snapped. It's worth a try. There *was* just a thin blanket draped over the two of us.

"No, you weren't."

My eyes narrowed. "Oh? Will you be monitoring my temperature now too?"

His mouth curved. Not a smile. More like the hint of one, like he found me mildly entertaining.

"It could be that you were scared," he said. "Maybe you trusted my body before you trusted my words."

The simple truth in his words was like solid punch through my defenses. The man never seemed at a loss for an explanation.

I scooted back and pushed up on an elbow, trying again to put distance between us. This time he let me, but his assessing look followed like a hand I couldn't shake off. "What time is it?" I demanded.

"Early."

"That's not an answer."

He got comfortable, like he had all the time in the world. "It's enough of one."

I huffed. "You're impossible."

"And you're mouthy," he replied.

I opened my mouth, ready to tell him exactly where he could shove that observation.

"But you're my type," he added, his voice rough with sleep and something else. "So I'll allow it."

Of all the things I was guessing he would say, that wasn't one of them. I froze for a minute, like my brain was buffering.

"Wow," I said, deadpan. "Thank you, Your Highness. I was a little worried I'd be executed at dawn for insubordination."

A corner of his mouth curved up. Just the faintest

sign he'd heard me.

"Keep talking like that," he murmured, "and I might change my mind."

"About what?" I shot back, even though my pulse had kicked up like I'd just run a mile. "Allowing me to exist?"

He shifted closer, a slow, deliberate motion. The heat of him pressed into my side. It wasn't enough to trap me, but it *was* enough to remind me whose bed I was in. Whose rules I was expected to follow.

"About letting you keep your distance," he said.

My heart sped up at his words, and I hated my body for noticing. For reacting like his words were a touch instead of a warning here. I sat up straighter, yanking the blanket up like it could cover my lost dignity. I'd slept in my clothes so not much besides my cleavage was revealed. "You're not funny."

"I'm not trying to be."

His gaze held mine in the dim light like he was making a point he expected me to understand without spelling it out. I forced my chin up. "You keep saying things like *you'll allow it* like I'm a dog you brought home."

"You're not a dog."

"Then stop talking to me like --"

"You're in *my* bed," he said, calm as a blade. "In my compound. With men outside these walls who would've used you until you stopped being useful."

My mouth snapped shut.

He didn't raise his voice. There was no need.

"That doesn't mean you get to --"

"It means I do," he said, and his hand slid to my hip, heavy and possessive. For one terrifying second, he held me in place. "And it means you can keep that mouth, because I like it… but don't forget who's keeping you breathing."

My heart hammered away in my chest now. Anger, fear, and heat all tangled together until I wasn't aware of anything else. I shoved his hand away, mostly because I needed to prove I still could. "I'm not thanking you."

He leaned back, unbothered. "Good. Gratitude makes women stupid."

I stared at him like he'd grown a second head. "That's the dumbest thing I've ever heard."

It didn't faze him in the slightest. "It's true."

"No," I snapped. "It's what men tell themselves when they want women quiet."

That got a reaction. It wasn't anger or amusement. No, it was a cold, assessing focus where he had decided a conversation is over and a decision has been made. He sat up slowly, the mattress dipped with his weight. "Listen to me."

My spine was rigid. "I don't --"

"You do," he cut in, his voice low and impatient. "I'm only going to say this once." The air in the room felt tighter, like it was holding its breath with me. "You're going to be my next old lady."

For a second, I honestly thought I'd misheard him. When I realized I hadn't, I barked out a laugh. "Oh my God."

Shade didn't move. Hell, he didn't even look offended. "I'm serious," he said. "I'm just letting you know."

"You can't just..." I gestured at him, at the bed, at the entire absurd situation. "You can't just *claim* me like I'm property. I'm not a puppy you found on the side of the road."

His hand landed on my thigh, heavy enough to stop my leg from bouncing. He wasn't squeezing me or stroking. Just pinning me in place. "I didn't claim you," he said. "Sinister Skin did. The moment Earle looked at you like you were for sale."

A chill rolled down my spine at how calmly he said it.

"I'm fixing that."

I blew out a breath. "By making me yours."

"Yes."

The bluntness of it stole my words.

He leaned in, his voice dropping into something rougher and darker. "You want to survive Oak Grove, you need a shield. You want to find your sister, you need power behind you. You can hate me all you want, sweetheart, but you're not walking out of this alone."

I went still. "My sister?" I repeated, the word scraping out of me. "How…" I pulled back enough to look at him. "How do you know about Claire?"

He wasn't offering apologies.

"Dylan," I said. It came out more as an accusation than question. I was quick to add, "I'm not mad at her. I just… *I* didn't tell you."

"You told my house," Shade said.

"What the hell does that mean?"

"It means you walked in here wearing the problem," he replied. "It was all over your face. And Dylan's the only one I trust to sit with you when I'm not there. So yeah, she told me."

It still hit me wrong. "It wasn't her story to tell."

"It *was,*" he corrected me. "Your sister isn't just *your* business. She's leverage. She's why you were at *Ned's*. She's why you'll do something reckless the second you think it will save her."

I couldn't find a clean lie fast enough. He'd already thought it through.

Shade's eyes narrowed slightly, like he'd caught

the attempt anyway.

"I'm not keeping secrets from you," I snapped, even though we both knew that wasn't the point.

He tilted his head. "You're not capable of secrets right now. You're running on pure grief and adrenaline."

The bastard had some nerve. "Don't talk like you know me."

"I know enough," he said, and his hand slid up to the side of my neck. His touch was light and controlling. "I know you were about to get yourself used and killed to save your sister."

I jerked my chin up, refusing to capitulate. "And you're what? Planning to save me from myself?"

"I'm planning to find *her*," he said.

I didn't care for the flash of hope in my chest at his words. "This is really about you helping me find my sister, so I owe you, right?" I scoffed, forcing the words out like they didn't sting. "That's what this is. You want me to be indebted to you. And then I end up your old lady because I *owe* you."

For the first time, something flickered behind his green eyes. Something dark, dangerous, and not remotely patient. One second there was space between us, and the next his body covered mine, pushing me into the bed flat on my back. His fingers spread along my jaw like he was holding me still for his own sanity.

All I could see was him. His body was rock solid, pressing me into the mattress. *Gorgeous bastard.* I wasn't even trying to push him away.

"Wrong," he said.

I wasn't prepared for his kiss, to taste dark need on his lips. His kiss wasn't soft or careful. It hit me like a punch, all heat and control. I could feel something feral beneath the surface, like he'd been holding himself back out of sheer will. His mouth claimed mine with a certainty that stole the air from my lungs. Every sarcastic remark and argument were gone in the moment.

I didn't recognize the sound that escaped from me. It felt like surrender as much as protest, and it made him deepen the kiss. His thumb pressed under my chin, angling my face to where he wanted it. Being directed like that, owned, sent traitorous pulses of desire through every inch of me.

I hated it. And I wanted more. Without permission, my hands gripped his shoulders. He inhaled hard like he was at the very edge of his control. I knew if I gave him an inch, he'd take everything. And maybe I wasn't entirely against that.

But then he pulled back to look at me. My lips tingled, and my breath was uneven. I couldn't form words at that moment as I stared up at him.

Shade's gaze dropped to my mouth once, then lifted again, steady and satisfied. "I'm not doing any of this because I need you owing me," he said. "I'm doing it because I *want* you. And nobody else gets to."

I stared at him, my chest rising too fast, and my mind blank except for the echo of that kiss.

He released my face like it cost him something, rolled away, and swung his legs off the bed. In the low light, he looked carved out of shadow and ink. He was so calm, like he hadn't just knocked every thought out of my head.

"Stay," he said, already heading for the bathroom.

The word should have made me angry, but it didn't. I stayed there, trying to get myself back under control.

The bathroom door clicked shut behind him. A

moment later, the shower hissed to life.

And I lay there in his bed with my heart racing, my mouth still burning, and nothing, absolutely nothing, to say back. It was a rare experience for me.

* * *

Shade

Snow's name lit up my phone a few minutes after I'd left Jazz in my bed, after her mouth stopped moving and she stopped pretending she wasn't affected by me.

I stepped into the hallway outside my room, shut the door behind me, and answered on the third ring. I'd been hoping to hear from the vice president of the Hounds of Hell MC over in Mercy.

"Speak." I put him on speaker.

Snow's voice came through deep and low. No small talk, and no preamble. "You were right to call."

My grip tightened on the phone. "Don't tell me that unless you've got something."

"I've got something," he said. "I ran your location through every channel I've got: shell purchases, utility spikes, burner clusters, encrypted comms. And I believe Sinister Skin has a holding property outside Oak Grove."

Vendetta stood at the end of the hall, leaning against the rail like he'd been born there. Ripper walked in to join him, watching my face.

I lifted two fingers. *Hold.*

Snow kept going. "It's quiet on paper. Too quiet. But the power draw doesn't match. Water delivery doesn't match. And the comms? They spiked the same night your girl's sister vanished."

I sighed. "That proves a house. Not a name."

"I know," Snow said, and I could hear the click

of keys. He was still working while we talked. "I pulled missing persons photos from local feeds and compared them to a private drop folder one of their buyers uses. You know, with metadata trails, image hashes, the whole thing."

Ripper's posture changed, just a fraction.

Snow exhaled once. "Shade… I'm about ninety percent sure I found Claire."

Everything in me went cold and clear.

"Ninety isn't sure," Vendetta said in a low voice.

"Then make it sure." Snow didn't miss a beat. "You need confirmation from a human."

I looked at Vendetta. "A recruiter?"

He nodded once. "Already tracking."

Snow's tone sharpened. "And listen, this isn't street work. This is high-tier inventory. It looks like a prep pipeline. They hold girls before sale. They don't move them right away because they're conditioning them."

My hand flexed around the phone hard enough to creak the plastic.

"How long?" I asked.

There was a pause. Somehow, I knew it wasn't because he didn't know, but because he didn't like the answer.

"They don't sell them out of the holding site. It's a place for breaking them in. Looks like you've got less than a week until the transfer starts. Forty-eight hours from then, they start moving the girls," Snow said. "After that, you won't see them again."

"When's the transfer start?" Ripper asked.

"Based on what I know," Snow said, "Friday."

Last night.

Vendetta's expression was dead calm. "We confirm. Then we burn it the fuck down."

In my head, I pictured Jazz's face when she said her sister's name like it was the last clean thing she had left. I could see Rick Earle's eyes on her like he'd spotted a price tag. I put the phone back to my ear. "Send me everything," I told Snow. "Maps. Comms. photos. Routes in and out."

"Already on it," he said. "One more thing."

"What?"

"That property?" Snow's voice dropped. "It isn't just a holding site. Which means… there are girls like Claire, who are younger and innocent, and other girls and women too."

Good. If I'm going to war, I want a reason that doesn't end the second we got one girl back.

I ended the call and looked at Vendetta and Ripper. "Claire's alive," I said.

Vendetta nodded. "Then we bring her home."

"She's not alone."

"Figured as much. We're bringing them *all* home," Ripper said.

I stood in front of my door. Behind it, Jazz was trying to pretend she hadn't just been kissed into silence. This intel changed things. I needed to know where she was at all times. Once she heard the truth, she was going to do something desperate, like offer herself for her sister.

Over my dead fucking body. I started walking. "Get Grim," I said to Vendetta as I passed. "I want a word with the recruiter by noon."

Vendetta's voice followed me, calm as a verdict. "Done."

Ripper fell into step on my other side. "What do you want me doing?"

"Lock the yard down." I kept moving. "Nobody comes or goes without me or Vendetta knowing. If there are rats in here, I want them to feel the trap closing."

Ripper's smile was thin and mean. "Finally."

I stopped in the kitchen, looking out the window as the sun was lighting up the horizon.

Claire, Jazz's little sister, was alive. And now, she was on a clock.

And Sinister Skin had just made one final mistake.

They'd reminded me of what I was built for.

Chapter Five

Shade

I was already leaning against the railing when Ripper, Grim, and Butcher came strolling back through the gate. They hadn't wasted any time. It was just after ten. Ripper's gaze met mine and I could tell from that look they fucking had something.

"The lake checks out," Grim said. "You said the girl went missing the night of the festival, right? The beach was packed that night. Bonfires everywhere."

Butcher crossed his arms as Vendetta walked up behind me. "Rental hut girl remembered seeing them."

"Rental hut girl?" Vendetta chuckled. "Livia Minor's been all over you for damn near ten years, and you don't even know her name?"

Butcher shrugged. "Not my problem."

Grim picked up the story. "The two girls weren't renting anything, but Livia saw them on the beach earlier in the festival, then later around the restaurant."

"She notice who they were with?" I asked. "If they were drinking or smoking something?"

"She didn't mention anyone specifically," Grim went on. "But there's a bar in the restaurant and Livia told us one of the waitresses slips drinks to the kids. Said they hang out with her quite a bit."

I shot Vendetta a look.

"You get a name?" Vendetta asked.

Grim answered without hesitation. "Frannie."

That name wasn't familiar to me, but I couldn't remember the last time I'd gone to Hazel Island. "She's local," Grim continued. "Everyone knows her. Friendly type. Livia said she always knows where there's another place to party."

No one spoke for a beat. That last bit really

caught my attention.

"So another recruiter?" Ripper asked. "Not a grab?"

"That's what it smells like," Butcher replied.

Vendetta looked at me. "We move?"

I shook my head. "Not yet. She calls her aunt first. I want to know if anyone has said anything to the aunt now that both her nieces aren't where they're supposed to be."

"And Frannie?" Grim asked.

"After," I told him. "First I want to reach out to the aunt. And we need to find out if Jazz knows anything about Frannie."

Ripper nodded slowly. "You think she will?"

I shrugged.

Vendetta pushed off the railing. "Then we're agreed."

I turned toward the barracks. Jazz was having breakfast with Dylan, and she had no idea how close we were to the truth.

* * *

Jazz

Breakfast sat untouched between us for a couple of minutes. The toast was cooling, and curls of steam rose from the coffee. The scrambled eggs Dylan made us were fluffy and warm. But it was the kind of normal I couldn't step into right now. Not after everything that had happened to me in the last twenty-four hours.

Dylan wasn't pushing me, and I appreciated the kindness in her expression. But I still needed to know something. "I know you told them," I said it finally. My voice was a lot steadier than I felt. "About Claire."

Dylan didn't rush to explain. "Yes."

I waited for an apology or an explanation.

Somehow, I knew I wasn't going to get one.

Instead, she folded her hands on the table. "I wasn't trying to upset you, Jazz. I had a good reason for talking to them about this, and that's your sister. And if your sister's still alive, and I believe she might be, these men are the ones who can get her back."

Her words weren't defensive or dismissive. That was the problem. I didn't want to get my hopes up, but what if she was right? Still, I huffed a humorless laugh before I could stop myself. "Oh. Wait. The bikers actually *listen* to you?"

Dylan shot me a knowing look. "Vendetta does. He also listens to Shade," she said simply. "And Shade listens to me when it matters."

Somehow, that didn't make me feel better. "Okay. He doesn't seem to hear anything I say."

"Shade's like that," she added after a beat. "You get used to it."

The words settled uncomfortably in my chest. What if I didn't want to? What if I didn't want to adjust myself to a man who took up all the space in the room and expected the world to follow?

Besides, I wasn't going to be here long. Right?

Pressing my lips together, I stared down at my plate. But what if getting used to it meant Claire ended up being found? Being returned to us?

We ate breakfast in the quiet of the kitchen. It wasn't awkward but it wasn't completely easy either. Dylan moved comfortably around the space, like she was waiting. Not pushing, but… open.

I didn't know what to say.

After everything that had happened last night, I was a little overwhelmed. Anger, fear, hope, and gratitude all battled each other but I kept my mouth shut. I focused on breakfast for now.

Heavy footsteps echoed up the hallway before I could find a thought to put into words.

Shade and Vendetta walked in together, cuts on, and their expressions locked down tightly. Another man was with them. Ripper. I had no idea where he got that name, and I wasn't sure I wanted to. He was a little smaller than the other two, but it did nothing to make him less intimidating.

Ripper leaned against the doorframe with the same easy confidence as the other two. He stared at me for moment too long to be polite.

Three men, each posing a different kind of danger. And now the kitchen table where I was sitting didn't feel like a respite. It was the calm before the storm.

Shade's green-eyed stare locked with mine, steady and hard to read. Everything in me went still. I tried to push the memory of that kiss out of my head for now. "You ready to make that call?" he asked. "To your aunt?"

No lead-in or pressure. Just the question.

I nodded. "Yeah."

Pulling out a chair to my right, Shade sat close enough for me to feel the heat of his body. His presence was solid and grounding whether I wanted it to be or not. Vendetta moved to stand next to Dylan at the counter, wrapping a muscular arm around her shoulders. Ripper stayed near the doorway, silent and watchful.

Shade set my phone on the table between us. I reached for it, but he stopped me with a glance.

"Before you dial," he said, "you need to listen."

Did I really have a choice? "Okay."

"You tell her you're safe. You tell her you're with people who know Oak Grove and are helping you search in the right places." The intensity of his words held me captive. "You don't give names or locations. And you don't speculate."

I already knew this plan wasn't going to go well. "She's going to ask questions."

"I expect her to," Shade said. "You answer the ones you can without giving her something to act on."

I frowned at him. "Act on how?"

"Calling the police. Driving out here. Telling someone who shouldn't be involved." His voice stayed calm and even. "We're not shutting her out. We're just keeping her from knowing anything that could get her hurt."

The idea of anyone hurting my aunt stopped me cold. No, I didn't want to put her at risk if I could help it. "And if she asks where I am?" I pressed.

"Tell her you'll explain it all later," he replied. "And you *mean* it."

I glanced at Dylan. She gave me a small nod of reassurance.

Shade slid the phone closer to me. "Speaker."

I picked it up, my fingers shaking.

Before I tapped the call button, Shade added, "If she tells you something we don't know, you let her talk. Don't rush her."

After tapping the screen, I put the phone on the table between us. It rang once. Twice.

"Jazz?" Aunt Susan's voice came through, worry and relief heavy in her tone. "Thank God. Are you okay? Where have you been? Can you tell me?"

I swallowed hard and nodded, even though she couldn't see me. "I'm okay. I promise I'm safe."

Shade didn't move or speak. But his presence at my side was impossible to ignore.

"Are you sure?" Susan asked. "After Ned called

last night -- and the police --"

"I know," I said gently. "I didn't mean to scare you. I just... I needed to be sure before I said anything."

A pause. It was so quiet at the other end. "Do you know something?"

I blew out a breath and I hoped I was doing the right thing. "I think I know where to start asking questions now. About the lake. About that night."

"The festival?" she asked. "That's what I've been telling them. They said it looked like a runaway situation, Jazz. Two girls together, no sign of a struggle..."

My stomach clenched hard.

"The police didn't do anything," she continued, frustration bleeding into her tone now. "Not really. It's been three weeks tomorrow."

Shade's hand rested on the edge of the table. I stared at it, scrambling to think of what to say.

"I'm not giving up," I said with conviction in my tone. "And I'm not alone in this."

Another pause. "Who are you with, Jazz?"

I chose my words carefully. Just like Shade told me to.

"I'm with people who know this town," I said. "And who care what happens in it."

The silence stretched out painfully.

"This is our town too," she said, and I swore I could hear tears in her voice. "I've never lived anywhere else. And you're telling me you're with people who know it better than us?"

Shade glanced at me meaningfully. I could almost hear his thought here. *Stick to what I told you.*

"You're right," I told her. "But they're familiar with parts of it that..." I couldn't look at Shade at that moment. What if I said something wrong? What if I fucked this up? "They know parts of it we're not so familiar with."

I looked to Dylan, then Vendetta. I saw the approval in his face and I sighed quietly. My aunt did the same, a quiet whisper on her end. "All right. Then you tell me what you need."

Relief at her acceptance, or as much acceptance as she could give me, rushed over me. "I'll call you again soon," I promised. "I wanted to let you know I'm fine. I'm asking you to trust me."

It was quiet for a long moment. My aunt *did* trust me. But putting myself in her shoes, I couldn't imagine the fear she had to be experiencing. One niece was gone without a trace, the other niece out of her reach and asking for her trust blindly.

"I love you, Jazz."

"I love you too."

I ended the call and sat there for a second, my hands still visibly shaking.

Shade didn't say *good job*. Or *thank you*. He simply turned his body fully toward me. "Tell me what you know about that night at the lake," he said, in a low, focused tone.

And just like that, I understood. The call I'd made had been for my aunt. What came *next* was for the truth. Taking a deep breath, I steadied myself, my hands wrapped around the coffee mug Dylan had given me.

"Claire and Scarlett graduated at the end of May," I began. "Scarlett's going to Wake Forest in the fall and Claire's going to Tech, so they wanted to spend time together this summer while they still could." I hated that emotion had my voice shaking. "They've been going to the lake festival for the last couple of years. It wasn't anything out of the ordinary for them. They'd hang out, see people they knew."

None of them interrupted, and my nerves climbed in the silence.

"Scarlett drove them that night," I went on. "Her car is a little blue Volkswagen Beetle she bought used last summer. She has vanity plates, something like 'Cutie Pie,' all one word and the I's are ones. But the car's gone too."

I didn't miss the look exchanged between Vendetta and Ripper. Shade's expression didn't change at all, his focus still on me.

"People remember seeing them at the lake," I explained. "Everyone said they were laughing and talking, moving between groups." I sighed, gathering the strength I need to finish it. "No one… No one remembers them leaving the festival. And no one remembered seeing them after nine or ten. And that's not a surprise to anyone. Claire and Scarlett were never party girls. They'd do movie nights together and do homework. Hell, I don't think Claire has ever had a beer. But at some point, they left and they… they were gone."

"And after?" Shade asked.

"They never called," I said. "Neither of them. Their phones went dark that night and never came back on. No pings. No posts. Nothing." I shook my head. "The police said it looked like they ran off. Two girls together enjoying the summer. No sign of a struggle."

I let out a short, bitter laugh. "Susan never believed that. Neither do I. That's not who my sister or Scarlett are."

Shade leaned back slightly, his arms crossed over his chest. He still watched me like I might change my story if he blinked.

"Anyone stand out?" he asked. "Anyone talk to them more than once? Anyone they trusted?"

I thought back, really thinking this time about the information we got from the police. Not with panic, but with intention.

"The last person they were seen with was a woman," I explained. "She worked at the restaurant. Frannie, I think? Frannie Parker? Apparently, a lot of people know her. I remember Claire mentioning her once or twice." I shrugged helplessly. "Someone said they saw her in the restaurant around quarter to nine."

Shade didn't react. But the energy in the room shifted.

"That's all I have," I finished. "That's everything Susan and I have. It was an ordinary outing, nothing they hadn't done before."

Shade's green eyes were unreadable. Then he nodded. "Good."

The word dropped between us like a weight. I frowned at him. "Good?" My voice came out sharper than I intended. "How is any of that good?"

Shade didn't look away. He leaned forward instead, one forearm braced on the table, bringing his focus down to my level. "Because what you told me lines up."

"With what?" I asked.

"With patterns," he said. "And patterns don't lie."

I had no idea where he was going with this, but my stomach dropped.

He gestured once with his chin toward Ripper. "Two girls at a festival. No witnesses saw them leave. The car is gone. Their phones go dark the same night." His focus returned to me. "That's a clean exit."

"Whoever took them wasn't in a rush," Vendetta added. "They had time."

"And access," Ripper said. "Someone the girls didn't question."

Wait. *Oh my God.* "Frannie?"

Shade didn't confirm it, but he didn't deny it either. "Good," he said again, and this time I heard what he really meant. "Now we know we're not guessing. Your sister didn't disappear by accident, and we have a trail we can follow."

My hands curled into fists on my lap. "You're talking about this like it's some map."

"It is," Shade replied. "And you just filled in the last blank."

A cold chill slid down my spine. "You don't seem happy about it."

"Maps work both ways," he said. "And now we know exactly how they moved your sister... which means they were careful."

Vendetta's voice came low and steady. "Careful people don't get caught."

The room went very still. I forced myself to ask the next question. "What happens now?"

Shade stood, slow and deliberate, the scrape of his chair loud in the quiet kitchen. He glanced down at me with certainty in his eyes.

He reached for my phone, but not to take it. He turned it face down on the table, like he was drawing a line.

"You did exactly what I needed you to do," Shade continued. "You told me the truth, didn't hide anything." His focus sharpened on me. "Now we need to find your sister."

My breath caught. "How?"

"We'll deal with that." Shade's voice dropped,

rough and absolute. "You're staying here with Dylan."

I opened my mouth.

"This isn't up for debate," he added.

Vendetta nodded, and Ripper was already moving toward the door.

Shade held my gaze a second longer. "Dylan knows where you are at all times." He said it like a command. "Under no circumstances do you leave this compound."

I went from hope to frustration in roughly ten seconds. But before I could say another thing, the three of them were out the door.

Oh. Hell. No.

I shoved back from the table and went after them. The hallway blurred as I moved, anger giving my legs speed. I burst out of the building just in time to see them crossing the yard, sunlight flashing off chrome and leather like they'd already stepped into another world. One I was apparently *not* allowed in.

"Shade!" I called.

He kept walking. It just pissed me off more.

"Shade," I yelled again, louder now. This time there was no mistaking the edge in my voice. "You're not just --"

He stopped. Just like that.

Vendetta and Ripper kept going for two more steps before Vendetta clocked it and then nudged Ripper ahead with a look. Neither of them turned around.

Shade pivoted slowly, his green-eyed stare locking onto mine.

The yard went very quiet.

"You shouldn't be out here," he said.

I planted my feet anyway. "You don't get to decide that."

He took in my bare arms, the way my hands were shaking despite my best effort to still them, then lifted his focus back to my face. "I *do*," he said evenly. "When it's about keeping you breathing."

"It's *my* sister we're talking about," I snapped.

"That's exactly why you're staying put."

I took a step closer, lowering my voice because suddenly I was aware of eyes on us, of men pretending not to watch. "I want to go."

"No." His fingers wrapped around my upper arm, firm enough to get my attention but not enough to hurt me. With me in tow, he marched back to the administration building, like he had to know I was back in that building before he could leave.

Shade didn't stop at the threshold. He walked me down the hallway, back to his room. Once I was through the doorway, he slammed the door and pushed me back against it. Before I could say another thing, his hand moved from my arm to my throat, his fingers wrapping around it and flexing just enough to get my attention.

"You're going to stay here," he said, leaning in closer. "I need to know you're here, with Dylan knowing where you are, so I don't lose my fucking mind."

The last part he whispered against my lips, still holding my throat with one hand. I gasped as his other hand plucked the front of my jeans open and slid down into them, into my panties. But I didn't make a move to stop him as those rough fingers started exploring me. The wetness that'd been there since that kiss earlier only made it easier for him.

He claimed my lips with a scorching kiss as he pinned me to the door, his fingers toying with my pussy like it was his. And God help me, maybe it was.

The green-eyed devil knew how to kiss me stupid, to wipe everything from my brain but *him*. I rolled my hips, moving with him, wanting more of his touch.

Abruptly, he ended the kiss, glaring at me now. Pulling his hand from my jeans, he brought his fingers to his mouth and sucked them clean. His breath was as labored as mine.

"Stay. Fucking. Here."

I was still trying to pull myself together as he marched out of the room, slamming the door behind him.

* * *

Shade

The lake looked harmless in the daylight. A day at the beach started with a couple of moms and a small flock of little kids with them. One was glued to her phone, the other was slathering her kids with sunblock as they tried to evade her. I saw people in a few boats out on the water, some fishing. I spotted a couple of joggers moving along the trail like it was just another day and nothing bad ever happened. All traces of the festival that was here three weeks ago, the music, bonfires, and laughter, were all gone.

That was fine. I preferred things stripped down. No matter how fucking sunny it appeared right now, there was still a mystery to solve. And the path led from this sunny place to the deepest shadows in human hearts. I pulled off my sunglasses and cut the engine of my bike. Those fuckers were going to realize they knew *nothing* about dark hearts once we got hold of them.

I could still smell Jazz on my fingers as I tucked my sunglasses into the pocket of my cut. I was hard enough to hurt, but that just drove me. I'd take care of business here so I could get back to the compound and take care of Jazz.

We parked where our bikes were visible from the restaurant windows. We weren't doing any shady shit. Nah, we were just present. Vendetta didn't even kill his engine right away. He let it idle a minute, and the sound carried.

Ripper checked his watch. "Ten on the dot."

The back door opened a minute later. Frannie Parker stepped out with a cigarette in one hand, fumbling with the ties of her apron with the other. She looked like she hadn't fully woken up yet. The T-shirt she wore with the restaurant's logo on the front was clean but looked like she'd slept in it. Her mostly pink hair was pulled back in a messy knot that was already giving up. A few loose strands caught the morning light, and the dark roots of her real hair color made her look more tired.

She took a drag, exhaled, and squinted toward the lot like she expected nothing more than another long shift and a headache she'd learned to live with.

Vendetta shifted his weight beside me, keeping his movements slow and easy. Ripper was quiet as always, his gaze already locked on her hands and the way her shoulders hunched like she was carrying some unseen weight.

They knew who she was. Not personally, but enough that they'd seen her around. I didn't have that history, so she was new to me.

She looked like she was on the wrong side of thirty. She was soft in places that came from comfort, not work. Her arms were strong from hauling crates and trays. She had tired eyes that learned how to smile on command. Nothing about her screamed criminal, and she sure as shit didn't seem like a woman who ruined lives for money.

No, she looked like someone who made change fast and remembered regulars' orders. The pink hair, nose piercing, and ripped jeans seemed like an attempt to appear younger or maybe relate to a younger crowd.

Her hand shook a little as she took another drag. Enough to notice.

Alcohol didn't seem to fit. Booze left its marks with sloppier edges and a different kind of wear. No, this was quieter. A habit that helped her work doubles and smile at customers while her body begged for a fix she could manage on her breaks. Pills maybe. Opioid addiction was still a problem in our stretch of Virginia and had been since I was a kid.

Frannie blew out a plume of smoke like she was trying to expel a rough year. Whatever she was on was probably prescribed to her once. Easy to justify, easy to hide. And when the prescription ran out, she had to get it somewhere. Then habit became a leash for the wrong people.

Rick Earle and the Sinister Skin fucks he worked for *loved* people like that. It was easy because they screamed when you tightened the chain.

She took one more drag and finally looked up. She froze.

She glanced first at Vendetta, then recognition had her waking up really fucking quick. She noticed Ripper, then me. She had no idea who I was. Now her movements were quick and shaky. She snuffed out the cigarette on the sole of her shoe. She carefully set what was left of it on the old metal drum next to the door.

Whatever she'd been expecting when she stepped outside this morning, it wasn't *us*. There was no panic yet, just recognition.

And that told me everything.

Vendetta swung a leg off his bike and stood. He didn't rush, but he didn't smile either. He waited, and he was good at that.

"Morning," Vendetta said casually. "We need a word."

Frannie's surveyed the empty lot, taking in the lake, our bikes.

"Ray isn't here until noon," she said, wiping her hands over the apron she wore. "Want to leave him a message?"

Ray was the owner, I was guessing. I couldn't blame her for trying.

"Not here to talk to Ray," Vendetta said. "We're here to talk to you."

"I... I'm working," she said. "I've got to open and --"

"You'll make time," Ripper cut in, as he climbed off his bike.

I stepped forward slowly. Frannie stayed where she stood. She was smart enough to realize running would be stupid.

"We're not here to hurt you," I said, keeping my voice quiet. "We're here because you know something."

Her dark eyes widened. "I don't --"

"Frannie," Vendetta said, now with weight in his voice. "Don't insult us."

She looked to each of us in growing panic as we moved closer.

None of us spoke for a moment, letting her fill the silence with her own fear.

"Two girls," I said finally. "They were here on festival night. At the beach, then at *this* restaurant. You talked to them."

Her hands fidgeted in front of her, twisting

nervously in her apron.

"I talk to a lot of people," she said, grinning and trying to put on the persona she used for her customers. "It was real busy that night."

"Funny thing about that night," Ripper said, moving closer. "A lot of people remember seeing those girls. None of them remember seeing them leave. And they never made it home."

"Oh." She looked away.

There was the crack. I leaned in enough to make her look at me again. "We already know how this works," I told her. "We're just giving you a chance to help yourself."

Frannie laughed weakly. "I didn't do anything wrong."

Vendetta's gaze sharpened. "Then this is gonna be very easy."

I shook my head. "No, it's not." She really looked at me then. And whatever she read there made her shoulders slump. "Let's start with their names, Frannie," I said. "You know them."

Her voice came out thin. "Claire and… Scarlett."

Ripper exhaled quietly through his nose.

I didn't smile. "Now we're talking."

I straightened and stepped back, giving her a little space to breathe.

"Let's go inside," Vendetta said. "You're going to tell us everything."

Frannie nodded, and I could tell her mind was running a hundred miles a minute trying to find a way out of this. We followed her in through the back door of the small restaurant, past storage and the dingy kitchen, to reach the front. Vendetta and Ripper walked around to take stools on the customer side of the front counter, where the barflies normally set up camp each evening after work.

I stayed behind the counter with her, cutting off her only escape route.

Her attention snapped to me. "I don't know what you think --"

"I think," I interrupted her, "you need to tell us what happened that night. You've worked here for years. You know everyone who comes to this restaurant. You talk to the kids like you're the cool older sister. You slip them drinks when no one's looking. Am I right so far?"

She stared at me.

"And I know," I continued, "that you were working that night of the festival. And you were the last one who talked to those girls before they disappeared."

Vendetta finally spoke. "Claire Scarborough. Scarlett Monroe."

The color drained from Frannie's face. I didn't miss the way she gripped the counter to keep us from seeing how badly her hands were shaking now. "I didn't --" Her voice broke. She took a deep breath and tried again. "Look, I didn't do anything to them… and I didn't make them do anything."

"I believe you," I told her. "You didn't force them. You didn't grab them or hurt them."

Her shoulders sagged in relief she didn't even try to hide.

But I wasn't done yet. "You just pointed."

Fear started bleeding back into her expression.

I stepped closer now, watching her anxiety climb. "You remember the night. Who stayed later. Who was looking for another party. Who told them it was fine."

Tears welled fast, spilling before she could stop

them. "I didn't know… I swear, I didn't think it'd be like this."

I didn't answer right away. My gut told me that Claire and Scarlett weren't her first recruiting efforts. Frannie knew. She'd known enough every other damn time. But *this* was the first one she hadn't outrun.

"Then tell us what you *did* know," Ripper said, staring her down.

Frannie shook her head. "They said they were going to meet someone. That was all."

Vendetta planted his forearms on the bar and leaned in. "Who said that, Frannie?"

Her eyes squeezed shut.

"Are you shaking because you're scared or because you need something?" It was a guess, but I knew I was right. "That's the deal, right? Painkillers are fucking expensive when you have to buy them off the street. Maybe they supply you for free if you supply them, right?"

Frannie's dark eyes flew open, terror blazing in them. Her mouth dropped open. "You think I want to be on them?" She glared at me. "I got T-boned pulling out of the bank parking lot three years ago and the pain just about put me on disability. My doctor put me on Tramadol, and I can't get off it without weeks of withdrawal symptoms. I'd lose my job."

Vendetta cut me a look. I had been right.

"If I help them out, I get all I want. If I don't… they'll cut me off." She unraveled right in front of us, swiping at her tears with the backs of her hands. "They said it was just introductions. If I run into any girls looking for a place to party --"

"Look at me," I ordered.

She did, shaking like a leaf. Her tears were flowing freely now.

"Where did they take them?"

Her lips trembled. "I never had the exact address. It's... outside town. An hour away, maybe two. Bobby Moore stays over at my place sometimes. He said it's a big place with gates."

It was hard to keep my anger at bay. "Why those two girls?"

Her answer came out broken. "They were clean. That's what pays the most."

Vendetta exhaled slowly through his nose, and I'm not sure Ripper had moved in the last couple of minutes. I straightened, every piece of the picture clicking into place. "How often does Bobby talk?" I asked. "Does he work for them?"

She didn't answer, but oh, she knew she'd fucked up.

"Here's what's going to happen now," I told her. "You're going to tell us everything. Names. Numbers. How you're paid. Who you talk to. Every time."

She nodded frantically. "Okay, I will... I swear. I'll help."

I held her gaze, cold and steady.

Leaning back against the wall, Frannie cried hard now, the truth finally too heavy for her to hold it back.

I spotted an order pad and some pens on a shelf next to me. I pulled out one of each and slapped them on the counter in front of her.

"Start writing," I ordered. "Make it fast."

The clock on two girls' lives had started ticking louder.

* * *

We rode back in silence. The road hummed beneath us, the wind stripping everything down to thought and intent. By the time we had hit the compound, the noon sun was high overhead.

And something felt wrong.

It was usually quiet around the compound this time of day, but now was too quiet. The second we walked through the gate, I felt it. The kind of quiet that sets in when something's already gone bad.

That's when I saw him.

JJ was laid out behind the old motor pool, half in shadow, half in the blazing summer sun. And he was *placed* there. His prospect cut was still on him, his hands posed over his chest like he was ready for the casket.

At first, I didn't see any evidence he'd even fought them. But once we reached him, when I looked closer, I saw rope burns marking his throat.

Oh, that was deliberate. *A reminder.*

Ripper stopped beside me, exhaling heavily. Vendetta didn't move at all. His focus was on the kid's throat, the rope burns there a shadow of the ones around his own neck.

It struck me that JJ was placed inside the perimeter. A clear message with no doubt in any of our minds who it was from. And that was when I knew it was true. Sinister Skin *still* had men here. In our compound. *In our club.*

I crouched, my gaze sweeping over him as I searched his pockets. JJ's phone wasn't there. His bike was still sitting in the yard, the keys where he'd left them.

Vendetta exhaled sharply. "Make sure everything's locked down."

Ripper was already moving, his voice snapping into the comms.

I straightened, shifting my focus to the fence line, the buildings, and the shadows between them. Someone *inside* had let this happen. Maybe they had fucking watched. Hell, they might have killed him.

I turned toward the administration building. Jazz safe for now, and unaware of how close the war had come to her door.

Sinister Skin was waiting for an answer. They'd just told us what the cost of delay looked like.

And I was fucking done waiting.

Chapter Six

Shade

Cowboy came up behind us, a paint bucket swinging from each hand. He halted when he saw us. It didn't take him long to figure out why we were standing there. He spotted his best friend lying motionless on the ground. The buckets hit the gravel hard, and he made a beeline for JJ, the cowboy hat flying off his head. In the next instant he was on his knees in his paint-spattered jeans. His hands were shaking hard as he checked his friend for a pulse he wouldn't find. His fingers traced over the rope burns on JJ's neck that were still red and streaked with fresh blood.

He didn't look up as we moved closer.

"I was only gone twenty minutes," he said with tears choking his voice. "Maybe half an hour. We were patching drywall in B-Barracks. JJ said he'd start sanding while I ran to the store for more paint." His throat worked as he swallowed hard. "He was fine. He was bitching about the paint color. Said it looked like hospital walls, all gray and shit."

Vendetta crouched in front of him, solid and steady. "You see anyone around here today that wasn't supposed to be here?"

Cowboy shook his head hard. "No. Nobody. Everything was normal. Hell, it was mostly just us." His voice cracked. "I came back and --" His voice broke off, and he scrubbed a hand through his hair, devastated. "I should've been here. I should have… why the fuck would anybody come after *him*?"

"We're going to find out," Vendetta said. "I promise you that."

Cowboy finally looked up, his eyes red and wild.

"His bike's here." He glanced at me like he needed confirmation. "That's not random, right?"

No. It wasn't.

"He lost his fucking phone," Cowboy said. "We'd been looking for it all morning. I told him he probably set it down somewhere stupid. We checked the break room, everywhere."

I didn't know JJ well. But as far as prospects went, he'd been a pretty sharp one. He never struck me as the scatterbrained type who was always losing something.

And a misplaced phone might not be an accident. Not right now.

Vendetta took a moment to look over the body, and I moved closer with him. JJ's face was swollen in a way that robbed it of expression. His cheeks were puffed, his skin stretched tight and mottled. Tiny red pinpricks dotted the skin beneath his eyes and along his cheekbones, angry and unmistakable once you realized what you were looking at. His lips had gone slack, slightly parted, the corners drooping as if whatever tension once lived there had simply let go.

The rope burns were obvious, dark and brutal against his throat. But it was what lay beneath them that caught my eye. Scratches and fingernail marks, shallow but frantic, raked into the skin under the bruising. JJ's hands were curled inward, his fingers stiff and half-clenched like they'd locked that way at the end. The nails were broken and rimmed with dried blood, the skin scraped raw where he'd clawed uselessly at his own throat. Paint still streaked his knuckles, white and gray smears from the job he'd been working on that morning.

Vendetta said nothing, but there was rage coming off him. The fucks who'd done this had done the same thing to him. His own club. But Vendetta had lived. And now he would unleash a holy shitstorm on the ones who'd struck JJ down. On Creep and Eagle and anyone else inside the compound who was helping them. I swore to myself I'd be right beside him.

He reached out and gently lifted one of JJ's eyelids with his thumb. The eye beneath was blood red, veins blown and ruptured, the white completely gone. Lowering the lid again with a steady hand, Vendetta sighed. His face looked carved from stone.

I straightened slowly, every detail of the kid's murder locking into place with sickening clarity. Hands, not weapons did this. It was up close and personal. They hadn't just killed him, they wanted us to understand how easy it had been for them.

Hell, the killer might have been someone living here in the compound. If that was the case, they knew the kid's routines already. Whoever the fuck did it had moved fast once Cowboy left on a paint run. The killer had strangled JJ before laying him out and posing him. They must have taken his phone.

Around us, other club members gathered, drawn by instinct. There were just a few brothers here this time of day because most had day jobs. Boots scraped concrete and voices dropped. They filled in behind us, forming a loose half-circle.

I turned slowly, my eyes sweeping the crowd. I had a pretty good idea of who was usually there in the middle of the day. I took notice of the ones standing still. The ones who hadn't shifted once since they arrived, watching *us* instead of the body. I also clocked the gaps. Empty spaces where there should've been brothers. Men who hadn't come running, who were suddenly busy elsewhere.

Grim stood off to my left. He was quiet, but his

eyes were sharp and calculating. He wasn't looking at JJ or Vendetta either. He was looking at his brothers, measuring them the same way I was. He was cataloging reactions and filing tells.

Good.

Butcher stood farther back with his arms crossed and his shoulders rigid. He shook his head, slow and deliberate, like the whole scene offended him on a fundamental level. Violence coiled in him, and it looked barely contained.

Vendetta stepped in, placing a careful hand on Cowboy's shoulder. "Go inside. Stay with Grim. Stay put until one of us comes to get you."

Cowboy hesitated, then nodded, letting Grim guide him away like his legs might give out any minute.

Vendetta turned to face the rest of us, his voice carrying. "All right. Listen up."

The men around me stilled. Even the ones pretending not to listen were listening.

"Lock it down," he said. "No one leaves. No one moves without checking in. Comms stay on. Shifts rotate, starting now."

Ripper was already barking orders. Gates slammed shut and men started moving with the practiced efficiency of an army unit.

Vendetta looked back at me, his fury barely contained. "We need to talk."

He tilted his head toward the command building, where his woman and mine were waiting. I fell into step behind him without a word.

That's when it really hit me. If they could do *this,* walk inside our perimeter in broad daylight, take one of ours and fucking leave him like a question we were meant to answer, then Jazz was in real danger. *What if they'd taken her instead*? The thought landed cold and vicious in my chest. Jazz didn't have JJ's size or his instincts. She wouldn't have heard them coming or known when to run. She would have been gone before anyone noticed a thing.

And now? There was no way she wasn't a target. Sinister Skin was back in Oak Grove, back in business. The first thing we did, loud enough for anyone watching to see, was pull a waitress out of *Ned's* like she was valuable. And she *was*. A waitress who just happened to have a sister with high market value and who was already in their hands. They weren't stupid. They'd already connected the dots. They had to know we were on their trail.

It wasn't just about stopping them anymore. No, it was about what they would do next to stop *us*.

The door slammed behind us, muting the noise from the yard and all the movement outside. We passed the kitchen to reach the room Vendetta used for an office. I didn't see Dylan or Jazz, but I heard their voices down the hall before I closed the office door behind me.

Vendetta dragged a hand through his hair. "This just got a whole lot fucking worse."

"Yeah," I replied. "It did."

He stopped and faced me. "We're on the clock for those two girls. And now we might have someone inside our own fucking walls feeding Sinister Skin." He exhaled sharply. "Every move we make now risks tipping them off."

"They *do* have someone inside our walls." There was no disputing it in my mind. "That's why they left us a message."

Vendetta shook his head. "Shade, if we move loud or take a step in the wrong direction, we'll lose those girls. They'll disappear, or worse."

"And if we move slow, we give Sinister Skin time to tighten their grip." He knew it and so did I. "Or risk them trying something with *our* girls."

"What if they move those girls somewhere else?" His gaze locked with mine. "Fuck, they've probably already done that."

Silence settled between us.

"We can't hunt both at once," Vendetta said. "Not openly."

He was right about that. "We separate the work."

Vendetta studied me, already knowing where I was going with this. "You want the rescue insulated."

"I want it fucking *invisible,*" I said. "Need-to-know only. Fewer people and no patterns. Anyone watching too close should see us turning inward, not outward."

Vendetta nodded slowly. "And the traitor?"

"You think there's just *one*?" I asked. "We let them think they're safe. We change routines just enough to watch who adjusts with us. Who knows things they shouldn't and who starts getting nervous when we don't move like they expect."

He smiled. "A slow squeeze."

"Until they slip," I said. "And they always do."

Turning back to his desk, Vendetta braced both hands on it. "Then this is how it goes. We don't announce anything. We don't retaliate *yet*. We let them think we're distracted."

"And we are," I said. "Just not the way they think."

He looked up at me, his eyes hard. "You keep Jazz close. They're gunning for her."

"I know." She wasn't leaving my sight until this shit was over.

The tightness around Vendetta's eyes didn't soften. If anything, it sharpened. "Good," he said. "Because I'm pulling Dylan out of here."

It was a good idea.

"This place isn't secure," he continued. "Not with what happened today. Rick Earle would *love* to get his hands on her, especially after I fucked him up to get her back. And if they're already willing to send a body as a message..."

"They'll escalate," I finished. "You thinking Mercy?"

Vendetta nodded. "They won't touch Dylan if she's with the Hounds. And she's been there before."

"Razor will end anyone who tries," I said. "If Deva doesn't beat him to it."

Vendetta grinned at that. "No shit." Scrubbing a hand over his lower face, his gaze met mine. "Jazz could stay there too, actually."

I didn't care for the idea, though it had nothing to do with my opinion of the Hounds. Jazz had a target on her back, and she was *mine* to protect.

I didn't respond to that.

"We can talk to Snow when we head over," I said. "See if he can update us."

Another beat of silence.

Vendetta straightened. "Yeah, do that. Fuck, *we* need a guy a like that. But if Snow can help us until we find one..."

"We hunt quiet," I said. "Once we move, it's final."

He nodded.

Outside, life in the compound seemed unchanged. Inside, the lines were drawn.

The clock kept ticking.

* * *

Jazz

I returned to Shade's room after talking with Dylan for a while. I'd told her I was taking a nap, but that was a lie. Even if I could put aside the hope that maybe these men would find my sister, the memory of that kiss lingered. I scrolled through videos on my phone for a little while, but I was barely paying attention to any of it.

Shade's words lingered too. *You're going to be my next old lady.*

Next. Meaning I also wouldn't be the last. And then I caught myself. Why was I thinking about the entirely ridiculous notion to begin with?

My mind was a hopeless tangle of worry. I shouldn't be thinking about him right now, but I couldn't get it out of my head. Would he be back soon? Would Claire be with them? Did they know where she was?

Was she alive?

I couldn't stop thinking about the conversation we'd had in the kitchen before Shade left with Vendetta and Ripper. They would talk to Frannie Parker. But the police had already talked to her a couple of times, and each time she'd told the exact same story. Everyone liked the woman. Claire had mentioned how nice she'd been to her and Scarlett a *few* times. It didn't appear that she was a suspect or had anything to do with my sister's disappearance.

Maybe *because* everyone liked her and Claire trusted her, *I* should have looked more closely at the woman.

I heard heavy footsteps seconds before someone unlocked the door. I knew it was Shade. He had the kind of purposeful stride that didn't belong to a man who ever second-guessed himself. When the door opened, Shade filled the frame like he always did, all broad shoulders and long, lean muscle. But just then, tension looked to be riding him hard.

His gaze found me immediately where I'd lain on my side in the middle of his bed, badly pretending to read my phone. He looked me over slowly before closing the door behind him.

There was something different in his expression, in the way he looked at me now. It wasn't softness. I wasn't sure he was even capable of that. No, he was more focused. It was like all the chaos outside the door had sharpened his purpose instead of rattling it.

"You need to pack up," he said, his voice low and rough.

I stared at him, confused. "I don't have anything to pack," I said after a minute. "Wait. Am I going home?"

Shade scrubbed a hand down his face. "No," he said. "But we can't stay here either."

The way he said it with absolute certainty filled me with dread. Why couldn't we stay here? This was the Cottonmouths' compound. What had changed since they'd left a couple of hours ago?

Shade remained standing. I moved to sit at the foot of the bed with my arms folded and braced myself for whatever bad news was coming.

"Things got worse," Shade said.

Just like that. No easing into it. No sugarcoating.

My chest tightened. "How?"

"One of our prospects is dead," he said. "Someone killed him and left his body where we couldn't miss him when we got back here."

The words left me stunned, and panic pressed down on my chest. "Here?"

He nodded. "Killed and left out in the yard of our own fucking compound."

My mind scrambled to catch up as a cold, crawling realization set in. "How... how long ago?" I asked, hating the way my voice shook.

Shade didn't answer right away, and that hesitation told me more than the words ever could.

"While you were gone?"

"Yes."

The room felt smaller, and taking a deep breath felt like a struggle. My gaze shifted instinctively to the door, then the window, like I was suddenly aware of how thin the walls really were.

"They brought him *here*?" I swallowed hard. "And killed him?"

Shade's jaw clenched. "No, he was here the entire time. So either someone came here and killed him... or someone who was already here killed him."

That did it. A rush of fear surged through me so fast it made my knees weak. I wrapped my arms around myself. My skin crawled and my heart hammered like it was trying to break free of my chest.

"They were *that* close," I said.

Close enough to walk through the yard. Close enough to *kill* someone. My thoughts spiraled. *They could have killed me or Dylan.*

"I'm sorry," I told him.

And I meant it. It was then I realized that the perpetual state of anxiety that I lived every day since my sister disappeared had me panicking first when it wasn't always the best initial reaction. Meanwhile, someone had died and I was worried about *myself*?

Shade's gaze softened a little but he didn't say anything.

"They didn't..." I took a deep breath. "They were

outside then, right?"

Shade stepped forward immediately, closing the distance like he could physically block the fear that clawed its way up my spine.

"You're fine," he said. "Dylan is fine. And we're not giving these sons-of-bitches another shot at either of you."

The way he said it, with so much control, told me something else just as clearly. They *could* have gotten to us, and he knew it.

The cold hard truth ran circuits in my brain. This wasn't retaliation but a message. Proof that whatever lines I thought existed between me and this war were imaginary. Hell, I'd been sitting in a kitchen drinking coffee while someone was murdered outside.

"We never heard anything." I stood and sucked in a shaky breath. "That could've been Dylan or me."

"It wasn't you. And it won't be." His eyes darkened, something fierce flashing there before he reined it in. "They strangled him. That's why you didn't hear anything."

The certainty in his voice steadied me more than it probably should have. But beneath it, the truth hummed like a live wire between us.

This wasn't only about my sister anymore.

"I know," I said. "This isn't just about me. It's affecting all of us. But I'm scared. Are they going to hurt my aunt now? Are we going to find Claire alive?"

Shade moved closer. The bed barely touched my calves, and he was standing so close to me that I felt his warmth. Slowly, he raised his hands and when I didn't stop him, he skimmed them lightly over my arms. His touch left a trail of gooseflesh as he slid them up and down, slowly and meaning to soothe. His thumbs traced reassuring arcs over my skin, like he was anchoring me to the moment.

"No," he said, his tone firm and absolute. "This wasn't on you."

I started to shake my head, but he leaned in enough that I had to look up.

"They didn't do this because I brought you here," he said. "They did it because we *know* and we're right."

"And your aunt?" he asked, his voice lowering. "She's not on their radar. Not yet anyway. They don't waste leverage they don't need."

That should have scared me. Somehow, it steadied me instead.

"As for Claire," he said, "she's the reason they're moving fast. And the reason they're sloppy right now."

His hands slid up, stopping at my shoulders, and his thumbs pressed in enough to make me feel solid again.

"Do you know something?" I had to ask. "Is she alive?"

Some emotion flashed in his eyes, but I didn't look away. I challenged him without words to tell me the truth or try lying to me. Shade didn't flinch.

"I don't know with a hundred percent certainty." The honesty in his tone had my heart speeding up. "But if I had to guess, yes, I think she's alive. She's valuable to them."

I was shaking though I didn't immediately realize it. His grip tightened around my shoulders, but his touch was gentle, careful.

"You didn't cause this, Jazz," he said. "You're carrying enough without adding to it."

My chest tightened and tears stung the backs of my eyes. But his voice stayed calm and controlled, like he'd already mapped every outcome.

"They wanted to show us how close they could get. What they didn't think through is that they showed me exactly who I have to protect now." His gaze dropped briefly to my mouth and throat before locking again with mine. "I don't lose what's mine."

"Why do you keep saying that?" I hated the tears and frustration in my tone as I asked that question. "I'm not your *anything*."

"You sure about that?" His green eyes darkened. "I could show you."

His mouth was on mine before I drew another breath. I braced for him to be rough and demanding. Instead, his kiss was heated but careful. It didn't feel like he was asking permission so much as he was giving me a moment to adjust, to accept him. I didn't kiss him back right away, but I wasn't fighting him either.

Shade took it as consent. His arms closed around me, and he pulled me into him. Instinct had me sliding my hands up the muscled wall of his chest as he continued to burn me down with his kiss. The man *did* know how to kiss. The hard length of his body was pressed against mine, and it felt good. His arms were like steel bands around me, holding me in place as he kissed me breathless. His lips were soft, and his tongue slid against mine.

He didn't push me back onto the bed so much as he dropped onto it and took me with him. My heart raced as his hands slid up into my hair, pulling the tie from the ponytail I'd been wearing. He dropped more kisses over my lips, and across my jaw. When his lips reached the space under my ear, I gasped. The weight of him pushed me into the mattress, and my body wound around him as I pulled him closer. The way he kissed and the way he touched me wiped away everything else that had been preying on my mind.

All I saw was him. I grabbed the back of his cut, trying to pull it off him. Oh, he stopped long enough to help me do that. But then his lips returned to searing my neck, trailing down my throat. I slid my fingers under his shirt, clutching at the muscular flesh of his back.

Shade pulled down the tank top I was wearing enough to free one of my breasts since I wasn't wearing a bra underneath. His large, rough hand smoothed over it first as his mouth danced around my throat in a way that left me struggling to breathe. He chained kisses down my throat, down to my chest. When his lips closed around the tight peak of my nipple, I froze. When he began teasing it with his tongue, a slow bestial slide, and it had me shaking beneath him.

My body moved with him, trying to get closer. I rolled my hips up into his, against the hard length of his cock encased in denim.

Shade moaned around my nipple, making me shiver. Impatiently, he lifted from me to grab the hem of my top and peel it up and off my body. I'd always thought my breasts were nice enough, but Shade was eyeing them with a hunger that should have scared me. He got his hands on them, then his mouth. I tangled my fingers into the long, gold curls of his hair, clutching as he tormented me in all the best ways.

Again, he abruptly stopped. I didn't try to stop him when he roughly pulled open my jeans, his strong hands grabbing the sides as he began to work them down my body. My panties went with them; my socks and shoes did too. Once I was naked beneath him on that bed, his hands grabbed my thighs and carefully pulled them apart.

I couldn't look down at his hands with his focus on my pussy and him mostly dressed above me. But I became a wild thing when he got his mouth on me. I cried out and gasped in turns while he took me apart, his tongue twisting in my folds as he slid a finger into my opening. The sight of his head between my legs nearly undid me, but I hung on with one hand clutched in the bed beneath me and the other in his hair. Shade was relentless, building me up until my entire body curled around him, a slave to his desires.

Just as I was on the edge of orgasm, he stopped. "Are you mine now?"

I was struggling to push thoughts through the haze of lust he had me in. "What?"

He grinned. The heat in his green eyes had the walls of my pussy clenching, needing more. "Are you mine now?" he repeated. "I want to hear you say it, Jazz." His lips claimed mine, smearing my lips with my own juices. He dropped his weight over me, one hand sliding between our bodies until his fingers were there, teasing my clit with a punishingly gentle touch. I wrapped myself around him. The rough denim of his jeans rubbed against the tender flesh of my inner thighs. My hands slid under his shirt again, skimming over his damn torso because I just couldn't help myself.

"I'm going to need to hear you say it," he whispered against my lips.

I was in a terrible way, but I wasn't giving him that. "No."

I felt his grin more than I saw it. "All sass and challenge," he said in a low voice. "And you wonder why I claimed you."

Tucked under him, needy as I was, I didn't dignify that with a response. I did try to encourage him, rolling my hips up into him. His jeans were already covered in my scent.

"That's how it is, huh?"

Shade lifted from me, tossing me over onto my stomach a second later. He shifted behind me, moving quickly. He stripped off his shirt. I heard the sound of a zipper, the rustle of denim as he shoved his jeans down his lean body. He stripped off as I watched from the corner of my eye. Just because I could, I waggled my ass at him, wanting him to hurry up.

He rewarded me with a sharp smack. There was more shuffling as he pulled something from the pocket of his jeans. In my peripheral vision, I saw him rolling on a condom. "Don't you have something to say?" he asked, draping himself back over me.

The length of his cock brushed against the cheek he hadn't just lit up. "Well?"

"Are you going to keep playing this game?" I said, not sounding as confident and sexy as I hoped. "Or are you going to fuck me?"

Another sharp slap on my ass had me gasping. "Careful." His voice was a deep purr near my ear as he dropped some of his weight on me, holding me to the mattress. "I can easily get mine and leave you hanging, darlin'."

The laugh came out before I could stop it. "I guess I don't have much of a track record." My voice wasn't as steady as I wanted. "Just a couple of bullet points on my resume. I'm pretty used to finishing by myself. Won't be the first time." I braced for his reaction to that challenge. Oh, I knew I was playing with fire. But I also really wanted the man and I had to try.

I felt the deep rumble of his laugh, the slight pulse of his body around me. "You're dynamite, aren't you?" he asked. One of his rough hands slid over my ass and into my slick folds. He teased me with his fingers until I started moving with him, wanting more of his touch. "As much as I'd like to spank your ass right now, I don't have the patience to wait."

He speared into me from behind in one slow, firm slide. It took my breath away as he sank into me, stretching my walls around him until he was fully sheathed in me. His cock split me open in a way that had me moving on him. I should have been embarrassed about the fact that I was fucking myself on him while he held still, his body a hard cage around me. Maybe he'd been trying to let me adjust. Or maybe he wanted to see what I would do.

While I was busy trying to work him against the right spot inside myself, his hands slid slowly over mine. He laced his fingers with mine, taking possession of my hands. He started moving within me. I closed my eyes, focusing on the way he filled me.

Shade took me for a ride, his body working mine into the mattress, my range of movement limited. Not that I wanted to move away. I tightened my fingers around his as I held on while he drove his cock in and out of me with a speed and force that hurt in a way that I'd be feeling later.

The first time I came left me panting beneath him, but he didn't slow or even miss a stride. He kept going, dropping heated kisses over my shoulders and upper back. When I got close the second time, as my pussy clamped around him, he pressed his lips to the back of my neck and over to my ear. "Want to tell me you're mine now?"

I was trembling and needy, gasping as release rode me hard. Somehow, I managed to utter, "No."

Again, he laughed. His thrusts came harder now,

faster. I came again, twisting and tightening beneath him. Shade kept driving me insane with his cock, teasing me with hot kisses that were too light and too fleeting.

After the second time, his body shifted. His fingers dug into my palms, and he dropped even more weight onto me like he meant to pound me into the bed. And he did. The pulses of my last orgasm were fading when he thrust harder, his breath hot in my hair. "Got one more for me?" he whispered in my ear.

What?

One hand released mine, sliding under me to touch my clit. The man knew what he was doing. It couldn't have been more than a minute until he had me dancing on his fingers, weeping around his cock. He was so close I could feel it. He moved faster, bringing a slight sting of pain as he took me like no other man ever had.

When I came that time, I was screaming. The edges of my vision faded to black as the explosion rocked my body. Mere seconds after I'd reached my climax, he pulled free of me, working himself with his hand. It only took him a few seconds to come, his breath coming in harsh rasps.

I shivered as the sweat dried on my skin. Shade tied off the condom and dumped it in the trash, then reached for his shirt, using it to wipe me down. He was careful about it, taking his time. The second he moved away, I grabbed the edge of the blanket I was on and pulled it over me for warmth. Maybe as a shield.

I didn't expect to see him standing at the foot of the bed, pulling on his jeans, and looking at me like I was something beautiful. Someone he valued. I could have been wrong. Shade wasn't an easy man to read.

"You said we couldn't stay here," I said. My

voice came out thin.

"We can't." He took a seat at the foot of the bed, sliding his hand up to cover my bare shin.

A chill slid down my spine.

"Dylan's leaving," he said next. "We're taking her somewhere safe."

Somewhere safe. He didn't say where. Dylan belonged to this world in a way I didn't. She was the club president's old lady. She was way more valuable than I was. "And me?" I asked.

For the first time since we'd been talking, Shade hesitated. "You can go with her," he said. "Same ride. Same protection."

"Where?"

"We're taking her to Mercy," he said, his gaze locking with mine. "To trusted friends. They're strong enough to keep both of you safe while we do what we've got to do."

"What are you going to do?" *Were they going to rescue Claire? Did they know where she was*?

Shade didn't answer. He rose and walked over to his chest of drawers and withdrew another T-shirt. He pulled it on, stretching it over those broad shoulders and all those ink-covered muscles. Did he have something against shirts that were his actual size?

When he didn't answer me, I sighed. I *could* go with Dylan to Mercy. It wasn't that far away. But I knew they were trying to get Claire back. If they did, I didn't want to be in another town. If my sister was alive, she'd gone through absolute hell. And I needed to be there for her. I couldn't do that if I went with Dylan. The Cottonmouths were dangerous men. Claire would be as scared of them as she was her captors.

If she was really alive. And I prayed with everything in me that she was. "No," I said, too fast. "I can't go to Mercy."

Shade's jaw flexed. "Jazz --"

"I can't leave," I said, sitting up in his bed, barely covered by the blanket. "I need to be closer. For Claire."

"You'd be safer," he shot back.

"A risk I'm willing to take," I said fiercely. "God only knows what *she's* been through."

Silence stretched between us, taut as wire. He was thinking about it.

"My sister is all we have," I said, softer now. "My aunt and me. She's missing because of this town. Because of *them*. I'm not running if I can do something to bring her back."

Shade studied me like he was measuring something he couldn't afford to get wrong. "You stay with me," he said. "You do exactly what I say when I say it. Do you understand?"

"I do." I was dead serious. "And I will."

"You better."

Sitting on the bed again, he tied his boots.

"Get dressed," he said. "Get your stuff. We're getting out of here."

"Because of the ones you can't trust here?"

Shade looked up at me. "Yeah. And because the clock's ticking. We're going to take care of business first. Then, we'll deal with the traitors."

An involuntary shiver ran down my body, not just at his words but the way he said them. I didn't even want to know how the traitors would be dealt with. Once I got Claire back, I wouldn't be around to find out.

Chapter Seven

Shade

While Dylan now knew about JJ's death and had to be shaken up same as Jazz, she never let anyone see it. That was the first thing I noticed. Vendetta's old lady moved through the room they shared like she was packing for a weekend trip instead of being evacuated because someone left one of our prospects dead in the yard. She packed a small bag with just the essentials.

As I stood in the hallway waiting for Jazz, she pulled everything together with the unspoken intention of not being gone long.

Vendetta stood in the doorway watching her for a second before turning to me. "Five minutes."

I nodded.

We'd already locked down a compound, but we knew we were most likely already fucking compromised. We didn't call the whole club or gather in the yard for this meeting. We weren't going to raise our voices.

Vendetta sent Ripper to grab only the men we were 100% sure of -- Grim, Butcher, and Cowboy. He also grabbed Crowe, Cain, and Riot, who had never done us wrong. That was it. We met in the motor pool bay instead of the admin building. The air was cold but there were no spectators or unnecessary ears. Ripper and I even scoped it out, just to make sure.

Cowboy looked completely wrecked, JJ's blood still under his nails. The others waited with him for our president to lay it all out.

Once everyone was there, Vendetta didn't waste time or words. "Someone wasted JJ. Right here on our own turf."

No one said a word.

"We have to assume we've got leaks," he continued. "That some motherfucker in our own ranks is in Sinister Skin's pocket. JJ was cut down before we got back from talking to someone they do business with."

Our president made no accusations or assumptions.

Ripper's gaze swept over everyone in our small group. Grim stood firm with his arms crossed over his broad chest, Butcher next to him, still as stone. Cowboy swallowed hard, but he was ready and listening.

Vendetta's attention shifted to them. "You will hold the line."

Cowboy stared at him like he misheard. "Sir?"

"You *stay,*" Vendetta said. "You want JJ's death answered for? You stay here, do your job, and keep your eyes and ears open. You do that and you'll find our rats."

The kid's eyes went wide at that, as he considered the orders. And he was right to be scared. But after a moment, Cowboy nodded.

Butcher stepped closer without being told. "I'm staying with him. I'd like to have one more."

Riot threw up his hand. "I'm in."

Vendetta nodded at each of them with approval. "Gate control is manual from now on. Nobody rides out alone. Nobody comes in without clearance."

Butcher grinned without humor. "If they try?"

"Fucking break 'em," I said. That part didn't need elaboration.

Vendetta looked at Grim next. "You're with us. So are Cain and Crowe."

None of them asked where. When the club was on the line, it didn't matter. Grim nodded. The other two men stayed quiet. All of them were steady and observant. All were the type of men who watched hands instead of mouths. They were well chosen, and exactly what we needed on this outing.

They were going to help us rescue Jazz's sister and any other girls we found tonight.

"Those of you coming with us," Vendetta said, "arm up. Travel light. Bring only what you're willing to use. We roll in fifteen."

"I'm pulling access codes," Ripper took it from there. "Wi-Fi goes dark in ten. Cameras rerouted to remote feed only. Patrol rotations change every hour."

"If someone's relying on routine?" Grim asked.

Ripper smirked. "Well, they won't have one anymore."

Good.

Vendetta stepped closer, lowering his voice enough that it didn't carry. "It's important that we look like we're bleeding right now. They're watching." A little misdirection at this point would only be helpful. "If anyone leaves this compound without my say-so," Vendetta added to those staying, "I want to know before they hit the fucking gate."

Cowboy straightened, scrubbing a hand over his eyes. "You will."

As far as plans went, it was clean and efficient. Nothing like the chaos that ruled when Eli Crizer had held the title of president.

Once everything was decided, we stepped back out into the yard. On the surface, nothing looked different. And that was the point. Men were still moving. It looked like business as usual from the outside. That was just what we wanted.

* * *

Jazz

I had everything together. It wasn't much. Dylan loaned me a change of clothes and a jacket since I literally had nothing with me, and I was grateful for that.

I really admired her. Once they told us what had to happen for our safety, she bravely accepted it. No questions. No demands or tears. She nodded and put together a bag for herself like it was just another day.

Was having to pack up and hide at any moment a natural part of this life? Shade wanted me to be his next old lady. After what happened between us earlier, I hoped it might be true. But could I live like that? Would it get worse?

"Where are you going?" I asked Dylan once we were alone. Vendetta and Shade had left for their meeting.

Dylan tucked a small makeup pouch into the side pocket of her bag. She zipped it up before looking at me. "Mercy."

"Mercy?" Shade mentioned that, and that we were taking her to "trusted friends." I wondered who those friends were. "Is there another club over there?"

"Yes. The Hounds of Hell," she clarified. "They have a chapter there. I've stayed with them before." A faint smile tugged at her mouth. "Deva's a friend. She's with Razor who's their president. It's safer for me there while the boys handle things here."

Especially considering that someone killed a Cottonmouth prospect in their own compound. Shade believed they had at least one traitor in their ranks.

"Are you the only old lady who lives here?" I realized I'd seen no other women here.

Dylan nodded. "Sure, although some of the other members have girlfriends. Maybe one or two are married. Those don't live at the compound. Most of those who do live here are single or just stick with the club girls."

"Club girls?" *That* didn't sound good.

Dylan sat on the edge of her bed next to her bag. "That's a story for another time."

"Wait." I hesitated. "Don't the Hounds and the Cottonmouths hate each other? I mean, that's the rumor."

Dylan huffed softly. "They did. This chapter of the Cottonmouths and the Mercy chapter of the Hounds were mortal enemies for a long time. But things are different since Vendetta took over. The priorities have shifted. Under my uncle, the Cottonmouths helped Sinister Skin traffic girls and run drugs, and apparently, they made good money from it. Under Vendetta, the club is trying to run that shit out of Oak Grove. The Hounds ran them out of Mercy before they could set up shop. Now the Cottonmouths and Hounds are trying to work together."

"Trying?"

Her blue eyes held mine. "There was a *lot* of bad blood. There are still trust issues. But right now, we don't even know who here in our camp is loyal and who isn't. I'm just hoping the truce with the Hounds lasts."

I understood that the Cottonmouths wanted to end trafficking. I hoped they made it in time to save Claire. But Dylan's explanation didn't exactly fill me with confidence.

She studied me for a second. "Are you coming with me to Mercy?"

The question sat between us, heavy and tempting. I *could* leave Oak Grove. Maybe I would be safer somewhere else. But the ticking clock in my chest reminded me that my own comfort wasn't the priority now. It was getting my sister back.

"No," I said.

Dylan didn't argue. She waited.

"I can't. I don't know where Claire is, but I feel like she's close. And if there's even a small chance that we could get her back…" My throat tightened. "I need to be here. I need to know what's happening."

Her expression softened, and she nodded. "Shade's not going to let you out of his sight."

"I know." And I *did*. I'd invited Shade in. Hell, my knees were still shaking slightly from the intensity of his loving.

"And you're okay with that?" Dylan tried not to smile.

Dylan *knew*. I didn't answer right away.

Was I okay with it? *Maybe*. But honestly, I trusted Shade more than the police who'd been running in circles for the last three weeks while my sister was still out there. At least he seemed to have a plan.

"I don't really have the luxury of being picky right now."

Dylan nodded. "Fair enough." She smiled. "You're stronger than you think, Jazz. Listen to Shade and Vendetta. They know what they're doing. They'll keep you safe."

I appreciated her honesty, and I genuinely liked her. I didn't know if Shade and I had any kind of future. I hoped so. If I ended up here for a time hanging out with Dylan, we'd get along well.

Boot steps echoed down the hall a second later, heavy and familiar, and the air shifted in the room.

It sounded like they were ready, and I was going with them.

I went back to Shade's room to get my purse and the tote with the extra clothes from Dylan. I heard

Shade walk in behind me. "Are you ready to go?" he asked in that deep voice.

I nodded. Out of habit, I looked through my purse to make sure I had my charger and my ID. The only thing missing was my phone. Shade still had that.

I did find a slip of paper in my purse that I *hadn't* seen before. My fingers brushed the paper and I froze, pulling it out slowly. It was folded into a small square, and my heart raced as I unfolded it. Three lines were written on it with no greeting or signature.

You want Claire alive?
Take her place.
The Mason Jar dock. Sunset.

My reality came to an immediate halt. I read it again, like the words might rearrange themselves into something less catastrophic. *The Mason Jar.* They wanted me to go to the restaurant at the lake. The last place my sister had been seen the night she and Scarlett disappeared.

My throat went dry, and so many realizations hit me all at once. They knew exactly where I was. The note hadn't been mailed to me. No, they'd left it for me here in this building within the Cottonmouth compound, in my purse -- which hadn't left Shade's room since he brought me here. The room Shade had told me no one else but Vendetta had a key to. Someone had been in here and touched my things. They'd stood close enough to unzip my purse. Close enough to look me in the eye later and say nothing.

My blood ran cold.

Take her place.

The ones who took my sister had delivered this to me, demonstrating how easy I was to reach. The words ran through my mind repeatedly as a rush of adrenaline hit.

If I traded myself, would they really let Claire go? Was she even still alive?

Hope flared so violently it almost knocked the air from my lungs.

Behind me, a drawer slid shut before Shade crossed the room. He moved without urgency, gathering what he needed for wherever we were going. The note in my hand froze me to the spot.

"What?" he asked.

I didn't answer. I *couldn't.* My fingers trembled around the paper.

Shade was beside me in two strides. "Jazz?"

He didn't ask again. He slowly took the note from my hand, and I didn't try to stop him.

Shade read it, and it felt like the temperature in the room had dropped. "They're not moving her."

I blinked. "What?"

"They wouldn't bait you if they planned to transfer her today." His gaze shifted to me now, sharp and focused. "This is pressure. Not an exchange."

My pulse stumbled. "They said --"

"They said what you needed to hear."

"Wait. You said 'transferring her.' You mean Claire."

Shade nodded. He read the note one more time before he looked up again. "Where did you find this?"

"In my purse." My hands still shook.

Shade's eyes sharpened instantly. "Your purse hasn't left this room."

It wasn't a question. "No," I whispered. "Not since you brought me here."

"When was the last time you looked through it before now?"

I thought about it. My mind raced backward. "Last night. When I grabbed my phone charger. I didn't see anything then."

"Today?" he pressed.

I shook my head. "Not until just now. I wanted to make sure I had everything."

A muscle at his jaw jumped. "You left the room this morning."

"Yes. Dylan made us breakfast in the kitchen. You found me there. Then we talked about Claire's disappearance."

"It was just you and Dylan before we came in?"

I nodded. "We were in the kitchen for a little while. Then I came back to the room."

"Did you bring your purse with you?"

"No. I left it here, on the chair."

His eyes flicked to that exact chair sitting by the window. "Did you get in your purse at that point? For anything?"

I nodded. "Yeah, for some lip balm. I didn't see anything then."

"Was the door to this room locked?"

"I... I don't know. I don't remember whether I locked it when I left.

Shade blew out a breath. "Did anyone else come into this room while I was meeting with Vendetta?"

"No." I hesitated. "If they did, I didn't know about it. I was across the hall talking to Dylan."

"Are you sure?"

I forced myself to replay everything in my mind. "I'm pretty sure. Dylan or I would have seen someone walk into the building from the kitchen, right?"

Shade stared at me intently. "How long were you in the kitchen?"

"Maybe an hour," I admitted.

"That's enough," he said quietly. "Did you talk to anyone else?"

"No. Just Dylan."

"In the kitchen?"

"Yes."

"Did you see *anyone* pass through?"

I'd been living in a state of hyper awareness since Claire had disappeared. If I'd seen something, I would have noticed. "No one."

He searched my face. "There's only one other door to the building. It's in Vendetta and Dylan's room, boarded up. They couldn't get through that without making a racket."

Still, Shade darted out of the room, dashing over to the room Dylan shared with Vendetta. After a couple of minutes, he returned.

"No one touched it," he said to himself as much as me. "It was someone who knows the compound very well. They didn't need to distract you or Dylan. They were comfortable here. Just walked the fuck in here like they belonged."

Folding the note he still held carefully, he slid it into a pocket inside his cut. "Whoever did this had access, and no fear of being questioned."

"You think it's someone who is still around from when Eli was president," I said, remembering Dylan's story. "Someone you thought you could trust."

"I know it is," he said with no hesitation. "We need to figure out who, and how many."

I wrapped my arms around myself, listening to him.

"Why leave a note?" I asked. "Why sneak a note into my purse telling me to trade myself for Claire? I was right here. They could have grabbed me."

Shade's eyes darkened, his focus returned to me. "That's a good point. And it tells me leaving the note for you was just a diversion. If we're distracted and trying to keep you safe, we won't be so quick to move against them." Stepping closer, he lowered his voice. "This wasn't about grabbing you. It was about making us choose."

It made sense to me. But the room felt much smaller now. "Sunset," I whispered.

Shade shook his head. "We're not waiting for fucking sunset."

And just like that, whatever fragile illusion of control Sinister Skin thought they had evaporated. The man standing in front of me? He wasn't rattled. He was about to go hunting.

* * *

Shade

I'd been in the Hounds' conference room before. Not too long ago, Ripper and I had made a break from Eli and the nightmare version of the Cottonmouth chapter he led at the time. We'd heard our friend Tank was dead, and I believed he'd died at Eli's hands. I almost had it right. Eli and all his trouble were coming for the Hounds, so we'd stopped in, wanting to tip them off before we headed out.

What we didn't expect to find that day was our old friend Tank, alive with a permanent rope burn around his neck and one hell of a story to tell. We made a plan that night between our two clubs to cut the cancer out of the Oak Grove Cottonmouths. We'd ended Eli and almost every man who'd sold us to Sinister Skin that night, led by Tank, reborn as Vendetta, and backed by the Hounds of Hell out of Mercy. We didn't get everyone. We knew Creep and Eagle were still around. A couple more, or at least one, still walked through the compound as one of us.

And we would find him.

In Mercy, we gathered around the same long table with its scarred wood and folding metal chairs. Maps were still pinned to one wall, a gun rack mounted on the wall across from it.

We wore different patches, but for the most part, our goals were aligned.

Razor sat at the head of the table. His long gray hair was tied back, and he took us in as we entered. Hero leaned back in his chair, his blond hair swept neatly back from his face. Snow's laptop was open in front of him, his fingers steepled like he'd been waiting all day for us. The harsh fluorescent lights overhead glared off his white hair.

Vendetta stayed beside Dylan. I stayed near Jazz. Ripper took position opposite Hero. Nobody wasted time on pleasantries. "Snow, is everyone up to speed on what's happening here?" Vendetta asked.

Snow nodded.

"Well, I've got something new," I said. "We've got another breach."

That got some attention.

"Do you now?" Razor asked.

I reached into my pocket and set the folded note on the table. "Someone left this in Jazz's purse earlier today."

Dylan's head snapped toward Jazz. Vendetta's expression didn't change, but I felt the shift in him. Ripper went completely still.

"It was left inside the compound," I said. "While we were in a closed meeting, following the murder of our prospect."

Snow leaned forward, eyes scanning the note without touching it. "Timeframe?"

"Fifteen, twenty minutes," I said. "Late afternoon."

Razor scrubbed a hand over his face.

"Sounds like an inside job," Hero said.

Vendetta finally spoke, his gaze on me. "First *we're* hearing of this."

"I didn't want that note to be discussed at the compound," I said. "It's compromised."

Jazz stiffened beside me but she didn't interrupt.

Vendetta reached for the note, unfolded it and gave it a quick read with Dylan leaning in to read it with him. Her hands came up to cover her mouth.

"Share with the class." Razor pointed to the note in my president's hand.

Vendetta read it aloud to the room, his eyes moving across the lines again. "'You want Claire alive. Take her place. Mason Jar dock. Sunset.'"

Snow leaned back slowly. "Well, that explains it."

"Explains what?" Ripper asked.

Snow turned his laptop toward us. A satellite image covered the screen. It showed a gated property outside Oak Grove. It must have been the house he mentioned. "I've had eyes on this place for two days. Their movement patterns didn't match a transfer window. I'd expected activity today."

"And?" Vendetta pressed.

"And nothing," Snow said. "They haven't moved."

Hero frowned. "Why not?"

Snow pointed at the note in Vendetta's hand. "Well, they were trying to pull her out."

Silence settled over the table.

"They were hoping she'd run," Snow continued, his focus shifted to Jazz. "If Jazz here showed up alone, they'd have grabbed her. You all would scramble. You'd lose focus and burn daylight."

"And Claire stays put," Razor finished.

"Yes."

Vendetta exhaled slowly. "So, she's still there?"

Snow nodded. "Probably. Yes."

Jazz sucked in a quiet breath beside me. I didn't look at her. Not yet.

Razor looked at me. "What's your read?"

"They're feeling pressure," I said. "Frannie talked. JJ's dead. They know we're close."

"And now they know you know," Hero added.

Vendetta cut me a look. "We have a traitor or two. They knew as soon as Frannie talked. Someone called it in, and they've got someone right under our fucking noses in the compound."

Snow closed his laptop. "If they don't move the girls before sunset, they'll move tonight. Probably after dark. The property isn't just a holding site."

I glanced at him.

"It's a transfer point," Snow said. "Foreign buyers. Clean handoffs. They batch girls before shipping them."

Jazz went very still.

Vendetta's voice dropped. "How many girls?"

Snow shrugged. "Could be a dozen or so."

Razor stood on that note. "Then we don't wait."

Hero nodded once.

Vendetta looked at me. "We hit it."

I inclined my head. "Quiet approach."

Ripper stepped forward. "What about the mess at the compound? We just have Cowboy, Butcher, and Riot manning the fort."

Snow didn't hesitate. "We send Crash, Outcast, and Player. They'll ride to Oak Grove, stage outside your perimeter, and keep out of sight."

Razor nodded. "If your insider makes a move

while you're gone, my boys help you catch 'em."

Vendetta gave him a sharp look of appreciation.

"And the house?" Razor asked.

"We've got a crew of six," I said. "Backup would be welcome."

Hero smirked slightly. "Axel and Ryder are itching for something ugly to get into. Want to send them?"

Razor nodded.

"Good," Vendetta replied. "We can use them."

The plan settled into place fast after that.

Crash, Outcast, and Player would ghost near the Cottonmouth compound back home.

Our crew, joined by Axel and Ryder, would move on the house. We'd move fast and quietly. No fuck ups and no second chances.

At my side, Jazz hadn't spoken a word. When I finally looked her way, her face was pale. She looked from Vendetta to Razor, then Snow, and back to me. But what she took from the discussion was bigger than fear. I realized then that it wasn't just possibilities we discussed anymore or hypotheticals. We were really going to take her sister back tonight, and now she knew it.

Dylan broke the silence. "Okay." Her gaze moved across the table before settling on Vendetta. "But where is Jazz supposed to be while all this is happening?"

The question hung there.

Razor leaned back slightly in his chair, one tattooed arm resting on the table.

"She's welcome to stay here." His voice was calm. "Mercy's safe ground. Deva will make sure of it. And if anything happens to a guest in my house, my old lady will personally have someone's ass."

A couple of the men in the room huffed in quiet amusement, but it didn't last long.

Jazz straightened beside me. "Thank you. But no."

Every head turned. Her voice wasn't loud, but it carried.

"I'm going," she said with zero hesitation in her demeanor, her words.

Dylan blinked at her. "Jazz --"

"I'm not staying behind while they all go find my sister." Her hands clenched into fists at her sides, but her voice stayed steady. "I know that area and the roads around Oak Grove as well as any of you. And if something goes wrong, I want to be there."

Her focus shifted to me then. "Claire is my sister. Not just another girl you're rescuing."

The room went still again. Snow's gaze flicked to me. Vendetta didn't say a word. And suddenly everyone waited to see what I would say. Jazz didn't move or look away. Her chin lifted. She was bracing for a fight if she had to.

I didn't answer right away. I studied her. Three weeks ago, her sister had disappeared and nobody had done a damn thing about it. Police shrugged it off. People told the family to wait, to hope and pray.

Now she stood in a room full of dangerous men, all of them prepared to kick in a door in and drag Claire out if we had to. And she thought I'd make her sit this one out.

I turned to face her. "You're not part of the assault." Her shoulders tensed immediately at my words. "But you're coming." She hadn't expected me to say that. "You stay in the SUV. You stay where I put you. You do exactly what I say the second I say it. No arguments. No running. No hero shit."

She swallowed nervously but nodded. "Okay."

Vendetta exhaled through his nose beside me like he expected that answer. Snow eyed us both, measuring something.

Razor scratched his beard. "Girl's got more spine than half my prospects."

My attention stayed on Jazz. Yeah, she *was* brave.

"Then it's settled," Vendetta said finally.

The meeting ended in a loud scrape of chairs and boots. Vendetta and Razor were already talking again before we even cleared the room, their voices low. The rest of the men shifted around the table to start working out details, routes, and timing.

Jazz gave Dylan a hug. Dylan talked to her in a quiet voice. Probably asking her again to stay here with the Hounds. Jazz waved her off, her gaze catching mine.

When Jazz made her way out of the conference room, out of the clubhouse, I followed. The air outside was cooler behind the trees that surrounded most of the Hounds' property. Engines idled somewhere out front, the quiet rumble carrying across the gravel lot while Vendetta's voice drifted through the open clubhouse door behind us.

Jazz didn't stop walking until she reached the back of the building. There was nothing but woods beyond it. She turned, her arms folded tight across her chest like she'd been holding something back that could poison her if she didn't spit it out.

"You knew," she said. It wasn't an accusation.

I leaned one shoulder against the wall beside her. "I did."

She studied me, trying to piece everything together. "Why didn't you tell me?" she asked in an unsteady voice.

"I told you when you needed to know." And that was true.

She looked away for a second. "I could've helped."

"No," I said. "You *couldn't*."

That pulled her attention back to me.

"If you knew, you would've pushed," I continued. "You would've wanted to run straight at that house the second you found out."

She opened her mouth like she thought about arguing. Then she closed it again. She knew I was right, and silence settled between us for a moment.

I heard Vendetta and Snow out on the porch now with the others. It sounded like they were mapping out something. But I couldn't walk away from the beauty who had upended my entire life in less than a week.

"Shade." Her bravado from the meeting remained, but now the fear underneath began to show. "Do you really think we can save her?"

Jazz her been through hell. Three weeks of fear and waiting, of imagining the worst.

I reached out and caught her chin lightly between my fingers, turning her face back toward me. "We're bringing your sister home," I told her with no hesitation or doubts. *We would.* "Claire's coming back with us tonight."

Her breath caught, but something steadied in her eyes. *Hope.* That was something that had been missing from my girl's life for too long.

I didn't expect her to push closer, to grab my cut with her hands and pull me into her. Jazz kissed me, her lips so sweet. I tasted desire and hope, and a hint of need.

When she deepened the kiss, I spun us so her back pressed against the wall and her smaller frame was hidden behind mine. No one saw us as she continued to kiss me breathless. I loved the feel of her hands roaming over my chest, down to clutch at my jeans. When one hand slid further down, she found my cock hard and wanting under the denim. Her need took me off guard, but I wasn't complaining. I allowed her to pluck my jeans open, gasping into her mouth when her hand slid in and wrapped around me.

I broke the kiss. "You sure about this?"

Her hand squeezed me a little tighter, moving up and down in a rhythm that stopped me cold. After a few more seconds of that, I was done waiting for an answer.

Grabbing the front of her jeans, I pulled them open and shoved them down roughly. Yanking one of her shoes off, I pulled the denim free, leaving the other leg alone. I already had the opening I needed. Grabbing her ass, I hauled her up the wall until I could line my cock up with the sweet opening of her pussy, warm and waiting for me.

Jazz was so wet that I thrust in, the tight heat of her taking my breath away, even as I started claiming her against the Hound clubhouse. She kept kissing me, my mouth, my jaw. She laced her fingers into my hair as I fucked her. Our movements were desperate, fueled by need as we moved together. We were racing toward a high we both needed.

When she was close, she slid a hand down to her clit, working it in a frenzy as I thrust into her a little faster. Orgasm hit her fast, and she clenched around me hard as she buried her face in my neck muffling the sounds she made. Sounds that belonged to me. I kept going, working her through it. I barely managed to pull free of her as I reached my own end, pinning her between myself and the wall as it shook me down hard.

We stayed still like that for a couple of minutes, trying to catch our breath as we held onto each other. In that small moment of peace before the storm, I realized what had happened. It was Jazz laying claim to me, maybe because she wanted me as much as I wanted her. Maybe because she understood now how committed I was to getting Claire back to her.

All I knew was that it felt right.

I gently helped her stand, tucking myself into my jeans while she put herself back together. She'd just zipped up her jeans when Vendetta called my name from the other side of the clubhouse.

It was time to move. I pushed off the wall and glanced back at Jazz.

"Stay close to me." Taking her by the hand, we headed toward the bikes and the SUV we were riding in.

Come hell or high water, we were going to take Claire back.

Chapter Eight

Shade

We cut the engines a quarter mile from the property Snow had found. We didn't want to announce our arrival yet. A sudden quiet settled over us like a held breath. Gravel crunched softly under our boots as we pushed the bikes the rest of the way down the narrow dirt road, headlights off, the house ahead of us sitting dark against the tree line.

Behind the line of bikes sat the full-size SUV Jazz and I'd brought. If this went the way we hoped it would, we wouldn't be leaving alone. We were going to need transport for the girls.

The place Snow had flagged using his technical wizardry was much bigger than I expected. It had two stories, a wide porch, and a detached garage sitting off to the side like it had money behind it once. Now it just looked quiet.

Too quiet.

Vendetta stopped first, scanning the house and the surrounding trees before turning back toward us. "All right," he said quietly, waving everyone closer.

We gathered around him in a loose half circle. Jazz stayed a few steps behind me, her amber-colored eyes locked on the house like she could see through the walls.

Vendetta pointed. "Front door's mine. The twins are with me."

Axel and Ryder nodded without a word.

"Shade, take the back," Vendetta ordered. At my nod, he said, "Ripper, Grim, and Cain, you've got his six."

The three of them had already stepped in closer, understanding where they'd be.

Finally, our president's gaze fell on the last man with us. "Crowe."

Crowe looked up from where he stood beside the SUV. Tall and slender, with jet-black hair and dark eyes that seemed to miss nothing, he carried himself with a quiet, watchful stillness that made people nervous even when he wasn't speaking. And he never had a lot to say.

"You're on the vehicles," Vendetta said.

Crowe nodded and stepped back toward the SUV, already scanning the tree line and the narrow road behind us.

Jazz immediately shook her head. "No."

Vendetta ignored her. "The engine stays ready. Anything moves on that road that shouldn't, you drop it."

Crowe rested a hand on the hood of the SUV, eyes already scanning the dark tree line.

Jazz stepped forward, not about to be ignored. "I'm not staying out here." Her voice wasn't loud, but it carried.

Vendetta didn't even look at her. "Not your call."

Her eyes snapped to me. "Shade." I turned toward her. She was trying to keep it together, but the fear in her eyes was impossible to miss. "My sister is in that house," she said.

"I know."

"Then I should be --"

"No."

Her chin inched up. "Shade --"

"You stay here." My gaze locked with hers. "That was the deal when I agreed you were coming. You do what I say. And I say you stay right here with the SUV and Crowe."

Jazz stared at me like she wanted to pick a fight.

I stepped closer, lowering my voice. "You go in there and something goes wrong, I can't protect you."

Her expression shifted, and she blew out a sigh. "You won't be protecting anyone if I slow you down."

It was the truth, and I was grateful she'd come to it on her own. I knew she hated it but she understood it. "Crowe's staying with you." I put my hands on her shoulders. "You stay *here*. You don't move unless I come get you."

Jazz looked past me toward the house again. "What if --"

"We'll bring her out." If Claire was in that house, and I trusted Snow's intel that she was, she was leaving with us tonight.

For a moment I thought she might start arguing again. She surprised me when she nodded and lowered her head.

Vendetta clapped his hands once, sharp in the quiet. "Arm up."

Metal slid softly as weapons were checked.

"Travel light," he continued. "No noise unless it's necessary." He surveyed the group of us. "We get the girls and we get out."

Vendetta had never been one for speeches. None of us were hesitating.

"Move."

I didn't immediately let Jazz go. I quickly pulled her into me, running my hands up and down her back. I felt the tension in her body and pressed a kiss into her hair.

"What if she gets hurt?" she muttered into my shoulder.

"They aren't going to aim for the girls," I said. "They're merchandise."

She released a shaky breath as I eased away from

her. "Bring her back to me."

I nodded. I had every intention of doing just that.

Our teams split. Behind me, Jazz stayed with Crowe at the SUV. I didn't look back again. If I did, I'd see Jazz standing beside the SUV, watching the house like she could will her sister out of it. And that wasn't going to help either of us.

I jerked my head toward the tree line. "Let's move."

Ripper fell in behind me, Grim and Cain spreading slightly to either side as we slipped through the dark along the side of the property. The grass was damp under our boots; the smell of cut hay and dirt hung in the air. The back of the house came into view a few seconds later.

Sliding glass doors opened onto a small patio. A grill sat against the railing, an empty beer bottle tipped over beside it. I moved closer and saw small embers inside the grill. Yeah, someone had been out here earlier.

I held up a hand to halt everybody. We listened for a few seconds but heard nothing.

Suddenly, a huge crash split the night open. The front door exploded somewhere on the other side of the house.

Vendetta.

Axel and Ryder followed right behind him, the sound of boots and shouting carrying through the walls.

Perfect timing.

Every set of eyes in the house would be facing the front now, gunning for those three.

I reached for the handle on the sliding door and found it locked.

Cain stepped forward without a word, slipping a

pry tool into the track. A quiet twist of pressure and the latch gave with a dull snap. The door slid open and we slipped inside.

We started in the kitchen. The lights were on, and the smell of stale coffee hung in the air. A mug was left on the counter next to a half-eaten sandwich.

Someone had left in a hurry.

Another shout came from the front of the house. I heard furniture scraping and a body hitting the floor.

Vendetta knew how to make an entrance. He was making damn sure everyone inside the house knew they had company.

Ripper pointed toward the far wall to what I was guessing was a basement door. It was locked but we could handle that.

Grim stepped forward and rolled his shoulders. "Move."

The frame shuddered the first time he hit the door with his shoulder. The second time the latch snapped and door burst open.

Cool air drifted up the stairwell. I paused, raising my weapon before slowly starting down.

I was halfway down the stairs when I heard it. Whispering. Thin, frightened voices layered over each other in the dark.

Grim's boots creaked softly behind me while Ripper moved along the wall, silent as a shadow. Cain stayed at the top of the stairs, covering our backs.

Another crash sounded upstairs, something heavy hitting the floor. Vendetta was raising hell up there, and the distraction was working.

If not for my Jazz, that front-end raising hell scene would have been my choice. It better matched my energy. As I paused just a beat at the bottom of the stairs, I felt energy shift. I felt the heavy weight of fear and desperation all around me and had an idea of what I was about to find. I took a deep breath. I had to do it. For Jazz and her family. For the other young women I knew I was about to find, trapped like animals at the lowest level of this house.

At the bottom of the stairs a narrow hallway stretched out ahead of us, lit by a single bare bulb hanging from the ceiling. The light flickered faintly, making the concrete walls seem like they were pulsing. The chaos from upstairs was ongoing but the sounds were more muffled down there.

The smell hit me first. A strong tang of bleach and stale air. And under that, something darker and medicinal. *Drugs*?

A man stepped into the hallway from a doorway at the far end, turning toward the noise upstairs with a scowl already forming on his face.

That was when he saw me. His hand went for the pistol tucked into the waistband of his jeans, but he was too slow.

I fired once, and the shot was deafening in the confined space.

The man dropped hard, his body hitting the concrete with a dull thud that echoed down the hall.

Aside from the dull noise from the top floor, silence followed. The whispering completely stopped.

Ripper stepped past me, grabbing the fallen man's gun and tucking it in the waistband of his jeans before glancing into the room beyond.

"Clear," he murmured.

I pushed the door open the rest of the way, revealing a room that was larger than I expected. It was cold with its concrete floor and cinderblock walls. A folding table sat against one wall with plastic cups, water bottles, and a tray of half-eaten food.

And in two uneven rows were eight metal cots, each with thin gray blankets that looked like they'd been bought in bulk somewhere cheap.

On those cots were the girls we were looking for, each of them staring at us like we'd just kicked in the gates of hell. A couple of them were sitting up. Others were curled on their sides, blinking sluggishly as if their bodies weren't able to keep up with their minds. As I looked them over, one thing was obvious. They were drugged. Not enough to knock them out, but enough to keep them quiet and docile.

One girl pushed herself up on shaky legs and immediately had to grab the cot beside her to stay upright. She was weak as a kitten. Another girl clutched her arm, whispering something I couldn't quite hear.

None of them moved toward us. If anything, they shrank farther back. They were trying to figure out if we were with their captors or if we were something worse.

Their eyes kept going to the cuts on our vests. The Cottonmouth cut. *Fuck*. From where they were sitting, men wearing patches like these weren't rescuers. They were buyers or worse.

One of the girls near the far wall stood up too quickly and staggered. Her long dark hair got my attention as it moved over her thin shoulders. She had wide brown eyes that looked familiar.

She backed away immediately when she saw me looking at her.

"You've *got* to be Claire," I said quietly.

She froze like the words hit her physically. Tears welled up fast, spilling down her cheeks before she could stop them.

"Why would you say that?" she asked, her voice

shaking.

Behind her another girl with red hair -- she looked familiar too -- grabbed her arm like she was trying to hold her up. I walked toward them, crouching down slowly so I wasn't towering over them. "You look just like your sister," I said carefully.

Claire blinked at me through tears. "My… my sister?"

"Jazz," I said. "She's outside."

For a moment the words didn't seem to land. Then her breath caught. "Jazz is here?"

"She never stopped looking for you," I said. "She's the reason we found this place."

Claire's legs gave out and she dropped back onto the cot, one hand pressed to her mouth like she couldn't quite believe the words.

The other girl, who I was hoping was Scarlett, tightened her grip on her arm. "What if they're not telling the truth?"

"She came for me?" Claire asked, ignoring her friend.

"Yeah," I said. "We all did."

Behind me Grim lowered his weapon, scanning the rest of the room. "Eight total."

Ripper nodded once. "Let's move them out."

The redhead hanging onto Claire looked at each of us with a bravery that I had to admire given their situation. "Where are you taking us?"

"Home," I said.

From upstairs Vendetta's voice thundered down through the floorboards. "Shade!"

"Got 'em!" I shouted back.

A moment later his answer came. "Good. Move!"

I stood and held out a hand toward Claire.

Her fingers trembled as she reached for it.

"Come on," I said. "Let's go see your sister."

* * *

Jazz

The waiting was unbearable.

Crowe stood beside the SUV with a pair of binoculars pressed to his eyes, watching the house like a statue carved out of shadow. Every few seconds he shifted slightly, adjusting his view of the windows, the tree line, and the long, winding drive that disappeared back toward the road.

I couldn't stand still. The night felt too quiet and too loud at the same time.

But the sounds carried. Somewhere inside that house a door slammed. A second later a crash echoed through the trees.

My heart jumped into my throat. "What was that?"

Crowe didn't answer.

Another sound, followed by a sharp crack that echoed across the fields. *Gunfire.*

My stomach twisted. I gripped the side of the SUV so hard my fingers hurt. What was happening there? I knew they were facing off against the guards in that place, the terrible men keeping young women like my sister hostage. How could you sell innocent people to predators and sleep at night?

But as the horrible symphony of sounds reached my ears, I had to wonder. Had they found Claire? Was Shade okay? My mind wouldn't slow down long enough to form a single clear thought. Every possibility slammed into the next one. I pictured Claire hurt, Claire dead. What if after everything we'd done, she wasn't even here?

Another distant shout carried through the night.

It was the silence that got my attention. It stretched long enough that my chest started to hurt from holding my breath. "Crowe…"

He didn't lower the binoculars this time. "Wait."

The seconds stretched until they felt like hours. Then Crowe stiffened slightly, lowering his binoculars. "They're coming."

My head snapped toward him. "Who?"

Crowe glanced at me once, his dark eyes calm and unreadable. "All of them."

The words hit me like a jolt of electricity. I turned toward the house so fast I nearly stumbled and fell. At first, I didn't see anything. Just the dark outline of the porch with its dull yellow light.

But then I saw movement. Figures emerging from the front door. My heart pounded so hard I felt it in my throat. There were four taller figures -- the men. Each of them was helping two girls down the stairs. The girls were slender, wraith-like figures struggling to keep up. They moved slowly, wobbling on their feet like they could barely stay upright. One of them was slung over Ripper's shoulder like she weighed nothing as he carried her toward the yard.

More shapes appeared behind them. Vendetta and the twins from the Hounds. All three of them scanning the property as they moved, weapons ready in case someone came out of the darkness.

But I barely saw them. As the girls and their protectors moved closer, I saw Shade heading our way. Beside him, I saw red hair. *Was that Scarlett*? And the slim figure between them… my heart nearly stopped. *Claire.*

Her dark hair hung loose around her shoulders, her face pale and thinner than I remembered, but I knew her instantly. Scarlett clung to her arm, the two of them leaning against each other as they walked.

For a moment the world narrowed down to a single point. I didn't see the other girls or hear the shouted instructions that were louder now. I didn't even feel my feet start moving. All I saw was my sister. "Claire!"

The name tore out of me before I even realized I'd spoken. She looked up. For a second, she just stared at me like her mind couldn't quite process what she was seeing. Then her face crumpled. "Jazz?"

I was already running. The distance between us disappeared in a blur of gravel and pounding footsteps until I slammed into her, wrapping my arms around her so tightly I was afraid if I let go, she'd vanish again. She clung to me just as hard. Her entire body was cold and shaking. She had on a T-shirt and jean shorts, no shoes on her feet. She held onto me so tightly it hurt, and I welcomed the pain.

"Oh my God." Claire sobbed into my shoulder. "Jazz…"

"I've got you," I whispered, my voice shaking. "I've got you."

Her hands trembled as they gripped the back of my jacket. "I thought," she started, her voice breaking. "I thought I'd never…"

"You're okay," I said. "You're okay now."

Behind us boots crunched over the gravel. "All right," Vendetta called out, his voice firm but not unkind. "I hate to cut this short, but we've got to move."

Reality crashed back in all at once. I loosened my grip just enough to look at Claire's face. She looked so exhausted. Her eyes were glassy like she hadn't slept in days. But she was here. *Alive.*

Scarlett hovered beside us, looking just as

shaken, her hand still gripping Claire's sleeve. Shade stepped up behind them, his presence solid and steady. "Get them in the SUV," he said quietly.

Vendetta and the twins headed for their bikes while Ripper and the other two Cottonmouths helped the other girls toward the vehicles. Claire squeezed my hand like she was afraid to lose it. "You really came for me," she said through her tears.

I swallowed hard. "We never gave up. Not me or Susan. Never."

Vendetta's voice cut through the moment again. "Now, Jazz."

Right. I pulled Claire gently toward the SUV. We were going home.

* * *

Shade

The gravel crunched under the SUV's tires as I turned into Susan's driveway. The house sat dark and quiet at the end of the short lane, a single porch light burning over the front steps.

Beside me, Jazz leaned forward in her seat like she couldn't quite believe we were really here.

In the back, Claire and Scarlett sat close together, wrapped in the blankets we'd grabbed from the house. Claire hadn't taken her eyes off her sister the entire drive.

Axel -- at least I thought it was Axel and not his identical twin Ryder -- was in the SUV's third row, keeping an eye out as I parked and shut the engine off.

My phone buzzed in my pocket. The screen lit up with Vendetta's number. I answered it without taking my eyes off the house. "Yeah."

"We're clear," Vendetta said.

The rumble of motorcycles carried faintly

through the phone along with the sound of wind and gravel.

"You make it back to the compound?" I asked.

"Just pulled in." His voice dropped a little. "It looks quiet."

To me, that wasn't a good sign. Too quiet meant someone had already covered their tracks.

"The Hounds still watching?" I asked.

"Yeah. Still set up outside the perimeter."

Good. Vendetta and Outcast were tight, and if my president trusted him and his friends, so did I. I hadn't really talked to Crash, but Player seemed like a good guy, always up for a fight. That they had eyes on the place made me feel a little better.

"Grim, Crowe, and Cain will help out," Vendetta said. "I haven't talked to Cowboy and Butcher yet. But if I had to guess, they had a slow night."

Something still didn't feel right.

"You see Rick Earle tonight?" he asked after a moment.

"No."

Which meant the bastard had slipped out before we hit the house. Someone, probably our about-to-be-dead traitor, had tipped him off.

Vendetta muttered something under his breath. "Figures."

Behind me the SUV door opened. Jazz had already got out, helping Claire and Scarlett out of their seats and steering them toward the porch.

The front door swung open, and a smaller lady with salt-and-pepper hair wearing a bathrobe stepped into the light. Jazz's Aunt Susan. For a moment, the woman just stared. As I watched, Claire ran straight for her.

I looked away and focused on the call. "Ripper

and Ryder headed to Mercy?" I asked.

"Yeah. Margot's ready for them."

That didn't surprise me. I didn't understand how Ryder and his old lady being a deputy sheriff in Mercy worked exactly. But it was pretty damned helpful right now.

"All right," Vendetta said. "Get those girls settled."

"I will."

"Call if anything moves."

"I will."

The line went dead.

I slipped the phone back into my pocket and stepped out of the SUV.

* * *

Jazz

My Aunt Susan didn't move at first. The porchlight caught Claire's face as she ran toward the house, and for a moment it looked like Susan couldn't breathe. Then she let out a broken sob. "Claire?"

Claire hit the porch steps at a run. "Susan! I'm home!"

They collided halfway across the porch, arms wrapping around each other so tightly it looked like neither of them would ever let go again. Scarlett hovered behind them, tears streaming down her face until Susan reached out and pulled her in too.

"Oh my God," Susan said. "Both of you… both of you…"

I stood a few steps away, suddenly unsure where to put myself. Claire turned, still clinging to Susan. "Jazz found me," she said through tears.

Susan's eyes met mine as I walked up. She crossed the porch and pulled me into the hug without hesitation. "Thank you, sweetheart," she whispered. "I don't know how you did it, but…"

I shook my head. "I didn't do it alone."

Behind us the SUV door closed. Shade leaned against the driver's door now, arms folded, watching the road the same way he always did. The Cottonmouth logo was easy to spot on the back of his cut, even in the middle of the night. He was always looking outward. Always protecting.

Susan noticed; her body went still beside me.

For years that patch had meant only one thing in this town: trouble and violence. The Cottonmouths were men you crossed the street to avoid. You warned your sisters, daughters, and nieces about them. For the last couple of years, they'd mingled with Sinister Skin as they invaded Oak Grove, and that was when things really started going to hell.

And now one of them was standing in her driveway like a silent guard. Susan's gaze lingered on the coiled snake stitched across the back of his cut. Then she looked at me. I braced for her reaction, but there was no accusation there, no anger. My aunt just looked thoughtful. Surprised even, like she was trying to reconcile the patch she'd always feared with the man who wore it. The man who'd just walked her girls back to her front door. There were questions in her eyes, but she didn't say anything else. She reached for Claire, then Scarlett, with shaking hands. "Come inside," she said.

The warmth of the house wrapped around us like the best memory when we walked into the living room. Susan watched them wrapping themselves in blankets they kept clutching before heading to the kitchen. "Have you eaten? You don't look like you have. I'm going to make you something."

Scarlett paused in the doorway of the kitchen. "Are you sure I can stay here tonight?"

Susan walked over, hugging her tight. "Of course. We'll call your mother first thing in the morning."

When Claire wandered in after them, my attention turned back to the man outside. I stepped back out onto the porch.

Shade was still where I left him. Axel had taken up position near the end of the driveway, watching the road with the calm patience of someone who'd done this kind of thing more than once. "You're staying?" I asked.

Shade glanced at me. "Yeah."

Relief washed over me before I could stop it. "Good."

Shoving his hands into the pockets of his jeans, he walked to the porch.

I went down to bottom step, unable to resist placing my hands on his strong shoulders. I hesitated for a moment, then leaned down and kissed his cheek. "Goodnight, Shade."

His hand caught mine before I could step away. "Get some sleep," he said.

"You too."

I turned to climb back up the porch steps. The screen door creaked as I reached for it, but before I could pull it open, it swung outward. Susan stood there holding it for me. She must have been watching through the window. For a second, she looked past me toward the driveway where Shade and Axel stood under the weak glow of the porch light. Her expression was careful but still thoughtful.

Then she lifted her voice just enough to carry across the yard. "If you need anything tonight," she called, "I'll leave this open. Help yourselves."

Axel waved, muttering, "Thanks, ma'am."

Shade only gave a small nod. But I knew he must have been surprised.

Susan didn't wait for an answer. She simply stepped back, still holding the door open for me.

I slipped inside, trying not to grin.

My aunt had spent years warning us about the Cottonmouths. But she was also the kind of woman who couldn't live with herself if she didn't offer someone a glass of water and a place to sit. Even if that someone was a biker standing guard in her driveway.

I looked back once before heading up the stairs.

Outside, Shade hadn't moved. He was still watching the road, keeping us safe.

And for the first time in weeks, with my sister and Scarlett safe inside the house, I was able to sleep.

Chapter Nine

Jazz

When I woke up, the first thing I noticed was the light. The first rays of dawn had filtered through the living room curtains, bathing the room in the soft light of a new day.

For a second, I didn't move. My body felt heavy, like I'd been dumped there and forgotten.

It all came rushing back to me within seconds. Going to that house hidden in the deep woods and then the raid. I sat up too quickly on the couch, my heart jumping into my throat before my brain caught up with reality. The house was quiet, and I felt like I could breathe again. Claire was alive and sleeping in her room.

I glanced toward the hallway. Claire's bedroom door was closed. Scarlett and Claire were in there together, the way they'd insisted on sleeping when we finally got them in the house. Scarlett had refused to leave Claire's side and none of us had the heart to argue.

A miracle had occurred last night, thanks to the bravery of men who I'd spent most of my life fearing. And I'd been there, watching my sister come back to me from the darkness. The impossible had happened and I felt tears threatening to come just thinking about it.

Susan's bedroom door was still closed too. The clock on the wall said it wasn't even six yet. No one else was awake. Except the men outside. I stood and crossed to the front door, easing it open so the screen door didn't slam. The cool morning air brushed my face as I stepped onto the porch.

Shade was still there, exactly where he'd been

hours earlier. He stood near the end of the driveway near the back of the SUV with his arms folded and the Cottonmouth logo stretched across his back catching the faint light of dawn. Ever since he dragged me out of *Ned's* that night, he'd been watching, looking outward.

One of the Suburban's passenger doors creaked open. Axel climbed out, stretching his shoulders as he stepped onto the gravel.

He didn't notice me, his attention on Shade. "Get some sleep."

Shade shook his head. "I'm good."

"You've been out here all night," Axel said.

"I said I'm good."

Axel didn't argue, but his expression said he didn't believe him any more than I did. He moved to the edge of the driveway instead, taking up the same watch Shade had been holding for hours.

That was my cue. I walked down the steps. Shade glanced over his shoulder when he heard me.

"You should still be asleep," he said to me, but in a softer tone.

"You stayed up all night."

"It had to be done." He said it like it wasn't even worth mentioning. Like watching the road for hours in case someone came to hurt us was the most natural thing in the world.

I stepped closer and reached for his arm. "Come inside."

He frowned. "Jazz…"

"You're exhausted." I started walking, a grip on his arm. But I wasn't dragging him anywhere. He was *allowing* me to move him.

He blew out a breath. "I'm fine."

There were deep shadows beneath his green eyes

and dirty-blond stubble covered the lower half of his face. But he did look *fine*. Yeah, he looked exhausted, in a brutally hot kind of way.

I tugged harder. "You're coming inside before you fall over in the driveway."

Shade's mouth twitched just a little at that. "Your aunt's not going to like finding a Cottonmouth under her roof."

I shrugged. "That Cottonmouth saved her girls."

His eyes met mine, and for a moment neither of us said anything.

"Maybe she'll come around," I added.

Shade studied me for another second before letting me pull him toward the porch.

Axel didn't look back. He'd already settled into the watch, scanning the road the same way Shade had all night.

Inside the house the air felt warmer and safer, even though I knew we weren't out of the woods just yet. There was a reckoning coming. Shade would insist on being on the front line, and I was going to make sure he had some rest.

I led Shade down the hallway and pushed open my bedroom door. "You can take the bed."

He leaned against the doorframe instead. "I'll take the chair."

"You're not sleeping in a chair." I kept my voice down because I didn't want Susan to wake up at this point.

"I've slept in worse." He walked in, carefully closing the door behind him.

I rolled my eyes. "Shade, get in bed. *Now*."

He hesitated, and then he smirked at me. Walking to my bed, I watched him sit on the side of it, the mattress creaking under his weight. He started pulling off his boots. He looked ridiculously large and dangerous in my girly bedroom with its fake ivy vines decorating the ornate white headboard of my bed and soft purple bedding. Once he'd pulled off his boots, he stretched out on his back on my bed, and I had to catch my breath. He looked so damn good. And the heat gathering in those green eyes as he looked me over had my body gearing up for things I shouldn't be thinking about right now with my aunt asleep across the hall and my sister just back from being held hostage by traffickers.

"Are you coming?" he asked.

"I got some sleep." I took a step closer to the bed.

"That's not what I asked." Shade's gaze moved over my face, then down my body.

Oh. Well, when he put it like that…

Still wearing the clothes I'd borrowed from Dylan, I unbuttoned my jeans and pushed them down before climbing on the bed with him. Feeling bold from the admiration in those eyes, I climbed over him, straddling his slim hips with the early morning light casting shadows on the floor nearby. I smoothed my hands over his muscular chest, leaning down to claim his mouth in a heated kiss.

"This bed make a lot of noise?"

I laughed quietly at that. "I don't know. I've never fucked on it before."

His grin got wider, as if that was all I needed to say. Wrapping his hand around the back of my neck, he pulled me down to him for another kiss. I loved the dirty, lusty way he kissed me while his hands were careful, skimming over my back before darting under my shirt so he could touch my skin. His hips rolled under me, his cock hard beneath his jeans. He nudged it up into the wet crotch of my panties, building a craving in my body for him. And it didn't take much.

When his hands grabbed my hips, I thought he meant to lift me enough to undo his jeans and free himself, to give us both what we both wanted. Instead, he pulled me up his body. I resisted a little, not understanding what he wanted, but he still moved me easily enough. I grabbed my headboard when my hips reached his chest, just to keep myself from falling.

By the time I figured out what he was doing, he'd hooked a finger in my panties and pulled them out of his way. When he got his mouth on me, it was all I could do to hang onto my headboard and not make a sound. It was the best kind of torture, the way he took me apart with his fingers and his mouth. It wasn't lost on me that I was riding the face of a biker, a Cottonmouth no less, in my childhood bed. My aunt was sleeping across the hall, my sister and Scarlett not far away.

Pleasure burned away any shame or hesitation I had. I fought to breathe as Shade made me come on his tongue. I covered my mouth with my hand, doing my damnedest to keep quiet. I clutched the dark gold locks of his hair with my other hand as I came down.

When I tried to move, Shade's strong hands kept me there. "Not so fast," he muttered.

I loved his whiskey-deep voice.

He let me go long enough to undo his jeans. And as he pushed them down his hips, I moved down his body. He fisted his cock just as I moved to straddle his hips again. He held himself up for me.

"Climb on. Let's take this bed for a ride."

"Let's keep it quiet," I whispered, hoping the bed wouldn't give us away.

I was almost afraid to find out as I lined him up to me and took him at my own pace. I loved the way his cock stretched me open, the way he filled me. Shade didn't try to rush me, but I could see the impatience in his face, waiting for me to completely swallow him.

And once he couldn't go any further, he started moving inside me. Despite an initial creak, the bed was relatively quiet as our bodies moved together. I planted my hands on the muscular wall of his chest, moving with him. His strong hands gripped my hips, moved me up and down on his cock. The wild blend of emotions in his green eyes made me feel seen and loved by this powerful man. A man who had risked so much for me and my family.

A man who looked at me like I meant something to him.

I shifted to work him against just the right place inside my pussy, and when I managed, I was close to seeing stars. Shade noticed it. He noticed everything. He thrust up into me harder and faster, not relenting until he brought me off again. I felt myself clenching around him, pleasure flowing through every part of my body like my blood. The room was a blur around me, but he anchored me there.

I felt his heart pounding against my palm as he continued to thrust up into me, chasing his own end now. I watched all the muscles of his upper body working, the heat in his eyes as he pinned me with his gaze. His grip tightened on me until it almost hurt when he came, his hips pumping relentlessly as he worked himself through it.

The only sound in the room was the harsh rasps of our breath as he patted his chest with a hand, and I leaned down to make myself comfortable there.

Shade's arms wrapped around me, his hands gentle as they skimmed over my back, drifted into my hair.

"You think you'll be able to sleep now?" I asked him. "Even for just a little while."

"Stay with me?"

I was in no hurry to move. For the first time since Claire disappeared, the house felt like it was breathing again. Claire and Scarlett were safe at home. Susan was sleeping across the hall for probably the first time in weeks.

And me? I'd found something, some*one,* I didn't expect. And I was safe in his arms. At least for now.

And outside, someone was standing watch.

For now, that was enough.

* * *

Shade

Somehow, I'd grabbed a couple of hours of sleep, got a shower, and made it out the door before Jazz's Aunt Susan knew any better. I was sure Jazz was right in saying her aunt might come around to having a Cottonmouth with her niece, thanks to the rescue. That didn't mean I could be one of those dumb fucks who took things for granted. Jazz was worth something to me, and that meant being respectful to her family.

I leaned against the porch rail when the truck came into view, sunlight glinting off the windshield as it rolled up the drive. Ryder was behind the wheel, and his twin brother walked up as he parked it. The woman in the passenger seat was familiar, and she stepped out the moment the engine died.

She was Ryder's old lady, Margot Donner. Even if I hadn't known her name already, I would've clocked her immediately. She carried herself like someone used to walking into rooms where people expected answers. Her dark hair was pulled back, and her eyes were sharp, taking everything in before she'd even closed the truck door.

Margot was a deputy sheriff. Ryder was an MC enforcer, and he came around the hood to stand beside her. I watched the way his hand hovered around the small of her back. She glanced over her shoulder just once, making sure he was there. I had questions about how *that* relationship worked.

Jazz stepped onto the porch behind me. Claire, Scarlett, and Susan were hovering just inside the doorway.

Margot's gaze swept across all of us, stopping when she spotted Claire. Relief flickered across her face before she masked it again.

"Ripper helped me get the others to Mercy last night," Ryder said.

Margot nodded. "Sheriff Sawyer logged them as trafficking victims this morning. Social Services is already involved. Their families are being contacted as we speak."

Susan joined Jazz on the porch and exhaled slowly, like she'd been holding that breath for days.

Margot had just started toward the porch when another car pulled into the drive, drawing everyone's attention. The sedan rolled to a stop behind Margot's truck. The red-haired woman who climbed out of it showed the same signs of exhaustion that Susan did. It only took me a moment to realize that she was Scarlett's mother. The second the girl saw her, she bolted out the door, her long red hair flying behind her.

"Mom!"

Her mother ran the last few steps and wrapped her up so tightly Scarlett's feet nearly left the ground. The sound that came out of that woman wasn't quite crying. It was something deeper. Something raw.

Scarlett clung to her mother, shaking.

Claire had followed Jazz onto the porch by then. She stood beside her sister, watching with red-rimmed eyes.

"No one called her mother before now?" I asked them as I watched the reunion.

"Scarlett's mom works at a data center over in Floyd," Jazz explained. "She's not allowed to have her phone on the job. We left a message so she'd know as soon as she got out."

Scarlett finally pulled back just enough to look at Claire. "I don't want to leave you."

Claire walked off the porch to them, reaching out and squeezed her hand. "You'll call me."

Before anyone could say anything else, Margot stepped forward. "I'm Margot Donner." She extended a hand first to Susan and then glanced around at the rest of us. "I'm a deputy sheriff over in Mercy."

Her voice was calm but carried the kind of quiet authority that made people listen.

Scarlett's mother wiped her eyes quickly, nodding as she shook Margot's hand. "I'm Marcy Wickline. Scarlett's mom."

Margot gave her a small, reassuring smile before shifting her attention to the porch. "Why don't we all go inside. It'll be easier to talk."

No one argued. We moved inside. Axel took a seat near the window, Ryder leaning against the wall beside him. Marcy and Scarlett joined Susan and Claire on the couch.

Jazz stood just behind her sister like she wasn't willing to let her out of reach again. I took a seat in a nearby rocker, giving me a perfect view of the front door and the hallway.

Margot remained standing. "All right. Let's start with the important part." Her gaze moved to Scarlett and Claire. "You're safe now."

Claire looked like she wanted to believe that but wasn't quite ready. Scarlett squeezed her mother's hand tighter.

Margot continued, steady and matter of fact. "We drove the other girls to Mercy early this morning. Sheriff Randy Sawyer, my boss and a good man, logged them as trafficking victims, which means they're under state protection now. Social workers are already involved and families are being contacted."

Scarlett's mother exhaled.

Margot glanced at Claire.

"You'll both need to come with us to Mercy too," she said. "Medical intake, statements, documentation. It protects you legally and makes sure no one can bury what happened."

Claire hesitated.

Jazz's hand settled on her shoulder. "It's okay."

Margot watched the exchange for a moment before straightening again. "I remember when Malcolm Dutton was the sheriff here in Oak Grove. He was a good man too. He took care of things. But when he died a couple of years back, things changed. Fast." Her gaze shifted toward me. "I was still a deputy here then."

"You left," Ryder said.

"I transferred," she corrected. "Now, the man who replaced Sheriff Dutton wasn't interested in cleaning up Oak Grove. He was interested in controlling it. And since Steve Belcher was elected sheriff here, things have only gotten worse."

Susan's brow furrowed. "I know a lot of people don't care for Sheriff Belcher. But you're saying he's corrupt?"

Margot didn't hesitate. "I'm saying Sinister Skin has influence inside that department. And that's the group responsible for this."

The room went still.

"That's why nobody looked for you." Margot turned to Claire and Jazz. "Two girls disappear after a lake festival, and it gets written off as a runaway situation?"

Claire swallowed hard as she listened.

Margot crouched slightly so she was eye level with her. "Tell me about that night."

Claire glanced at Scarlett before answering.

"We were at the lake festival," she said. "Scarlett and me."

"Did you talk to anyone you didn't know?"

Claire shook her head. "No. We just hung out with our friends. Then we talked to Frannie. She's a lady who works at the *Mason Jar* up there. It's a restaurant."

Jazz stiffened behind her.

"She was always nice to us," Claire continued.

"Yeah, she always remembered what we ordered," Scarlett added. "A couple of times she slipped us beer. But just a couple of times."

Someone serving alcohol to minors was just the first red flag.

"Was that night one of those nights?" Margot asked.

Scarlett nodded before Claire could say anything. Margot cut me a look. Yeah, Frannie'd slipped them drugs that night.

Margot didn't interrupt. "What happened after that?"

Claire frowned, trying to remember. "It got

blurry. I remember Scarlett laughing… and then I felt really dizzy."

"You said you had to go to the bathroom." Scarlett's voice faltered. "But three men came in and… we left after that."

"Can you tell me what they looked like?" Margot asked.

Claire shook her head. "I couldn't see. They had something over my face."

Scarlett hesitated. "I saw them."

Every head in the room turned toward her.

Margot's voice stayed calm. "All right. Tell me what you remember."

Scarlett closed her eyes for a second.

"One of them was really tall," she said. "Like… he looked sick. Really skinny and pale. He had dark stringy hair and his teeth… were messed up."

Creep.

I didn't move.

Scarlett continued. "The other one was bigger and bald. He had a bushy beard and… some kind of bird tattooed on his arm. Oh, and a scar across his cheek."

Eagle.

Ryder shifted against the wall.

Margot noticed. "And the third?"

Scarlett frowned. "He didn't look like them."

That made my stomach tighten.

"How so?" Margot asked.

Scarlett shrugged. "He looked… normal, I guess." She glanced between Margot and her mother nervously. "He was shorter than the other two. He had dark hair. He was kind of quiet. He didn't say a lot."

Her brow furrowed as she tried to remember.

"But he kept watching the door. Like he was

making sure nobody saw us."

I took a deep breath, kept listening. And Scarlett kept going.

"And when Claire started getting dizzy, he told the other guys to hurry."

The room had gone very still.

Scarlett looked at Margot with uncertainty. "I'm sorry. I don't remember his face very well."

"That's all right," Margot said. "You're doing great."

But I wasn't listening anymore. The way she described that third man… The quiet one, the one watching the door. He was making sure nobody saw them, huh? She didn't say all of them seemed worried.

That sounded an awful lot like Cain. And if Scarlett was right…

Then this whole thing started a lot closer to home than I'd thought.

I must have made some face because Axel and Ryder were both studying me then.

"Anything else?" Margot asked

Claire's voice dropped. "They blindfolded us and shoved us into, like, a van or the back of a truck."

Susan's hand flew to her mouth.

I just shook my head. Frannie had dosed them good.

"There were other girls." Claire's fingers twisted together in her lap. "Already there at that house when we got there. There were nine of us at first, but one girl got sick. They said they were taking her to the doctor. But she never came back."

Ryder cut me a look. That had me wondering once that house and its grounds were thoroughly investigated if a body or two would be found.

"Men came and went. Guards." Claire stopped to

brush a tear off her face. "They talked about… buyers."

Margot's expression hardened.

Claire started blinking back tears, the recollection pulling all her emotions back in. She jumped to her feet. "Sorry, I need to throw up."

With that she flew from the room with Scarlett on her heels. The bathroom door slammed down the hall a second later.

The room went quiet.

Susan stood, taking a step toward the hallway instinctively, worry written all over her face.

Margot lifted her hand gently.

"Let her," she said. "That's probably going to happen a few more times."

Susan looked back at her. "What do you mean?"

Margot exhaled before answering. "The girls were drugged. Not just once. Repeatedly."

Scarlett's mother paled. "What kind of drugs?"

Margot shook her head. "Hard to say yet. Could've been sedatives. Opioids. Whatever kept them compliant." Her voice stayed calm, but there was no softening the truth. "After three weeks of that, their bodies are going to react when the drugs stop."

Susan crossed her arms. "React how?"

"Withdrawal," Margot said.

Axel shifted near the window but didn't interrupt.

Margot continued. "Nausea. Shaking. Headaches. Trouble sleeping. Anxiety. Mood swings." She glanced toward the hallway where Claire had disappeared. "Vomiting is pretty common."

Scarlett's mother pressed a hand to her mouth. "Oh my God."

Margot's tone softened slightly. "It's manageable. But it's another reason we need to get them to Mercy."

Susan frowned. "For a hospital?"

"For medical intake," Margot replied. "Doctors can monitor them, make sure the detox doesn't turn dangerous."

Margot glanced at me before finishing.

"And it officially documents what happened to them."

Susan looked toward the hallway again, torn. "They've been through so much already."

"I know. But the sooner we get them help, the easier this will be on them." Margot's attention was on Susan and Jazz. "Did they talk about anything else that happened?"

The way she asked the question was delicate. Susan nodded. "Claire doesn't remember anyone... violating her. Not saying it couldn't have happened, but she said most of that time they kept her in a cot in a room with the other girls. She said the guards weren't really allowed to touch them."

Margot lowered her voice. "The girls they choose, like Claire and Scarlett? They're not random victims."

Everyone in the room went still.

"From what Snow has been able to learn, this is a premium trafficking group," Margot continued. "They look for girls who are young and clean. Untouched. It's important because they have foreign buyers looking for that. There's also, apparently, more money paid for religious girls."

The words hung in the air like rotten things.

"All of them were already sold," Margot said. "Including Claire and Scarlett."

"Sold where?" Susan asked.

"Overseas buyers."

Ryder ran a hand through his hair.

"So, Earle wasn't just running a holding house," I said.

"No." Margot's gaze shifted to me. "He was preparing an international shipment."

The real meaning sank in. Rick Earle hadn't just lost hostages. He'd lost an entire transaction worth millions of dollars. And men like him didn't walk away from losses like that. They came looking for blood.

Down the hall the bathroom door creaked open. Scarlett appeared first, leading Claire behind her by the hand. Claire looked pale, her eyes watery, but she was breathing a little easier.

"All right. Let's get these girls somewhere safe." Margot didn't waste time once Claire came back from the bathroom.

Within minutes she had everyone moving. Scarlett and her mother got in their car while Margot spoke quietly with Susan about Mercy, doctors, paperwork, and the kind of attention the girls would need in the coming days.

Claire leaned against Jazz for a moment before Margot separated them.

"We'll take good care of her," Margot promised.

Jazz nodded, though her grip on her sister tightened before she let go.

Claire wrapped her arms around Jazz one more time. "You're coming home when this is over, right?"

"I will," Jazz promised.

Scarlett hugged her too before Margot ushered both girls toward the vehicles.

Susan hovered nearby, wanting to hold on to them all.

Jazz hugged her aunt next.

Susan held her tight for a long moment before pulling back just enough to study her face. "Where are you going?"

Jazz glanced toward me before answering. "To finish it."

The words made Susan's expression tighten. Her worried gaze shifted from me to Jazz and back again. "Why do *you* have to go?"

Jazz's voice stayed calm, but there was something firm underneath it. "Because I need to see it end. I need to know Claire's safe for real."

Susan's focus drifted to me again. "And you think he can promise that?"

Jazz didn't hesitate. "Shade won't let anything happen to me."

Susan didn't look convinced. But after a moment she nodded slowly anyway. "Are you coming back here after?"

It was the same question she'd asked the night before when Jazz had tried to explain where she'd been and couldn't.

Jazz glanced at me again. "This time I will."

I gave Susan a small nod. That seemed to settle it.

Margot climbed into the driver's seat of Ryder's truck while Ryder took the passenger side. Susan and Claire climbed into the extended cab. Scarlett and her mother were following in their car.

Claire gazed out the window one last time as they pulled away. Jazz stood in the driveway waving until the vehicles disappeared down the road. Then she exhaled.

"All right," Axel said from behind us. "Let's go."

We headed for the Suburban. Jazz slid into the passenger seat while Axel climbed into the back. I started the engine and turned the vehicle toward the road.

A few seconds passed before Jazz spoke. "Did you know any of those men Scarlett described?"

I kept my eyes on the road. "Two of them."

Her head turned slightly. "Who?"

"Creep and Eagle," I said. "They made it out when we took the club back. They were from Eli's inner circle."

Jazz went still beside me. "And the third?"

I shook my head once. "Not sure." That wasn't entirely true. But saying the name out loud didn't sit right yet. "It can't be who I thought."

"Why not?" Jazz asked.

"The man I'm thinking of rode with us last night." Hell, Cain had been with him, Ripper, and Grim in rescuing the girls.

Silence filled the SUV for a moment. Then Axel spoke from the back seat. "That actually makes more sense."

Jazz turned halfway around. "How?"

Axel leaned forward, resting his arms on the seat. "If someone inside the compound was feeding information to Sinister Skin," he said, "the safest place for him during the rescue would've been with us."

I glanced at him in the mirror. Axel was watching me.

"Think about it," Axel continued. "If he stayed behind, everyone would be watching him. But if he rode on the raid?" His gaze shifted toward Jazz. "He hears the plan. He knows the timing. He knows exactly where everyone is."

The weight of that settled in the vehicle like a storm cloud.

Jazz shook her head. "And he can warn Rick Earle."

Axel nodded. "Exactly."

I tightened my grip on the wheel. If Axel was right… then the traitor hadn't just been close to us. Cain had been riding beside us the entire time.

Chapter Ten

Shade

The compound came into view just past the tree line. It looked like every bike in the club was already there. That was the first thing I noticed. There wasn't a single empty spot along the fence as we drove up.

And it was way too quiet. An unusual silence had settled over the Cottonmouth compound, almost like a funeral rite. There was no music or shouting. Usually, someone had an engine running. But there was nothing at all.

Our men stood in small clusters around the yard, cuts on, arms crossed, most of them watching the gate. "Looks like your whole damn club showed up," Axel muttered from the passenger seat.

"They did." I rolled the Suburban through the gate and killed the engine. The second I opened the door the tension was so high it felt like stepping into a storm.

Vendetta was already walking toward us. Grim and Butcher flanked him a few steps back. Crowe stood near the garage doors, eyes scanning the perimeter like he expected trouble to come through the trees any second now. That wasn't a good sign.

And standing halfway across the yard with the rest of the club were three other brothers, all of them I'd seen at *Ned's* the night we took Jazz. That just made my case stronger.

Cain.

He wasn't talking to anyone. He was watching and waiting.

I shut the door and came around the front of the SUV.

Vendetta stopped in front of me. "You're late."

"Margot came to take the last two to Mercy," I said.

He understood what I meant. *Claire.*

Vendetta nodded. "Good."

A flash of relief passed through the men behind him. Still, the yard was tense with something darker.

Vendetta's eyes moved past me toward the SUV just as Jazz walked around to join us. She stepped out on her own before I could answer.

"Why aren't *you* in Mercy?" he asked her. "With Dylan?"

Every head in the yard turned in her direction. Some of the guys looked curious while others seemed impressed. A couple of them were trying not to stare too long.

Jazz ignored it all, and walked straight toward me. "I'm not hiding in the truck," she told him.

Vendetta huffed quietly. "Somehow I didn't think you would."

I scanned the yard again, and Cain hadn't moved.

When I spotted Ripper and Cowboy walking toward us, I waved the prospect over. I had one important thing to take care of before *anything* happened. "Cowboy."

He looked up immediately. The kid was still a wreck, walking like he was carrying the weight of the world. He stepped forward anyway. "Yeah?"

I jerked my chin toward Jazz. "You're with her."

Confusion was easy to read on his face. "With… Jazz?"

"Yeah. You keep her with you," I said. "Inside the barracks. Nobody goes near her unless you say so. You understand? Some shit is going down tonight."

Cowboy straightened, and his shoulders firmed

up. "You got it, Shade."

Jazz looked between us. "I don't need a babysitter."

I leaned closer to her. "I need you to stay breathing."

Her mouth opened to argue. And I braced for the fight, because she would have it right out here in the open. I knew she would.

Just as quickly, she sighed. "Fine."

Cowboy stepped beside her like he'd just been handed a mission. "Come on with me," he said awkwardly.

Jazz hesitated for a second before following him toward the barracks. The look she threw over her shoulder at me was a witch's brew of concern and frustration. But she went along with Cowboy who was walking half a step ahead of her like he was trying to remember how to be a bodyguard.

I watched them until the door shut behind them in our administration building. Only then did I turn back to Vendetta. My president and VP were watching me, and the yard had gone even quieter.

"What do you mean some shit is going down tonight?" Vendetta asked.

"I figured out one of our traitors," was all I said.

Vendetta followed my gaze. "You sure?"

"Yeah."

Across the yard Cain smiled. He hadn't moved. He already knew what was coming, and he honest-to-God looked like he was anticipating this.

Vendetta exhaled slowly as Axel took his position behind me. "Well, let's hear it then."

I walked straight toward Cain while the entire yard held its breath. And still Cain didn't move an inch. Gravel crunched under my boots, the sound carrying in the still evening air. Nobody said a word or even moved. They just waited to see what would happen next.

Cain's long arms were loose at his sides. His expression was calm, the energy in his eyes looked gleeful. He stayed still, waiting for me. And that told me everything I needed to know. Innocent men didn't wait like that.

I stopped a few feet in front of him, and for a moment we just sized each other up. "You were at the lake the night of the festival," I said. It wasn't a question.

Cain's mouth twitched slightly. "Maybe."

I felt the club tightening all around us. I heard the boots shifting, and someone exhaling slow through their teeth. The possibility that Cain wasn't the only one knifing the club in the back ran through my mind. But at that moment, I was ready for anything. I didn't take my eyes off him.

"Three men walked into the *Mason Jar* that night," I said. "Two of them were Creep and Eagle."

Cain's gaze lowered briefly toward the dirt, then back to me.

"And the third?"

Silence stretched between us. Cain smiled. "So that's what this is about."

Vendetta stepped closer behind me. "Answer the damn question."

Cain ignored him, his stare locked on me. "You killed Eli," he said.

The yard stiffened. I didn't look away. "Yeah, I did."

Cain nodded slowly like he wanted confirmation. "Thought so."

For a second, I didn't think he'd say anything

else. But then something in his face shifted, transforming it into anger. *Real* anger. "You know who he was to me?" Cain asked, his tone tight and bitter.

"No."

Cain laughed under his breath. "Figures." He ran a hand over his jaw. "My mother used to work this compound. Back when Eli ran things."

Nobody interrupted. The compound was as silent as a tomb.

"She was a club girl," Cain continued. "One of the ones Eli liked to keep around back in the day. But you and Vendetta and Ripper wouldn't know anything about that, would you? You weren't from Oak Grove. You just showed up and fucking *took over*." His eyes hardened. "I didn't know who my father was for most of my childhood. But eventually my mother told me. And his name was Eli Crizer."

A ripple moved through the yard, and Vendetta went still behind me.

Cain shrugged. "I didn't come here for revenge."

That part surprised me.

"I came here because I thought maybe… if I earned the patch… Eli might actually see me." Cain's voice dropped. "But the old man never even remembered my mother." The bitterness in his words was like acid. "Didn't remember her name. Didn't remember me."

I stared at him then. Was he Eli's son? The eyes were the same color but set differently. Cain didn't have the same nose. But the way he stood, his tall, wiry frame? Yeah, that was *all* Eli.

Cain stared me down. "And then *you* killed him."

The accusation hung in the air. I don't know what he expected. But I didn't flinch. I had zero fucking regrets. "Your father sold women and children," I said. "He sold drugs on the streets -- to *kids*."

Cain's eyes flashed. "I don't give a fuck about that. You took the only chance I had. And you, Shade, you committed the ultimate club sin, didn't you? You killed a brother. Your *president*."

I took a step closer, watching as Cain took the smallest step back. "When club members turn greedy and put the club in the crosshairs of the law to line their own pockets, they break the bond of the patch we all wear. And when they got called on it? They tried to hang *our president* in the woods and leave him to die."

Cain wasn't letting it go. Angry color flooded his face. "Vendetta is still alive. My father isn't."

Vendetta finally spoke. "Did you kill JJ?"

The question cracked across the yard like a gunshot. Cain didn't hesitate. "Yeah, I did."

The words landed like heavy blows. And they were the reason I'd sent Cowboy off to protect my Jazz. In the state the kid was in, he'd lose his fucking mind if he heard that.

"He needed killing," he said flatly.

My hands curled slowly at my sides. "Why?"

Cain's stare drifted past me for a second, toward the barracks where Cowboy had disappeared with Jazz earlier. "He still fucking believed in this place," he said.

The yard shifted uneasily.

Cain shrugged like the answer was obvious. "Dumbass kid thought the Cottonmouths stood for something now. Thought Vendetta cleaned it all up." Cain's mouth twisted slightly. "But the way I see it, the club died the second Eli hit the ground."

A ripple moved through the men around us.

Cain went on like he didn't notice. "JJ was running his mouth about loyalty. About how things are gonna be different now. So, I showed him what loyalty really looks like."

I took one slow step closer. "You fucking strangled him."

Cain didn't even blink, his focus on Vendetta. "Figured it was fitting."

The words hit like a punch to the chest. Vendetta's voice came low behind me. "You were warning Earle."

Cain's smile crept back. "Had to let him know you boys were poking around his shipment. Especially after you took that little whore waitress out of *Ned's*."

"Too late to stop it," I said.

Cain shrugged again. "Late… but not too late."

A sharp crackle from the walkie clipped to Ripper's jeans broke across the yard. Everyone heard it. Outcast's voice came through. "Movement on the road."

The yard went still.

"Three SUVs. Coming in hot," Outcast said.

Ripper lifted the radio. "Confirm."

A pause. Then Outcast again. "Earle's in the lead." Another beat. "He's not alone."

Ripper's eyes lifted from the radio. "Sinister Skin."

Cain chuckled under his breath. "Right on time."

The roar of engines cut through the quiet a second later. Gravel exploded at the gate as the first truck tore into the compound.

And Rick Earle rolled in like he owned the place.

* * *

Jazz

The office door was open just enough for me to see the yard. I knew I shouldn't have been watching, but I had to.

Shade had told Cowboy to keep me inside and keep me safe. Technically, that's *exactly* what he was doing.

Cowboy stood beside the door like he wasn't sure whether he was guarding me or holding himself together. He was about my age, maybe a year younger. He was tall and lean, with bright blue eyes and dimples, the kind of boy who'd probably had girls chasing him all through high school. The cowboy hat he wore over his dark hair had seen better days, but it suited him.

Right now, there was nothing easy about him. The grief of having his best friend murdered had hollowed him out. His entire body was wired tight, and his jaw was locked so hard I could see a muscle ticking. He was a man barely hanging on by his fingernails.

We both listened while the entire compound held its breath, starting the minute Shade had marched over to Cain.

Outside, Shade stood near the center of the yard, squaring up to Cain. I could hear most of it. Not every word, but I heard enough.

"Did you kill JJ?" Vendetta's voice carried across the gravel.

Cain didn't hesitate. "Yeah, I did."

Cowboy went completely still beside me. For a second, I was worried he might collapse. That's when the shaking started in his hands and shoulders.

Sharp static from the hand-held radio drew our attention to the table where Cowboy had placed it. "Movement on the road," someone said. Every muscle in Cowboy's body went rigid at those words. "Three SUVs. Coming in hot."

I felt the air change. The coming danger was a tangible thing, even through the walls of the barracks. "Confirm," Ripper's voice came over the walkie.

"Earle's in the lead," the first voice continued. "He's not alone."

My stomach dropped. *Rick Earle.* Just hearing his name made my skin crawl. I could still see him leaning across the bar at *Ned's,* smiling like he owned everything in the room, including me. Like women were things to buy and sell the same way he'd bought that bar.

The same way he bought and sold girls like my sister.

A flash of anger burned through the fear. Earle had nearly destroyed my family. And now he was dragging the Cottonmouths back into the same filth they'd just fought to tear out of. Earle was here for revenge, and for Vendetta and Shade.

Cowboy shifted beside me. "They're really doing this."

I didn't answer him. Instead, I leaned closer to the door. Rick Earle wasn't there to talk. He was here to take back what he could. And if the way he'd always looked at me before was any indication, I had a pretty good idea what. By now the man had figured out their "shipment" was out of their reach, thanks to the Cottonmouths. He and his crew wanted to end this feud today so the MC wouldn't be there to interrupt their operations in the future.

The loud roar of engines pierced my awareness, getting louder by the second.

Cowboy moved toward the door.

I grabbed his arm. "No."

He tried to shake me off. "Let me go."

"They want you angry," I said. "They want you to make mistakes because of it."

Cowboy's eyes were bright with rage. "That sumbitch killed my best friend."

"I know." I squeezed his arm harder. "He sold my sister, and if not for all of you I'd never have seen her again. I don't care if he dies, but listen to me. If you run out there right now, you'll die before you even get near him."

That stopped him. *Barely.*

Outside, the SUVs tore into the compound yard. Voices rose and doors slammed. Men started shouting, and I leaned closer to the crack in the door.

Rick Earle stepped out of the lead SUV like he owned the place. The two men who got out behind him wore Cottonmouth patches. One was gangly and sick-looking, the other bald and bearded.

Were they the ones Scarlett had described at the house? The ones who'd taken her and Claire?

Behind them were more men dressed in mostly black and armed. There were a lot of them. *Sinister Skin.*

My anxiety rose as I watched three Cottonmouths step forward, but not to Vendetta. No, they walked over to join Earle. Shade had been right all along. The club *did* have traitors.

"Cowboy," I whispered.

He followed my gaze. "Shit."

Numbers. That's what this was about now. Vendetta's men were good, but Earle had come ready for war. Cowboy's voice dropped. "We're outnumbered."

I didn't answer. My mind was still going, remembering how men like Earle had regarded at me in that bar. The way predators always did when they saw something they wanted. They grabbed it and used it. And they liked nothing better than having the upper hand.

What we needed was to disrupt that somehow. I turned slowly toward Cowboy. "Where would you shoot from if you were going to surprise them?"

He just stared at me. "What?"

"If someone found me and dragged me out there, where would you shoot from to break things up?"

His face went pale. "No."

"If someone *did*," I tried again.

"Jazz, if something happens to you, Shade will kill me."

"Where?" I pressed.

He blew out a frustrated breath before pointing toward the line of SUVs in the yard. "There. Behind the second one," he said, his voice barely a whisper. "I'd have a clear shot."

I nodded. That was all I needed to know.

Outside, Earle's voice carried across the compound. "… my Cottonmouths back in power."

Vendetta answered with something I couldn't hear. The tension outside was a living thing, ready to snap. I reached for the door handle.

Cowboy grabbed my wrist. "Don't."

I looked up at him. "You want justice for JJ?"

His eyes filled with something raw. "Yes."

"Then trust me." And before he could stop me, I stepped out into the yard. I wasn't quiet about it, and every head turned.

Rick Earle's eyes locked on me like I was exactly what he'd been hoping to find. A slow grin spread over his face.

* * *

The vehicles rolled through the gate like they owned the place. All high-end SUVs, dark colors and big engines.

Rick Earle rode at the front of the pack, slow and deliberate, making the kind of entrance a little coward like him craved, loud and flashy. Creep and Eagle flanked him like a pair of ugly shadows, and behind them came a dozen more Sinister Skin goons spreading out across our yard.

Vendetta didn't move. Neither did I. We'd been waiting.

Boots hit the ground as Earle climbed out of the passenger side of the lead vehicle, his gaze sliding across the yard like he was already counting bodies. His smile widened when three men stepped out from the Cottonmouth line and drifted toward him.

It didn't even surprise me. All three of them had been sitting at the bar at *Ned's* the night we pulled Jazz out of there. *Figures.*

Earle followed my gaze and laughed. "Well, look at that," Earle said. "Some of your boys still remember who actually runs Oak Grove."

Vendetta's voice came calm and deadly beside me. "You lost the right to run anything when you started trafficking here."

Earle shrugged like that was a minor inconvenience. "Business is business. You boys cost me *millions* last night."

Cain stepped forward then, moving to Earle's side like he'd been waiting his whole life for the moment. "Don't worry," Cain said. "They're about to lose even more."

Earle tilted his head. "Oh?"

Cain smiled. "Your waitress is here, sir."

For the first time since he rode in, Earle looked genuinely pleased. "Well now," he said. "That *is* a nice surprise." The fucker's gaze swept the compound buildings. Then he raised his voice. "Bring her to me."

The order rolled across the yard like thunder. One of the Sinister Skin men headed for the vehicles parked near the barracks.

My muscles tightened, every instinct in my body screaming at once. If they laid a hand on her...

Earle looked back at me, that greasy grin spreading across his face. "You should've stayed out of my business, friend. Now I'm taking back what's mine."

Movement caught my eye. And like a vision from a nightmare, Jazz stepped out from the barracks where Cowboy was supposed to be keeping this from fucking happening. For a second the whole yard seemed to freeze. She walked forward slowly, shoulders squared even though I could see the tension in every line of her body. The wind tugged lightly at her hair as she came to a stop out in the open yard.

My blood went cold. What the hell was she doing?

Earle's grin spread wide as he took her in. "Well, look at that," he said. "She came out all on her own. Guess she knows who she belongs to."

I started forward before I even realized I'd moved. One of the Sinister Skin men stepped toward Jazz, reaching out like he was about to grab her arm. The distance between us vanished in my mind. Three steps. Two. The man's hand lifted and --

A split second later, a gunshot cracked across the yard. Earle jerked hard where he stood as the bullet slammed into his shoulder. His grin vanished as he lifted a hand to the wound, pulling it back to see the fresh blood coating his fingers.

Total fucking chaos exploded then.

Cowboy, who was supposed to be guarding my Jazz, stepped out from behind the line of vehicles, smoke curling from the barrel of his gun. And right behind him came Outcast, Crash, and Player moving like hell had just opened its gates.

Player's grin was downright joyful.

Axel fell in beside his fellow Hounds as the Sinister Skin men scrambled for cover. Jazz ran like hell away from the action, and I didn't move until I was sure she was out of harm's way.

The entire yard erupted in gunfire. Sinister Skin scattered for cover, some diving behind the SUVs, others dropping to a knee and firing blindly toward the barracks. The Cottonmouths loyal to Vendetta answered immediately. The music filling the compound yard around us was a symphony of determination and pain, with shots cracking, fists landing, and men shouting over each other.

Vendetta moved first, closing the distance on Earle like he'd been waiting for this since the day he crawled out of the grave Eli'd left him in. Earle barely got his weapon up before Vendetta drove him backward into a parked bike. The two of them went down hard, fists and steel flashing in the dirt.

Creep fired toward the vehicles, trying to push through the perimeter. Outcast returned the favor from his position, his shot punching into the dirt at Creep's feet and forcing him back.

Player whooped like this was the best day of his life. "Christmas came early, boys!"

Then Cain came for me. He moved faster than most men in the yard. A knife flashed in his hand as he closed the distance between us, rage burning in his eyes.

"This was my father's fucking club!" Cain snarled.

I sidestepped the first strike, catching his wrist and driving my elbow into his ribs. Bone gave under the impact, but Cain barely slowed.

"You killed my father!"

The knife flashed at me again. I blocked it, drove him backward, and the two of us slammed into the side of an SUV hard enough to rock it.

"Your father trafficked kids," I snarled. "For money. He was a piece of shit."

Cain spat blood. "He built this place!"

He came again, wild now, grief and fury blinding him. I caught his arm, twisted, and the knife clattered into the dirt between us.

Cain swung with his other hand, but I hit him first. The punch snapped his head sideways. He staggered but didn't fall, swinging again, desperate now.

I grabbed his collar and slammed him down into the dirt hard. The air rushed out of him in a broken gasp. In those seconds, the yard seemed to narrow to just the two of us.

Cain glared at me, hate burning through the blood running down his face. "You took everything from me… The chance to finally know my father."

I pulled my gun. "And he never gave two shits about you." It was true. "All you had to do was be faithful to the club that let you in, and you couldn't even fucking do that."

The barrel settled between his eyes. But before I could pull the trigger a voice cut through the chaos behind me.

"Don't."

Out of the corner of my eye, I saw Cowboy standing a few feet away, chest heaving, gun shaking in his hands. Fury and grief twisted together to form a mask of pain on his face.

"He killed JJ," Cowboy said hoarsely.

Cain's gaze flicked toward him. Recognition dawned, but he kept his mouth shut. Cowboy's hands tightened on the gun he held. "You killed my best friend."

After a moment, I lowered my weapon.

Cowboy stepped forward. The yard was still blowing up all around us with shots fired and men shouting. For him, the world narrowed down to just one thing. Justice for his best friend.

Cain tried to rise.

Cowboy pulled the trigger, and the shot echoed across the compound.

Cain dropped back into the dirt and didn't move again.

Vendetta and Earle were still battling it out. Neither of them had guns in their hands anymore. The arm at Earle's injured shoulder hung uselessly at his side where Cowboy's bullet had torn through. Blood soaked the sleeve of his coat, but the bastard was still smiling through it with bloody teeth.

"You should've stayed dead," Earle snarled.

Vendetta didn't answer with words. He just drove forward. The two men collided hard enough to send gravel spraying under their boots. Earle swung first, a wild right hand fueled by rage more than skill. Vendetta took the hit across the jaw and answered with a punch to the ribs that folded Earle over like paper.

Earle staggered back, breathing hard. "You cost

me fucking millions."

Vendetta wiped blood from the corner of his mouth. "You were making money off the suffering of girls and women, you selfish asshole."

Earle laughed, a harsh, ugly sound. "Don't pretend you're better than the rest of us."

Vendetta stepped in again. This time his punch landed square across Earle's face, snapping his head back. The second one dropped him to a knee.

For a moment Earle just knelt there, breathing hard, with one hand pressed to his bleeding shoulder. Then the bastard looked up and smiled.

"You think this ends here?" Earle said.

Vendetta grabbed him by the collar and hauled him upright.

"It ends when you stop breathing." Vendetta's fist drew back.

Before his fist could land again, an engine roared. One of the remaining Sinister Skin men barreled into the yard in one of the SUVs that had been idling outside the front gate. The door flew open and two men jumped out, grabbing Earle under the arms.

Vendetta tried to hold on. But Earle twisted free just long enough to shove himself backward toward the vehicle. Blood ran down his face as his men dragged him toward the open door.

Earle's gaze found Vendetta, then me. Pure hate burned there. "This isn't over," he rasped before the men managed to shove him into the back of the SUV and slam the door.

The engine screamed as the vehicle tore through the open gate, gravel spraying behind it as it disappeared down the road. Outcast fired shots at it, trying to take out a tire. He hit a couple of the windows, and I sincerely hoped one of those bullets hit the bastard.

The other SUVs made it out just as fast, one with just the driver in it, who was covered in blood. There were two in the other. One was Creep, hauling ass up the road like the devil himself was chasing them.

Silence slowly returned to the compound. Vendetta stood in the middle of the yard, his chest rising and falling, staring after the taillights fading into the trees. Then he spat blood into the dirt. "Next time," he muttered.

Around us our brothers began to regroup. Men moved through the yard, checking bodies, kicking weapons away from limp hands. Six Sinister Skin members lay scattered across the compound now. Eagle was one of them. Two of the three Cottonmouths who'd stepped over to Earle's side weren't getting up either.

The third one had run with the SUVs.

Good. Let him carry the story of what had happened here. We knew who he was and we'd sure as hell remember.

Grim wiped blood off his knuckles and glanced toward Vendetta. "We're okay. We have a couple shot, but no one down."

Relief didn't quite settle me, but it loosened something in my chest. I still looked around, silently doing a head count. I spotted Butcher and Crowe, talking to Riot who had taken a beating and was sitting on the ground. Ripper ended up with the four Hounds, laughing about something. They were still here.

Cowboy. The thought hit hard and fast, and I turned, scanning the yard. I looked over the vehicles and barracks, the shadows between the buildings. Realization hit me like a gut punch.

Where was she?

My head snapped toward the barracks again just as Cowboy walked in my direction. He still looked wrecked, and his hands were still shaking from the shot he'd taken. But the kid was still standing.

Alone.

The anger came fast and hot. I started toward him. "What the hell did you --"

The words died in my throat. Jazz came out from behind him. She crossed the yard fast, running straight toward me, breathless but unharmed. For a split second I didn't move. I just watched her.

She slammed into me hard when she reached me. My arms came up automatically, pulling her tight against my chest. My girl was shaking like a leaf, but she was alive.

Behind her, Cowboy finally exhaled, pulling off his hat and running a hand through his hair like the weight of the world had just lifted from him. Vendetta glanced over at the three of us. A slow, tired grin pulled at the corner of his mouth. "Looks like we won," he said.

And for the first time since this whole mess started, I knew he was fucking right.

Epilogue

Jazz

The compound looked completely different when it wasn't a battlefield. Tonight was a special occasion. We were celebrating our victory against Sinister Skin. Music drifted across the yard from a couple of speakers someone had dragged out onto the porch. A grill smoked near the fire pit, and the smell of burgers and beer hung in the air. Bikes lined the gravel lot in uneven rows, chrome flashing in the glow of the string lights me and Dylan had strung between two buildings. We could have done a better job, but we'd had a couple of mojitos while we did it.

If someone had told me a couple of weeks ago that I'd be standing in the middle of all this… I would've laughed in their face. Now, on this warm Friday night it felt strangely normal.

Ripper, Butcher, and Riot were sitting around the fire pit, empty beer bottles piling up under their camp chairs. Player, Ryder, and Axel had come over from the Hounds. Player's booming laugh was contagious. Grim and Crowe were listening outside the main circle. Grim had somehow ended up with a beer in each hand while Butcher argued loudly with Player about his favorite NFL team getting robbed last week. Player laughed, telling him he was full of shit. Crowe was losing interest in the tall tales, instead noticing a few club girls dancing near the speakers.

I was at one of the picnic tables where Vendetta, Shade, and Ripper were talking with Ryder and Margot. Dylan sat across from me with her hand resting in Vendetta's while she and I talked to two of the Hounds' old ladies. Heather was a tall, black-haired beauty who looked plenty capable of dealing with the presence that was Player. Sadie was with Axel, and she was a gorgeous redhead who was one of the sweetest people I'd ever met.

And Cowboy…

Cowboy was hovering. Not in a creepy way. Just… hovering. He leaned against the railing nearby, pretending he wasn't watching me while also very obviously watching me. Every time our eyes met, he looked away too quickly. It was almost adorable.

"Kid's got himself a problem," Ripper muttered, following my gaze.

Shade's head snapped in Cowboy's direction so fast I almost laughed.

Ripper barked out a laugh. "Relax, man. He's just got a crush."

Shade's eyes narrowed like he was mentally calculating how far he could throw the poor kid.

Player, who had wandered over with a beer, was quick to pick up what was going on. "This is the best entertainment we've had all week."

Shade didn't look amused.

I slipped my hand into his, squeezing lightly. "Cowboy helped save my life."

Shade stared at Cowboy hard, but his expression softened just a fraction. Still, Cowboy suddenly found somewhere else to stand. I hid a smile.

The night stretched on, warm and easy in a way that felt almost surreal after everything that had happened. Eventually the music faded into the background as the crowd thinned. One by one the club members and their significant others drifted off toward the barracks or made their way home. Dylan and I wrapped up food and cleaned up what we could, deciding to tackle it tomorrow.

Shade and I ended up walking toward the

administration building, heading toward his room.

I leaned against him as we walked. "I told Susan I'm staying over tomorrow night too. If that's okay."

Shade almost smiled. "You know it's okay."

"She's coming around," I said.

"She will." He sounded certain in that quiet way of his, like once he decided something it was a matter of time before everyone else caught up.

We walked a few more steps in comfortable silence before I glanced up at him.

"You know, you could move in here," Shade said, "if you wanted. Dylan would probably love having another old lady here."

Well, he was direct.

"I bet she would," I said, smiling.

He stopped walking, and something in his expression shifted just enough to make my stomach flip. "Is that still something you think you'd want to do?"

I nodded. "Maybe. Once my family is okay with the fact that I'm in a relationship with a Cottonmouth."

Shade studied me for a second. "Or we could get our own place. I was thinking maybe something more permanent."

I didn't expect that. "Oh." A laugh slipped out of me before I could stop it. "You know what the funniest part of that is?"

He raised an eyebrow.

"I don't even know your real name," I admitted.

For a second, he just stared at me. Then he sighed like a man accepting his fate. "Paul," he said. "Paul Miltner."

I tried it out. "Paul."

It felt strange. It was far too normal for the dangerous man who I was coming to care about more every day.

I tilted my head, pretending to consider it. "Mrs. Jasmine Miltner," I said thoughtfully. "That sounds… respectable."

The look he cut me made me laugh. "Yeah… no. I like Mrs. Shade better."

For the first time all night, Shade broke into a full smile. It transformed his entire face, as if he wasn't handsome enough.

"That's more like it," he said.

Shade pulled me into him for a scorching kiss, and he didn't give a damn who saw us.

Jamie Targaet

Jamie Targaet is the author of the motorcycle clubs of the *Hounds of Hell MC* multiverse. She's anxious to introduce you to these gorgeous, dominant men and the lucky women who surrender to them. The ride is going to get wild at times, not going to lie. But there's thrilling action, scorching hot sex scenes, and all the feels.

Jamie writes erotic romance for Changeling Press, a little fanfiction on the side, and she's an aspiring horror writer in another life. She enjoys time with her family (including the fur babies). She likes good horror movies and shows, emo, metal and classic rock, and time spent in other worlds writing and reading. She loves hearing from readers and is looking forward to hearing from you.

Cottonmouth MC is part of the Hounds of Hell MC Multiverse.

Jamie at Changeling: changelingpress.com/ jamie-targaet-a-227

Changeling Press LLC

Contemporary Action Adventure, Sci-Fi, Steampunk, Dark Fantasy, Urban Fantasy, Paranormal, and BDSM Romance available in e-book, audio, and print format at ChangelingPress.com - MC Romance, Werewolves, Vampires, Dragons, Shapeshifters and Horror -- Tales from the edge of your imagination.

Where can I get Changeling Press Books?

Changeling Press e-books are available at ChangelingPress.com, Amazon, Apple Books, Barnes & Noble, Kobo, Smashwords, and other online retailers, including Everand Subscription and Kobo Subscription Services. Print books are available at Amazon, Barnes and Noble, and by ISBN special order through your local bookstores.

ChangelingPress.com

www.ingramcontent.com/pod-product-compliance
Lightning Source LLC
LaVergne TN
LVHW020522100826
845148LV00010B/1308

* 9 7 8 1 6 0 5 2 1 9 7 0 7 *